ORDINATION

Book One of the Paladin Trilogy

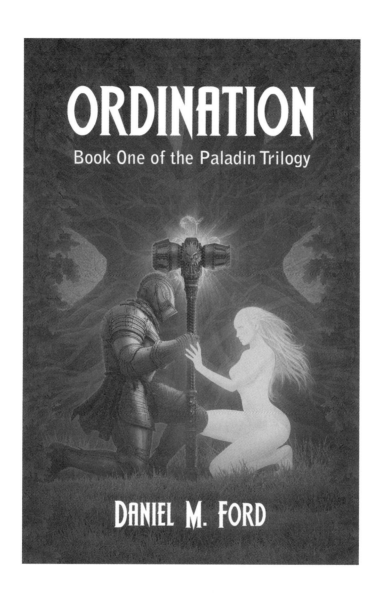

ORDINATION

Book One of the Paladin Trilogy

DANIEL M. FORD

sfwp.com

Copyright ©2016 by Daniel M. Ford
All rights reserved.

Library of Congress Cataloging-in-Publication Data

Ford, Daniel M., 1978-
    Ordination / Daniel M. Ford.
        pages cm. — (Paladin ; Book One)
    ISBN 978-1-939650-34-4 (pbk.)
    1. Fantasy fiction. I. Title.
    PS3606.O728O73 2015
    813'.6—dc23
                                                    2015016691

Published by SFWP
369 Montezuma Ave. #350
Santa Fe, NM 87501
(505) 428-9045
www.sfwp.com

Find the author at www.danielmford.com

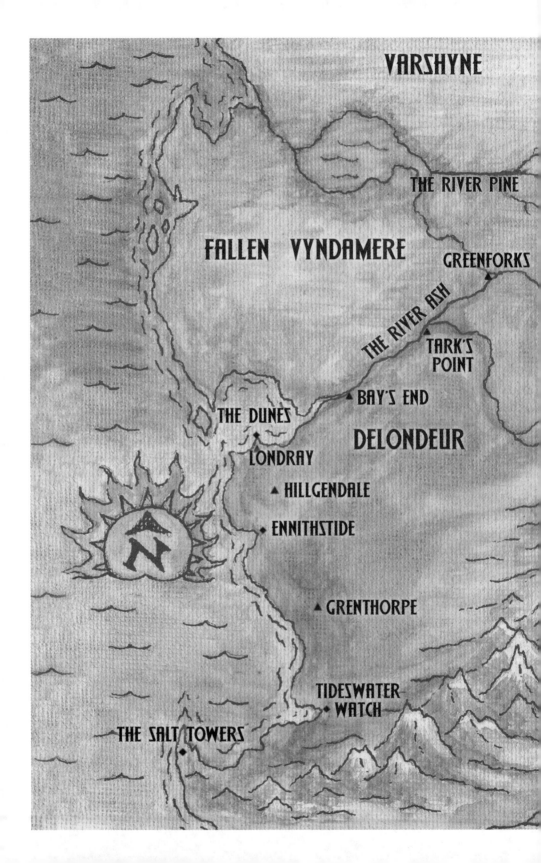

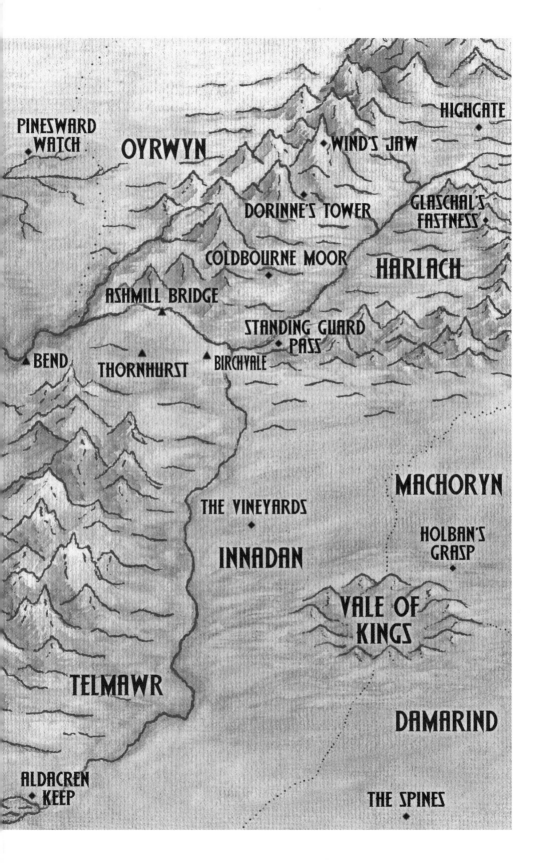

For my father, for everything, but especially for
reading me *The Hobbit* when I was four years old.
I hope some of you who knew him recognize him in this book.

Table of Contents

I had not thought to take the talk of war in the Baronies seriously when I set out to visit them. They might be populated by a backward and barbarous lot, but what people could make war on themselves for two-score years with nary a pause? Surely, I told myself, it was just the odd Warband, or petty lords divided by ancient insult having a whack at each other once or twice a summer.

The first three roadside villages I came across put the lie to that, with their burned fields and their missing sons and lost daughters. Soon, I came to believe that their war was not simply about a throne without a king. After all, their last king had been dead since soon after the war began. Rather, their Succession Strife had become the life's work of generations that had been taught nothing but war.

Excerpted from A Bard Abroad, *by Andus Carrek*

Prologue

Deep within wet, salt-kissed stone walls, a man in blue robes worked in a room without candle, lamp, or lantern. The only radiance in the room was a dark, blood-colored light emanating from underneath the man's fingernails. The dim light moved along in slow trails with his fingers, offering little illumination and no heat.

He was bald and thin, with drawn cheeks and eyes hidden in pools of shadow. His sight was not, it appeared, hampered by the dark.

The same could not be said of the slim boy that stood at his side. He was similarly robed and bare-headed, but fumbled for things in the darkness. For tools, mostly, all of them sharp, and more than one command to fetch ended with a bleeding finger.

The bald man bent over a table upon which a lamb bleated and shat, squirming to get out of the grip of his left hand. "Hook."

The boy peered into the darkness of the instrument case, thought he saw the right shape, reached out, pricked his finger. He bit away a curse and reached more carefully.

"The hook. Have you not learned the Seeing Dark yet, idiot boy? It is right in front of your face." The man's voice was smooth, nearly a hiss. The boy found the hook, his fingers only just managing to avoid the wickedly sharp point, and brought it quickly to the extended hand.

"I do not know what Gethmasanar sees in you. Great potential, he tells me.

The most powerful will he has ever touched, though it all remains unconscious." The man took the wooden handle of the hook and, almost casually, plunged it into the soft, bare belly of the lamb. The frenzied bleating became awful, magnified in the silence of the otherwise still room. He twisted once, twice, then yanked. A huge stain, dark even in the darkness of the room, pooled in a hollow in the middle of the table upon which the man worked. The lamb quickly grew still, though its pitifully diminishing cries left the boy trying, and largely succeeding, not to flinch. His eyes betrayed him, nearly closing as the muscles of his neck tightened.

"So he tells me, Bhimanzir, you must teach the boy. And yet you still quiver at the haruspicy table." He leaned forward over the dark mass he had spilled on the table and pulled the hook free; where the gore touched his fingertips, it smoked.

Whatever it was that Bhimanzir saw, he did not like, for he howled his disapproval, and mashed at the spilled organs and entrails with the flat of the hook until the table was spattered with pulped innards. "No. It must be wrong. This cannot be."

"What does it say, master?" The boy's voice was cautious without being obsequious. He did not, in truth, wish to know the answer.

"What all the rest have said," the sorcerer bellowed. He turned and seized the boy with bloodstained fingertips, and the lad felt heat rising from them. "*All of them*. Death, they have said. They have said that death comes."

Not a moment too soon, the boy thought.

"Go upstairs. To the guards. Tell them to bring me one of the new maids."

"Maids, master?"

"Are you defying me?" Bhimanzir's voice was low, and the boy knew, very dangerous. "Go and tell them to bring me a woman. One who has borne at least three children. Be quite clear on that. Go now. And if you question me again, Gethmasanar be damned." The boy felt the vile, insidious touch of one of the sorcerer's fingertips through his thin robe. "I will boil the blood in your heart. Go."

The boy knew this was no idle threat, and quickly, his bare feet slapping the stones, he vanished.

The sorcerer turned back to the table, taking a deep, steadying breath. *The lamb was wrong*, he thought. *The lamb was wrong. And the goat. The cat. And the birds. All wrong. Death does not come. Death does not come for such as me and my kindred. Not now. Not ever.*

* * *

Hundreds of leagues away from the haruspex lurking in the bowels of one castle, two men shared the late afternoon watch on an outer tower of another. Where the first had been the color of sand and stood facing a great bay leading to a greater sea, this one was a mottling of greys and browns that stood high on a mountainside, commanding multiple views of three ascending paths, its fourth side a sheer cliff face.

The men guarding the particular tower wore, like others dotting the walls and gates, dark grey tabards over mail, and they carried spears and heavy shields. Shields and tabards all bore the same device, a black peak outlined against the grey. Leaning against a crenellated wall, they watched a figure descending one of the paths, leading a string of animals. Even from this distance, one of the animals stood out, an exceptionally massive grey destrier.

"What if the baron turns us out to search for him?" one man muttered to the other.

"I'll not go," said the second.

"Liar," the first responded.

"Fine, I'll go," he admitted. "But I'll make no haste."

The sound of boots from the stairs leading to the top of their tower reached their ears, and they turned, straightening spears and shields much the way they straightened their backs.

The man who emerged was pale, wearing a black-and-silver barred surcoat over riding leathers, with a finely wrought sword belted at his right hip. Twin braids of fine blonde hair framed his face.

Their spears closed against the shields at precisely the moment their booted heels met. The knight returned their salutes with a faint wave and joined them at the wall. He wasn't winded from the rush up the stairs, but a sheen of sweet glimmered on his forehead. The watchmen fairly streamed with it beneath their mail and arms.

The pale knight drew breath as if to yell. The taller and older of the two soldiers cleared his throat.

"Begging pardon, m'lord of Highgate, but he'll not hear you from this height. Leastways, not so he could answer you."

The knight sagged a bit against the wall, but soon he stood upright again. "He would not turn back anyway, Bannerman Lamarck," he said.

"No m'lord," the older soldier replied, "I don't think he would."

"Two men tried to detain him at the main gate," the knight added, watching the figure grow smaller in the distance. "An order got to them fast enough, to try and stop him alive and unhurt, no blades."

One soldier's eyes found the other's, and they winced in near unison.

"How did that end, m'lord?" asked the younger soldier.

The knight grunted. "How do you think it ended, Chosen Man…?"

"I'm Ingil, m'lord. Ended poorly, I suppose."

"Nothing was broken, or so the chirurgeons thought. But neither will be fit for duty for a day or two," the knight replied.

"Sounds like they may have gotten away lightly, m'lord," muttered Lamarck.

"Aye. On his way out of the gate, they say he made sure to explain that he bore them no ill will, but that he could not be detained."

Ingil sighed. "M'lord, that's two knights gone this year, and it's not yet high summer…."

"I wouldn't count Sir Casamir a great loss, Chosen Man Ingil," the knight replied. "Yet any loss is regrettable."

An uncomfortable but brief silence prevailed, until finally the knight sighed and pushed away from the wall. "Dammit, Ally," he muttered, as he headed for the steps. Further muttering was lost to the two soldiers, who slumped and leaned on their spears.

* * *

The southern border of Barony Oyrwyn was all hills, valleys, and occasional mountains.

Which made it perfect ambush country.

The lone figure currently crossing that border, atop one horse and leading another, along with a mule, avoided cresting any hills. Likewise, he never descended to the bottom of any valley he crossed. There was only so much caution he could take, though. Soon, he knew he was being watched.

Nothing for it but to keep riding, he thought. His current course cut across a hillside. He meant to follow it down around its rounded, western edge, which would lead him to the north bank of the Ash. *Then cross it and leave Oyrwyn behind*, he thought, calling to his mind a precise and detailed map of the area. On it, he knew the fords and the passes, trails for cattle and game, the narrow spots and the steepest hills. What to defend, where to attack from, how fastest to move an army across it, or how to keep an invader mired in it.

So when he spotted six armed men coming around the side of the hill he was making for, he stopped and studied the ground a moment.

Too steep to risk a hard run on the grey, he told himself. He narrowed his dark blue eyes, nearly squinting, at the approaching men. *No pole-arms or spears*, he noted, though there was an assortment of knives, hand-axes, and one short sword.

The mounted man was unarmored, but armed with a grey-faced shield slung off the pommel of his saddle and a long and heavy-bladed sword strapped to his back. When he decided to stop and await the men, his hand fell to the hammer at his side. It was an ugly thing, a heavy dull maul atop nearly two feet of wooden haft, the last foot or so of which was bound with iron rings riveted into the oak.

He rested his hand on the hammer's head for a moment, feeling the warmth the metal had soaked in. The day was hot, brutally hot, though not yet midsummer. *Not going to be any cooler in the lowlands*, he reminded himself. With a snort, he drew out the hammer and laid it across his legs, resting his right hand lightly on the haft to keep it in place.

And he sat atop his palfrey and waited.

This seemed to give the other men pause; they stopped and conferred briefly, most appearing to defer to a tall man in the middle. It gave the lone horseman time to study them. The places where armbands had once been tied securely around their upper arms, or where stripes had been sewn onto their sleeves and cut off, were obviously discolored. One still wore a red tabard, a few ragged holes pocking it where insignia had been ripped off.

Deserters, he thought, with derision curling his lip. *What does that make you, then?* he scoffed to himself. He turned in the saddle and looked behind at the impressive mountain range in the distance, imagining the roads that picked through them, seeing in his mind's eye the towers that guarded them, the keeps and halls and villages they led to.

Then he turned back to face the group of deserters, squaring his shoulders.

At a distance of ten yards or so, the men drew to a halt, and the tall one took a step forward. His shoulders still had a military bearing, and his back was straight, but the rest of him looked shabby, and a patchy black beard had started filling in his cheeks.

"Good afternoon, friend traveler," the man began, his voice inflated with feigned joviality. "What brings you out t' this country?"

The mounted man thought for a moment, his lips pressed into a thin line beneath a nose that had been broken more than once. Enough times, indeed, that it had started to splay to the left side of his face.

"Traveling," he finally said, calling out in a deep, polished tone.

"We can see that well enough. Travelin' t'where?"

Another pause. "West, and then south."

"So to Delondeur, then? Wouldn't advise it, friend. Lots of trouble in that part of the barony these days."

"What sort?"

"Reavers," the man said. "Slavers, some say. Deserters gone bad. That sort of thing."

"What other kind of deserter is there?"

A thick, tense pause was followed by reactions among the men that ranged from angry, to quiet, to the one in the red tabard dropping his gaze to the ground.

"Maybe you take a look at yerself and answer that," the bearded spokesman finally shot back. "Maybe prove ya've worth by sharin' wi' some fellow...travelers."

"Sharing what, exactly?"

"Well, yer mounts. Why d'you need two when there's but one o' you? And all those bags look heavy. Too much for one man to carry."

"I think I will be keeping both mounts. And the bags," the mounted man replied.

"Big grey looks worth a lot."

"You will find that he is worth more than you are willing to spend."

"Wasn't lookin' t' spend anything, come to it," the bearded man spat. "But you can still walk away. Cold, you could still ride. On the mule." He looked back at the men behind him, forced a laugh. Most of them chuckled with him, nervously.

"I think you will find that you would spend quite a lot," the man replied. He lifted the hammer up with his right hand, extended the head, and pointed it straight at the bearded man.

"Y'reckon pointin' yer hammer at me's goin' to 'ave me pissin' my pants?"

"Just measuring my distance," the man said, lowering the hammer to rest against his leg, then adjusting his grip, settling his fingers a few inches above the bottom of the haft.

"Are you daft? There's six of us and one o'you." The bearded deserter's voice sped up and rose in pitch.

"I can count," the man replied, his voice deep and calm. "How willing are you to make it five against one?"

"You're dreamin' or you're mad. What're ya, some great knight out of legends, able to kill half a dozen brigands wi'out breaking a sweat?"

"Well," the man said, "I am already sweating, so that rules out one part of the legend. And I do not imagine I can kill all of you. But what I will do," he said, raising the hammer and pointing it again at the bearded man, "is be sure of you."

"My lads'll 'ave you," the man warned, shifting his feet, trying not to glance behind him at the others, who seemed altogether less ready for action than he did. None had seized a weapon or spread their feet into a readied stance, and one had started to edge away from their spokesman.

"So they might," the horseman allowed. "But you and your...lads...have neither bows nor spears, which means getting good and close. I may not be on my warhorse, but this little one will still give me height and speed against a man afoot, and I will put my hammer through your skull like the dull end of a breakfast knife through an egg shell."

His warning hung in the hot, close air a moment. He began to tense his thighs against his saddle, started to lift his hammer.

One of the deserters blurted out, "You've knives just for breakfast?"

The mounted man laughed, though it was a dry and humorless sound. "Some do," he replied, but, with the laughter, the tension seemed to slip away. One of the other deserters slapped at the one who'd spoken, and the bearded leader turned to face them, glaring.

It was an opening, and the mounted man seized it.

"Listen. Traveling in this heat is thirsty work," he called out. "I am willing to trade you a full skin of wine and a sack of biscuit for more of the news you spoke of. And nobody has to die."

"We could take all your wine and your biscuit," the bearded one muttered darkly.

"I'd rather be one of six splittin' the drink than dead while three do it," one of the other men countered.

"Your man sees sense. I would rather kill none of you. Hot though it is, I have no wish to go to the Cold today. I doubt you do either."

If the bearded one wasn't ready to relent, his men were, and he could sense it. "Fine. We'll 'ave the wine."

"News first, then I leave the wine and the biscuit and ride away."

"Fair enough. I don't know all o' the whys, but seems like Delondeur has let the whole north of his barony go to seed," the bearded one said.

"Word is that some slavers are workin' the villages, takin' what the press gangs haven't got already. Villages up here've not seen a green-hat or a baronial messenger in years anyway, just men in armor rounding their sons up to fight," put in one of the others.

"And he's engaged down at the southern tip of Innadan and Telmawr, and with islandman pirates at his back." The bearded man picked up the thread without missing a bit. "Cold, they even say there's a town out where the Ash gets huge that's calling itself its own barony now."

"I heard there was a den of robbers and river pirates out there," the mounted man said. "Been rumors of it now for twenty years or more. But a town?"

"Aye," the bearded man said. "They're buildin' walls, wearin' livery. All that rot."

"I have a hard time believing that Baron Delondeur could let it all go that far. And I thought he made peace with the islandmen?"

"Those in lost Vyndamere, sure," the red tabarded man replied. "Rammed it right down their throats. And he's put enough weight in the pockets o' real islandman swords-at-hire t' call it peace, I s'pose. But make good wi' one batch and another'll come along, shoutin' and burnin' and killin' for the Sea Dragon."

The less Lionel is looking this way, the better chance I have to get across his barony, the horseman noted silently. Then, cynically, needling himself, *To get where?*

"Well," he said aloud, "it is west and south for me no matter what. There are still some villages across the Ash, aye?"

"Might be. Might be that some of the villages that are standin' today'll be burnin' tomorrow," the bearded man said.

"West and south it is anyway." The horseman slid down from his saddle, hammer still in hand. He walked to his mule and rummaged in the packs, pulling free a small sack and a bulging skin. He set both down on a sun-warmed rock, stood, took his saddle, and said, "I shall be off now."

"You might be ridin' t' yer grave," the bearded one said, trying to keep one eye on him and one eye on the food. "Safer up here in Oyrwyn, most like. Plenty of places t' get lost in all that mountain."

"For you, maybe," the man said, as he gathered up his leads and gently nudged his palfrey back into motion. *I could never get lost up there*, he thought.

"Thanks for the food an' drink…you got a name?"

"You are welcome to it. And I do."

"Goin' t'let us know it? I'm Malken."

Silently, the man rode off, giving the deserters a wide berth, descending further down the hill than he would've liked, but round it all the same.

* * *

The lone horseman pushed on as far as he could before nightfall. The day was long and the sun stayed with him, so he had a good view of the Ash River valley as he tied his animals up for the night and began brushing them down. He had found a camp at the thickly-wooded top of a lone, rounded hill. He knew it as a good place to set bowmen who wanted to harass a host heading north.

In the distance, as the air around him darkened, he could see an unusually bright glare of flame, and the deserter's words came back to him.

"Standing today, burning tomorrow," he muttered. "Or tonight." He stood and watched the distant flame for a while. At least he was a full day from the village that was burning now. *And that's if I give the larger towns a miss completely.*

He studied it a moment more, then nodded faintly. "Good a place as any to get lost, I expect." He turned back to his own meager fire, made more for the form of the thing than anything else, settled his back against a tree, laid his hammer over his lap, and slept lightly, fitfully.

A ghost-glow of the distant fire lingered on the backs of his eyelids most of the night.

CHAPTER 1

The First Step

The farmhouse was empty.

He was sure of that, because he'd watched it from the cover of the treeline for a solid half-turn of the glass. Empty of folk, anyway. There was livestock around, cows and chickens and some dogs that roamed around outside, sniffling every so often at the ground, staring off down the road toward the village proper.

When he'd risen before the sun the previous morning, he could still see this hamlet burning in the distance. For a day and a quarter he had followed the smoke, as he forded the Ash, crossed the High Road, and finally found himself at the mouth of the slight valley that this village nestled within. It was well wooded on both sides, with stands of old growth as ancient as any he'd ever seen. A few farms clustered around its northern end, spread out along a packed-dirt road.

From what he'd seen from higher ground, the village center followed a bend in the road as it turned west, leading to the inner plains of Delondeur and the distant rise of the Thasryach Mountains, a thin range that divided Delondeur neatly in half. The road continued south beyond it as a smaller track, making it a kind of crossroads, if old and unused.

Sweat trickled down his face and back and finally, with a snort and a shrug, he put himself back on his horse and led his other animals down the road. He kept his hammer loose at his side as he rode, dust turning up under the palfrey's hooves.

The smell hit him before he even rounded the turn, past a gently sloping meadow with a hillock at its top—woodsmoke, a huge and powerful punch of it. But the air held another odor, something burnt and foul.

You do not wish to admit to knowing that smell, he thought darkly as he continued riding.

Aside from the ill-omened, ink-black birds that hopped and flitted about, he decided that he and his animals were the only living things in the smoking remnants of the village center. Instead of taking flight as the man and his retinue trotted by, one of the carrion birds turned a baleful eye on him, yawped menacingly, and resettled itself on a charred wooden beam.

The man was large, but it was thickness of chest and broadness of shoulders, rather than height, that gave the impression of an imposing stature. He was no longer young; thin strands of grey mingled with his dark hair. He sat on the smaller of the two horses with his back blade-straight and dark blue eyes alert, though restless.

Finally, he dismounted, swinging easily out of the saddle, with the economy of motion that comes of having done a thing a thousand times, and more. Dirt mushroomed up as the heels of his boots hit the ground. The larger horse and the heavily laden mule that rode on leads behind him crowded closer, seeking treats, but had to be content with muzzle rubs as the man walked alone further down the track.

Before he did, he took the reins of the smaller lead horse, dropped them to the dirt, and stepped on them; the small shaggy palfrey whickered knowingly and stood in place. The larger horse and the mule followed suit.

Around him, buildings smoked and smoldered, adding to the heat of the day. The reavers who'd burned the place had been thorough. Dark stains marked the once carefully swept stones in front of some of the buildings. Few of the charred buildings had once boasted two floors, and only one that he saw had been taller.

As he neared the source of the smoke and the stink, he instinctively slipped his hammer free of its loop. *A hand is better filled than idle*, he thought.

The village green was now green in name only. It had become a mass pyre, and a sloppy one. Corpses lay piled atop one another, more than a score of them. Many were scorched to the bone, while others were simply burned to blackened husks.

"More than a score," he murmured aloud, sinking to one knee on the track, a foot or so from the green. The road circled around it, forming a large oval shape. At the far end from where he knelt, the largest building he'd yet seen in the village smoked fitfully; though in the main it was built of stone and its walls still stood, the roof thatch had long since burned away, and several of the framing timbers bowed threateningly.

He rose and contemplated the green and the pile of ash, char, bone, and flesh at its center. "Not enough of them," he finally pronounced aloud, though no one else was near to hear it.

Edging around the green, looking to the ground before his footprints, something drew his eye back to the horror at its center. He shook his head, spat into the dust, and started back towards his animals, murmuring again. "Too many to bury. Be here for days."

Could be back to the High Road and following it east in two days. At Innadan's border in a week if luck is with me. He took a deep breath, careful to inhale through his mouth and not his nostrils.

The stink got into his nostrils anyway, and his mouth, and his expression soured. *Nothing a good half- barrel of Innadan red and someone to drink it with couldn't wash away.* His own jaded voice prodded him into action. He spat, trying to rid his mouth of the foulness. *The bodies on that green are not all the folk of this village,* said another part of him. *And there are deep wagon-wheel ruts in the dust leading west.*

"Wine to the east and slavers to the west. An easy decision, I call that," he said aloud, gathering himself to take a step back toward his horses and to the best vineyards in the baronies.

The smell of burnt flesh was too thick in the air to step away from. It coated his mouth, sick and sour at once.

He turned back toward the pyre.

A few steps onto the green, then he again dropped to one knee. He picked up an arrow sticking at an angle from the lightly charred grass, turned it around in his hands, and spat again. "Shoddy." He snapped it between two fingers and tossed it away as he stood. Idly, he tapped his hammer against his calf, letting it dangle head-down from his right hand.

"They have, what? A day and a half? And a wagon or two. A lot of water and food to haul. You do not mean to follow them, you old fool." He looked back at the pile of charred bodies.

He began edging around the green, heading more or less toward the large stone building he'd decided must have been the village inn. It had, despite the missing roof, empty window frames, and scorch marks, the look of a settled and comfortable place. Or, he supposed, it had had such a look two days ago.

Suddenly, impossibly, over the cawing of the birds, the rustle of the wind, the whickering of his animals, he heard a thin voice crying.

He ran. He was not fleet of foot and wore heavy leathers, weapons, and worn riding boots, but his legs churned with power, if not grace. He gave the pile of charred bones a wide berth and quickly reached the gutted building. "*Ware the house,*" he yelled, the force of his voice suddenly cutting the quiet and sending birds flapping away in annoyance. "*Where are you?*" Even as he asked, he was ducking under the stone doorframe, knocking aside a few charred sticks.

There was no answer, only another tiny sob, fainter than the first. He sprang again, letting out a piercing whistle. The distant *thunk* of several pairs of hooves told him his call had been answered.

Several paces across the room ran a long, low counter, also made of stone and with a hammered metal top, now laden with ash. Piles of shattered crockery surrounded it. He scanned the room. The charred stairs leading upward would not support his weight. He turned his eyes back towards the bar.

Wagering silently against himself, he ran, planted his hands upon the bar, and leapt it, sword rattling against his back; he landed hard on one knee on the other side, exhaled sharply, and looked for the source of his wager. Staying low, he swept his hands across the floor, scattering jagged shards of wine jars, soot, and charred pieces of wood.

He didn't see it, but his thickly calloused fingers felt it: an iron ring set into the floor. *Cold well,* he thought, and pulled upon it. It gave, but it did not open.

He dropped his hammer to the sooty ground, set his left hand to his right wrist, and squatted with one boot planted to either side of the trap door. He pulled again, pushing upward with his legs; the trap door flew open and the quiet crying that had twice teased his ears suddenly filled the building.

Flinging himself down, he chanced a look in. The well appeared to have been dug out from some kind of natural spring, large enough to hold a keg, though none was in it now. Instead, in the cool waters he saw a small, nondescript shape, covered in soot, shivering and soaked head to toe. He reached in, seized thin shoulders, and hauled the child up and out. Laying the small and nearly limp form against him with one arm, he ran for the door and the snorting horses that gathered just beyond it.

CHAPTER 2

Mol

Later, the lass, for so the shivering child proved to be, dozed as close to the fire as the man had dared to put her. He squatted across the spitting and crackling flames, hastily made with scraps of unburned wood from a nearby, unravaged cottage. His sheathed sword rested on a stone beside him, and he watched her intently. There was no telling how long she'd hidden in the chill waters of the inn's cold well, and he wasn't entirely sure she'd wake. He'd chafed her arms and legs, dried her, and wrapped her; the soaked, homespun dress she'd been wearing now dried on rocks beside the fire. Reluctantly, for a while, he had stripped his chest bare and held the girl against his skin inside a blanket, hoping all the while that she didn't wake and find herself being held by a strange, half-naked man.

The horses whickered impatiently from their hasty picket a few yards away by a bare-branched tree, wanting tending. With a wary eye still on the girl, he moved to them and began loosening straps and uncinching girdles. Soon a small hillock of gear piled up near the edge of the firelight.

The heaviest bags, taken from the mule, clanked as he set them carefully down. As he strapped small feedbags around the animals' mouths, a sharp cry spun him around. The girl was sitting bolt upright, backing away from the fire, her wide eyes huge dark circles in her pale, shadowed face.

The man had the presence of mind to stand where he was and to slowly lift his hands, palms out. "Peace, child," he said, his voice a careful rumble. "You are safe now," he continued, but she shook her head hard, side-to-side.

"No. NO," she repeated sharply. "Who are you? What were you doing in the inn? In the village? Be y' another slaver, followin' to be cert none were missed?" She scrambled around, one hand holding the blanket to her, the other searching behind her; finally she brought it up, brandishing a stone.

"One question at a time, young miss," the man said, his voice still slow and careful. He moved no closer. "My name is Allystaire. I am no slaver, nor brigand, blackguard, pirate, or thief. I came down into this valley because I saw the smoke yesterday morn." He paused, then added, "And the fire the night before." He lowered his hands, but stayed rooted to the spot, watching the girl carefully, narrowing his eyes.

She watched him just as carefully. There didn't appear to be any guile in her appraisal, but her eyes didn't flinch away from him, and he had the sense of being studied, weighed somehow. He broke the silence.

"Have you more questions? Shall I guess at them? I heard your cries as I searched your green and I pulled you from the well because..." He paused, shrugged, "because if I did not, then I would be some measure of blackguard, aye?"

The child nodded slowly, lowering, but not dropping, the stone she clutched. Her eyes moved over the fire, to the pile of gear across it, lingering over the arms. "Yer a knight." Half statement, half question, as her gaze lingered over them.

Allystaire grimaced lightly, hoping the child wouldn't see it in the dark. "No," he said, after a pause.

"Ya have food?"

She moves on quickly, this one, he thought, and nodded.

"What can I call you? I cannot go on with "lass" and "child" for long."

Her turn to pause, eyes still moving between him, the packs, and the sword, shield, and hammer. "Mol," she said, uncertainly.

"Mol, then. A fine name. I am going to come back to the fire now, Mol, and sit on the other side of it from you. I will not touch a weapon, and I will get meat and bread for both of us. I prepared some hot broth while you slept."

With that said, he took slow, measured steps until he could squat back down by the packs he had unloaded from the mule and began rummaging.

"Y' must be a knight or a lord to have three horses," Mol finally said.

"I have neither title nor land. What you see is everything I own," he replied, sweeping one arm in a gesture of mock grandiloquence.

"Then why d'ya have three horses? Man can't ride more'n one at a time," she countered, lifting her chin.

"Well," he replied, pointing back towards the picketed, munching beasts, "there are in fact only two horses, and one mule. The mule carries packs, which neither of the horses could do as well. The larger horse, well, he is only for riding in battle or…" He stopped short, and went on. "The smaller one is a riding horse; he can bear a rider at better speed for longer than the destrier might. The right animal for the right task, you see," he added, smiling tightly. Finally, he found the bag he was looking for, and dug out hard bread and dried meat, holding it out toward the girl.

Unselfconsciously, Mol leaned forward to reach over the fire for the food and asked, "What are their names?"

Startled enough by the question, he almost let a chunk of meat fall into the fire, but caught himself. "What? Names?"

"Horses have names," she said, nodding authoritatively.

He shook his head, handed over the food, and sat back. "I have never thought on it. It does no good to get too attached to an animal. They are well-trained and healthy. All that matters." He dug out food for himself.

"Ya talk about them like they're tools," Mol frowned, a piece of bread held halfway to her mouth. "They aren't shovels. They deserve better'n that."

"They are considerably more expensive than shovels, so they get better than that."

She ignored him for a moment, staring at the animals, her head cocked to one side as if listening to some distant noise. Then she shrugged, began gnawing at her food, and was silent for a moment.

"Where were ya bound?" she suddenly asked around a mouthful of bread and meat.

Allystaire shrugged, shook his head, and relaxed, sitting back on the ground and stretching his booted feet toward the fire. "Nowhere certain. I told you; I saw smoke in the valley, and so instead of skirting it, I sought the source."

"'Twas foolish," the girl said, and went on before he could protest, pointing at him with the chewed bread in her hand. "What if they'd been there still?"

"I suppose I would have had to fight," Allystaire replied with the gentlest of shrugs.

"And if there'd been a dozen? A score? A warband turned to banditry?"

"In order then," he said, raising a finger, "were it a dozen or a score—makes little difference, I suppose—if they were organized, had bows, knew how to use them, I would likely die." He shrugged. "If only some or none of those were true, perhaps I could scatter them. A warband, though?" He nodded. "I should like my chances better. Likely to have a career man-at-arms or two, even an officer or landless knight among them. I could have parlayed with such as that, perhaps talked them down, or challenged one to a single fight. A warband would kill me, but I could make them understand that some of them would die, too. Those sorts of men do not throw their lives away cheaply."

"Y'know a lot o' warbands," Mol said, turning her head and studying him sidelong. He wasn't certain, but perhaps there was a tiny accusatory note in it.

"I do," he allowed. "I have had occasion to learn of them. I might even be headed to join one, for all I know."

In short order the child worked her way through the food he had given her and scooted closer to the fire, now staring straight at him. "Ye'd seek to join such a group? Even if y'came upon them at the slaughter?"

He thought a moment, narrowing his eyes. "Perhaps." Then he raised a finger. "Only if I saw some men among them, not just rabid dogs. Understand that even a good soldier, a man of strong guts with good intents, he can go a bit mad at the wrong time. Especially if he follows the wrong man."

"And ya'd be the right man then?" Her eyes narrowed as well.

"Where are all these questions coming from, Mol? None of these things happened, did they? But I will answer this last one: no. But if I were aware of *who* the wrong man was in such an instance? The man who did that?" He hooked a thumb over his shoulder, to the distant, shadowed shapes of her ruined village. "I would see him into the ground and on to the next world, if there is one."

"Slit 'is throat then?" Finally, she tossed aside the rock she'd been holding onto.

"Cold, lass! I said I would answer one more and I did!" There was more laughter than heat in Allystaire's voice, but it quieted, and he said, finally, softly, "I have never slit the throat of a man who did not know what was coming. If I found the man who did that, he would die with a weapon in his hand. But he would die."

"Sure o' yerself," Mol said, a note of reproach in her voice.

Allystaire laughed lightly. "I suppose so." He reached into the small stack of wood at hand and tossed some into the flames. "You probably need to sleep. Question me more in the morning, if you must." He stretched his legs so that his boots just brushed the stones defining the firepit.

Mol was silent a moment as she considered this. Then, with a yawn she didn't try to contain, she stretched back out on the ground. Her head lifted up, and she quietly asked, "Y'll still be here in the morning?"

"I will," Allystaire said, his own voice slightly weary.

"Promise me," she said urgently, leaning forward to peer at him across the fire.

"I promise, Mol, that I will be here in the morning," he said. The words rolled out of him more easily than he expected.

That seemed to satisfy her, and she settled her head down on pillowed hands, and soon her breathing eased.

With a small sigh, Allystaire leaned back further against his saddles and packs. "Fool," he murmured, almost silently. Unbidden, a voice whispered to him, *You could leave the child. You fed her and warmed her. What more do you owe her?* He sneered at no one, at his own thoughts, and stood up to see once more to his animals. When their feedbags were stored, their coats given a quick brushing, he sat back down across from Mol, pulled his hammer across his lap, and let his mind drift.

He slept, but lightly. Every so often he would stir himself awake, tensing his legs against the ground as if he'd need to spring to his feet. Each time he looked across the fire, Mol was sleeping well, but the sense of being watched and measured never left him.

CHAPTER 3

The Second Step

Dawn broke weakly, pushing thin, reedy stems of light through grey clouds. Mol woke shivering; the fire hadn't quite died, but it threw little heat. Immediately her head snapped up so she could see where Allystaire had been sitting last night, but he wasn't there. She sat bolt upright, eyes searching the camp, until she heard the solid thump of his boots in the dust.

"Food in a moment," he said suddenly, without turning to look back at her. "Your dress ought to be dry enough if you want to slip it back on."

She stood up, blanket still held around her shoulders, and half-circled the fire for her homespun wool. Quickly, she dropped the blanket and slipped the dress back over her head, shivering again. "S'damp from the dew, y'fool. Why'd ya not pack it 'fore you slept?"

Allystaire pulled the strap of a saddlebag closed and turned slowly around. "Do I look like a washerwoman to you, that I should know this?" He tried to soften his words with a smile, but it was an expression that sat uneasily above his heavy, lightly stubbled jaw. Mol glared at him. He sighed, changed tack, hefting a sack in his hand.

"Hungry? Bread and cheese. And a piece of this, which I suppose you could do with." He lifted his other hand, which held a long, mottled white and brown cone and a pair of hinged, dark iron pincers.

Her eyes widened and she took a few quick steps toward him. "Sugar? How d'ya have so much of it?"

"Long story." He held the sack out to her to forestall more questions, then applied the nips to the sugar loaf, breaking off a few small pieces and tipping them into his other hand. Loaf and nips went back into the saddlebag; he held out the sugar to her, and she took it. Quickly, she stuck a piece into her mouth, but didn't chew, instead letting it sit in the center of her mouth and melt, her eyes closing as she concentrated on the unusual sweetness.

"While you eat," Allystaire said, walking back to the fire and retrieving the last things he'd left there, the shield and warhammer, "think about where you want to go." He slung the shield off the pommel of the larger horse; the hammer slid into a loop on the saddle's right side. "We could be back out of the valley by noon if we cut straight for the High Road. Have any kin around these parts? Ashmill Bridge? Birchvale? Those are the nearest towns I know."

As he spoke, the girl's eyes opened again, fixing on him steadily. Her tongue tucked the sugar chunk into one side of her mouth. "I've no kin except what lived here in Thornhurst," she said, carefully. "And those places are the wrong way, too far upriver."

"Too far upriver?" Allystaire puzzled over this for a moment, brow furrowing. "Oh no. No lass. No. You do not mean what I think you mean."

"Frozen Hells I don't!" she yelled. "'twere slavers came through and they've my family and I mean ta find 'em! They're takin' 'em downriver meanin' to sell 'em and you know it!"

Allystaire raised a hand, shaking his head gently. "Lass… Mol. I mean no cruelty to you. You have suffered, I know. I have seen this happen to villages such as yours before." *Ordered it done, you mean,* he thought, wincing. "And if you could find them, what do you mean to do? Be enslaved? Let me take you somewhere out of their path."

"Come with me," the girl said, suddenly, passionately. "Track 'em. We'll find 'em and kill 'em, free m' folk so we can come back and rebuild." Her words came out in a rush, the sugar he'd given her crunching between her teeth.

He sighed heavily, looking to the ground for a moment. "There were how many? I am one man, and they have a head start."

"Y'can move faster than they can. And what was it you told me last night? Y'came riding for the smoke knowin' it could be a dozen or a score. Y'sounded plenty confident in the dark. Not so much in daylight."

Allystaire grimaced, then forced his features to relax and took a deep breath. "How many were there?" *You are not considering this.*

"Near a dozen, wi' two big covered wagons. Came to our inn, it was run by my dad and nuncle. Stayed two nights, drinkin' their weight and then refusin' to pay. Then when nuncle told 'em to pay and leave…"

"They turned violent. And the covered wagons turned out to be a cage, aye?" Allystaire raised an eyebrow at the girl, watched as she nodded slowly, turned her eyes toward the ground, tears gathering in her eyes.

Freeze. "Listen. Mol. If we trail after them—*if*—mind you, understand that I am no hero of legend. There might be no rescue, no help we can give." Allystaire knelt, so that his face was closer to hers, but stopped himself short of reaching out to touch her. "Your kinfolk would not thank me for delivering you to the slavers you escaped."

Mol lifted her head, sniffling, and wiped at her eyes with the sleeve of her dress. "I don't fear that. And I haven't other kin to go to. Leastways if I find 'em I can be with 'em again."

Until they sell you to a brothel or a whoremonger. "I cannot convince you to ride with me somewhere? To a church?"

She shook her head defiantly, eyes suddenly agleam. "Folk here didn't hold with any gods. What good've they done us? I'm followin' my kin whether you come or no. If I have to walk after 'em while you ride away, I will." Then, as if to prove the point, she started stomping off, her small bare feet kicking up dust clouds.

He sighed, stood, briefly rubbed at his closed eyes with two fingers. The famous vineyards and friendly women of Barony Innadan seemed further away than ever. Allystaire looked eastward over his shoulder. *Could put her in a sack and tie her to the mule*, he mused. *And then how would I be any different from the reavers?* Finally, he looked back to her; she was several paces away and showed no signs of slowing. He took a deep breath and called out to her.

"Mol, lass! Can you sit a horse?

* * *

"These reavers leave a trail one of the Blind Priests could follow," Allystaire remarked, as, a day and a half later, he and Mol followed them steadily east.

"D'ya think there's a ship waitin' for 'em?" Mol sat on the smaller horse, the stirrups shortened in a way that might have been comical, if she weren't sitting in the saddle so seriously, so competently.

The man shook his head, walking alongside the warhorse a few paces ahead of her. "No. Not much further, another day and a half if I make my guess, 'til we come to the bend in the Ash and the town I have heard now squats upon it."

"What town? I had 'em just makin' for the bay..."

Allystaire shook his head, frowned up at Mol. "No getting to the bay without going straight through Londray, and they will not be able to move slaves through there. The baron's law will see to that, at least."

"Baron's law?" The girl twisted in the saddle to look down at him. "Don't have a baron."

"You do. His name is Lionel Delondeur. And for a whole new town to have raised itself up beyond the reach of his laws, he or his lords must be taking regular payments from whatever thug has back-stabbed his way to running the place, and so Delondeur's knights, wardens, and rivermen pretend not to know what goes on there."

Mol reined in the palfrey, her face suddenly contorted in a rage that was somehow unchildlike; it was no temper tantrum, but rather a sudden, bright anger that took Allystaire aback.

"He's supposed to protect us if he's our baron," she shouted. "What good is lordship if—"

"Do you want everyone else on this road, or within a mile of it, to know where we are?" Allystaire interrupted her brusquely. Dropping his voice, he added, "Yet in truth, lass? You are right. That is what lords ought to do. But he is busy fighting wars to move his borders and win honors, and the gold from pirates helps him do it. Slavers, though? I would be surprised if Lionel would brook such as that."

"Ya say his name like ya know him. If that's so, then why not go t'him, after m'folk are rescued, and tell him of it."

He sighed, dropped the reins he held, and walked to the side of the palfrey, tilting his head just slightly upward. "Child, I am going to tell you something true. Something you should remember." He paused, pressed his lips together for a moment. "Do not expect the great folk of this world to care what happens to you. The only place kings and barons give a damn about farmers and laborers is in legends."

"But yer a knight and ya do care or y' wouldn't be here now," Mol insisted, pointing a stubborn finger down at him.

"I am no knight," Allystaire said wearily. He turned, abruptly ending the conversation, picked up his reins, and starting walking the destrier again.

"Then how d'ya know the names of barons and so much of the land? Those'r the kinds of things knights know," Mol persisted.

"I am merely educated," he replied, through nearly clenched teeth.

"What's that mean? Y'can read, n'cipher?'

Allystaire nodded. "That and more."

"What more is there?"

"Doing sums, reading maps, memorizing heraldry and bloodlines. And music, and dancing…but I was never any good at those."

"And where'd ya learn all this?"

He shook his head sharply. "Nowhere you know, Mol."

"Well y'know a lot o'things farmer folk dunno. And yer rich," she went on, blithely. "Either of yer horses would cost more'n the entire lot our village would sell on fair days. And ya've more sugar than I've ever seen aside from oncet a dwarf caravan came through."

He looked back, frowning. "Enough. I have answered as many of your questions as I intend to. Now let us have silence."

The man on foot, the child on the easily trotting palfrey, they followed a pair of obvious wheel-ruts driven deep into ground by the heavily laden wagon the villagers had likely been imprisoned in. The ground was wetter here. The previous day's rainfall and denser tree cover gave the travelers a slight but welcome respite from the late summer heat. The equally welcome silence, Allystaire suspected, was destined to last but briefly; he was proven right after only a few more moments of plodding along.

"Can I try ridin' the big horse again?"

"No."

"He won't try n'bite me again, m'sure of it."

"He did not try the first time. He warned you. If I put you on his back again, he will take a finger."

That bought him another few moments of silence. Mol looked around the landscape and at the huge destrier and mule trailing along behind the palfrey she sat upon, but her eyes always seemed to settle on Allystaire.

"Who're the Blind Priests?"

Startled, he looked back over his shoulder, sweaty brow furrowed. "What?"

"You mentioned Blind Priests earlier. Who're they?"

He shrugged, the heavy, stiff leather he wore creaking. "Priests. Serve the god Urdaran." He blinked. "Has one never come to your village?"

She shook her head, then immediately followed up with, "Why're they blind?"

He shrugged again, looking once more at the road ahead. "Some fool dogma or other. Urdaran urges his followers to 'look inward' and eschew—ignore—the world. So his most devoted priests blind themselves."

Mol gasped sharply. "That's horrible! Why would a god demand that?"

"I have known more than one scholar to waste his life trying to answer that, and lass, I shall not try. I avoid the gods and anyone who pays them more than lip service. I counsel you to do the same."

The silence that followed in the wake of Allystaire's sullen advice was relieved only by plodding hooves, creaking leather, and jingling tack.

CHAPTER 4

Bend

The next day, Allystaire drew them to a halt with the sun blazing hot and bright above them. A voice he knew well spoke up within him, speaking from an instinct he knew well not to ignore. *Get some Freezing steel on.* In answer, he murmured, "Sound advice, that." So he led them off the muddy track of a road and pulled a heavy pack free of the mule's load and set it down on the side of the road.

As he tugged it open, heavy-looking pieces of dark, oiled metal were revealed. Mol crowded over his shoulder to look; suddenly she pointed excitedly at the breastplate.

"I knew you were a knight," she crowed.

"Quiet!" Allystaire looked back over his shoulder at her while his hands deftly pulled the plates free—front and back, curved to contour around the body to deflect impact, but undecorated. Overlapping segments would protect the sides of the ribs from the waist to the armpit. A great confusion of straps and buckles connected them.

"Say those words again that loud, and you may bring trouble, girl. I am not a knight, and we do *not* want anyone in this town thinking I am, understand?" He stood, laying the plates aside, and shrugged his sword off his back and set it down. Mol reached for it, but after a stern look, stepped back and tucked her hands behind her back.

The heavy boiled leather vest he wore came off, landing in the grass with a muffled thump, but the sleeves stayed in place. Underneath it was a padded shirt, visibly sweat-soaked. Allystaire knelt, giving a muted grunt as his left knee thunked into the ground. Carefully, he slid an arm, then his head, through the tangle of buckles and let the weight begin to settle onto his shoulders. The cuirass remained unbuckled on his left side, so he turned and began fitting leather into metal.

"Listen lass, and listen well," he said with a grunt, as he pulled a strap tight against his side. He leaned forward awkwardly, gathered up sword and vest, and stood in one swift movement. "This is vital. When we reach the gate, say nothing. *Nothing*. Do you understand? Let me talk, and only me. You are my mute, addled niece." He stuffed the vest into the sack in place of the cuirass he now wore, and resettled the strap of his long scabbard back over his shoulder.

As he tied the sack back into place, he continued. "Like as not, folk will assume I have brought you here to sell you." Immediately he shook his head, holding his hand up to forestall her. "Not a word. I have no intention of buying or selling you. Besides," Allystaire tried on a lopsided grin that didn't particularly fit his face, "what kind of price could I possibly get for a soft-brained mute, eh?"

Chuckling at his own gibe, he didn't see Mol's hand dart to the ground; there was no warning, only a thump as the stone, cunningly thrown, connected with his shoulder. "Aghh! Peace, lass," he said, reaching to rub the spot with his opposite hand. "Peace. It was meant in jest." He pulled himself into the saddle of the destrier, and indicated that she should do the same on the palfrey. Gathering the leads of both other animals, he began trotting them the last two miles towards the timber-walled town he saw rising in the distance.

A haze of smoke sat heavily above it in the afternoon air, and Allystaire could smell the place before he could see it clearly. Brackish water dominated, but the air carried notes of sweat, piss, wet burnt wood, and moldering garbage.

When they neared, Allystaire felt his stomach clench as a pair of men in leather, carrying poleaxes, with fluttering cloth badges pinned to their chests, stepped into the road. From his belt, he plucked a pair of heavy leather gloves with iron studs along the knuckles, and slipped them on. *Could just leave her and go.*

"Remember, say nothing," he whispered without turning around, as they neared the outermost earshot of the guards.

The sight of three animals and two riders had certainly drawn the attention of the guards, as they stood on either side of the road with their spears held out, blocking the path beyond. About twenty yards beyond them stood a crude gate made of tree trunks lashed together that a few men working together could draw closed, against a similarly constructed timber palisade. Allystaire was taken aback by the gate, having expected a miserable clutch of tents and shacks. And while tents crowded up against both sides of the wall, beyond was a hotchpotch of buildings built on no plan, and far more of them than there should've been. While hides strung on poles predominated in the front, driftwood and wattle-and-daub hovels seemed to spring from them.

Beyond those, buildings of better timber and many of stone stood crowded together, practically touching, above muddy streets. In the distance, Allystaire thought he could descry some buildings of brick.

Great deal bigger than I had ever imagined, Allystaire thought. *This must have been growing since I was a boy.* Then, with a faint sneer, he thought, *Could probably raze it with two-score and ten good men.* He reined to a stop in front of the guards.

"Down off the 'orse, yer lordship," sneered the nearer spear-bearer. A thick brown beard covered his cheeks, and a leather cap ringed with iron sat atop his head. His clothing and equipment were as mismatched as the town he guarded: a studded leather jerkin, sailor's pantaloons tucked into tough hobnailed boots, and an archer's buckler strapped to his left arm. The badges pinned to their chests appeared crudely sewn, some kind of blue blotch on white. "'Afore yer enterin' Bend, yer packs need t'be searched and anything yer sellin' valued for, ah, excise duty." The man pronounced the last two words with extreme precision.

"I am not selling anything," Allystaire said, carefully. Leather creaked as the fingers of one hand curled slightly. "And I doubt the baron would be very happy to hear that someone else is claiming taxes in his lands."

"Well yer can ask him yerself, Lord Broke-beak," the other spearman piped in, chortling nasally at his own wit. This one was younger, thinner, with pockmarked cheeks barely covered with hair. "Baron Windspar o' Bend don't hold no court but sure'n a lordly one such as yerself can knock on his door and tell him all about his duties n'taxes n'like, no?"

With a sigh, Allystaire turned and fixed his dark-eyed stare on the younger man, leaning one hand on the pommel of his saddle. The destrier under him snorted, stamped one hoof on the rock-strewn road. "Baron Windspar? Must not have been in the most recent books of lineage." His eyes narrowed, bored intently on the younger man, who returned the glare, if only for a moment. *Only the older one's a threat. See the rust on the boy's spearhead? See how he has three daggers all lined up on a baldric on his chest, where they do him no earthly good? Kill the old one first.*

Finally, Allystaire smiled atop his horse and reached to the purse tied securely to his hip. He tugged it open, and, with glove-thickened finger tips, carefully extracted a round circle of gold. He held it up where the afternoon sunlight glinted brilliantly off of it for a moment, let them see the sky through it as he twisted and turned the bright metal loop in the air.

"Surely a gold link will more than pay Baron Windspar's excise tax, eh?" Then, making sure both men had time to see the glint, he casually flicked his wrist toward the younger guard, tossing the link off the road into the weeds, a yard away from him.

The older man was faster to react. He dropped his spear and bulled his way across the road toward the tall growth. Only a tug on the reins kept Allystaire's horse from lunging with its teeth for the man as he passed so near. Soon enough the younger one got the gist and dove for the link. Allystaire nudged his destrier's flank and gently whistled; all three animals started up again in unison and stepped past the gate, and the palisade wall.

Behind them were some muted curses, some thumps as blows were exchanged. Allystaire paid them no mind and, as soon as they were well within the timber wall, slid down off his horse. As he gathered the reins in his left hand, he used his right to pull the warhammer out of its loop on the saddle, and clutched it with the head pressed against his hand.

With Mol obeying—for now at least—the instructions to keep silent, Allystaire led them into the city, such as it was. The streets were unplanned, unpaved, and teeming with locals.

They were a mix of folk: rivermen, laborers, miserable types Allystaire guessed were refugees from the borders with Innadan, Oyrwyn, or the coast that Islandmen were known to raid. Some might have trickled down out of Vyndamere, long since given over to the same raiding Islandmen.

Many were armed, and he saw more than one wearing armor or livery with telltale fading framing a place where badges, devices, and rank sigils had been ripped away. They stank, and they glared at him, but most gave him a wide berth, and a circle began to form around him and his animals; the destrier, disliking the crowding, snapped and stamped at anyone who stepped too near. The circle around them widened.

Tracking down an inn didn't take long, as what passed for streets seemed to be organized mostly by what could be bought or sold there. When they came across a row of tents over which hung the unmistakable miasma of fermenting beer, Allystaire turned down it. Tents became huts, built long with low, sloping thatched roofs and holes in the middle to let out smoke.

A two-storey building of stone caught his eye as soon as they made their way round the tents and the huts, and he guided them towards it. Looping the reins casually around the post outside, he strode up to the door and nudged it open with the head of his hammer.

"Innkeep!" His voice rolled into the room and could be heard several yards into the street, pitched to carry without bellowing. "I need a groom to show me to your stables." Letting the door close, he strolled back to the street and quickly dug again into his purse; two circles of silver, looped together, dangled from the fingers of his left hand. A wiry, cross-looking man in a grease-spattered apron threw open the door and opened his mouth to speak.

Whatever words the innkeep had been about to say died on his lips when he caught the glint of silver. "Right this way m'lord," he murmured.

Allystaire turned and offered a quick grin towards Mol, tucking the silver links into his clenched fist. The stables stood behind the inn and, while not large, appeared more sturdily built than most of the surrounding dwellings.

"No need for any titles. Call me Allystaire." The horses followed and Allystaire backed up to help Mol dismount. "How long have you been here, goodman?"

"Two years less a score, m'lord. Sign o' the Stone Wall was the first inn to open in Bend."

"The town has been here that long?"

"Aye, though it was a fort and a watchtower or two first," the innkeep replied. He led them on a well-tamped path around the side of his building to a small wooden outbuilding with a sagging roof. "Most o'the stones that make the place up were part o'the outer wall."

The man pushed open doors that swung easily on their hinges, a sign Allystaire took well.

Stinks, Allystaire thought, for indeed it did, as the stables were small and the day hot, *but at least it's an honest stench.*

"Now, that'll be three stalls, half a silver link each a day, and I'll throw in hay and waterin' free. Rooms, well if yer wantin' to throw a roll down on a floor, be two lead bobs a head. Private room with a proper bed, 'ave to be a silver link." His lips parted in a stump-filled, hungry smile.

"Your prices do not worry me, goodman, but it will not be three stalls. One will do; all three of my animals stay together. Surely you have stalls for oxen, aye?"

"No m'lord, that won't do. I've no stalls large enough…"

He trailed off as Allystaire smiled at him and raised his hammer speculatively; he reached out to tap a nearby stall door with its thick, scarred head. "I can fix that. Or you can manage somehow."

It was all the man could do not to tug a forelock. "Aye, m'lord. There's a stall that'll do but it'll be close quarters, it will."

"All well and good. Two silver links a day while we stay, and this as a token of my appreciation." Allystaire tossed the two links he'd already held out at the man; they glinted in the air, catching a beam of sun that poked through a warped roof slat. The innkeep's hand flashed out and caught them like a hawk striking a rabbit, and they disappeared before his hand was back by his side.

"Very well m'lord, I'll have me sons out to deal with the horses. Will yer, ah, daughter be in the same room?" The innkeep swallowed delicately as he flicked his eyes to the silent, wide-eyed Mol, who had drifted closer to Allystaire.

"My niece. She will. I am not a lord. Tell your groom to be careful of the big grey. Very careful." Allystaire and the innkeep led the mule, then the palfrey, and finally the destrier into a stall. Quickly Allystaire pulled the saddlebags off both horses and slung them over his shoulders, then took up the heavy bags from the packhorse, tossing two of the lighter sacks into Mol's waiting arms.

* * *

"Why'd ya make 'em stable all three animals together," Mol asked around a mouthful of bread that, while not fresh from an oven, was at least not as dry as what they'd had on the road.

Allystaire tore a piece of bread off the loaf and dragged it forcefully through the bowl of butter, leaving the white surface pebbled with crumbs, then shoved it into his mouth. He half-swallowed and answered, "If anyone has a mind to steal them, the grey will show a right nasty temper—bite, rear, kick. He does not care much for people."

"He likes you."

Allystaire snorted, swallowed the rest of his butter and bread. "He knows that I do not care much for people either. And besides, he is used to my hand and my weight, so he tolerates me."

"He likes you. Trust me," Mol insisted, thumping a fist down on the table and rattling crockery. "And that's a lie, you not carin'," the girl added in a mumble, before lifting a bowl of barley in broth and drinking from it noisily. A rivulet of the brown broth left a small grease streak down the side of her chin. When she set down the bowl, she mumbled again. "Horse has a name, y'know."

"Enough with that." Allystaire stood up and once more paced around the room. It didn't take long: two short steps from the fireplace to the bedding, currently occupied by the armor he'd happily traded for the leather vest; turn, one step 'til the slanting roof forced him to hunch over the table that held a fired clay basin half-full of water, a small chest for more bedding beneath it.

"Why d'ya keep doin' that?"

"Thinking. Now that we have got here, what do we do next?" He pulled his gloves from where he'd tucked them in his belt and slapped them against his palm. "Thinking that I do not want to leave you alone here, but I need to be able to move about the place unhindered."

"Why d'ya do that? Talkin' as though I'm not here? D'ya often talk to yerself? Nuncle Tim says that's a sign of madness," Mol said, and resumed slurping from the broth bowl.

"I talk to myself because…" He stopped, slapped his thigh with the gloves. "I simply do. It helps me reason things out." Another few paces and his booted toe rebounded off his saddlebags where they were piled against the wall. He stared at them for a moment. "I could hire a guard." Allystaire knelt, pulled open a flap, and started digging in the bag.

"Wi' what? Sugar? Is yer purse endless?"

Without lifting his head, Allystaire slowly turned to fix his eyes, dark, upon her. "No. But I have enough that may do for now." Turning back to the saddlebag, he pulled free another purse, much like the one he wore on his belt, but fatter. He tugged it open and dug a finger in, pulling free a chain of gold links that trailed back into the purse. He dropped it back in, pulled the leather tightly closed, and raised a finger toward the girl. "Not a word. Now, come down with me to the taproom. You will sit with me quietly, silently, no matter what it is that I do."

"A pint'd buy lots o'silence."

He fixed her with a narrow look and opened the door of the room.

Mol shrugged and followed him toward the door; when they passed nearby she briefly raised one hand as if to take his, but he, busy at tugging on his iron-studded gloves, did not see. Once downstairs, in the not yet very crowded taproom, he guided her to an unoccupied corner and sat, the bench creaking slightly under his weight.

A barmaid soon came to them promptly and stood, waiting impatiently, one hand cocked on her ample hip.

"Too early in the day for charm, then?" Allystaire offered a grin, but she was having none of it and simply sighed heavily. "Fine. Whatever you have that is more wine than water, and not at all vinegar, for me." A pause, as he looked at Mol. "And a mug of small beer for my niece."

Soon enough, the drinks were set down in clay cups that matched the basin in their room. Allystaire sipped between frowns. Mol happily slurped. And so they sat through the afternoon. Shadows gathered, as did the crowd. There was a hearth across the room, but the fire in it was barely lit, for the more bodies that filled the room the less it was needed. Allystaire watched the crowd grow and change. He noted where men sat and who shoulder-heaved whom aside. He watched who apologized and who didn't, who sat at tables that had remained empty and who crowded around the bar.

Finally, something seemed to please him, and he nodded to himself; two men, one of a size with him and one taller, but slimmer, sat together at a table in the center of the room. They wore woodsmen's greens and long knives. The taller one pinched each serving woman who passed by close enough and received tired grins and forced laughs; the stouter one simply leered at them with broken teeth. Most of the men gave their table a wide berth, though some stopped by to share a bit of news or a joke. Allystaire noted with interest that two of their first four rounds were stood to them.

Very quietly, his mouth barely moving, he said to Mol, "Say nothing. Just nod." She nodded. "See how the room moves around them? See how boorish they are, and yet no one says a word? Folk are scared, and want to be thought their friend for fear of the opposite. Toughest men in the room, or so they want everyone to think." He took a quiet, deep breath and rolled his shoulders; one popped audibly. Then he stood and shuffled oddly towards the bar.

Mol watched him, eyes wide and shining in the rushlights that the barmaids were now lighting. He leaned heavily on the bar, had his mug refilled, and dropped an entire silver link to pay for it. He held the broken circle of metal up where everyone could see it before tossing it to the barman. Then, once again shuffling away, he moved with the walk of a man slipping into his cups, but not too far gone. With exaggeratedly slow and careful steps, he passed by the table of the two men and suddenly tripped on a chair. The mug of wine fell onto their table, splattering them both.

"So sorry lads!" Allystaire turned as bright a smile as he could upon them. "Well, likely the pair of you were due for a bit of a wash anyway, hey? Just sorry it had to be my wine!" He laughed, loudly, at his own feeble joke.

The silver had caught their eye, and the spilled wine had drawn their ire. The insult seemed to get their backs up, Mol saw. They shared a look, then the taller one stood up, looking down at Allystaire, who smiled placidly back at him. "It'll be costin' ye more silver now, fellah," he warned, rolling his tongue around his teeth as he talked. "We're drinking on yer weight the rest of the night, aye, and we'll be fergettin' about this, right? That's a good man."

Allystaire pursed his lips and shook his head; Mol was watching him so intently that she saw his stance widen, his back straighten, and his arms relax. "Afraid I cannot do that, my friend. Now if you will excuse me…" He turned his head as if to look back at the bar, but not, Mol noted, his feet.

"No yer don't," muttered the taller man, as the stout one stood up and started to move to the side. "We'll be having enough silver to see us through the week, we will." As the scene developed, drinks were lifted off tables and the crowd drew back to the edges; Mol was forced to stand up on the bench to look over the now rapt audience.

The tall man started to reach for Allystaire, and had one hand on his shoulder when suddenly his breath rushed out of him in one great cough. The iron-studded punch Allystaire had driven into the middle of his stomach hadn't been fast, but had traveled a short distance with no wasted motion. His hips and trunk turned into the blow, and before Mol knew it, the taller man was leaning against his table for support.

That is, until Allystaire seized the back of his head with one hand, pulled him back by the hair, and then slammed him, face first, against the table. A smattering of cheers broke out, but quickly died at the sound of steel drawn.

By then the stouter man had come on, knife in hand. "Be yer blood now ye bastard," he snarled, all pretense of drunkenness gone, Allystaire stepped away from the table, raising his hands, fists clenched. The room fell quiet enough to hear the leather of his gloves creaking.

"Put the blade away, man. Or I will hurt you." His voice was low and angry, filling the now hushed room. His feet were spread the width of his shoulders, and he crouched slightly, his weight shifting from one leg to the other.

The man lunged, blade first; Allystaire stepped toward it, catching the stab with his left arm; the bracer beneath his sleeve turned the blade, and he snatched for the man's wrist, squeezing it once he caught it.

The man grunted in fear and anger, but perhaps to his credit, wasn't out of the fight; he stepped close in and snapped his head forward into Allystaire's face.

"*Damn* it man," Allystaire bellowed, though his yell didn't drown out the small yet sickening *crunch*. "That hurts every freezing time." Mol saw his nose was splayed to one side, and so did the stout man, who laughed and drew back his head again, before suddenly letting out a shriek.

Allystaire's eyes had shut when his nose had broken, but the grip of his hand around the man's wrist suddenly tightened. In the relative hush of the room, the sound of bone grinding against bone was loud and chilling, and the stout man's shriek became a whimper. He fell to his knees, but Allystaire, eyes still closed as the pain of the broken nose washed over him, did not release his grip. When his eyes finally blinked open, he drove an iron-studded fist into the knife-man's dirty, stubbled face once, then twice, then a third time.

By the third, spots on his cheek and a streak of flesh above his eye socket had been torn open. Allystaire struck him once more, in the jaw, and he collapsed in whimpering heap as the knife clattered away.

The taller man was starting to push himself off the ground. Allystaire shook his head and took a step, saying, "Stay down, man. Stay—" Then, with a shake of his head and a muttered, "Freeze him," he launched a kick straight into the man's stomach.

Allystaire stood for a moment, sucking great lungfuls of wind, and, ignoring the rising murmur of the crowd, bent to collect the forgotten knives from the ground. With one in each hand, he stuck the blades fast between planks on the table the men had occupied, then bent them toward each other till the blades snapped and tossed the wooden hilts to the ground.

"Surely even this dung heap holds better men than this," he said, suddenly addressing the crowd, who immediately hushed again. "Or will I have to look elsewhere?" He scanned the crowd a moment or two, which parted as he went back to where Mol was standing. Without meeting her wide-eyed gaze, he gestured, and she hopped lightly down off the table and scampered back up the stairs to their room.

CHAPTER 5

An Oath

"Why'd ya do that? Those men'd done ye no wrong," Mol accused as soon as the door was closed.

He sighed, nodding. "I know, lass. I know; but you saw how they behaved, aye? They were bullies, and they had it coming. You grew up in an inn, aye? Surely you have seen their type before."

Mol shook her head side to side, her face set in stern disapproval, arms crossed fiercely over her chest.

"You have never seen men turn violent in your father's inn?"

"No. There never was any fightin' there that I saw. Not until…" The girl trailed off, the stern anger melting as she remembered.

Allystaire sighed. "I had more reason than merely punishing bullies."

She dropped her arms to her sides and glared at him, awaiting an answer.

He sighed, reached up to his nose, and, with a deep breath, tenderly pushed it back into place until it popped. He released the air with a grimace and a bitten curse. "Two reasons, in point of fact. First," he held up one finger, "everyone is less likely to give us trouble. Second, word will spread that I mean to hire men, and handing the likes of them a beating helps with the weeding. If I can handle them, then only tougher sorts—skilled sorts—will come see me."

"Why d'ya need a guard for, since ya can beat up all these bullies, hrm?"

"I do not. You do. I need to move around this place and find where your people are." *If they're still here*, he thought. "If I do leave you alone, you will probably join them in a slave pit even faster than if I take you with me."

"If the whole town's so horrid, why d'ya expect a guard to stay with me?"

"Because I know people, Mol. I do. Or at least I know the kind of men who make a living with swords. I can find a man who will stay bought. Trust me."

She didn't answer; instead, she turned to stare into the very dim coals that barely filled the small fireplace with their glow.

"Listen; even here, the slavers have to make the gesture of staying hidden. Sure, the pirate who calls himself 'baron' and the thugs who work for him know, and maybe most of the common folk suspect." Allystaire reached up and gingerly pressed around the edges of his nose with two fingers, wincing and sucking in his breath. "But they will be hidden, at least a little, and probably close to the docks, because most of the buyers will want to load their cargo quickly, and—"

Mol suddenly whirled on him, raising an accusing finger. "They aren't cargo," she hissed, "they're *people*. They're whatever's left of my family and friends. Don't call them cargo!" She stamped a foot and stepped toward him, raising a finger in anger. "If I don't come wi' ya how do I know ya'll even save them, and not just come back to tell me they're gone from here and toss me to yer priests t'be blinded?"

Taken aback by the sudden ferocity of the girl's outburst, Allystaire found his mouth pulling into a sour frown. "I have done everything I told you I would do. Why do you doubt me now?"

"Because ya still think on leavin' me," the girl said, her voice rising angrily. "I can see it when yer thinkin' it. Ya won't say it, but you're afraid that watchin' me and findin' my people'll kill ya. Part o'ya is hopin' to find that they're already dead or gone so you can wash yer hands of it, maybe sail off somewhere you can earn gold bein' a bully 'stead o' spendin' it while fightin' em."

The child's keen insight startled him, and anger bloomed inside him. *She is right*, he told himself. *That's why I am angry.* His anger faded as swiftly as it had flared.

Before he could answer, Mol stepped forward, jabbing a finger up at him. "Yer own words t'me, about the great and powerful? T'not expect 'em t'care for the likes o'me? So y'were a lord or a knight then, aye? And y'just can't wait t'be one again, I s'pose."

Not anymore, he thought.

With his dark blue eyes solemn above his swollen nose, Allystaire went down on one knee in order to look Mol in the eye. "You are right, Mol. I have had the thoughts you accuse me of, and it shames me. My apologies." He took a deep breath, still fixing his eyes on her. "I have broken oaths in my life. Yet I tell you this and I mean it truly; if your people are to be found, I will free them, or I will die in the attempt."

The solemnity of the gesture was somewhat hampered by the swelling on his face, but Allystaire's gaze was even and his voice soft. "I need you to be guarded, because if I find your folk, to successfully free them, I will un-doubtedly be forced to kill men. Maybe a lot of them. And I cannot do that and protect you at the same time. You have my word that I will not leave you behind."

"Or give me t'the blind priests."

"No," Allystaire assured her. "I will not give you to any priests, blind or otherwise. I promise."

Mol sat watching his face in the shadowed darkness of their room, then stepped forward and put her arms around his neck. Allystaire knelt stiffly, un-sure of what to do; before he could try to return the gesture, she had pulled away, unwittingly nudging his recently broken nose with her head. He stifled a grunt, and she laughed lightly.

"If yer such a great warrior, why's yer nose been broken so much?"

Chuckling, an uncomfortable sound in his throat, Allystaire stood and brushed his hands on his leather-clad thighs. "I lead with my head."

Before Mol could say more, a timid knock sounded at the door. Allystaire stifled a curse and lifted a finger to his lips. "Yes?"

The obsequious voice of the innkeep dripped, "Thought ya might want supper, erm, Allyst…er…m'lord. Wi' my best wine, bottled stuff it is, been storin' it. Ya did a good thing down in me taproom."

Allystaire allowed himself a brief, satisfied grin before opening the door. The innkeep stood, tray in hand, and with his free hand eagerly held up a thick, squat, glass bottle toward Allystaire.

"We would be happy to accept, goodman," Allystaire said. "Have you a lamp in the house, or only rushlights?"

The innkeep glided in, practically bowing, a feat he managed neatly despite his full hands, and set tray and bottle down on the small table. "I should be able to scare up a lamp, m'lord, if you give me time." Without asking, he moved to the pile of firewood and tossed a few sticks into the fireplace, then seized a poker and stirred the coals. He cast a brief glance at Allystaire before adding, "Don' keep such in the bar no more; too expensive to keep replacin', if y'understand, m'lord."

"You want to know if those men will be back, and whether I would chase them off again?" Allystaire tilted his head slightly, eyes narrowed as he considered the man. "They will not be; they have been shamed in front of folk they thought cowed. They will not darken your door again, if I am any judge of their kind."

The innkeep nodded, sighing a little. "I may miss their weight but I shan't miss them. Too bad ya din't kill 'em, m'lord."

"I do not kill over bad manners, goodman," Allystaire said icily. "I had not seen them do anything that warranted real blood." He stepped quickly over to the table to survey the tray—fresher bread and fish instead of broth. "Soon enough there may be folk in your taproom to see me. They drink on my weight, but I want a strict count kept of how many each man has, aye?" The innkeep shrugged, but nodded, his hand straying of its own accord toward his forelock.

"As y'say, m'lord."

With that, he was off down the stairs. Allystaire barred the door and leaned against it, pressing his ear to it. He nodded, satisfied, at the sounds of boots clattering away.

"He may have heard us talk, lass. We must be more careful from now on."

Mol nodded solemnly. They sat around the small table, Allystaire on the floor, the girl on the single stool, and ate silently. Allystaire looked out the small window, covered with only a small grill of four iron bars.

While chewing, Mol watched him sidelong, but intently, as though figuring a calculus well beyond her years.

CHAPTER 6

Finding a Shadow

Back downstairs in the taproom roughly half a turn later, twilight had given way to a sultry summer night. The regular crowd was still drinking, laughing, and talking, albeit slightly subdued and gathered mostly on one side of the room. The smoke of pipes, rushlights, and hearth filled the air.

The corner table Allystaire and Mol had occupied earlier had been left unoccupied, with two mugs, a pitcher, and a lit oil lamp set upon it. Allystaire couldn't quite stop a misshapen grin from tugging at his lips, but he quickly forced it away when he saw the gathering at the side of the bar nearest the door.

There were eight men, so far, and a few exchanged muttered small talk as if they knew each other. *Probably do*, he thought. *Like as not they're reminiscing about the murder they've done together.* It was true that, regionally, soldiers, warriors, and swords-at-hire generally came to know each other by reputation or type, if nothing else. At the least they'd likely served in bands that fought each other, or for the same lord. They were of a piece, leather-clad and well-armed. Some were tall, others short. Some whip-thin, others threateningly broad. All shared the same air of bored menace.

"Go sit. I will be along." Allystaire shooed Mol off to the table and walked to the bar, thumb absently hooking behind the head of the warhammer he'd slid into its iron loop on his belt.

"Good evening, gentlemen," he murmured, taking their measure. "I am glad to see word traveled as fast as I had hoped, and that you have been enjoying the hospitality." At this, he paused briefly, expecting perhaps a small, sarcastic cheer; there was merely restless shuffling. "Now, I am only looking to hire one man, not a band. I will talk to each of you in turn, but before I do, I have a simple question. How many of you are on your third round or better since walking in the door?"

They looked oddly at him; one spat on the floor. Another finally spoke up. "Why'n the Cold does that matter?"

"You interested in my weight or not? Answer the question now, all of you, unless you cannot count to three." Allystaire paused, then spat out "Now" once more. His voice was calm, his expression placid, but there was something in the way he said the word, some snap of command, that reached down to the place in a man's soul where orders were obeyed.

And he was. Among the eight gathered there, five men nodded, lifted a hand, or spoke a word of assent.

"Then thank you for coming and be on your way. There is a time and a place for drinking, gentlemen, and moments prior to trying to convince a man to hire you is *not* that time and place. *Out.*" Once again, Allystaire's voice, even in a single syllable, conveyed a ring of power and authority; the five men left quietly, but swiftly.

"Now then. One at a time, I will speak to each of you over there." Allystaire pointed one thick finger toward the corner table that, he supposed, was now his. "From now on your drinks are on your own account."

He left it to them to settle the order. *Probably need to reject the first as too eager.* He sat down, offered Mol a disapproving stare as he saw her sipping from one of the cups, and lifted the pitcher to pour into his own. He slipped the warhammer out of his belt and stood it on its head by his right foot, with his hand leaning casually on its iron-shod handle. Not long after, the first man walked to his table. Of indeterminate age with a mouthful of blackened, yellowed stumps and a face marred by pox, he didn't cut an imposing figure, but the hilt of the sword on his hip was well worn, the metal scales sewn onto his jerkin polished.

"Where have you served?"

"Wi' Thanar, up nor' apiece," the man mumbled through his wreck of a mouth, the name coming out 'Dannar'. "Keepin rivers clear mostly; nor'ern rivers go' a bi' cold for me now."

"Never heard of him. Battles? Towns?"

"When I firs' come down 'ere, found me place in one o' Baron Vyndamere and 's ou'fi's."

Allystaire leaned forward, his hand flexing against the handle of the hammer slightly. "What battles with him?"

The man scratched at his stubbly neck. "When we forced da crossin' up in Greenforks."

"Baron Vyndamere's men slaughtered a mob of peasants in their haste to escape the Islandmen. I need a man who can do more than that."

"I figh' whoe'ers in fronna me," the man fairly spat. "So longs's ey's go' a weapon an' ain' wavin' no flag."

Allystaire studied the man's face, arms, hands as they sat on the table. *Has a pox. Thick wrists; probably quick sword. A survivor. But he will cut down a child if he has the scent of blood in his nose.*

Finally, Allystaire shook his head. "You will not do. Next."

With a simple shrug, the man was off, rejection rolling off his back like rainwater.

Allystaire beckoned toward the bar and another man started forward. This one was large, larger than Allystaire across the shoulders and a good head taller, making him the biggest and tallest man in the room by far; he carried an enormous single-bladed axe that was taller than most men and swung it ahead of him in one hand like a walking stick. Meanwhile, still at Allystaire's side, Mol had drained her cup, and, between the wine and the warmth of the nearby fire, had begun drifting to sleep against him.

"Sooner you start your questions the sooner we can be drinkin' to our arrangement," the big man said, a broad, gapped smile splitting his beard as he sat. Something about the smile seemed uneasy, ill-suited to his features, much as it seemed on Allystaire's own face. It parted his grey-threaded brown beard like a fissure in a stone, and it didn't reach his eyes.

Islandman, thought Allystaire. *Confident.*

"Who are you and where have you served?"

"Nyndstir Obertrsun, Trollsbane, and Giantslayer," the man boomed. "Far north, just off the tundra. I was at Wroolst for the winter of mist and wolves; I've chased river pirates, hunted bandits, and killed every kind of man, dwarf, beast, and fey creature what walks this world. I'm your freezin' man."

Allystaire shifted backwards in his seat and studied Nyndstir. "Who did you serve with and what has brought you to this part of the world?"

He paused, took a slight breath, and answered, "I was with Daegan's Hounds for nigh a dozen years. Followed the captain down to the Keersvast Archipelago when they started throwing gold around."

"Daegan's Hounds?" Allystaire's eyebrows shot up. *Why are so many bold men showing their back to the tundra? What is scaring them away?* "Heard of them," he allowed with a nod. "More good than bad. What happened?"

The larger man leaned his axe across his knees and pretended to study the blade. "When the captain died, we made a poor accord and fell out over it. Bad blood boiled up." He looked up with a shrug, flicking a thumbnail against the blade of his weapon. "Everything ends 'cept the tide, the waves, and the Sea Dragon what made 'em. No use lookin' any closer'n that."

Allystaire nodded. *I like this one.* "The job is simple, Nyndstir. I need you to protect a child. My niece." He gestured to the girl sleeping soundly at his side.

Nyndstir snorted, the whiskers around his mouth blowing indignantly. "I'm no freezin' wet nurse. Who's she to be protected from?"

"I do not know. Anyone or anything that poses a threat. I need her safe and guarded while I am off on business in the town and environs."

Nyndstir turned and spat at the ground, making no effort to aim for a spit-bucket. "I'll protect your precious *niece*." He twisted the word, made it something ugly. "But it'll cost you. You're a lordly type and no mistakin'," he drawled. "I will want gold or gemmary for this, mark me."

Allystaire fixed his eyes again on the large man across from him, blue gaze narrowing. *He might be worth it. His eyes are hard and his hands are sure with that axe.* He was about to open his mouth to speak, when he suddenly felt Mol's small hand settle carefully atop his; for all her youth, her palm and fingertips were calloused. Her nails dug sharply into the skin of his hand, but he saw from the corner of his eye that she'd not opened her eyes or done anything to shake the pretense that she slept. The pressure on his hand was insistent, steady, and warning. Allystaire reached for his cup and took a long swallow, buying time.

Finally, he settled on a question. "If a brace of crossbowmen were to corner the two of you at the mouth of a clear street, Nyndstir, would you be willing to die for my gold?"

Nyndstir sat back, a hand tightening around the smooth wooden haft of his weapon. For a moment, Allystaire readied himself for violence, sitting up straight and curling his fingers around the hammer that rested against his boot. Then the other man relaxed.

"No. No, I don't think I would, and that's the plain truth of it. A time not so long ago, my word for gold and I would've had their scalps after taking three bolts, and later over mead I'd have claimed it were a half dozen." He shook his head, and stood. "But that man died in Keersvast." He extended a huge, gnarled hand. "Sorry to waste your time, sir."

Allystaire stood and took the proffered hand. "No need for pardon. You were honest, and you know who you are; not many men can claim that." Shaking Nyndstir's hand was like having a gauntlet shaped around his fist by a clumsy blacksmith.

Nyndstir nodded, turned, and walked out of the inn, holding his axe blade in front of him and studying it closely.

With a weary wave, Allystaire called over the last man. As he was sitting and reaching for his cup, he heard dry laughter and a voice he knew too well.

"Oh if this isn't rich. This'll be just the thing to get me back in his lordship's good graces, it will."

Allystaire's eyes sparked coldly. "Casamir," he snarled, "Walk out of this place before I kill you." In a flash, the warhammer was resting in both his hands, his shoulders tensed, his feet shifting.

The man across from him was of medium height with a head scraped clear of hair; a hawk-like beak of a nose; and narrow, dark grey eyes. His arms were thick through his swordsman's wrists, plainly visible as he raised his hands. "No, you won't." He took a half step back from the table, keeping his arms in the air. "You won't because everyone sees you, because that'd make you a murderer, and you like playing the hero. You won't kill me in front of the child, whoever she is." He dropped his hands, but kept them well away from the sword and dirk resting on his hips, his eyes flitting to the stirring, blinking Mol, then back to Allystaire. His voice dropped, but the crowd was intently watching them; Allystaire, gritting his teeth, lowered his hammer.

"I know you're a killer, Allystaire. But you always worried about things like times and places and observances. And knowing your whereabouts is more valuable to me than taking the chance on gutting you now." He laughed again, a fuller, throatier sound than his dry chuckling. "Rich indeed." He leaned forward, eyes gleaming as they caught the light from the table's lamp. His voice dropped into a grating whisper. "And so will I be, once I take this news back to his lordship. Oh I'll bet he raved when he heard you'd fled—unless he exiled you, too?" The man smiled then, and what on Allystaire and Nyndstir was merely an unusual expression was disturbing on Casamir's face. "I can only imagine what your lapdogs'll say to him to placate him. He'll never let you walk away, you know, not like me. Not the invincible lord." His lips twisted into a sneer that played oddly with the shadows on his face. "And if I kill a horse or two, I can get back to Wind's Jaw in what, a week? Ten days?"

As Casamir spoke, Allystaire's expression didn't change, but his hands curled, white-knuckled, around the haft of his hammer. The threat of violence rolled so powerfully from him that several onlookers made hasty, silent exits. *Kill him. Now.*

Casamir sneered back at Allystaire, lips curling away from his teeth. "One day, mayhap, I'll take that hammer away from you and mash your stones with it."

"No time like the present to give it a try." Allystaire's voice, though eerily calm, belied none of his fury.

"I've a long ride to start. Use the time to get further away, if you're smart. But then, you never were." Casamir, still smiling cruelly, began to back toward the door, his hands still held carefully away from his hilts. "I'll be sure to give Audreyn your best."

Allystaire watched Casamir until he was gone, then lowered his hammer back to the ground and sat back on the bench, moving with deliberate care. Removing his hands from the hammer took effort. *You'll have to kill him one day. Should've been today.* He placed his hands on the table and tried to steady them by lacing his fingers together, then wrenched them apart, seized his clay cup in one hand, flexed his wrist, and shattered the cup. Mol started and looked up at him strangely, but said nothing. His eyes fixed upon the table, and his breathing rose and fell audibly.

"The cup's not what made you look a fool," put in a quiet, rough, and rasping voice from across the table, "though breaking it makes you seem more so." Allystaire's eyes lifted from the table, and he dropped the broken pieces stuck in his palm. Across from him sat a woman whose age he was hard-pressed to determine. A braided leather band encircling her forehead kept her dark hair swept back from her face; her eyes were deep pools in a shadowed face, but Allystaire thought he saw thin lines of scars on her chin, hard lines against dark brown skin.

"It also seems like you've chased off all your best options, and I suppose now your schedule's a trifle tighter. So why don't we come to terms?" The woman leaned back in the chair and stretched her legs under the table, crossing her feet at the ankles.

Allystaire cleared his throat, and, almost delicately, plucked a shard from his right hand, grunting as it tore free of his skin and brought a droplet of blood with it. He curled his fingers closed, cleared his throat. "Terms?"

"Yes. I assume you still want a guard for the lass?" The woman pointed with her chin toward Mol, who now sat awake and bright-eyed. "I don't work cheap, but I won't cheat or steal, either."

Allystaire cleared his throat again and sat straighter, regaining a measure of his composure. "Who have—"

"Nowhere you've heard of, with no one you've heard of. I don't collect trophies, names, or titles, but I'll work for a silver link a day plus room, board, and wine, and I'll keep the child safe. I heard every question you asked the first two, and everything the third said, in case you were wondering."

She leaned forward, bringing her face closer to the lamplight. Her brown cheeks were high and broad beneath narrow eyes, and she was handsome despite the scars that started at the left corner of her mouth, ran down to her chin, and appeared to snake along the side of her neck. She looked younger than Allystaire would've guessed from the rasp in her voice.

"I wouldn't be fool enough to lead her into a clear alley where a brace of bowmen could corner us, and I've killed my share of peasants, but only when they were trying to kill me."

"How did you get into that chair?"

"I sat."

"I meant without my noticing," Allystaire half-growled.

"You were too busy murdering the crockery while wishing 'twere that other fellow's neck." She rapped a knuckle on the table and went on. "Silver link a day. Make a decision."

"First I have to decide if I want to hire you. I have to learn something about you."

The woman sighed and leaned back again, shaking her head. "Go ahead. Ask your stupid questions."

"Casamir. If he showed while you were guarding the girl, what would you do?"

"Put a knife in his back—from ten paces away, if possible. He had that air of knowing how to fight about him." She suddenly pointed a finger across the table at Allystaire. "So do you. So if I couldn't do that, I'd lay low with the lass and wait for you to show up and club him to death."

"Are you saying you are a coward, then?"

"I'm sayin' I never fight fair if I can help it. At the least I'd try to put a knife into an arm or a thigh before I went blade to blade with him."

"If it came to it then, how would you fight me?"

She tilted her head to one side, grinning, which brought her scar into sharp relief. "Knives in the dark if I could. If I couldn't, stay well back, try to keep something between us, let you tire yourself. Hide. Slip it into your back between a gap in your armor; you're the kind that wears a lot of steel, I can see that."

"That is an unseemly way to fight," Allystaire remarked, his voice a mix of admiration and disapproval.

"Could be, but it's a freezin' good way to kill a man who's stronger and better armored than I am," the woman retorted tartly.

I like this one. "You are hired. One silver link a day, meals, shelter, wine." He stood up and extended his hand toward her; the skin of her answering grip was every bit as rough as any swordsman's Allystaire had ever known. "I am Allystaire."

"Idgen Marte," the woman said. When she stood, she was of a height with Allystaire. "You've hired your niece a shadow."

CHAPTER 7

Mercy and Strength

With Mol left in bed and Idgen Marte to guard her, Allystaire was soon out in the warm, moist night air, sweating beneath the cuirass he had put back on, along with the studded gloves, bracers, and a metal-banded leather cap. Sword on his back, hammer in belt loop, and shield clutched in his left hand, he set off in no particular direction, letting his mind wander the same as his feet.

"Were I a slaver, how would I do business?" He asked himself this question aloud, though only just. He considered the answer while his strides methodically covered the hasty, unplanned roads.

"Down at the docks, of course," he replied to himself after a bit more walking. "Still, I cannot simply kick open every bracken-slimed warehouse." He paused a moment and added, "Every warehouse with a door big enough for a wagon, anyway." Leather-clad fingers drummed idly against the top of his hammer.

Struck with a sudden thought, his strides became more purposeful; rather than wandering, he raised his eyes to the few roofs that hovered above the street. The dim outline of the palisade wall rose, a heavy shadow against the night sky. Following its outline, he moved his gaze along until the taller shape of a watchtower emerged; he mentally marked the spot and headed straight toward it.

Bend's streets had other ideas; none of them, it seemed, ran in true directions for more than a handful of yards. They spiraled, they dead-ended, they coiled back on themselves and made abrupt turns. But with his eyes fixed directly on the tower, a store of patience, and gritted teeth, Allystaire soon found himself at its feet.

"Ware the guards," he called, his voice quiet, but pitched to carry. Then, with a deep breath, he started up the planking that led to its top. They bent under his weight, and the sound of his ascent carried quickly. Two muzzy voices called down, each rising over the other to be heard.

"Stand away lest we shoot!" shouted one. "Bugger off!" warned the other.

Shoot at what? The darkness? "I would speak with you good watchmen if you have a moment." Allystaire paused. "There could be silver in it." *Your purse isn't endless.*

Good that I do not plan to pay them, then.

Soon, a beam of light shone down from the tower as one of them lit a lantern and two pairs of boots bowed the planking. They were of a piece with the guardsmen he'd met before—dirty, noisome, wearing mismatched gear. Both carried crossbows and wore the same clumsily sewn badge.

As soon as the light appeared, Allystaire took two large steps away and put a hand over his eyes to shield them from the approaching lantern beam. He rolled his shoulders; spread his feet; and took deep, even breaths.

He didn't look up until the guards were close enough that the light from the lantern was ambient, rather than direct. By then, he could smell the sour reek of wine off the guardsman directly in front of him.

"Gentlemen. Glad you could see your way clear to giving directions to a poor lost soul. Let us say I was interested in bringing some new volunteers to milord's host. Particularly, let us say I wanted…" He shrugged expansively, raising his free hand, "oarsmen."

"Eh? We'll be havin' no freezin' press-gangs in Bend," said the lantern bearer. The other, whose free hand carried a heavy, sloshing skin, snorted.

"He's not here to press anyone, Rogit. He's lookin' t' buy 'em." He turned toward Allystaire. "Ain't ya, yer lordliness? Well, we can help but 'twill cost. A silver link'll keep us in wine fer a few long nights o'watchin' an' guardin', what say?"

Allystaire smiled, hoping the shadows concealed his gritted teeth. "If the information is reliable, then yes, a silver link will do as you described."

"Fine. Ye've the look o' weight on ye." He coughed, spat to the side, then popped open his wineskin with a flick of his thumb. "Down by the quays. Cross the Street o'Sashes from the harbormaster's office is a big warehouse. Wains full o'goods can drive right in. Or out. Any night three lanterns are burnin' above the door, they's lookin to sell."

"Truth straight from a man who knows, that is. Three lanterns, Street o'Sashes. Now about our link?" demanded the lantern-bearer.

Allystaire clicked his tongue, and if the lantern had been closer, they might just have seen his smile turn a little fuller, his jaw unclench. "What a shame."

"Eh? What? What's a shame?"

Allystaire shook his head. "That you got so drunk on duty that you fell while trying to descend from your post to piss." Then, without warning, he stepped forward toward the winebibber and swung his shield straight up. The solid thunk of its iron-rimmed edge biting into the guardsman's jaw brought a release of tension and fury that he wanted to stop and exult in.

Wineskin's jaw snapped closed so hard and so fast that his teeth bit clean through the tip of his tongue. A bit of flesh flew into the night, a trail of blood behind it, to land wetly on the ground. Allystaire didn't stop there; he swung his right fist overtop of the shield, straight into the jaw he'd already slammed shut, and the man dropped like his legs had been cut from under him.

Lantern was so befuddled by what was happening, and his night vision so ruined by having stared into a light source on the way down, that he barely had time to register Allystaire stepping forward, sweeping back his shield, and bashing him straight across the face. He let out a broken whimper after the audible *crunch* of his nose breaking, and he, too, fell to a moaning heap on the ground.

As the men dropped, Allystaire immediately relieved them of their crossbows, heaving them toward the wall as hard as he could. He wouldn't swear that either made it over, but they were as good as gone in the darkness. He picked up the wineskin, still half full, and poured the rest of it over their prostrate forms. Wineskin was, by now, attempting to struggle to his feet; for this he earned two sharp kicks in the ribs.

Smash their heads. Slit their throats. Stop leaving live enemies in your wake. "Those who would profit from the sale of men and women might as well be slavers themselves. I should not suffer your kind to live." His hand wrapped about the head of the hammer and began to draw it free, his right arm tensing with the need to swing. "I should spatter the dirt with the meager brains in your heads." *Am I out to prove Casamir right? I may be a killer. Am I a murderer? They are beaten men.*

Allystaire spat on the ground, then raised his voice in the direction of the nearest other tower, its faint outline barely visible. "Help! Help! Fallen guardsman!" His baritone voice carried well and strong.

He turned back to the prone forms before him and dropped his voice, though he couldn't keep anger out of it. "At least neither of you will bleed to death. Remember that. Remember that I could have killed you, and I did not. Sometimes mercy is strength."

His words were met with slobbery moaning. He trotted off with quick steps.

* * *

Three raps on the door, a pause the length of a heartbeat, then two more. Allystaire stepped back, waited; he heard the sound of the bar being moved back, and then the door opened into a darkness that was lessened only slightly by the dimly lit coals of the small, banked fire. Idgen Marte stood just inside the door, slipping a long blade with a very slight curve into a scabbard held lightly in her free hand.

"Any luck?" she asked quietly, as Allystaire moved slowly past her into the room and set his shield down against the door, followed by his cap.

"I learned something of what I needed to know." Soon, the large and heavy sword he wore joined shield and iron-banded cap. He took a deep breath, pulled off his gloves, pushed back his sweat-slicked hair. "Where is the Street of Sashes?"

Idgen Marte snickered as she lowered herself back onto a stool. "You didn't hire me just so you didn't have to take your niece whoring with you, did you?"

Allystaire, thankful of the darkness, felt a flush creep into his cheeks. *You should have guessed that, idiot.* "No. What I learned is that the business I have to do is on that street, and I did not want to blunder about looking for it in the dark." He moved over to settle down in front of the bedding gathered upon its crude wooden frame; upon it, Mol slept without a sound.

Carefully, Allystaire leaned back against the low wooden board, not entirely sure it would hold against his armored weight, but it did. He drew out his hammer and laid it across his lap.

"I will need you for at least the rest of the next day. Go get some rest. Report to me after breakfast."

Idgen Marte laughed very lightly. "Report to you? You're used to being in command and no mistaking." She stood, stretched a bit, and slid the sheathed sword she still gripped onto an iron frog on her belt. "Don't tell me you're gonna sleep sitting up in your armor like you're expecting a stand-to in the dead of night."

"It is not the first time I have slept like this, and I suspect it will not be the last. Casamir could decide he wants to bring my head back to his lord, after all."

She shook her head and started for the door. "There's a story there I mean to hear before this is done."

"You will be disappointed."

Idgen Marte laughed that light laugh again and left without another word. It took Allystaire a moment to realize that he needed to heave himself back to his feet and shut the door; when he stood, a sharp clicking in his left knee led to gritted teeth and a muffled curse. He shuffled over, closed and barred the door, then arranged himself back in place, hammer in hand.

He couldn't help but think over Idgen Marte's words. *No man ever regretted being prepared.* But he would be stiff in the morning, the armor perhaps a touch heavier, the hammer slower. Sleeping like this was barely enough, now. "Then barely enough will have to do," he murmured to the room, to himself, to Mol sleeping above him. Allystaire leaned his head back against the board and inhaled deeply; with the quick ease of long practice, he slipped into a light and dreamless sleep. He thought that he heard, perhaps, a voice whisper an answer: *It will.* But he was too tired to wonder at it.

* * *

Allystaire awoke all at once. No grogginess to shake away, no yawns to suppress; he had slept, and now he was fully awake.

There was stiffness, though, and his knees and back protested with violent cracks as he pulled himself to his feet. The room was filling with dirty grey light and the promise of thick morning heat. Mol had surfaced from underneath the bedding, her forehead beginning to run with sweat. Allystaire spared a glance for her, then shuffled away from the bed. He set the hammer that had lain all night in his lap on the small table and stretched his arms toward the ceiling, sighing as tight shoulders released.

He was staring fixedly at the dead ash of the fireplace when he heard Mol stir. "Did ya find m'folk yet?"

Allystaire sighed and turned to face her. She was sitting up in the middle of the bed, her eyes large and bright even in the dimness of the room.

"Perhaps. I think I have found out the place where slaves are sold. More than likely, your kin are there…or those doing the selling will know where they are." Allystaire paused, then drew a stool toward Mol's bedside.

"I am going to watch the place today to see what I might do at nightfall. I need to know things. How many guards and at what intervals." He waved a hand dismissively. "At least, I will feel better knowing them. It is time for some plain truths, though. First is that they may already be gone, or tonight may be the night of sale. I hope neither are true. Second…"

He hesitated, choosing his words carefully. "I might not be able to rescue them. If there are ten or a dozen men in there, armed and competent, and I simply walk through the door and set to killing them, I mislike my chances." Mol opened her mouth to protest, but Allystaire shook his head, then leaned forward to put a hand gently on her shoulder. "I cannot help you if I die foolishly."

Smiling gently, Mol patted the back of his large hand with her small one. "Ya'll not die. I know it. Once ya get inside, ya'll know what to do. Y'always have so far."

Allystaire stood and patted her shoulder. "I wish I could say your faith is comforting, but it sounds too much like the empty words of a priest telling me to trust in Braech's rough justice, or Urdaran's great wisdom, or Fortune's whim."

"If faith isn't comforting it isn't anything, and m'words aren't empty. Ya'll see," Mol insisted, jaw set defiantly.

"Well, if I am going to die today I am not going to do it on an empty stomach. Bar the door and do not open it unless I tell you where I found you, aye?" With that, Allystaire was off to rouse the staff.

Downstairs, there was only a bleary-eyed groom sitting by the front door, but the smell of bread drifted in with the increasingly sticky heat. Soon, the haggard looking innkeep, another day's growth of grey stubble on his cheeks, stumbled out into the room, brightening considerably when he saw Allystaire.

"An early start t'yer business then, milord? There'd be fresh bread for you and yer niece, or yesterday's bread fried in ham fat if ya prefer." He paused, rubbed a cheek, and added, "And ham. Tea? For a little extra copper I might find some honeycomb—"

Allystaire cut him off with a wave of a hand. "Yes. All of it. I am famished. But I do not wish to wait long. While you get it ready, send someone to fetch the woman Idgen Marte. If she complains, tell her that as long as she works for me, her day starts early. Are my animals well?"

The innkeep winced slightly and pulled his hand away from his forehead. "Er, yes, m'lord, though my grooms all have a fear o'the big grey. They say he bites and stamps, they come too near."

Allystaire met his words with a quick smile. "Which is precisely what he is trained to do. Tell them to show some spine, but for their fingers' sakes, do not rile him. I want the horses saddled and ready to run after the sun crests today, unless I return to tell you otherwise." With that, he was tromping back up the stairs. He rapped gently on the door, cleared his throat, and said, "Cold well." The bar was thrown back, slowly, and the door opened, Mol tugging it with both hands.

While he walked through the door, the girl wandered over to where his shield leaned against the wall. She reached out a finger and traced the slight nicks that the guardsman's faces had put in the paint last night. "How'd these happen?"

Allystaire had walked past her and begun staring out the small window, frowning as he felt the heat rolling in on him. "Eh?" He turned around to face her. "Shields get nicks in them."

"This one din't have any before," she insisted. "I saw. 'twas all smooth grey." She rubbed a finger across a spot where the grey paint had been scratched. "What'd ya do last night, t'learn where m'folk were?" She turned to him, mouth serious beneath large brown eyes. "Who'd ya hurt?"

Allystaire stared at her for a moment. *How exactly did she…Doesn't matter.* He let out a quick sigh and spread his hands. "Some guards. They knew where slaves were kept and wanted silver for the benefit of the knowledge."

"You kill 'em?"

Allystaire shook his head slowly from side to side. "No. I hurt them. Anyone who profits from the sale of people is little better than a slaver himself. But I did not kill them."

"Ya've killed men afore, tho?"

Allystaire frowned deeply. "What kind of question is that?"

She shrugged. "Why bother t'hide it? Ya told me t'save m'folk ya'd have t'kill men, lot of men maybe. So ya've done it afore."

He shrugged and waved a hand helplessly. "I have, yes."

"So why'd ya not kill them?"

"Killing a man and murdering him are two different things. I will do one, but not the other."

"What about tha' man from last eve, Casmir? Would he?"

"Casamir," Allystaire said carefully, correcting her pronunciation and drawing a scowl for his trouble. "And yes. For any reason he could seize upon. He enjoys it."

"And ya don't?"

"Cold, lass, but you are a thorough inquisitor. I could have had use for you once upon a time."

She set her hands on her hips. "Answer me then."

"I do not enjoy killing for its own sake, no."

"I dunno what that means," Mol said, her eyes narrowing. "But 'tis not an answer."

Allystaire was spared further questioning when breakfast and Idgen Marte both arrived.

She looked considerably less awake than Allystaire, but for all that, her face, neck, and hands bore the scent of recent washing, her hair was carefully bound back, and her clothing and weapons were all in good order. Looking at her in the daylight, Allystaire could see more of the warrior in her. Her limbs and torso were long and leanly muscled, her wrists thick. She wore knee-high riding boots over dark trousers and a dark grey arming jacket that looked to have gussets of armor stiffening it here and there, but not so as to slow her down. In the light, her scar was more pronounced, vivid against her brown skin, far darker than any barony native.

Most telling, to him, were her eyes. Wide and brown, they had the cold, hard look of a seasoned warrior. Despite the sleep that lingered in them, they saw everything in front of them, and much else besides.

"Am I to play governess again today?" Idgen Marte asked him, as she poured tea into a mug and claimed the stool. Her voice was quiet, but not soft. It sounded as though it grated against her throat.

"I suppose so. I think, with luck, I can conclude my business today. But I may need your help a day further."

"What is your business?" She took a swig of steaming tea, heedless of the heat. "You aren't whoring. You're not here to buy passage or you'd just take her with you." She leaned back, appraising him with cool eyes. "Whatever business you mean to do, I'm guessing the weight is blood, right? But you're no assassin. Hunting a deserter or a renegade, mayhap?"

Allystaire met her stare with his own. He tried to be cold, but he held no malice toward Idgen Marte, so, while his facade didn't crack, neither did hers. Something about her prevented him from flinging his usual air of command, of expected obedience.

"I've had every kind of stare there is in the world directed at me, Allystaire. By men and women, rich, noble, killers, madmen, artists, and teachers. You have no chance." She grinned lopsidedly as she answered him. "Ya've trusted me to guard the child, and if you trust me that far, trust me with this."

He sighed, dropped his gaze, and moved to the breakfast things. He helped himself to fried bread and ham, then took a large bite and chewed thoughtfully. "Slavers," he finally said.

Idgen Marte's eyes flickered dangerously. "You aren't buying—"

Allystaire waved away her words. "No. Her people," he said, pointing with his chin toward Mol, who sat on the bed watching silently. He turned his eyes to her for a moment, narrowed his lips and swung a hand toward the table full of food; she quickly darted over and generously doused a piece of fresh bread with honey. "Her village was attacked and her people were taken. We followed them here."

Idgen Marte set down her tea. She tilted her head and studied Allystaire for a few moments. "Then are you a lord? A knight? These your liege's people?"

Allystaire snorted and took another huge bite of ham and bread. He'd barely swallowed when he answered, "Look around you. We are a handful of days from Londray itself, not far from other Delondeur keeps, and this place lives under its own laws. Would any barony liege lord send a man-at-arms, much less a knight, to track down a few peasants?"

Idgen Marte shrugged. "Still, it doesn't make sense. These folk are under your protection, then?"

Allystaire reached for more fried bread. "They are now. And they are here, or at least I think as much. We were but two days behind the slavers, three at the worst; I doubt they have been sold yet. I mean to find and free them."

"D'ya mean to just cut your way in?" She sounded incredulous.

"I am not a subtle man."

"That shortcoming seems like to get you killed."

Allystaire smiled slightly. "I do not mean to die today."

Mol had settled down cross-legged next to the table. Allystaire lowered his eyes pointedly toward her, and Idgen Marte followed his gaze. He said, "There are things in my saddlebags you can sell, if it comes to that. Valuables." The swordswoman chuckled, but she nodded, and he saw an answering promise in her wide brown eyes.

He poured himself a mug of tea, drained it in a go, and set it back down. "I guess I will be off then."

Allystaire was pulling the bar from the door when Idgen Marte called him back, a curious note in her voice.

"How valuable?" She stood and walked over to him, every movement an economy of grace.

"Can you at least wait till I am dead?"

Idgen Marte's hand darted out lightning-quick and cuffed his ear.

It stung, but Allystaire knew it wasn't nearly as hard as she could've hit. He rubbed his ear gently and shook his head ruefully, hiding his admiration. He'd known few warriors who could cuff his ear by surprise.

"I'm no thief, you daft crusader. What I meant was…" And she smiled widely, revealing surprisingly white teeth, "valuable enough to buy a whole cargo of slaves?"

* * *

Decked out in more steel than was probably necessary, Allystaire found himself rattling the locked gate of the large warehouse on the Street of Sashes until he thought the poorly built, rattletrap business might fall down on him. It was still a few turns from midday, but the late summer sun was out in full force and had burned away the morning mist. This close to the quays, the stench of salt and fish was pervasive, and the air clung wetly to his armor-and-leather-clad body.

He was just about to switch from rattling to banging with the haft of his hammer, when the doors beyond the gate swung open and a dirty, leather-clad man with long knives on either side of his belt stuck out his pale, bleary-eyed face.

"Freeze off," he bleated.

"I want to inspect some merchandise," Allystaire called back, pitching his voice just loudly enough to carry. "And I am ready to pay for the privilege." He stuck two gloved fingers inside the curve of his cuirass and tugged out a purse, shaking it to set the links inside jingling.

The man blinked a few times and spat a thick, brownish gob to the ground. "I'll talk to the cap'n. Wait."

"Every moment I wait means a lower price for the doorman. Hurry."

The man simply grunted and stumped off, coughing as he went.

"Is it always too early for civility in this rathole?" Allystaire shook his head as he murmured aloud. He rolled his shoulders, turned his wrists, shuffled his feet, and checked to see how easily the hammer moved against its loop.

Soon the doorman was back, with a taller man who was cleaner and better armed. The newcomer wore a brigantine coat, the steel scales sewn onto a backing of leather dyed a dark, rich green. On his belt was a sword slimmer than the one on Allystaire's back, but of a similar length. *The hilt worn smooth. Pommel's clean. Every bit of metal on him shines. Dangerous.*

"What is it you're after?" The 'cap'n,' if that's who he was, affected a leaned-back swagger, and his voice dripped with contempt. *Maybe not*, Allystaire amended his silent assessment. *Never known a dangerous man to care that much for his pose.*

"As I said, inspect merchandise. Maybe make an early offer," Allystaire answered quietly. "Can it hurt to let me in?"

With an exaggeratedly small shrug, the captain turned away. "He gets half a turn of the small glass. Let him in."

The doorman, or Hacker, as Allystaire was already labeling him for all his coughing and spitting, trundled out to the gate and produced a long key. He fit it carefully into the crude lock that held the gate shut and held his hand out, even while turning his head to launch another gobbet of spit.

Allystaire produced his purse, dug inside it till he found two greening copper links, and flicked them directly toward the most recent gobbet, enjoying a twinge of satisfaction when the two joined rings landed with a moist plop. He walked on unconcerned.

Then the smell of the interior hit him; it was a raw human stench that mixed unwashed body odor with the heavy stink of shit, the tang of dried urine, and an almost palpable aura of fear. The interior was built like a barn, and smack in the middle of it was a cage of crude iron-fitted wood nearly as tall as the ceiling. Two large, box-like wagons, their coverings down to reveal similar constructions, sat to either side. Thin, poorly constructed walls led to anterooms and chambers in both the front and back, but the doors allowed a clear view into the center of the room. The stark reality of just how little these men needed to do to conceal their slaving was driven home.

If it's off the street, it isn't happening. That's the plain truth of it.

And the cage was full. Of people. Of misery. Stuffed into a space too small to contain them, a few dozen men and women sat and laid about, defeated and broken.

Poorly fed, likely beaten, and in utter despair, they were the folk of Thornhurst, Mol's kith and kin, he was sure. Most of the men, especially the younger, sported bruised faces. There were fewer younger men than old, and more older women than he would have expected.

Such anger rose in Allystaire's chest and throat that he very nearly drew his hammer to hurl at the nearest sleeping guard. He forced himself to calm, to patience, swallowing the anger like sour beer. And like sour beer, it roiled in his stomach.

"Well, you've not got much more time." The Captain leaned against the edge of the cage, arms crossed over his chest. "We'll be selling tonight, but you can have a few minutes to examine the cattle. What are you after buying?"

"Oarsmen." Setting his jaw, Allystaire strode over to the cage and began circling it; he spent far more time looking through the bars, avoiding the dead-eyed gazes of the prisoners within, and taking stock of the men that dozed or sat about. Besides the Captain and Hacker, he saw at least a half-dozen more, all armed. He counted two crossbows and, with both a professional regard and a sinking recognition, realized that they were posted in opposite corners of the room. Most of the men looked hard, their weapons well cared for. He also saw a few coiled whips hanging from swordbelts.

Still, he had to make a show of inspecting the people he supposedly meant to buy. But all he saw were grown men, women past their youth, and a few young men. "Where are the young women, the children?"

"Gonna strap the boys and girls to oars, then?"

Allystaire snorted, and hated himself when the answer came easily. "Even chained to an oar, a man might earn a reward, no? My liege lord's soldiers have needs and who better to service them?"

"A man who thinks ahead, then. Good. Looking to buy in bulk, then?"

Peering into the cage, forcing himself to look into the huddled bundles of misery packed into it, Allystaire mustered a shallow nod. "Perhaps. Any that cannot row or whore will have to come cheap." The folk gathered in there refused to hear any of his words; they clutched one another, turned their beaten faces away, or stared into the middle distance. He looked away, his stomach boiling over with his choked-down rage.

"The older women, those who've born children, they're of no use for you, aye?"

Allystaire was taken aback by the question, and shrugged. "Farm wives come strong. Mayhap some of them could do double duty aboard ship, aye? Take me to see the women. The *younger* women," he added, leaning forward and leering slightly.

The Captain smiled and waved a hand as he pushed away from the cage; Allystaire followed him. *One quick strike into the base of his spine and he's down.* His anger, the miserable faces of the caged folk, and now his own advice—all things he simply, for now, ignored. *Patience wins more battles than it loses so long as it never becomes cowardice.*

Beyond the big central room were several smaller antechambers, separated with flimsy wooden walls, the doorways covered by ragged blankets. The Captain led him to one such room, inside of which slumped a half-dozen young women; they were less bruised and cleaner than those in the central cage, with no ropes or chains holding them in place.

As if he knew the first question he was likely to be asked, the Captain immediately said, "If one of these tries to do a runner, balks at her work, we kill one of the older folk in the cage. They haven't tested us since the first night." He waved a hand at the younger women, who all had turned their faces from him the moment he entered the room. "This lot are all broken. You can have one for a silver link. Two for a silver and three copper." The man winked at Allystaire, a leering smile cracking his sneering, stubbled face. "Not t'keep, of course. Just to test. You're a soldier yourself, after all. Unless you're interested in something more expensive?"

Allystaire made a show of looking at the captives—bony, strong farm girls whose eyes wouldn't meet his. *Not sure I could stand it if they did.* "More expensive?"

"Aye. A few of them, real choice. Maidens. Planning to have a special auction for them, couple of nights from now. And ya know," he stepped closer, sensing camaraderie, "just because you want to keep one a maiden for a few days more doesn't mean she can't be taught what else she's good for, eh? Cost considerable more than these culls, though."

It was only by picturing, with a craftsman's attention to the details, what this sneering reaver's face would look like after a few of his best hammer blows that Allystaire was able to summon a smile. "It just so happens my lord has a weakness for, as you say, maidens. And one of his sons for boys. He had not thought to find such luck in Bend, but if I bring him back a new string to break it would do me no harm at all. I will have the lot: maids, culls, oarsmen, hags for the scullery if need be. Let us talk price."

"Gonna have to be a lot of gold for this," the man said, slowly shaking his head in hesitation. "Won't be much discount, if any."

"How do you feel about gemmary? Loose stones?" From underneath his breastplate, Allystaire produced a leather purse that bulged oddly. He pried the opening loose with two fingers and reached in. When he pulled his hand out, three items nestled in his palm: a heavy silver band, big enough to fit a man's thumb, with a sapphire set in the middle that was almost crude in its size and rough cut; a much larger carnelian with a woman's likeness engraved in fine detail upon it; and a gold ring, smaller than the other, but with chips of ruby circling a brilliantly deep red garnet.

Allystaire saw greed fire the Captain's eyes; though it was quickly suppressed, he knew he'd won.

* * *

"Cost me two rings, a handful of gold links and the deepest blue piece of unworked lapis I have ever seen," Allystaire declared, as he re-entered the room where Idgen Marte and Mol awaited him; a deck of cards were spread out on the table as the former apparently was teaching the latter a game. "But I bought your folk. When we can clear the city at nightfall, they will be free. Bastards would not deliver until dark."

Idgen Marte smiled coolly at him. "See? Wasn't that easier than playing 'storm the wall' and getting feathered for your trouble?"

Allystaire laughed, but his heart wasn't quite in it, so the sound fell flat and tinny. "I suppose." He turned to Mol, expecting a smile, but she threw a withering glare at him before turning away and storming off to the bed, her feet stamping violently against the floorboards.

"Is beggaring myself to free your people not enough?" For the first time since he had pulled the child from the cold well in her family's shattered inn, a note of real anger crept into Allystaire's voice.

Mol whirled on him, angry tears streaking her face. "You *paid* them! It's what they *wanted!* What they did *worked* and they'll just do it again. You liar. Oathbreaker!"

Allystaire stood stock still as Mol's angry words stung him. *She's right, you know. You just financed their next expedition.* He wetted his lips with his tongue, and finally said, in a smaller voice than he imagined himself to be capable of using, "You are right." Then, firmer, but still softly, "I will see to it."

Ignoring Idgen Marte's stunned and almost palpable silence, he turned for the door and clattered back down the stairs, tossing two considerably lightened purses onto the small table as he left.

The swordswoman looked from the open door to the defiant girl with her tear-streaked cheeks, and sighed. "Fool," she murmured.

CHAPTER 8

Pain Can Wait

Neither a woodsman nor a thief, Allystaire lacked the subtlety or the grace required for genuine stealth.

But of patience, he had some store. And it was patience that served him as he skulked in the alleys that viewed the wide, crude gate that protected the slavers. "If I can lay siege to the Harlach and Delondeur towers at Standing Guard Pass with three hundred men, I can besiege this place with only myself," he said to himself, for perhaps the dozenth time that afternoon. Midday had fulfilled the morning's promise of heat, and the air still hung like rain that was falling only halfway to the ground; inside his layers of metal and leather, he steamed.

Deep inside, though, he was cold. The roiling stomach of his earlier venture into the den was gone—now, he was calm, blue eyes fixed on the gate, occasionally moving to a different alley, or going inside one of the many taverns to sit, order wine, stare out the window, and not move. Once, he left his watch to find a common well and pay a copper link for a bucket. When he had poured as much warm, dirt-flavored water into his mouth as he could swallow, he emptied the rest directly over his face, where it ran down his neck and soaked the quilted tunic he wore beneath the cuirass.

Occasionally, men left the warehouse; he saw the Captain leave at least once, and many others besides. In total he counted thirteen different men that left the building and returned laden with supplies. Casks of ale, rope, chain, nails, tools, mended armor and clothing, sharpened weapons, baskets of bolts, large burlap sacks sewn tightly around salt-crusted sides of beef, and so on.

Already planning the next trip. And I freezing paid for it. Another word flitted over his brain, in Mol's sob-wracked voice: *Oathbreaker.*

The past few days played out in his mind again. Mol's tears. Her hand pressing his, warning him against hiring Nyndstir. Her constant questions. The stench of burnt flesh that hung over Thornhurst. The angry ravens. The impossibility of having heard Mol's voice from across the green while she lay hidden in the cold well.

That one kept coming back, but then again, his ears had always been sharp. *When a man's senses are primed, they grow sharper. You know this.*

Given his habitual muttering and the way his gloved hand kept returning to the hammer, passing folk gave him a wide berth.

A smarter man would've followed them as they left and killed them one, two at a time, his thoughts offered, as the summer sun finally, mercifully, started to give way to sooty darkness.

Where were you three turns ago, he countered himself.

Finally, he judged it close enough to the time that his delivery was promised. A quick glance told him the street was empty enough. Onlookers might come running, eventually. But for now, he might as well be alone with the slavers in pitch darkness. With heavy strides, he crossed the street and started rattling the plain shield on his left arm against the gate.

Soon enough, Hacker opened it up and met him with a broad, brown-toothed smile that was soon interrupted by coughing.

"Yer cargo's nearly ready, Lordship," he finally puffed out. "Never seen the cap'n so pleased with hisself. Bonus shares for e'ry man. Ahh, if only work came so easy every day, eh?" The man pattered on as he came to unlock the gate. The instant he turned around, Allystaire slipped the hammer out of its ring. For a moment, he pressed his fist against the black iron head, feeling its weight against his curled hand. Then he turned the head toward the ground and let most of the haft slip from his grip until he was holding it at the end, the head reaching past his knee.

Hacker turned back toward Allystaire, his lips parting to spit, when the hammer swung in a straight, short whip-like upward arc and took him on the bottom of the jaw. His jaw and teeth shattered in a spray of bone, blood, and flesh that left his mouth obscenely distended. The shocked and wretched howl that immediately followed was abruptly silenced as Allystaire, in a practiced motion of iron-strong fingers, turned his grip and brought the hammer back down straight on the top of Hacker's head.

The *crack* was audible on the quays across the street. Hacker dropped, and another short, quick hammer blow left his brains leaking into the dirt.

Allystaire used his gore-spattered hammer to push open the cutout in the wagon-sized door and stepped almost delicately inside.

The central room was bustling; the cage had been emptied, and both wagons were being readied for transport, their wheels tested and canvas coverings hammered into place. The slavers moved about with lazy, assured purpose. More than one whip was in hand, and though the light was meager, Allystaire felt sure they gleamed wetly.

The second man on the door was slow to realize anything was amiss. He sauntered over, hand resting casually, ineffectually on the sword at his hip.

Allystaire turned on him with a snarl, sweat and flecks of Hacker's blood rolling down his lip and into his mouth. Suddenly crouching behind his shield, he rushed the man; though the distance between them measured but a few steps, the shock of his armored weight met the man's casual stance and knocked him flat on his back, and the impact of the shield took his wind.

And the hammer that swung down over the shield crushed his breastbone and left him gasping for a breath he would never catch.

"Are you all going to die like cattle?" Allystaire muttered. The sight of him—gore dripping from the hammer in his hand, his face set in animal rage—along with the horrid, wet sounds of their comrade flattened at his feet, set two men running. Three others stood frozen in stunned disbelief.

The first to fully assess the situation was the Captain; he whipped out his sword in one hand and deftly produced a dagger from behind his brilliant green brigantine with the other. His feet instantly assumed a classic fighting stance—spread, weight shifting between his front and back foot. "I'll brook no cowards in my band! After him!" He pivoted sharply and hurled his dagger straight into the calf of one of his own men, one of the two who were fleeing. The man went down with a sharp curse. His companion thought better of doing a runner and turned to join the fray.

Meanwhile, Allystaire had reached the next nearest slaver, one who had drawn a thick, straight-bladed short sword and was busy fumbling to get a targe into his other hand. Shortsword was no coward; as Allystaire closed the distance, the man lunged forward and swung his blade in a wide arc, cutting the air audibly until the moment it rebounded hard off of Allystaire's grey shield.

As Allystaire felt the shock move up his arm, he let several inches of his hammer's haft fall through his hand, effectively shortening both the distance and power needed to swing. He took another blow off his shield, and with his shortened grip, raised his hammer and started chopping it down straight onto his opponent's shield—once, twice, three times, again. On the fourth blow, the targe was knocked clean out of the man's hand, and the next quick, chopping blow took him in the cheek. He dropped, his sword clattering from suddenly limp fingers.

Move, bellowed the voice of Allystaire's thoughts, and instinctively, he skittered two steps to his right and one step back. A sword cut through the space he'd just been standing in, swung in a wild two-handed grip; a mad-eyed, red-headed, bearded man in reeking boiled leather had charged him, thinking to split him from appetite to asshole.

But the sudden wild swing into air had unbalanced Ginger, and Allystaire reared back and lifted his right leg in a short, sharp kick directly on the seat of his pants. The man pitched forward, tripping over the unconscious form of his compatriot.

He spared a quick glance for the state of the field, sweeping his vision from one end of the huge room to the other. The Captain was hanging back, hoping, perhaps, to see his men earn their gold. The moment he had doubtless dreaded, though, was unfolding: men were running for the crossbows propped in opposite corners, dozens of feet apart from each other.

Without hesitation, Allystaire broke into a run for the nearer of the two would-be archers. *He's going to reach the crossbow before you reach him,* his own thoughts dryly informed. And he was, in truth. It wasn't a huge, belly-braced weapon and wouldn't need a windlass or claw to crank, but at this distance, it would do. By the time Allystaire was a dozen paces away, the man had reached the bow, calmly and expertly stuck his foot through the stirrup, and pulled back the bowstring. Deft fingers plucked a bolt from his belt and he turned, smiling, pleased with himself, to line up what he expected to be an easy shot.

Allystaire's hurled hammer, thrown stiff-elbowed from ten paces, took him square in one cheek, shattering the bones on one entire side of his face, forever destroying one eye. If not dead, he was done for, and the bolt fired up at the high roof as he fell.

Allystaire turned; his sprint had put the cage between himself and the other crossbowman, who didn't appear eager to fight.

Suddenly, both breath and thought were squeezed out of him as something hard curled around his neck and cut off his air. One of the slavers carrying a whip had employed it and was standing at the end of its length, smirking as he gave it a tug, assuming, likely, that as it tightened, Allystaire would fall.

Instead, with no time to waste and no trace of panic, Allystaire seized the taut length of hide in his free right hand and pulled as hard as he could, twisting his legs and leaning backward.

Stunned bewilderment replaced the slaver's smirking visage as he stumbled weakly toward Allystaire, pulled nearly off his feet. Allystaire pounced as the man stumbled. Reaching for Bullwhip's belt, he seized the hilt of a long, bare knife thrust through it. He tugged it free, pointed the tip up, and drove it into the base of the man's throat with one quick stab, then sawed it back and forth, tearing open Bullwhip's throat with a wound that would kill him instantly.

The whip immediately slackened around his own neck, and Allystaire tugged it off, gasping for air and feeling some blood seeping from thin, torn skin. He had little time to rest, though, for Ginger had gotten back to his feet, gathered up his two-hander, and was charging again, wild-eyed and brandishing his sword above his head. Quickly, Allystaire took a step forward, raising his shield as if to absorb the blow—then just as quickly stepped to the side, lowered his arm, and drove the rim of his shield straight into the man's stomach.

Between the momentum of his sprint and the force of Allystaire's blow, Ginger folded around the iron-rimmed shield and vomited as he fell. Discarding the shield, Allystaire reached over his shoulder and drew his sword with both hands. It was of a size with Ginger's, who lay gasping on the floor.

With bored efficiency, Allystaire reversed his grip and drove the point of his sword through the back of Ginger's ribcage, underneath the left shoulder, where he knew it would interfere with something vital. He drew it free and dropped its point down a second time, above the small of his back.

His odds were better now, but still bad; across the room planning his demise were another crossbowman, the irritatingly competent Captain, and at least two more men. The Captain appeared to be directing maneuvers in a low voice. Allystaire spread his feet and lifted his sword, which was heavier and less sure to his hand than the hammer that still lay in a corner. He held the blade in a cross-body guard running from his left shoulder toward his right hip, crouched slightly, and waited.

* * *

Meanwhile, just outside the gate, a newly laden string of pack mules, led by three members of the reaver band, was just arriving. The men were bored, well armed, and lightly but effectively armored in studded leather jacks.

The leader stopped the string and pulled a thin-bladed hatchet off his belt. "What in the Cold?" He pointed at the gory scene at the entrance.

* * *

"Throw down your weapons and come forward, you treacherous dog!"

"I was about to say the same. I have already butchered half your rabble," Allystaire called back. "I will make it the lot of you if I must."

"And the odds are still against you. Why'd you turn on our bargain? Come to recover your gold and gems? The former's mostly spent and the latter sold!"

Allystaire suppressed a wince at the thought of his wondrous lapis gone to waste, never seeing a craftsman's hands. "I never meant to bargain. I came here to keep a promise."

A moment of silence followed, during which Allystaire peered through the bars for flickers of movement, but most of the men appeared to be standing still. The one with the knife in his calf was still down, but the Captain, crossbowman, and the one who'd thought better were standing, clustered, opposite the far corner. Then, suddenly, the slim figure in green let out a harsh laugh.

"These folk under your protection then? They mean something to you, aye?" He gestured with one hand. "Daevat. Get on that wagon and start killing folk. Start with children."

The man hesitated, but bowed to the order and drew a hatchet and a long knife from his belt as he ran for a wagon.

If you go to meet him the crossbowman'll have a shot, he thought. Then he thought of Mol's anger, her tears.

"So be it," he muttered aloud in reply to his own thoughts, turning to intercept Daevat. The instant he was free of the cover of the cage, he dove for the ground in an awkward, painful roll toward the wagons. The crossbow thrummed with the release of its deadly tension, and a line of hot pain striped across Allystaire's foot. The bolt, shot in haste and low, had scraped across his boot, tearing leather and skin both. But then Allystaire was engaging Daevat, and the crossbowman had no clear shot.

Daevat was wiry and fast, and he alternated the point of his knife with the edge of his axe in blows that were designed to keep Allystaire away as much as do him injury. Even so, unshielded and with the larger and clumsier sword, Allystaire was forced to defend mostly by throwing his bracered forearms at the weapons. Twice the knife point skidded off them to draw blood—once from the back of his right hand, the other time digging a shallow gash on his left upper arm.

Daevat was emboldened by scoring a hit, and he lunged, leading with the point of his knife. Allystaire let it squeal off his breastplate, which turned the point, and leaned back, extending his arms to chop the heavy, dullish, final foot of blade above the hilt into Daevat's neck.

Dullness notwithstanding, it opened the slaver like a cleaver cutting ham, snapping his delicate collarbone and unleashing a fountain of blood.

Allystaire roughly kneed the dying slaver off his blade, grunting as he was forced to stand painfully, for a moment, on his bleeding foot.

* * *

Outside the slaver's den, the three who'd gone to lay in supplies stood over the door guard's mangled, lifeless corpse in silence. All had filled their hands, though. Two held knives, and the third grasped a stout cudgel with a metal cap riveted to one end.

"Figger the cap'n finally tired o' Morrys's spittin' n'coughin'," one suggested.

"Morrys? He'd never—"

He never had the chance to finish his statement. His knife fell from suddenly nerveless fingers at the same time that his neck sprouted four inches of slim, razored steel that was withdrawn as quickly as it came. He burbled blood from his mouth and the wound and sank to his knees.

Behind him, a tall, slim form swung the sword that had killed the first man in a quick arc, spraying the cudgel wielder with hot blood and blinding him for a crucial moment.

She whirled, her arms a blur, her sword a curved gleam. A long gash opened on the cudgel wielder's neck, and he, too, fell to the ground, clutching at the blood that poured from him.

The second knifeman readied himself to attack, but she had three times the length of steel in her hand, and he was cut three times before he could even begin to fight back.

The last thing that any of them heard was a husky feminine voice saying, "Your captain doesn't carry a hammer heavy enough to split rocks. Idiots."

* * *

Kicking the twitching body free of his blade was, Allystaire realized almost instantly, a tactical error, because it left him wide open for the crossbowman, whose weapon *thrummed* with the release of a bolt, immediately driving the breath from Allystaire's lungs. He expected, as he threw himself between the wagons, to feel the bolt tearing its way into his abdomen. But when he put his back to a wheel and looked, he realized the bolt had skipped off a bracer, lost much of its force, and simply put a large dent, rather than a hole, into his cuirass.

It still hurt.

It can hurt later, he willed himself, forcing the pain to some other part of his mind where he wouldn't feel it here and now. He knew very well how to be hurt, and to keep fighting.

But what are you going to do about the crossbow, you old fool? At this distance, he couldn't charge. The Captain, who'd been waiting all of this out, watching his men fall, appeared fresh and unhurt, and too calm by half for Allystaire's liking. And now the green-jacketed reaver was calling out to taunt him. "Come on, you fool avenger. You've had your share of blood. You can still take what you paid for and leave. I'm a civilized man and will allow you that. But my generous offer is good for only a few seconds."

Allystaire heard the deep *thrum* of the crossbow immediately following the Captain's words, and splinters quickly showered him. A bolt lay quivering in the bed of the wagon mere inches from his lightly-armored head.

Move!

He spun out from under the wagon, and as he stood, something caught his eye. Charging forward, he bent and scooped up the hatchet that Daevat had been swinging at him. With the same grip, the same straightened arm and downward motion he'd used to throw his hammer, he threw it at the archer.

Luck was with him, or the crossbowman must've been green; instead of using the stirrup, he had pressed the stock against his stomach and pulled the bowstring back with his hands, then slotted a bolt in and lowered the weapon. A panicked move.

The hatchet *thunked* straight into the understock of the crossbow and relieved the bowman of all the fingers that were curled around it in the bargain. He dropped his weapon, and the quarrel rolled free; then he fell backward, clutching at the bleeding ruin of his hand.

The Captain laughed contemptuously, stepped toward his fallen man, and casually skewered his throat with the heavy point of his blade. Then he stepped away, smartly raised the bloodied weapon in a salute, and began circling, nimbly shuffling his feet and shifting his weight.

Allystaire instinctively did the same, moving to his right as the Captain moved to his left, though each step caused a small jolt of ever-worsening pain in his bleeding foot.

"You've done me a favor, you know," the Captain sneered at him.

"Not yet," Allystaire replied through gritted teeth. "Come a little closer and I shall."

The Captain laughed again and lunged forward, swinging his sword in a swift, sidelong arc. Allystaire's blade caught it and flung it aside, and the Captain danced backward.

"Oh not at all, my bloodthirsty friend. Indeed, what you most obligingly did was lower my costs." The smile widened, the sword point danced. He tried another lunge with an overhead chop, and once again it was turned away. "Dead men draw no wages and drink no beer, you see."

Allystaire tried a long, slow swing, but he aimed it at the Captain's left side and put some heft into it. The Captain danced to his own right, backing toward his dead crossbowman in the corner, and Allystaire shuffled to bring them square.

"After I kill you, I'll still have my cheerless chattel, my profit will be doubled, and I'll have no shares to pay." He followed his taunt with a lunge and a low sweep.

Allystaire knocked it into the ground, but it nearly took him at the knee.

"You're getting slow. Your body's finally feeling what it's done," the Captain taunted. He tried a quick slash, then again on the backhand, which drew a sizzling line across Allystaire's forehead, just beneath his cap. Blood began to trickle toward his eyes.

At least he fights with style, Allystaire thought, even as he felt warm droplets tickle his eyebrows. "You talk too much." He stepped forward with his left foot and ran his blade like a spear at his opponent's stomach. The Captain, instead of parrying, stepped aside like a young man dodging a bull in the ring at a village festival. He even rose to his toes, bringing his feet closer together until they touched.

If Allystaire's thoughts could've smiled, they would have, but he stopped the expression from showing on his features. *Style is for dead men.*

With a light laugh, the green-coated Captain swung his sword in another slash, this time parting the leather on Allystaire's left upper arm between bracer and cuirass, opening a shallow gash on the layers of muscle beneath.

This may hurt. Allystaire gathered himself and drew back his sword almost clumsily, showing his opponent another spear-point lunge. As he'd hoped, the Captain started to draw his feet together, but instead of lunging, Allystaire threw his sword at the Captain's face. A desperate gamble, and intended merely to befuddle, but in his startled confusion, the nimbler and fresher swordsman overbalanced and stumbled.

Allystaire pounced like a bear on a suddenly vulnerable baiter. His left hand went for the right wrist and managed to seize it as he drove the Captain back into the wall, but not before the slaver had managed to drive the point of his sword deep into Allystaire's left shoulder. *Doesn't matter now, does it?* Pain bloomed down his arm.

It would wait.

His left arm was weakened by wounds, and blood trickled along his eyebrows, but Allystaire had the benefits of mass, momentum, and surprise. He drove the Captain back into the wall and was rewarded with the sound of a sword, punched out of a hand by unyielding stone, clattering onto the floor.

"You…Talk…Too…Much." With each seething word, Allystaire drove his balled up, iron-studded fist straight into the hateful smirk. His first punch wasn't quite square, but the rest lined up the iron studs perfectly and tore open the man's skin. Between the shock of the assault and the impact of the first blow, the Captain raised only meager defenses; he couldn't get his knees beneath him to push Allystaire away, and by the time he was raising his arm the second blow had fallen, stunning him to near insensibility. His arm rising and falling like a man sawing a log, Allystaire threw every ounce of his fury, every moment of suppressed rage of the past few days, into his punches. Each satisfying thud of his gloved fist against flesh was another sight of the charred bones in the village green, was a sword biting into Casamir's neck, was Mol's shrill accusation from earlier in the day.

Like a baker punching down an over-proofed dough, Allystaire punched until his arm burned, pressing the Captain's increasingly limp body against the wall with his knees and his wounded left arm. He stopped only when he realized his fist, spattered with red and gray gore, had just thudded into the stone of the wall.

He let the limp, nearly headless reaver leader drop in a heap, and turned back to survey his grisly handiwork. Blood had seeped into his right eye, half blinding him. Trying to wipe at it with his sleeve did no good, so he simply closed the eye and turned his head to see what he needed to.

A whimper, and not from the wagons, caught his attention. Allystaire turned; the man who still had a knife in his calf was crawling toward the back rooms, and, presumably, a way out.

"Stop," Allystaire commanded, his voice hoarse and quiet, his left arm hanging limp, his right coated with blood up to the elbow, his face spattered with his blood, and others'.

The slaver stopped. With painful effort, he flopped over onto his side. "You're a good man, I see that. And ya've bested all me mates," the man blubbered, as Allystaire advanced on him. "I don't deserve yer mercy but I cry for it anyway. Surely ya won't strike down an unarmed and wounded man who surrenders, aye? I surrender! I surrender!"

Allystaire nodded slowly, and his voice sounded very far away. "No. No, I will not kill a wounded man who cannot defend himself, pleads for mercy, and surrenders." He turned and walked back to the corner where he'd just done his grisly work. He picked up the hatchet and the Captain's sword.

Slowly, painfully, he walked over to the nearest wagon, turned the hatchet around in his hand, struck with it once, twice, a third time. A section of wooden cage, poorly made and bearing a sturdy iron lock set in the middle, cracked sharply. He pulled it away, and the door of the cage swung open. The maids who had not been bound hopped down onto the floor, blinking and crying.

"I will not kill an unarmed man," Allystaire repeated. With shaking hands, he held out the hatchet and sword to the women he'd freed, who took them uncertainly. He turned back to the wounded slaver. "*They* might," he added faintly.

Then Allystaire pitched backward and knew no more.

CHAPTER 9

Not a Lord

Allystaire awoke in a pool of pain, and no small measure of surprise that he was alive to feel it. His body was slick with sweat, and his back glowed with the agony of lying down too long and too limply. He struggled to sit up. When he started to lever himself up on his hands, his left arm immediately gave way, reminding him pointedly of how much steel had passed through it that day. Or was it yesterday. Or…He could not fathom how much time had passed. He fell back to the bed, gathered the blankets with one hand, and tossed them away.

"How in Fortune's name did I get here? And where is here?" His voice was a dry, painful creak.

"Yer at the Sign of the Stone Wall, m'lord," a voice offered meekly.

Careful to rise using his right hand now, Allystaire cast his gaze around the suddenly familiar room and located a girl, grown into womanhood but probably not yet twenty, sitting on the stool before the fire. Her hair was honey-brown and appeared recently brushed, and her days of captivity had not entirely robbed her skin of its summer tawniness.

"You got here because the woman Idgen Marte commanded us to carry you on one of the wagons," she added.

"Why was she there? I hired her to watch Mol, nothing more." Frowning, Allystaire swung his legs out of the bed and prepared, slowly, to push himself to his feet. The young woman whirled on the stool to face the opposite direction, and it was only then he realized he was stark naked.

"My apologies, lass," he said, flushing. "Though I daresay I have never encountered a shy farmgirl before." He couldn't help but tease her, but all the same he lowered himself, gratefully, back to the bed and pulled a blanket close around his hips. "You may turn around now. Tell me what happened?"

Sitting up on the edge of the bed and aching, Allystaire noted that the wounds on his left arm were bound in clean strips of cloth, and as he felt around them there was little sign of swelling or heat. His fingers moved to probe the wound on his forehead; he was amazed to find it neatly stitched in tiny, tight threads.

As he checked his wounds, the woman spoke cautiously and carefully, still looking at him only sideways. "Well, after you opened our…our wagon, m'lord, and thank you…after that, you fell to the ground and we thought y'might bleed to death. Was only us and the children in there and we tried to do what we could. But then the woman Idgen Marte strolled in, and, casually as you please, like a man squashing bugs with 'is thumb, she put her sword through the neck of e'ry man lyin' there. Or nearly. I think you'd done for most of 'em, true, but…"

Allystaire withered in the face of her talking. But just then, the door opened and in strode Idgen Marte herself, carrying a steaming tray. Allystaire's stomach leapt and growled audibly, and she set the tray down with a laugh.

"You can leave, Leah. I'll explain." With a simple nod of her head, Leah stood flush-faced and hurried out, closing the door behind her.

"Woman acted as though I was like to bite her."

Idgen Marte pulled the table to the bedside so that Allystaire could reach to the tray and eat. He seized a cup that steamed and smelled of beef; it proved to be strong, thick beef tea, which he drank down in sizzling gulps.

"Bear in mind that the first time she saw you, she thought you were haggling to buy her. The second time, she watched and listened from a cage as you maimed and killed a roomful of armed slavers. She's wise to be afraid."

Allystaire shrugged, then flinched when the motion tugged at his left arm. "I suppose so. Still, I mean her no harm."

Idgen Marte sat and stared at him for a moment as he reached for more food, seizing bread and cheese in his right hand. He winced again as pain, this time from swollen and possibly broken knuckles, coursed through him.

"You can be a terrifying man, Allystaire. And you don't even know it, do you?"

He paused with a great hunk of cheese halfway in his mouth, bit down, chewed slowly, and then said, "Terrifying?"

"Did you forget that you punched a man to death with those awful iron gloves of yours? Or the other nine or ten you killed before? And you did it so badly, with such poor planning, I don't know how you aren't dead."

Allystaire lifted one finger of his left hand and said, "First, I survived, which means I did not do it *badly*. Second, I told you I was not a subtle man." He stuffed more cheese into his mouth, ate it quickly, then looked around the room, puzzled. "Where's Mol?"

"With her kinfolk." Idgen Marte quickly pointed to his bandages. "Hurt? Itch? Swelling, burning?"

"None of those." Allystaire lifted his arm, bending it at the elbow. He turned his head to sniff at the dressings. "No rank smell, either. What did you clean it with?"

"Boiled wine. Had the maggots ready. Didn't need them, as it happens." She leaned forward and, with a light touch, felt at the stitches on his forehead, her fingers cool and practiced.

Allystaire started to nod, but she tightened her fingers and stopped him. "Stay still." He stuffed a piece of bread into his mouth and chewed slowly and carefully.

"Killed them all, then? The whole crew?"

Idgen Marte stood and walked to the fireplace and grabbed the stool, then dragged it to join the table at the bedside. She looked at him for a moment, frowning slightly, then turning her eyes to the window, said, "All but one."

"What? The one their Captain wounded? I thought they would take care of that."

Idgen Marte shook her head. "No. They aren't killers, and handing them an axe and telling them to take revenge won't change that. Nor would it do them any good. I wouldn't let them."

Allystaire grimaced, eyed the swordswoman carefully. "Why not? And what were you doing there, anyway?"

"If *you* won't kill an unarmed man who's begging for mercy, what makes you think those farmgirls would?" Idgen Marte smacked her open hand on the table, and the crockery jumped. "I was there because Mol persuaded me."

Allystaire nodded, closing his eyes a moment and murmuring, "You are right." Then he laughed, albeit gently, to avoid pain. "*Persuaded* you? How did a child of ten summers persuade *you* to do *anything*?"

Idgen Marte frowned and looked back toward the window, covered now in oiled paper. "Lass was more convincing than she had any right to be. And I think I'm not the only one she's persuaded to do something, eh?"

Allystaire chortled again, nodding and wiping at his sweaty forehead. "True enough, true enough. Where is she? I should like to talk to her. And her folk."

I don't know whether…" Idgen Marte pressed her lips into a thin line and sighed. "That child has seen a lot of things these past days. Lot of worry for a child to take on, aye? I do not know…"

Allystaire started to rise, though he kept the blanket wrapped around his hips. "What is wrong with Mol?"

Idgen Marte stood up and shoved him back onto the bed with the heel of one hand, then sat down. "The girl is fine. Her health. But her mind? I don't know. She hasn't spoken since her kinfolk returned. She's mostly slept. They're too happy to see her alive to be worried. But I think something in the girl snapped like bad cordage." She held up a hand before Allystaire could interrupt. "That's a bad figure for it; likely 'tis only frayed. She'll come to in time. She eats, she grasps onto her uncle and cries, but…" Idgen Marte paused a moment in thought. "Let her rest for now, mind and body. See that you do the same."

Allystaire sat silently for a long moment, long enough for the sounds of the wooden floor creaking in the heat and the distant rattle of voices and movement down the stairs to reach their ears in soft, slow waves.

"I have seen that happen once, to a man. His mind did not come back."

"The young heal faster than we do, no?"

"In mind as well as body?" Allystaire shook his head and sighed again. Most of the burst of strength he'd felt when he stood had deserted. He lowered his head, took another deep breath. "What of the living reaver? What do we do with him?"

Idgen Marte frowned again. "That, too, is out of our hands. The rabble of a guard have him. We were hauling away when they came upon us—he wanted to make a complaint."

"A complaint?" Allystaire felt a spark of strength return, fueled by a sudden anger. "A complaint? He was part of a gods-damned reaver crew, a slaver, and he wants to make a *complaint?* He is an outlaw!"

"Aye, in an outlaw city, where his crew had paid the right people the right prices." Idgen Marte wet her lips a moment before continuing. "And there's worse."

"Of course there is." Allystaire lifted his swollen right hand and gestured toward himself with it. "Out with it. All at once now."

"When the guards asked around, probably backed by reaver gold, they found a couple of sots from one of the taverns across the Street of Sashes who'll say they saw you murder the door guard, spring from ambush and crush his skull."

"Say to whom? I doubt any magistrates answer to this false baron, and I doubt Delondeur has any justiciars riding a circuit here."

"No," Idgen Marte allowed, "no justiciars, no magistrates. But there is a man who calls himself the Baron of Bend, and he seems to think he can bring you before an assize. Making threats about blood gold and damages and so on. He's got the folk from Thornhurst cowed, and no mistake."

"An assize? Some up-jumped river pirate thinks he can put me to his law when he allows *slavery?*" Allystaire's hands curled into fists, despite the swelling in the right.

"He has the numbers in this fight."

"So did the freezing reavers," Allystaire reminded her, his voice searing his throat.

"He'd have the numbers even if it were you, me, and every man from Thornhurst holding a spear and knowing which end to stick with, which they wouldn't. You probably can't bludgeon your way past this." She paused, shifted on the stool, and said, "I could sneak you out."

"But not the Thornhurst folk. And if they do not get home with time to salvage before the season starts to turn I will have done them no good."

Idgen Marte sighed and stood. "I was afraid you'd say that. I've kept them at bay since yesterday by saying you were gravely wounded, but they'll want to see you soon enough. You may have to appear before this so-called Baron of Bend and do what you can to appease him."

"Oh I will appease him till he is a foot Cold-damned shorter, and I am not feeling particular about which end to pare from."

"Go back to sleep, Allystaire. I'll send another lass to watch you." She made a show of leaning forward as if to peek past the blanket, and lifted an eyebrow. "Mayhap I'll send one who doesn't blush so easily."

Allystaire grimaced, and with his chest bare, couldn't hide the flush her jibe had raised. He *harrumphed* to clear his throat, then lifted his bruised and swollen hand. "Anything we can do for this? Is there a cold house in Bend anywhere? Maybe some fish oil? Willowbark?"

Idgen Marte shook her head as she opened the door. "Could be. But I'm letting that one sit. I want you to remember it."

It wasn't long before Allystaire allowed himself to fall back on to the mattress, but he did pause to finish wolfing down every bite Idgen Marte had brought up. He tossed aside all of the covers but the lightest one and let his head fall back to the pillows. He ached with fatigue, but glowed with relief. He had held to his word, and for once in his life, the blackguards had suffered and the weak had prospered.

You're much the poorer for it. You can't swing your sword for two days at least and these peasants are still in danger. You're a freezing hero all right.

"Bloody cheerful one, I am," Allystaire said aloud. "I did the hard part," he offered in counter.

Killing's always the easy part and you know it. Always has been.

He found no answer for that, so he let his eyes close and soon drifted into a deeper sleep than he was accustomed to.

* * *

When he awoke, it was with a start, his right hand snapping up to grasp the wrist of a hand that lingered just above his bare, sweat-slicked chest. His fingers closed around the arm and held fast as he sat up, opening his eyes to find varying degrees of shadow in the room, with the only light a tiny fire of tinder. The arm his fingers closed hard around was slender, and its owner let out a startled cry and tried to fling herself away, but he held tight, until his eyes adjusted. When he recognized the same nervous creature who had sat at his bedside that afternoon, he let go.

She drew back her hand and started rubbing her wrist with the other one, swallowing a sound too close to a sob for his comfort.

"I apologize, lass…Leah, is it? You startled me. I did not mean to hurt you."

"You didn't…not…'t won't last." She paused and straightened up. "I've had worse. These past days." She rubbed at her wrist again, adding, "You're awful strong, m'lord, for a wounded man who was just asleep."

"I am a light sleeper," Allystaire replied, though he knew, in this instance, it hadn't been true. "And I wake quickly. My apologies." He sat up, propping his back against the backboard, careful to keep the coverlet drawn to his navel. "What turn is it?"

Leah, still at his bedside, folded her hands behind her. "Three turns past the innkeep's dinner bell," she replied. Though it was dark in the room, he had a sense of her studying him carefully.

"Why are you at my bedside again, Leah? And why all the way over here instead of sitting by the fire, or with a lamp?"

She turned her head away, and said, "I…I dunno, m'lord. I just…you were so fearsome back in that warehouse last eve, I wasn't sure…I wasn't sure you were a man at all and not somethin' out of a story." Her voice was thin, apologetic. She took a half step away from the bed.

Going to let this one keep calling you m'lord, then? Allystaire was glad of the darkness, given the flush that his thought sent creeping up his neck.

"I am not your lord, Leah, or anyone's. And I promise you," he said, trying to lighten his words and smiling for all the good it did in the darkness, "I hurt too much to be anything out of a story except a corpse."

Leah laughed a little desperately and inched back toward him, turning her gaze once more upon his face. Suddenly she stepped even closer, bent down, and moved her mouth over his, kissing him inexpertly, but enthusiastically. She pressed a timid hand against his bare chest.

Opposing forces immediately began to war in Allystaire. On the one hand was the sudden, wild urge; he remembered suddenly and all too well the shape of her cheeks and the soft gold glinting of her hair that afternoon, the curves beneath her peasant's dress. On the other hand, something nagged at him intensely. He reached up and gently pulled her hand from his chest and tugged her away from him.

"Leah, lass…what do you think you are doing?"

"Kissing you, m'lord. In gratitude." Even in the darkness, he could see her face move in a smile. "And gettin' kissed back if you don't mind me sayin'."

Allystaire chided himself inwardly. "Leah, I am not a lord. Please remember that. And…" He felt his flush deepen as he straightened up on his bed, painfully aware of the drumbeat of his pulse. "…this…has nothing to do with gratitude."

Leah sniffled slightly at his mild rebuke, but she found her courage and replied, "'Tis not the first time I've kissed a man, you know." A pause. "Well maybe the others were boys, but still."

Allystaire suppressed a laugh, even his stunted instincts telling him it was the reaction that would sting the most. He tried a gentle tone. "Leah, I am probably old enough to be your father. Why would you want to kiss an old man?"

Leah sat on the bed, bringing her face into his vision. "You aren't that old, Allystaire, and 'tis my eighteenth summer." She looked intent, her eyes wide circles, darker than the shadows around them.

Two thoughts nearly collided: *At least she's using my name* and *Freeze me, I am old enough to be her father*. He swallowed, finding it hard to meet her gaze, even shrouded with dark as the room was. "Leah, I think you should probably go back to your own room, or to your kin, and sleep. In the light of day you will think better of this."

Leah darted from his bed and out of the room in a flurry, leaving the door open behind her.

With a sigh, Allystaire stood, his legs aching from disuse. He fumbled at the table for the lamp and lit it from the fire with a twig. After setting it on the table, he rummaged through the saddlebags that were pushed against the wall, coming out with a clean pair of trousers and a plain but finely made linen shirt. He pulled them on, seized the lamp, and trudged down the stairs.

The taproom was neither crowded nor empty. Idgen Marte sat at a corner table in front of a window with its oilskin untacked, and Allystaire could feel the breeze wafting in. By the time he had crossed the room, the lean warrior had turned to face him, and the innkeep was dogging his steps with a pitcher of wine.

"Did you send her back to my room?"

Idgen Marte gave the innkeep a nod of thanks, set down the pitcher and poured a cup for Allystaire. "Good eve to you too. Send who?" She pushed the cup toward him with a finger.

Allystaire sat down and took the wine, but did not drink. "The lass. Leah. Did you send her back to my room?"

Idgen Marte shook her head and spread her hands. "Not at all. Why? You scare her off again?"

Allystaire took a long drink of wine; it had been chilled, and its coolness, along with the slight breeze, made the taproom a smidgen more tolerable. "Not quite. She was rather less shy this time."

Idgen Marte fell into such a deep laugh that she had to lay her head in her hands. "And how did you handle that, you brave knight, you?"

His face warmed again, less in shame than anger. "I told her that trying to kiss me had nothing to do with gratitude and that she should leave. That the morning would show it to be as bad an idea as it was."

"You can walk into a room full of hardened reavers and start killin' 'em with no plan, but you can't kiss a farmgirl for a bit, eh?"

Allystaire slapped his right fist on the table lightly, then winced at the pain. "Dammit woman, that lass had more than kissing on her mind," he hissed. "I did not rescue her from life as a chattel whore only to try and make her my own."

"You're an idiot."

"Am I paying you to insult me? I would have sworn I hired you just to guard Mol."

The swordswoman waved a hand. "Stop trying to change the subject. Think. Think about why the lass was kissing you, hmm? You were frightening at first, yes, but in your own words, you rescued her. *And* what was left of her entire village. Do you think she came there on her own? Or do you think mayhap her mother, or another woman, or even her father, sent her up to your room? Did you even wonder why they sent a fetching lass like Leah to watch you in the first place?"

Allystaire narrowed his eyes and pressed his lips together. "Just what are you suggesting?"

"They are simple folk, but they aren't dull-witted. They see you as a lordly type, and that's what you are, no matter your chaste squeaking otherwise,"

Idgen Marte said, forestalling argument with a raised hand. "In their world, a lord never does anything for free. And if a comely maid is the price they must pay, well…" She trailed off, lowering her hand. "Do ya see? And supposing you took a particular liking to her; well then, who knows what might happen?"

Realization dawned on Allystaire, yet something about Leah's wide, knowing eyes still troubled him. "I see, I think." His second pull at the wine emptied his ample cup. "Even if it was her own idea, it would be wrong."

"You tryin' to get me to tell you what to do?" Idgen Marte chuckled. "You won't like the results."

Allystaire shook his head, and reached for the pitcher. "No. I rarely come to an answer without speaking aloud. Old habit."

The woman gestured to his hand. "Swellin's gone down. You didn't get someone to bring you some fish oil, did you? I meant what I said."

Allystaire lifted his right hand, suddenly surprised at how easily it had been working. "No. Appears to be healing fast on its own." Then he turned narrowed eyes on Idgen Marte. "Not that I would need your permission if I *did*." Then, quickly, "That brings me to a question. Why are you still here?"

Idgen Marte shrugged. "You seem like an easy mark and I aim to keep milking you till the links stop flowing." Allystaire's face darkened, and she waved a hand. "Relax, crusader. I don't mean to bilk you. You'll pay for the work I did, and I think I earned a bonus share for hauling you out of the warehouse and keepin' you alive afterwards." She swung one booted foot up on the table, and tilted her chair back casually, keeping her eyes fixed on his face. "But I'm still here because I want t'know how this ends."

"How what ends?"

"You, Mol, Bend, the Thornhurst folk, the Baron of Bend…all of it." She waved a hand to indicate the space around her, and presumably the town that slumbered beyond the stone walls of the inn. "I've always had a head for stories. Liked hearin' 'em, rememberin' 'em."

Allystaire snorted. "You're a bard, then? A minstrel? Where's your harp?"

Idgen Marte leaned forward and scowled, dropping her foot back to the floor. "Mind what you say. I said nothing about singin' 'em. Said I like hearing and remembering. That's all."

Allystaire raised his hands in a conciliatory gesture. "Apologies. I did not mean to strike a sore spot." He waited a moment before adding, "You were saying?"

"Right. Stories. Stories and songs are probably the reason I'm not a farmwife or a whore, and thank Fortune for that," Idgen Marte said, raising her cup, her cheerful insouciance returning in a heartbeat. "For the former, anyway. Whore and sword-at-hire are much the same except whores probably get cut less." A pause. "Most places. Anyway…" She tilted her cup back again, draining it. "I like stories. And I think *you* are one, now. Never before seen one as it unfolded."

Allystaire shook his head, closed his eyes. "There is no story here. And even if there were, it would not end well."

"Who's to say there isn't some charmed fate leading you on? Perhaps Fortune awaits you with wealth and fame? Ever hear the stories of Elinthanar? 'The Blade of Oaken Fire' n' those?'"

Allystaire nodded, his head tilted to the side. "Sure. What is your point?"

"My point is that story makes much of Elinthanar facing and killing ten men in open combat, on his own."

The man shrugged his broad shoulders, glancing down in surprise at how little the movement hurt. "Still sounds as pointless as a tourney lance."

"You faced ten men in open combat, alone. You killed nine, the tenth yielded, and you're still here."

Allystaire snorted in derision. "Most were rabble. Reavers who were used to culling sheep. The only one who knew what he was about was the Captain." Allystaire rapped the table with a knuckle as he thought. "A popinjay he was, but dangerous. And fast."

"You were faster?"

Another shake of the head. "Hardly. If anything I was a good deal slower. But he wanted to fight with style, as if fencing masters were standing by to assign points. Now *there* was a man who thought he was in a story."

"How'd you defeat him, then?"

"Well, he did me the favor of waiting till all his men were dead." *He didn't exactly wait,* he reminded himself, remembering the Captain's blade tearing out the throat of the crossbowman he'd maimed. In his strangely vivid memory, he saw the pain in the young man's eyes, how pale his cheeks were beneath the stubble it had likely taken him days to grow. "Decided it meant he would not owe them shares or wages."

"And it meant you were wounded and slow. So how?"

"As I said, he wanted to fight with style." Allystaire shook his head, his lips curling in disgust. "Style is for the *mêlée* or the yard, not for hot-blooded battle."

Idgen Marte sipped from her refilled cup. "And what do you fight with?" She quirked her lips. "Besides, apparently, your nose."

"Patience," Allystaire replied, smiling lightly. "And a willingness to get hurt."

"That'd explain the nose, then."

"Hardly a fight unless this gets broken," he responded, reaching up and tapping a finger against his splayed, slightly-leftward pointing beak.

She laughed, drained her cup, and stood. "I'm for bed. Tomorrow you'll need to see the baron, who, ah, thinks I'm your second or your castellan or your major-domo. Whatever the Cold you northern lordlings have. I've let him think it because it meant you got to rest."

"I am not—"

"A lord. I know, I know," Idgen Marte said, heading for the stairs. "Ya talk like a lord, have the armor and weapons of a lord, the horses of a lord, the links and the gemmary of a lord, and the bearing of a lord. But, nay, by all means, you are not a lord. If you aren't a lord, you had better decide what you *are*, because a lord is what we've got every reason to think ya are." She didn't wait for a response as she nimbly hopped up the wooden stairs, her soft boots barely making a sound.

"If I knew I would tell you," Allystaire said—to the swordswoman who was out of hearing, to the innkeep asleep on his feet behind the bar, to his cynical thoughts, to himself. Then he heaved to his feet, his knee twinging as usual, and marched toward the stairs.

Once inside his room, he set down his lamp and stared at the door for a long moment. "If I leave it unbarred and Leah wanders in, that is not my fault, right?" *Right.* He closed his eyes, steadied his breathing, barred the door, and fell into a fitful sleep.

CHAPTER 10

Ardent

Allystaire awoke the next morning shortly after dawn. He dressed simply: linen shirt, leather vest, riding trews, boots. He paused before the door, frowning. *Feel naked without any steel on.* He considered the armor neatly piled with his bags, and he finally stuffed his arms through the bracers and buckled them tightly. He sighed contentedly. "Better."

He considered the weaponry, picked up the sword with a less happy sigh, and unbarred his door. He could hear the buzz of conversation in the common room from his door, but as soon as he'd descended the stairs, it hushed in profound silence.

He soon realized it was full of the folk he'd rescued, given their plain homespun, their stooped backs, and the awe and surprise on their faces as they all, in unison, stared at him. Taken aback, Allystaire could do naught but return their stares.

Finally, one man stood and whipped off the shapeless hat he wore, his huge, gnarled knuckles clutching it against his chest. This precipitated a wave of standing, kneeling, curtsying, and forelock tugging.

Cold, Allystaire thought, unable to keep from wincing, though when his eyes swept the crowd and fell on Leah—who was positioned rather near the stairway and curtsying in a way that left the neck of her already low-pulled blouse open to his eyes—his grimace became a bit flustered. He waved his hands, motioning everyone back into their seats, and pitched his voice to fill the room.

"None of that, folks, none of that. I am not your lord and you owe me no obeisance." The sea of blank looks that met his gentle admonition compelled him to add more firmly, "You do not need to bow and scrape. Go back to enjoying your breakfasts."

That order, they understood, and most of them obeyed, though very few without turning to glance surreptitiously at him once or twice. As an undercurrent of whispering filled the room, Allystaire couldn't shake the certainty that most of it was about him.

Unlike the others, Leah stared openly at him, her eyes wide and dark, her back straight, and her face and form all the more alluring for being in the light of day, instead of shadows and insinuations in a shadow-filled room.

Close your eyes and think of Dorinne if the farmgirl's interest seems so awful, he thought, shortly followed by a burst of intense self-loathing. He found Idgen Marte at the corner table, her brown eyes full of barely contained mirth at, he suspected, the way his cheeks flushed.

"Did you make it through the night with your honor intact?" she asked, before he could even sit down.

"Not amusing."

"Y'haven't the faintest idea how amusing it is."

"It is *not* amusing," Allystaire insisted, his voice starting to growl. "That lass has been to the iciest reaches of the Cold and back. Her folk have no right to try and shove her into a stranger's bed."

"It's how their world works," Idgen Marte said simply. "Besides," she ventured, "perhaps it was Leah's own idea. Have you considered that?"

"Even so, it would be a bad one. I would not see the girl hurt any more than she already has been."

Idgen Marte turned her head to one side and studied him for a moment. "You actually mean that, don't you? You are dead certain it'd be wrong to bed the lass, and now that your mind is made up, nothing will change it."

"Not certain about anything in this world," Allystaire answered honestly, his voice calming. "But…yes, you mostly have the right of it. It would be wrong. I will not do it."

"Have you always been this way?"

"No," he replied without the slightest hesitation.

"How you got from there to here is a story I'd like to hear."

"You could die waiting for me to tell you that story."

"We'll see," Idgen Marte chirped brightly, as the innkeep toddled over rather unsteadily. His eyes were weighed with heavy bags, and his fringe of hair flopped in wild disarray.

"M'lord, I'll be bringin' yer breakfast soon. But, ah…there are a few matters. First, there's this letter from the Baron o' Bend, just arrived, and his courier is waitin' in the stables for an answer. And, uh, second…" As he spoke, the innkeep rummaged in his grease-spotted apron and pulled out a piece of parchment folded to a square and sealed with wax.

"These folk are eating you out of business, aye? I will get you some gold to cover it, goodman. I promise. Their debt to you will be paid in full." *What am I saying*?

The innkeep sagged with relief so visible that Allystaire was afraid the man might faint. In fact, both he and Idgen Marte had half-risen to catch and steady him, but his eyes blinked back into wakefulness. "Thank ya m'lord, and thank ya, warrior," he half-murmured. "I'm run off me feet tryin' to do for 'em all."

"You are indeed a proper host, goodman. I believe I can secure you some help." Allystaire stood, and he and Idgen Marte eased the harried man to a chair. Then, clearing his throat and once again filling his voice with a ringing note of command, he boomed, "Folk of Thornhurst. I believe that your gracious host is unused to housing quite so many under his roof at once, and is performing, dare I say it, heroically, in the face of the challenge. Of course, there is no thought in his head of turning any of you out. But he has need of assistance. Everything from sweeping and fire-tending to feeding animals, beating the rugs, washing linen, and grooming horses needs doing. I am sure he will find no lack of volunteers." With that, he gave a small nod to Idgen Marte and held up the letter from Baron of Bend, then walked toward the front door, scabbarded sword and belt in his other hand.

He emerged into a day that was promising to be blinding in its brightness and oppressively humid. He tore open the letter, piercing the blue wax stamp without a thought for its elegant design, and read it in the sunlight as he headed for the stables. Idgen Marte followed a few steps behind.

"Damned if we don't need a great storm to blow away this heat," the warrior grumbled, as Allystaire paused to read:

Sur Alastare,

Yew arr hearwith commandid to present yourself before the Baron Windspar I o Bend at yor earlyist conveenyance. Yew arr too ansur charges of murdur, assalt from ambush, theft, and enturing the citee of Bend undur fals pretens. Yew may be kalld upon to ansur at an Assize aftur the Baron's enquest. Make yur arrangement with my messengur.

Baron Tallenhaft Windspar I of Bend

Halfway through the letter, Allystaire's laughter turned to a fury as cold and bright as the sun off thick ice. His pace had quickened, and his hands had started to pull the sword from its sheath, when Idgen Marte dashed around him and pushed her hands onto his chest.

"*Stop*. If you go into that stable and kill his messenger, you'll only prove your guilt."

"He has no right to judge me," Allystaire snarled, slamming the foot of steel back into the scabbard.

"That may well be true, but he has the *means*, and that's what matters. Ya can't cut your way out of this. Frightening as it sounds, your best weapon is your brain. Y'have to outsmart the man." She paused, tried a grin. "Or let me outsmart him for you."

To remove the temptation, Allystaire swung the belted sword over his shoulder and cinched the buckles at his chest, wincing only slightly as he moved his bandaged left arm. "Where would you start?"

"Give him exactly what he wants. Play the lordling, the knight. What you are is as plain as day—so let him see it all bright and polished like a tourney jouster's armor. Call him *baron* and treat him like a peer."

"And if he calls an assize, what then?"

"Pay him off, if you must. I think if he wants to see you convicted, he will. But I think if he wanted to kill you, his watchmen would've been swarming this inn yesterday."

Allystaire thought over her advice, wetting his tongue with his lips. His stomach roiled sourly, but he nodded. "Aye. Very well. I will return his message." He stalked into the stables, throwing open the loosely swinging doors as he went. In the corner, a man in blue and white livery lounged on a barrel. Allystaire pointedly ignored him in favor of checking on his animals.

The huge grey was the first to notice him, and it whickered and lightly stamped in the stall. Allystaire reached out to stroke along its neck, and soon the riding horse and the mule were clamoring for his attention. He could hear Idgen Marte barely avoiding snickering behind him, then the *thump* of the messenger sliding off his barrel and his footsteps stumping up the hard-packed dirt floor of the stable.

"Lordly animal, there. Mayhap the gift of it might calm my lord baron's anger at you, sir," the man intoned nasally.

Idgen Marte must've seen or sensed the way Allystaire's back and shoulders tightened as he whirled on the messenger, the way his hands quivered with the impulse of violence, for she instantly glided between them, her face suddenly a smooth gambler's facade.

"You are a fine judge of horseflesh, and do your lord baron credit, but the value of a fine-blooded, war-trained stallion such as that is far beyond any damages incurred to his interests."

The messenger sniffed, a cavernous nose twitching as he did, and hitched his hands onto his swordbelt. "And you are?"

"Her name is Idgen Marte, and she is my man-at-arms and servant," Allystaire said, drawing himself to his full height, within a hair of six feet, and spreading his shoulders and chest to their full and imposing breadth. "She can be assumed to speak for me in all matters unless I say otherwise, and she is correct: my animals are part of no discussion with your lord baron." Once again, his authoritative tone rang in a note of easy command that simply assumed whoever heard it would leap to obey.

When the liveried man grinned lecherously at *man-at-arms*, Allystaire made ready to interpose himself between him and Idgen Marte, but her face remained impassive, hands calmly at her sides. "As you say, m'lord. What news shall I take back to the Baron of Bend? Will you require ink and quill?"

The messenger unslung a leather satchel that rode under his arm.

Idgen Marte turned toward Allystaire and gave a slight nod, encouraging him to play along. He, in turn, nodded graciously, though imperiously, toward the messenger, who rummaged in the bag and brought out a fresh sheet of parchment, a quill, bottles of ink and sand, and a smooth wooden plank.

Allystaire accepted the items, found an empty crate, and perched upon it, placing the board upon his knee. The ink was thin and runny, but serviceable, and the quill well cut. In moments he had scrawled out a response:

Lord Baron Tallenhaft Windspar I of Bend,

I received your message this morning and commend your messenger for his speed, bearing, courtesy, and demeanor. I will be happy to present myself at your Lordship's residence later this morning after I have had time to attend to matters of private business; I will be accompanied by one servant. I do hope that your Lordship does not believe I have done him any injury. If you do, there is, of course, a simple expedient by which men of our standing may discharge such grievances. I do assume that such arrangements will be unnecessary but I stand ready to receive your Lordship if necessary. As to the matter of standing before an assize, if your Lordship is able to provide a suitably neutral magistrate that both sides would approve, I would be willing to argue a case and accept the ruling. I must, however, insist upon a neutral presiding judge.

At your service,

Sir Allystaire.

He sanded the ink, blew upon it, waved the page in the air, and, satisfied it was dry, folded it with a careful delicacy that seemed odd in his thick, calloused fingers. He handed it to the messenger. The liveried man seemed to be waiting for something else, but Allystaire merely raised an eyebrow. The man tipped up his huge nose, fetched a small shaggy horse not unlike Allystaire's gelding, swung into its saddle, and trotted out the open stable doors.

"I would have thought that his lecherous insinuation would have angered you," Allystaire ventured, once the sound of hoofbeats on uneven cobbles faded.

Idgen Marte snorted. "If I wasted my time killing every fool who suggested I was bedding the man I worked for, my blade would never be dry."

Allystaire chuckled a bit, and then shared the contents of the letter he'd written.

"You just couldn't resist implying that you'd be happy to face him in a duel, eh?"

"If your judgment is accurate, the mention of a duel will delight this so-called baron, though he is unlikely to accept such a challenge. The essential thing is that he believes me to be taking his nobility seriously."

"What if he accepts?"

"I kill him. Problem solved. Wine all round."

"What if he turns out to be a great river pirate who carved his way to the top of this mess?

"He kills me. Problem solved. Wine all round."

Idgen Marte laughed and gestured toward the stall that held Allystaire's mounts and mule, saying, "Go and tend to your horses." She started for the door, then turned back around. "By the way…before she sent me to find you, Mol said she'd figured out the big grey's name."

Allystaire smiled and turned toward her, his hand gently on the muzzle of the very animal. "Oh?"

She nodded, solemnly enunciating the word as she repeated it—"Ardent." The swordswoman shrugged her rangy shoulders and stalked into the bright morning light.

Allystaire resumed petting the horse, trying out the name. "Ardent." The grey continued looking at him, flicking an ear. "Where did a lass like Mol ever hear a word like that?" He cast his eye around the stables till he spied a small basket of hard green apples; he went over, seized a handful, and tried the name again. "Ardent."

The grey charger turned to stare at him intently. Allystaire shook his head to clear it, murmuring, "It is only because I am holding apples."

CHAPTER 11

The Baron, the Priest, and the Soldier

Barely more than a turn of the glass later, Allystaire and Idgen Marte were mounted and letting their horses pick their way through the heat-dazed crowd on the winding and muddy streets of Bend. Allystaire was streaming sweat; his shirt was soaked through, the wounds on his left arm itched fiercely, and the heavy weight of his sword was irritating.

In short, he felt in a perfect mood to confront Baron Windspar of Bend.

He rode his grey warhorse, and Idgen Marte sat atop a lean, dark bay courser that responded to every twitch of her hand or press of her knee and seemed to gather itself to break into a run whenever space opened in front of it; she occasionally had to tug the reins to keep it in check. The destrier, meanwhile, was happy to be free of his stall and apparently wanted to find, or start, a fight; his muscles bunched under Allystaire, he tugged on the reins, and he snapped at the courser any time it ventured close.

Unlike Allystaire, Idgen Marte seemed calm, even happy, as they rode in the brutal, damp heat. While he mopped his face and grunted, she smiled, glowed.

"Where the Cold's his bloody house? Rather, where is the *Baronial Residence*," Allystaire called out.

"Oh you won't miss it. Trust me. It's in *Old Town*, as those with the links call it."

"And what do those without the links call it?"

"Brick Town."

"Imaginative lot," he snorted. "I find it hard to credit that this place has grown so large in so short a time."

"Been growing a score of years now. You people've been so busy with your wars for…how long, now?"

Grimacing, Allystaire said, "Forty-one years. Though, to be precise, it is one war, not wars."

"Could've fooled me. What is it you call it? The Succession Strife? But there's no king to fight for or against anymore," Idgen Marte pointed out. "I'm just a southerner ignorant of your ways, of course," she added, smirking, "but seems to me now what you've got is a lot of little border wars caused by old men trying to write their names bigger on a map."

Allystaire said gruffly, "There is more to it than that."

She waved a hand dismissively. "There always is, and it rarely matters to the folk who flee from it. Best I can tell, Bend has been giving them a place to flee to for most o'that time, though only in great numbers for the past score of years."

Allystaire grunted. He felt the steps of the horse beneath him change as dirt and gravel suddenly gave way to more regular cobbles. The streets widened, as well, and the construction of the buildings improved; instead of motley shacks and shanties built almost atop one another, stone and brick of a more or less regular size and dark brown color began to appear.

Beyond them, a much larger building loomed straight ahead, surfacing in the swimming haze of the morning heat. A vast house—too large for the space it occupied—squatted, froglike, at the end of a street. Instead of brick, it was fashioned from a hotchpotch of grey, white, and brown stone and looked like an idiot's approximation of a fearsome castle, only far too small and vulnerable. Allystaire stopped his destrier and leaned forward to stare at it, blinking slowly.

"Is that a *moat*?"

"Six feet deep and three wide. A fearsome barrier," Idgen Marte laughed. "Don't forget the barbican and the portcullis."

The effect of this martial edifice was singularly absurd: the moat surrounding it was no impediment; the barbican was a squat tower of less than two full stories high, and the portcullis appeared to be a flimsy thing, with a sigil—clumsy river upon a field of white—carved from wood and hung upon it.

One part of the comical concoction appeared to be legitimately fortified—an old watchtower with a crenellated top, situated for a good view of the Ash River. It stood at the north corner, and was both the most dilapidated and the most secure part of it all.

Allystaire shook his head as he took in the full measure of the baronial folly before him. "This is what happened to the fort that once squatted here. An ignoble end."

"Probably an ignoble building," Idgen Marte offered.

"Men died to hold this place once," Allystaire reflected. "Their lives depended on the walls and on the tower this farce has been built around."

"And look at the good it's done them. No one remembers their names and nobody cares about the fort except the pirates and poor folk who've fled the wars altogether. Wonder why the baron's let it go so far."

"Nobody north of the river here worth fearing, I suppose. Lionel put down the Islandmen who had conquered Vyndamere, and pretty hard at that, some years ago. Nothing up there but fish, fur, and misery."

"Lionel?" Idgen Marte tilted her head to one side as Allystaire mused aloud. "The Baron Delondeur."

"I know his name. Just don't often hear him referred to that way. Familiar n'all," she said, peering at him. She grinned then, lightly, then looked back to the "so-called castle" and sighed. "Doesn't it strike fear into your warrior's heart?"

Allystaire slumped over in his saddle laughing for a moment, the absurdity of the castle capping, as it were, the absurdity of the day's mission. Finally, he drew a deep breath and said, "I have knocked over more impressive keeps with morning wind after a breakfast of eggs and beans."

It was Idgen Marte's turn to lean over the pommel of her saddle laughing, but for only a moment. They exchanged a glance, stifled their grins, and rode on with impassive faces and erect backs toward the gate.

They drew close enough to see a pair of gate-guards. Allystaire rode ahead, Idgen Marte falling behind and to his right. "Ware the gate," he called, while they were still a few yards distant.

The guards stepped forward, shouldering spears. Unlike the other watchmen Allystaire had seen in Bend, these both wore hauberks that appeared in fighting trim; they gleamed with oil and scouring, and bore neither brightwork nor rust. "Announce yourselves if you wish entrance," one called, his voice bored.

"Baron Windspar is expecting us," Allystaire answered, as they drew to a halt just out of spear's thrust.

"Tell us your names and titles and we will see if he is inclined to receive you," the guardsman said, his tone still distant and unconcerned. His bearded face streamed with sweat under his coif.

Allystaire drew a deep breath. *This idiot baron is like to be impressed by titles. What have you got left to lose?* "Lord Allystaire Coldbourne, of Coldbourne Moor, Lord of Coldbourne Hall, lately Castellan of Wind's Jaw Keep, seat of Baron Oyrwyn, and with me is my man-at-arms and servant, Idgen Marte."

He heard Idgen Marte's jaw snap tightly shut, and could all but feel her eyes boring triumphantly into the back of his head.

The bearded guardsman stared hard at him a moment, then nodded respectfully, bending his head and shoulders carefully under their hot weight of mail. "Sir Allystaire. I bid you welcome to Windspar Castle." Though he acquitted his duty with what Allystaire found to be impeccable courtesy, the guardsman couldn't keep the sigh out of his voice, or stop his eyes from rolling a bit as he spoke. "I will see to your animals." He nodded to the other guard, who tromped across the drawbridge in three quick steps and pounded on the portcullis.

It rattled like an ill-fitted door and soon rose on thickly knotted rope. Allystaire swallowed another snort as he carefully climbed down from his destrier. He heard Idgen Marte's soft boots land lightly on the cobbles behind him. They walked forward, led their horses across the tiny drawbridge one at a time, and emerged from the gate into a courtyard that was, like the castle surrounding it, a mocking miniature of a real courtyard. The guard followed them and held out a hand for their reins.

"Your mounts will be properly seen to while here, m'lord," the bearded guard said, as he wrapped the reins around his hand and started to lead the animals to what Allystaire could only assume was the stables, a structure built against the inner wall and smaller than the stables attached to The Sign of the Stone Wall.

"He seems like a veteran. What is he doing here?" Allystaire wondered aloud quietly.

"Probably the best wages in town," Idgen Marte guessed with a shrug. She paused a moment, then added with the slightest smirk, "Castellan of Wind's Jaw, eh?" Her timing didn't leave him a moment to respond, for by then the guardsman was on his way back, having handed the horses over to a groom.

"Follow me, m'lord."

He led them to the building Allystaire assumed to be the castle keep, though it was naught but a two-storey wooden house looming at the far end of the courtyard. The only defense it boasted were two more guards and a row of useless iron spikes upon the roof. He and Idgen Marte both looked ahead resolutely, fearing that to exchange a glance would prompt a collapse into laughter, but they made it across the few dozen yards with little difficulty, and soon they were handed off to another guard and ushered into a parlor. A liveried servant, in blue and white with the same crude badge upon his chest as the guards, scurried off to fetch the Baron of Bend.

Allystaire and Idgen Marte were left to cool their heels in the room that was empty, save for a lone guard. A few trophies hung on the wall—a mounted shark, naval banners, and the like. Allystaire focused on the guard that watched them; like the first, he had an air of competence, moved easily in his heavy hauberk and coif, and carried his spear and wore his sword with casual ease.

After a few moments had passed, the servant returned and with an unctuous gesture, indicated that they follow him. Their boots clattered up a short staircase to a large hall with a sizable fireplace at one end, dominated by a long, rough, wood table. The latter was set with a bounty of crystal and silver—but Allystaire quickly realized that *set* was the wrong word; the stuff was heaped and piled without organization. Captain's decanters with flat, wide bottoms sat next to delicate long-stemmed glasses; plates rose in poorly stacked towers a foot or more above the table surface; and silver spoons and knives lay in tarnished heaps.

"Pathetic, eh? What many of the local captains pay me in tribute. Technically the value is acceptable but there aren't enough folk of quality about to use it all." The voice, over-smooth and careful, came from behind them, and

Allystaire and Idgen Marte turned to find themselves faced with Baron Tallenhaft Windspar I of Bend, all five feet and twenty-odd stone of him. Flanked by a pair of his poorly liveried guardsmen, he waddled towards them from one of the room's many doorways.

He wore, even in the summer heat, a crushed velvet doublet of deep blue with yellowing lace at the cuffs; it was meant to be loose on a taller man, and instead, it strained to hold in his stomach. His pale yellow hose looked ready to burst at the seams and spill milk that had been left in the sun for a week, and his fringe of browning hair ringed a pate from which sweat streamed in heavy rivulets. Still, there was a suggestion of forgotten strength about his neck and shoulders, and his wrists had a warrior's thickness.

"Lord Baron," Allystaire intoned, deeply and slowly, inclining his shoulders—but not his neck or eyes—in a bow that was barely acceptable. Idgen Marte did much the same, but slightly deeper, as befitting a servant. "I have come to discuss this complaint as per my letter. And the possibility of an assize."

"Straight to business with you then, Sir Allystaire? Would you like a bit of refreshment? Stay for lunch perhaps?" The baron's tone leaned toward obsequious and a bit whinging.

"Perhaps there could be pleasantries later. For the moment, business lies between us." Allystaire paused, drawing himself a little straighter as he spoke. He waited to let the implied threat sink in; when there was no visible reaction from the baron, he added, "I would see it resolved." Another pause. "Peacefully."

The baron sighed and walked into the room, sinking heavily into a cushioned chair at the heaped-up table. "If you must, Sir Allystaire. But I insist on hearing about Wind's Jaw Keep and Oyrwyn. How exciting!"

A rapacious manchild brooding and fuming in an ugly stone tomb is about the size of it, your corpulence, he thought, but said, "Perhaps, my lord. For now, if there is to be an assize, there are many things that I, as a landed knight and lord, have a right to know." *Had a right.*

"A landed knight and lord, you say? Yet you announced yourself to my guard as *lately* Castellan of Wind's Jaw Keep." The baron's fat, sweaty face peered closely at Allystaire, his deepset eyes suddenly shrewd. "Could it be that, like so many other residents of my fair city-state, you've found the caress of Fortune to be less than pleasant? I do wonder if you're a landed knight at all, Sir Allystaire.

Wind's Jaw and Barony Oyrwyn are far from here indeed. A week's journey on fresh mounts just to the foothills. Could be a long time till we got word of your *rights*, if I chose to send word to my fellow baron."

Allystaire barely suppressed a snort at the thought. "Neither of us have that much time, my lord, though I will tell you the truth; I no longer bear office or position. Whether I still have land, I do not know, for no decree stripping me of it has reached my ears." Behind him, Idgen Marte fidgeted, very slightly, rocking on one ankle.

"Coldbourne Moor, I believe you told my guard, and Coldbourne Hall. An ancestral manse?"

"A peat bog guarded over by an overbuilt hunting lodge, my lord."

"A what?"

"A peat bog."

"What in the name of the Sea Dragon is that?"

"A marsh. A fetid, waterlogged mix of soil and dead plants."

The baron tilted his head quizzically; the gesture reminded Allystaire of nothing so much as a small, fat, stupid dog. "And people live in such a place?"

Allystaire allowed himself a small smile. "Not if they can help it, my lord."

Snorting, the baron shook his head and slowly levered himself to his feet, exhaling heavily. "Peasants ought to be happier with their lot in life. No hard decisions to make, no expenses, no pirates to fight…"

With a surge of anger, Allystaire took half a step forward, his arms tensing for violence, but his left arm twinged in pain, and Idgen Marte cleared her throat pointedly. He stopped, set his hands firmly on his belt, and said, "My lord, may we discuss an assize?"

"Yes, we bloody well may." Spittle gathered at the corner of the baron's mouth as his voice leapt suddenly into a full-throated roar. "You owe me *weight* or you owe me *chattels*."

Forcing a deliberate calm into his voice and concealing a cold so deep it seared his veins, Allystaire said evenly, "Slavery is outlawed in every barony, my lord. It has been for some time." *As if the peasantry isn't practically enslaved already*?

"I don't give a bowl of beggar's piss what's outlawed where! I take duties on all goods in and out of my barony and I mean to have it for that chattel!" The baron calmed his own voice and continued. "Perhaps you can pay a simple blood price, eh? My messenger told me you had a fine destrier, a lordly animal; I do fancy a new mount." His deep-set dark eyes glittered with avarice as his hands rubbed together like a child's.

"As I informed your servant, none of my animals are for sale."

"I decide what is and is not for sale here! You are in *my* keep!"

Allystaire's hand, unbidden and unchecked, suddenly crashed down on the tabletop, sending plates rattling. One chunky glass fell off the edge and *thunked* to the ground, but did not break. "Cease to give me orders, my lord! I am *not* your vassal. I could have slipped through your gates but I did not, for I intend to make restitution if it is decided I owe it. Decided by a neutral magistrate. That is what your letter suggested and what I came here to negotiate in good faith."

"Oh you'll *make restitution*! You'll bloody well pay!" The baron had worked himself into a lather and had to tumble back into the chair he'd recently vacated, which groaned precariously beneath him. To one of the guards, he wheezed, "Fetch the priest."

The guard nodded, murmured, "Yes m'lord," and stomped off, jingling.

Allystaire turned to Idgen Marte and mouthed *priest?* She shrugged. The guard returned quite swiftly, followed by a man of impressive height, who was broad-shouldered, though skinny. He had a thick and well-salted beard and a head of grey hair to match, but above an aquiline nose sat sparkling sea-green eyes. He wore a fine, dark blue robe trimmed with seal-skin, and around his neck sat a heavy silver chain; from it hung a heavy amulet also wrought in silver, of a horned and serpentine face atop swelling waves encrusted with sapphires. He fairly crackled with unspent energy.

"My Lord Baron of Bend," the man intoned in a deep, resonant voice, inclining his head and shoulders. "Sir Allystaire. Goodmen and woman," he added, looking to each in turn and inclining his head, though each less deeply than the last, till the acknowledgement of Idgen Marte was barely more than a nod. "I am Symod, Choiron of the Church of Lord Braech the Sea Dragon, Braech Wave-Father and Storm-Maker, Braech the Master of Accords and Mover of the World."

His voice an instrument of precise command, Symod's words rolled out and filled the room, as one hand rose to stroke his heavy silver amulet. When the words had sunk into the walls and the floor, he went on. "I understand there is a dispute over goods of value and that one party feels deprived; likewise that said goods were stolen by means of ambush and murder."

"That is but one side of the story, Choiron," Allystaire said; he forced himself to meet the tall priest's gaze. Usually meeting a man eye for eye was no difficulty, even one who, like Symod, stood half a head taller than he, but something about this priest seemed to beat the eye away. The baron, his guards, and Idgen Marte turned away.

Nevertheless, Allystaire looked on steadily.

"Such is always the case, Sir Allystaire," Symod rumbled. "And should you and our gracious host both consent to my terms I will hear both sides at the assize."

"Then what are your terms, priest? I'd like this done and my duties paid by dinner," chuffed the baron.

Allystaire remained silent, his face set as close to a dicer's blank as his rage would allow, and watched the priest. Some part of him felt as though he could not help but watch the priest, that his eye was drawn to the man and the aura of power that coruscated, just the other side of visible, around him.

The corners of Symod's mouth lifted at the baron in the tiniest ghost of a smile. "These things take time, my lord." His voice gave an impression of vast depths and frightful volume without resorting to either. "I should say tomorrow at the earliest."

"Tomorrow will suit me well," Allystaire offered, casually. *No reason not to get on his good side.*

"For me as well," the baron sniffed. "So long as you bloody well remember who's the *Baron* in this city!"

The blue-robed priest's smile widened very faintly but did not reach his eyes. Allystaire knew the expression well; he wore it often himself.

"I certainly could not forget, my lord," the priest practically purred. "But you have not yet heard my terms."

"The day is hot and the glass pours. Pray, do not keep us in suspense any longer," Allystaire snapped, a little more loudly than he had intended. The baron snickered in surprise; the priest of Braech turned the full weight of his gaze down upon Allystaire.

"The Father of Waves makes haste only when it suits him," Symod said; throughout the entire conversation his hand had not stopped stroking his amulet. "And when he does, ships are ruined, and men lost. Do not attempt to get in his way."

Loves to hear the sound of his own voice, this one, Allystaire thought.

"Out with it! 'Tis nearly luncheon and all this talk has worked up a powerful hunger in me!" the baron shouted. "And the cook just bought a good pork shoulder," the baron added, licking his lips childishly and staring for a moment into the middle distance.

Symod's words snapped his attention back. "I will require the both of you to be Godsworn for the following terms: that you will answer my questions honestly; that you will abide by the judgment the Sea Dragon, in his ageless Wisdom, leads me to; that neither of you will seek vengeance upon the other for an unfavorable outcome."

"I will be sworn if it will bring an end to this," Allystaire quickly answered.

"The sooner I am paid the better. On with it!"

"You will Swear tomorrow before the assize. As will any who give testimony. We will begin at the onset of the High Tide after midday, when the Sea Dragon's strength is waxing fullest. Be here promptly." The last three words sent a tingling jolt through the room.

"I shall." Allystaire bit off his words without swallowing his contempt and stormed out of the room, Idgen Marte close behind. He brushed briefly against the choiron and felt an intense surge of power. He would have described it like a powerful spark hitting his skin, but there was no pain and no tingle, just a heavy looming presence pressing upon his mind, weighing down on him. It vanished quickly, but the shadow remained, and wrote its presence upon his face.

Still in the room, Baron Windspar sputtered something about propriety, gasping for air as he pushed himself to his feet; neither Allystaire nor Idgen Marte bothered to look back. They quickly departed the ridiculous townhouse "keep" and were several steps across the courtyard before either spoke.

"Was that your idea of mannered?" Idgen Marte remarked, as dirt from the sun-beaten ground blossomed with each footstep.

"I showed him every possible courtesy. I used his title and I respected his authority while demonstrating that it did not reach to me."

"I suppose so." Suddenly Idgen Marte stopped, looking intently at him, her eyes narrowed in concentration. She pointed uncertainly to his right boot, the heel of which had just stomped into the dirt as he turned to face her. "Shouldn't your foot hurt?"

"What?" Allystaire looked down to it, then back to her, confused, distracted.

"You took a crossbow bolt across that foot less than two days ago, and yet you walk on it as if it pains you not at all."

Allystaire lifted his foot, shook it speculatively, and shrugged. "I heal fast," he offered uncertainly.

Idgen Marte took an unconscious half step away. "You haven't the lepra, have you? I once saw a man in a troupe of freaks with that; they said he felt no pain and would cut and burn himself for money…"

Allystaire's eyes narrowed, his lips pressed into a flat line. "Be sensible. Had I any disease, surely you would have seen it when tending my wounds." He tried a laugh, found it weak, but continued. "Believe me, I feel pain." He rolled his left shoulder and grimaced convincingly, secretly surprised at how little it hurt.

Idgen Marte seemed mollified, and she sighed, nodding and avoiding his eyes. They collected their animals in silence, mounted, and were out the gate and over the bridge in a few moments. As they passed the guards, Allystaire stopped and wheeled his destrier, pointing at the guard who had escorted them in before.

"You there. Answer me a question, if you would."

"I am at your service, m'lord," the guard replied with a curt nod.

Allystaire folded his hands on the pommel of his saddle and leaned forward. "You seem to know your business; your armor is clean, your weapons well kept and I daresay sharp. You have done a bit or two of real work, been blooded, or I am no judge of armed men. Why in the name of Fortune are you serving *here*?"

The man thought a moment, fighting, for duty's sake, a smile that started to form on his lips. "I ask myself that same question every day, m'lord."

"And your answer to yourself?"

"Haven't got one better than that I need the silver, m'lord," the man admitted, with a frown and a rattling shrug.

"For what?"

He shrugged heavily. "Beer. Food. The odd woman, I s'pose."

"What is your name, guardsman?"

"Renard, m'lord."

"Renard, you can do better. I daresay you have done in the past." He sighed faintly and nodded, as if confirming something to himself. Then he turned his horse and rode for the Sign of the Stone Wall.

* * *

Later that afternoon, Allystaire sat brooding at a table set near the hearth, turning over in his mind the events of the morning. In the stifling, drenching heat of the day, no fire was laid, and no breeze came up through the opened windows of the inn.

Godsworn, eh? Lovely dead-end you've fought your way into now. "Even my own thoughts mock me," Allystaire said. A few of the folk bustling around the inn, Thornhurst folk who were sweeping, hauling, carrying, and dusting, turned to look at him when he spoke, but all quickly returned to their tasks. Food, mostly cheese and bread, as well as a small pitcher of wine, sat half finished in front of him.

"Can I fetch you anythin', m'lord?" A timid voice floated in from a few feet away. Allystaire looked up and quickly caught sight of a carefully displayed bosom, bent toward him, and a round-cheeked face surrounded by honeyed hair. He quickly looked away, shaking his head.

"No, Leah. I have my mid-day meal, thank you." The girl glided away, but Allystaire swore he could feel her eyes upon him. He thought a moment, then waved a hand to call her over; he was careful to look her in the eye. "Upon second thought…I would like to speak to one of Mol's kin. A parent? Uncle?"

She looked blank for a moment, and Allystaire said, "Mol. The girl I found in the Thornhurst inn, she has kin here, somewhere, aye? Adults? Go find one." Finally, Leah nodded and trotted off.

Act of pure will not to watch that lass walk away. Allystaire scowled at himself and tried to briefly drown the thought by pouring the last half of a pitcher of wine down his throat.

Soon, a man close to Allystaire's age, shorter and not quite as broad, was approaching his table cautiously. He had curly hair salted with grey and several days' stubble on his cheeks; the knuckles on his large hands were scuffed and scarred, his clothing simple and oft-mended. He stood near the edge of the table and, for lack of anything better to do with them, tucked his strong hands behind his back.

"Ya sent fer me, m'lord?"

Allystaire indicated the seat across the table and stood to offer his hand to the other man. Instinctively the man took it, and Allystaire felt a strength in the grip that wasn't unlike his own. They both sat, the man seeming more at ease.

"Are you Mol's father, or—?"

"Uncle," the man answered quickly.

"Uncle Tim? I heard about you," Allystaire said with a slight, hooked smile. "Mol told me that you thought speaking to oneself was a sign of madness."

The man grunted a laugh. "Aye, well, our Mol's a bit of a tale-teller, I'd say."

"She is a strong little lass." Tim looked back at him, confused. "Willed, I mean." Still blank. "Stubborn."

The man shrugged, a gesture that spoke of pain in its slow caution. "If you say so, m'lord. I haven't had the raisin' of her. Till now, I s'pose."

"What do you mean?"

Tim sighed, looked down at the tabletop. "Her da died when they took us. She hasn't heard it yet, but I saw them cut his legs out from under him before they started hurlin' torches."

"What of her mother?"

Tim shook his head. "Hilde is dead three years'n more. Glad of it now, in a way. She didn't live t'see this happen.".

Allystaire sighed, lowering his head and staring, for a moment, at his curled hands on his lap. "Was it you that hid her in the cold well, then?"

Tim looked up quickly. "I didn't see her. I was wrestlin' wi' one o' them reavers when it all broke out. Lass might've been smart enou' to figure it out herself. Was all confusion and blood, and then suddenly fire. Most o' us never really knew what was happenin'."

"How many souls in your village?" Allystaire leaned back in his chair, hardening himself for the answer.

"More'n a hundred, but closer t'that than t'two hundred."

"How many back from the warehouse?"

"Fifty, lessen' two. Plus Mol. Makes forty-nine of us left," Tim said with finality.

"Was everyone else killed?"

Tim shook his head, his grey hair swiping against his head as he moved. "Some o' the younger folk ran oft, their kinfolks yellin' at 'em to do so. They sent one o'their men t'track but I don't think he e'er came back." He smiled a bit, showing missing and crooked teeth. "Could be one o 'our lads got 'em."

More likely he just decided to cut his losses, or rounded up a couple of children to sell for himself, Allystaire thought, but he smiled and nodded, rapping the tabletop with a knuckle, and said, "Good on them. Mayhap a few will be found when you return. Now, if I may ask, what of Mol?"

Tim shook his head and spread his broad hands, his wrists popping as they turned. "I can't say. She sleeps, eats, cries some, like she's a babe again. M'wife s'takin' care o'her."

Allystaire nodded. "When the girl comes round, I would like very much to speak to her, if I could."

"Anythin', m'lord." The man cleared his throat and said, "Might I ask you a question, m'lord?"

Allystaire nodded encouragingly and leaned forward. "Of course, goodman."

"Everyone's wonderin' it…not just when we'll head back to Thornhurst, but…wha' then? We rebuild, what's it matter if reavers come again? Where will we get the money or the tools? And are…ya've already bought us our lives, but if…how long d'ya plan to stay?"

"I have not given it any thought," Allystaire replied carefully, knowing it to be a lie as soon as he spoke. *Stay? Stay and wait for Casamir and half a dozen men-at-arms to find me there and burn what still remains?* He sighed. "Tim… Timothy?"

The man shook his head. "Timmar."

"Timmar, then. I do not mean to mislead you; I do not plan to stay on in Thornhurst."

Tim seemed to deflate a bit, his carefully buttressed hope melting away with a slow nod.

"I would only be in the way if I did," Allystaire said gently. "I am no carpenter or laborer or farmer; I would be a mouth to feed, with horses that ate three times the cost of what I did. I would be of no help. He leaned forward conspiratorially, adding, "In truth, I might only attract trouble." Suddenly uncomfortable, Allystaire stood and offered his hand; Timmar shot to his feet and took it, his grip lacking the earlier vitality. He walked away, shoulders slumped, defeated.

As he was leaving, Idgen Marte entered the taproom with a slow and measured pace. She arrived at Allystaire's table and sat down, looking at the wall behind him as if it were miles distant.

"What? No quip? Nothing about kicking these folk while they are down?"

She looked at him and frowned. "I heard what you told him and you weren't wrong. Better not to deceive them into thinking you're their new lord protector now."

"What about you? Plan to stay behind in Thornhurst while it rebuilds?"

She snorted, her face split by a sneer. "I'd sooner be a monk. At least in a cloister I might drink myself into the grave in peace and quiet." She turned away from him again, took in a deep breath, and said, "What happened this afternoon? That priest, that choiron. There was something—"

"Power. He almost glowed with it."

She shook her head hard enough to send her braid halfway over one shoulder. "Glow is the wrong word. He held it like you hold a hammer, ready to bludgeon aside everyone in his way. His voice weighed on my mind." She grimaced uncomfortably and added, "That's why I asked if you'd the lepra. Foolish, entirely, I know. I know. But I was…my mind wasn't right."

Allystaire nodded, his face darkening as she spoke. "When I brushed against him on the way out I felt something menacing and huge ready to perch upon me like a carrion bird that wanted a choice bit and was not prepared to wait till I died. I did not like it."

"Does he speak for his god?" Idgen Marte's face blanched a bit at the thought.

"I could not say. Most of the priests I have known were whoremongers, drunkards, or spendthrifts, except for the few who were all three. I knew priests of Braech and Fortune both as I grew up. They alluded to being able to call upon the powers of their gods, yet I cannot say I saw them do it."

"I have heard tell of it; priests of the Sea Dragon who call the waves or who move the reefs down in Keersvast. And I know of Braech's holy warriors, said to be the most fearsome foes alive. Never seen them, though," Idgen Marte admitted. Then she raised a finger to him. "And you agreed to be Godsworn by him, you fool."

"The baron did the same. Neither of us have the advantage. And I doubt if the choiron could be bought." Allystaire fiddled with the edge of his plate. "And if he can, I doubt the Baron of Bend can afford him."

Idgen Marte laughed a bit, some of the usual warmth returning to her voice, her features reviving. "True enough. What a vile little frog."

Allystaire nodded his agreement. "How did such a frog hop to the top of this mountain of shit?"

"We may never know. I asked about somewhat, and most think he was a fearsome river pirate in his day. Life on land doesn't seem to have kept him any too sharp."

"He was," put in a new and unexpected voice. "And he was no fool then; but now he's rich and fat and stupid, like most whom men call lords. If I may say, m'lord."

Allystaire and Idgen Marte had been too absorbed in their talk to notice the man who'd entered and sidled up to them. He wore no armor , but the great brown beard and the blade-backed bearing were quickly recognizable.

"You are the baron's man. What are you doing here?" Allystaire tensed himself in the chair, ready to spring, pressing his hands to the arms. Idgen Marte had leaned forward, getting her toes under her, hand creeping toward her blade.

"I was the baron's man. But your question set me thinking, m'lord." He cleared his throat and said, "I've sold my spear for five years, but I've never been a reaver or a slaver. And I'd never taken their links, till now." He swallowed, forcing his eyes to meet Allystaire's. "Didn't sit well, once I studied on it. I heard what you did. We all heard. And we knew the baron was thinkin' o' simply sendin' men after ya till Fortune found him a lucky moment. That didn't sit well either. I think those slavers got what was comin' to them, and I started wondering what man I'd rather take orders from. The man who eats from reaver tribute, or the one who kills ten slavers." He swallowed again, shrugged. "I don't know that you'll want me, m'lord, but if you'll have me, I'm your man."

Allystaire blinked, confused; Idgen Marte merely smiled triumphantly. Finally, Allystaire found a response.

"I cannot afford to pay you, Renard."

"Y'don't have to pay me, at least not yet. I want a chance t'feel…t'feel clean, again. Like a man ought. Give me that, it'll be all the pay I need till we decide otherwise." A flush rose in Renard's bearded cheeks, like a boy caught out in mischief.

"Sit," Allystaire said, pushing out a spare stool with one foot. "You said that you sold your spear for five years, but you have been a soldiering man for more than twice that. What did you do before you sold it?"

Renard sat stiffly and managed to raise his brown eyes to meet Allystaire's face. "I was a soldier for Baron Delondeur."

"Saw battle? Earned rank?"

"Bannerman First, third company, Chimera's Spears," Renard answered, a hint of pride creeping into his voice.

"Lord Inglaren's men?"

"Aye."

There was a brief silence; Idgen Marte's eyes flitted between the two of them, watching carefully. Finally, Allystaire cleared his throat.

"You heard, earlier, my name? Who I am?"

"Aye," Renard said.

"So we have been on opposite sides of the field, then, as it were."

Renard shrugged. "Not my fight anymore, m'lord."

"Not a lord anymore. Just Allystaire now, if I can make anyone understand it." Another pause. "I do have one more question. Bannerman Firsts have to serve a term of ten years after their appointment—"

"'Twere but five when I took the gold link," Renard said fiercely. "Proclamation came down to change it in my last year. Didn't think it right, changing the terms o'what I agreed to without askin' me."

"Aye," Allystaire said, nodding. "Still, lots of places to get lost in or out of Bend."

"I tried t'go home. Had a farm out in the western lee of the mountains, my kin. Wasn't there when I went back."

Allystaire sighed and lowered his eyes. "This was how many years ago?"

"I know what you're askin' m'lord, and yes. It were Oyrwyn men that done it, back in that summer when you got 'em around the mountains in the south and tried t'push north to Londray."

"Renard, I—"

"No, m'lord, I'm not here looking for revenge. Hadn't even thought on it. I know the men who did it hung for it. That's enough for me."

"I am still sorry."

"Happens to folk like us all the time, m'lord," Renard said with a small shrug. "Our time in the world s'like a winter's day. Short and dark."

Allystaire struggled for words again, but Idgen Marte said, "Welcome to the company, Renard."

The soldier nodded and stood. "I have my gear and mount outside. I can pay my own way here."

Allystaire spared a brief glare toward Idgen Marte, but quickly turned to Renard and recovered enough to stand and shake the other man's hand. "I have immediate work for you. Tomorrow morning I want you"—he paused and swept a hand to indicate both warriors—"both of you, to get these folk together, get them out of the city, and start them back to Thornhurst." Idgen Marte rose to her feet in protest, but Allystaire cut her off with a raised finger.

"No. I will go before the assize alone; if it goes badly for me there, none of you need to share the cost. Provision them and get them all out of here." Mentally, he began totting up figures and wondering just how thin his purse had gotten.

Idgen Marte looked ready to protest further, but Allystaire added, "I will not discuss this." He stood for a moment, watching them, then held up his hands and said, "What are you waiting for? Get to work and be quick about it." His voice snapped with command; Renard practically leapt away.

Once the bearded man was out of earshot, Idgen Marte swung her gaze toward Allystaire and pointed a finger at him. "Story," she said, grinning like a cat that finds herself well supplied with cream.

"What do you mean?"

"What I just heard. It's a Cold-damned minstrel's tale, and a song or three to boot." Idgen Marte lingered and pushed outstretched fingers into his chest, punctuating her words. "And it better not end in that farce of a castle, fool crusader. I mean to hear more."

Allystaire grunted with the force of each poke. "Be calm. He may make a pauper of me, but I do not think that choiron intends my death."

Idgen Marte lowered her eyes and shook her head. "I don't trust him. Be careful of him. Who knows how the moods of a man who worships the sea might change?"

Allystaire snorted derisively. "Where I come from, *the sea* is spoken of by men who want everyone else to see them as heroes, when they are drunkards too afraid to face the real difficulties of life. They look to the water to hide them and even kill them if they lack the courage to do it themselves."

"He doesn't come from the same place you do," Idgen Marte warned darkly, as she turned and started to walk away, head still shaking.

"Do me one more favor, if you would. Take my animals with you. They may beggar me, but neither of those bastards—not the fat one, not the dangerous one—will have my horses."

Idgen Marte laughed very lightly. "Nothing is stopping you from leaving, too. I'd wager you could find a way to terrify the guards at the gate into letting you past. Cold, we could just hide you in a wagon."

Allystaire shook his head. "I am staying. I want to see this through. Wherever it goes."

Idgen Marte nodded, and as she walked away, offered, "That's the kind of thing a hero in a story would say."

"Do you always need the last word?"

"Yes," she called, just as she ducked outside.

The next few turns were a flurry of activity as the folk of Thornhurst packed and prepared. Allystaire engaged in a general policy of walking among them, nodding approvingly and doing absolutely nothing to direct them or hamper them. *Renard and Idgen Marte are good sergeants, and good sergeants always run the camp*, he thought to himself. And indeed the bustle was in many respects similar to moving a small warband. *Less cursing and fewer whores, though.*

The village folk kept looking to him for guidance; he answered each question by directing them to whichever sergeant was closer. If neither were in sight or hearing, he would simply say, "Carry on as you think best."

He did grow a great deal poorer. By the end of settling with the innkeep, his first purse was entirely depleted and the second held but two gold links and a palmful of silver. His bag of gemmary, loose and worked, was none the lighter since he'd "bought" the village folk in the first place, but even that much distressed him.

You're no beggar, but poorer than you were but a handful of days ago. Couldn't you have at least spent a little of it on a woman? Thoughts of Leah leapt to his mind, but he shook them away in self-loathing and wandered back into the Sign of the Stone Wall to take a flagon of wine to his room to accompany him into sleep.

CHAPTER 12

The Assize

Shadows still hung in his room when the barred door was set rattling by a none-too-gentle fist. "Allystaire," called Idgen Marte's only slightly muffled voice, "get up. We're leaving, but there's a problem."

He rolled out of bed, bare-chested but trousered, and quickly moved to the door to lift the bar, blinking sleep out of his eyes. "What? The frog baron decided to do us in after all?"

Idgen Marte shook her head. "No. It's your horse, that giant grey monster. It won't listen to anyone. Not me, not Renard. And it scared away the village folk."

Sighing, Allystaire nodded. "I will be down."

He started to close the door, but Idgen Marte's boot stopped him. Her hand darted toward his chest and stopped just short of poking the wound on his left shoulder. "This is healing faster than it ought." Carefully, she probed it, Allystaire abiding it sleepily, both of them frowning. "You've some manner of luck, anyway." She slipped out with a curious backward glance.

A few minutes later he was tromping into the stables, flexing his foot in his boot and rolling his left shoulder. Aside from his usual morning stiffness, he felt almost no pain. The two wagons were pulled up in front of the inn with folk milling around them. His palfrey and mule were placidly tied by leads to one wagon, but the grey remained in the stables. Idgen Marte and

Renard were there, and Timmar, but most of the village folk were staying well away.

"Hey. Hey, calm," Allystaire said to it, raising his hands and walking toward the beast. Almost instantly it trotted over to him, tossed its head, and whickered. He reached up to seize the bridle and started to walk it toward the door as the other three watched curiously. The destrier followed him, and he casually said, "See? Nothing to it."

He led it out front toward his other animals, meaning to tie it in the same spot, but instantly its legs straightened and its muscular neck pulled away from his hands. Scowling, Allystaire grasped the bridle again and said firmly, "Now is not the time to be stubborn."

"He doesn't want to go. He means to stay. And you should call him Ardent, because that's his name." The voice was quiet and came from a few paces behind him. Allystaire turned around, incredulous; Mol was standing by the front of the wagon, looking at him intently.

Her eyes were wide and dark and seemed to stand out in circled hollows in her small, pale face. The huge horse whickered and tossed his head when she said *Ardent*, and something seemed to fall into place in Allystaire's mind—the click of a door unlatching, or the clean rasp of a weapon drawn.

The villagers, including her uncle, stood watching Mol in silent shock.

Allystaire smiled at her a bit uneasily and said, "Mol, I am glad to see you're up…" and would've said more, but Mol cut him off with a shake of her head.

"Stay with him," she said, though whether she was speaking to the horse or to him, Allystaire wasn't sure. Then she took two slow steps backward, turned around the edge of the wagon, and scurried into it. Every one of the villagers paused in their bustling, stared at him for the briefest moment, then turned their eyes away and scurried off twice as fast.

Heaving a sigh, Allystaire walked the destrier back into the stables, rubbing its neck along the way. "Ardent it is then, eh? Damned if I know why, but you seem suited to it." He secured the horse in its stall and fetched a small apple, held it in the flat of his hand, and let the stallion devour it quickly.

Once he was back out in the street, he sought Renard and Idgen Marte, who were both leading their own horses. A short, curved horse bow was loosely tied to Idgen Marte's saddle, and a quiver of short, darkly fletched arrows rode on her hip, opposite her sword. Renard's spear rested in a boot attached to his right stirrup, and on his belt he carried a handaxe and a long dirk.

"You two," Allystaire said, waving them over. He tilted his head toward the ground and said quietly, "According to what Timmar told me, there may still be a reaver or three out there. Scouts and such. And some of their own folk, boys I suppose, who ran off when the town was taken. Keep a sharp eye."

They nodded, listening with the careful, loose intensity of practiced soldiers. Allystaire continued, "Renard, do you know who guards the gate this morning? And more, how many men in towers within crossbow range? Or how many that know how *not* to shoot their feet?"

Renard chewed on his lower lip for a moment. "Men on the gate will stand down to my challenge, I expect. As for the other…" He smiled wryly. "You know a bit more of Bend's guards than I would've expected, m'lord. How is that?"

"Ask me again later. Now. How many men in bowshot?"

After another speculative chew on his lip, the bearded warrior answered, "No more than four. And their chances of hittin' anything moving in less than bright noon? Poor."

Allystaire nodded. "Good. Then if the gate guards attempt to impede your progress, cut them down. If any of the villagers know how to use a bow…never mind. No time to find and buy bows."

Idgen Marte twisted her lips and narrowed her eyes. "You think I was idle while you slept, crusader? I was able to salvage most of what the reavers had. Obviously," she added, waving a hand to indicate the wagons. "There are crossbows under the buckboards and I managed to find a couple of short-bows. Inferior stuff, bad wood, and no horn, but they'll do. At the very least the farmers can *look* menacing." She leaned forward and grabbed Allystaire's right arm with her hand and gave it a rough, friendly squeeze. In a much softer voice, she added, "Kill that choiron if you can. I mean it. I don't want him as an enemy."

"Mayhap he does not want me to be his enemy," Allystaire said, though he wasn't sure what he felt or meant by it. He nodded, clasped both of their hands, and retreated to the inn. As he climbed the stairs he could hear their voices calling out, Idgen Marte's strong, laughing rasp, Renard's low and rumbling, cracked but strong, like an old wooden shield—split in places, but held together with iron bands. Soon the sound of wagons rolling off, underwritten by horse's clopping hooves, drifted to his ears.

Once in his room, he did the soldierly thing and went back to sleep.

* * *

A few turns later, sun blazing overhead, Allystaire sat atop Ardent, wrapped in steel over quilted gambeson, and armed with sword, shield, and hammer. No half measures this time, no bracers hidden under sleeves or leather cap. His plate armor didn't gleam or shine; it was dark, pitted, functional stuff. Scarred and beaten, yes, but strong. His helmet was slung from the pommel of his saddle. He worked his jaw as sweat already streamed down his freshly shaven cheeks, stinging the raw, reddened flesh.

Heavy grey clouds sat thickly on the horizon, and the smell of rain promised respite from the heat. The crowds parted for Allystaire and the broad destrier. They were of a piece, both with a size that projected beyond them and was due as much to breadth as to height. In his armor, Allystaire even shared a color with the horse, more or less.

He rode almost absentmindedly to the so-called castle, picking out the way with surprising ease. For his part, the horse seemed happy to be out again, but his gait was more contained than the previous day; he didn't have to be reined in or held back, and proceeded with the same quiet determination as his rider. When he reached the gates, Allystaire dismounted and wrapped his gauntleted hand firmly around the reins as he marched toward the guards.

"I am here for the assize. Make way."

Whether it was his tone, the fact that he was armed like a knight—albeit fresh off a campaign and not in the lists—or simply his presence, the gate guards snapped to his words. The portcullis quickly lifted, the pathetic gate swung open, and soon Allystaire was leading Ardent into the courtyard. A liveried servant trotted forward, hand out for the reins. Allystaire had halfway handed them over when Mol's words from the pre-dawn morning echoed in his mind: *Stay with him.* Whether she'd been addressing him or the destrier he still didn't know, but he shook off the servant and led the horse himself.

He didn't have far to go. A crude stage had been erected in the courtyard itself, a wooden platform upon which three chairs sat. The largest of the three had been raised on a slight and none-too-sturdy looking dais of three steps in the center, at the back of the square wooden platform; one chair sat to its right, and another directly in front of it.

It occurred to Allystaire rather quickly that the entire affair bore more than a passing resemblance to a gallows platform, minus the pole. Probably it was Bend's gallows without the pole erected and with some hasty additions. He pushed the thought from his mind.

Stepping slowly but resolutely across the grass, he reached the edge of the platform, dropped Ardent's reins to the ground, and stepped on them; the well-trained mount settled down and started picking at the nearest grass. Allystaire relaxed himself by resting one hand on the head of his hammer and flexing the other around the strap of his shield. He relaxed his knees, rolled his shoulders, and waited as stormclouds gathered overhead and the first distant rumbles of thunder echoed over the river.

He knew very well how to wait.

Time passed, neither very much nor very swiftly, and others started to gather. The Baron of Bend hobbled out, dressed up in finery that could only be drenching him in sweat—bright blue robes and a creamy white scarf that seemed, somehow, to signify his office, or at least his wealth, with its yards of silk. Servants scuttled around him like tenders swarming around a massive ship of war. Some bore pitchers of wine, others trays of food, another a towel, and two more carried a large cushioned chair, which they quickly placed on the ground. When the baron sat, it sank visibly into the hard earth, its legs pushing into the ground.

Once he'd been served wine, the baron saw Allystaire waiting and waved him over, wearing a haughty expression that Allystaire guessed was intended to convey magnanimity.

"Could still forget all this bad business, y'know, Sir Allystaire," the baron tried, his voice as grating to the ear as a knife dragged across a whetstone. "Just pay me what I'm owed and be off wi' no trouble."

"I will let the choiron decide what, if anything, I owe you," Allystaire replied. He paused, let the silence hang in the air for what he knew was a beat too long before adding, "My lord."

The baron's face darkened, and his jowls shuddered as he said, "And when he decides to hang you? What then?!"

Allystaire smiled the careless smile of the puissant man, and said, "I will not hang today. And if the choiron decides that my life is forfeit, then, *my lord*, we will learn how many of your men are willing to die for their silver." Seized with a sudden anger, he turned toward the nearest liveried servant, though the man bore nothing more than a dagger on his belt. He thrust out a finger like a spear and barked, "You! Will you lay down your life for the man whose wine you pour?" The man blanched and took half a step back. Allystaire turned toward the next servant. "And you? Will you stand against my hammer for this *pig*?" His finger became an open hand and he swept it toward the baron, who sputtered in his chair.

Neither of the servants, nor their blue-and-white-clad fellows, answered. Most turned away their eyes.

Allystaire turned toward the grossly corpulent man and said harshly, "See, *my lord*, how loyal and daring your body servants are. It would behoove you to remember that should you care to make any more threats. I am not Godsworn to 'take no revenge upon you' *yet*," he finished, dropping his hand and whirling away before the baron could recover his own fury to muster an answer.

When he turned, he found himself eye to eye with Choiron Symod, dressed still in his seal-skin trimmed finery, the huge amulet around his neck gleaming under the stormclouds with its own light.

The Sea Dragon's priest smiled coolly at him. "Do you come to the assize armed, as if it were a trial by combat? I did not offer such terms."

"Well for the baron you did not," Allystaire replied, once again forcing himself to meet the priest's intense, sea-green gaze. "But no. I came here wearing steel and bearing arms because I come as myself and that is who and what I am."

"Few men know truly what they are, and I doubt you are one of them," Symod replied loftily. Softening his tone and smiling that chill smile again, he added, "But you may be nearer to it than our friend the Baron of Bend. And mayhap today's assize will play some part in helping you to discover it."

Allystaire misliked the way those particular words fell from the priest's lips; he liked less the rumble of nearer thunder that followed them. Thunderheads had advanced till they hung over Bend like an army readying to shatter its pathetic wall.

"We will never know if we do not begin," Allystaire replied, letting the last of his anger drain from his voice. "And the weather bodes ill if we are not quick about it."

Puffing as he sat up straighter in his chair, the baron said, "Aye, for once I am in accord with this brute. Choiron, let us take this affair indoors afore we are all soaked through."

"Nonsense," the priest replied, in a tone that, though quiet, brooked no dissent. "The coming storm is a sign of Braech's favor, that the Oath you are about to make in His Name will be well and truly bound with His power. Now attend me, both of you."

You could probably crush his skull before he had anything to say about it, whispered Allystaire's pragmatic self. But that tingle of power he remembered, that unsettling note of vast authority in Symod's voice bid the thought remain a thought.

The baron had to be helped to his feet and tottered over with the support of his servants. The choiron reached into the bag he wore over one shoulder and removed a thin, flat piece of wood with parchment tacked to it, and a pen with a bright copper nib. He held the board and parchment and pen toward one of the servants, the gesture of a man used to being obeyed without question, regardless whose colors the men around him wore.

"Unless all of your servants wish to be sworn under my Lord Braech as well as you, milord, it is best that they move off for the nonce." The choiron raised his hands and threw back his head then, his arms wide to encompass Allystaire and the Baron of Bend. The men in livery beat a hasty retreat, leaving Tallenhaft Windspar standing unsteadily under his own power.

The wind picked up and the first intermittent splashes of rain began to plink against Allystaire's armor as Symod began to half-chant, half-shout into the grey midday air. They were small drops, and few, the mere vanguard of a mighty host.

"Braech Sea Dragon! Father of Storm and Wave! Lord of Trade and Master of Accords, cast Your Ears and Eyes upon the shore of this river, a piece of the great water that is Your demesne. Fix Your sight upon these men as they swear to hear

Your judgment! Grant me the cunning and the wisdom to see the truth of what they shall tell me, and to apportion out blame and praise as You would see fit. Let them swear to abide by the judgment of Your wisdom and to seek no vengeance if they find it bitterer than sea-water. Let those who swear be placed beneath Your baleful curse should they by will or weakness see their word and bond not held. Let their wealth and wares dwindle, their nets fail, their sails tear, their hulls break apart on the rocks, and all their plans and means come to naught. Under Your eye do we consecrate this agreement. In Your ear do we declare the terms. In Your sight do they sign. Let no man later deny to what he now agrees."

As the priest spoke, Allystaire felt the wind intensify, tugging at his hair, while another drop of rain slapped at his raw cheek. He felt the tingling charge of lightning building to strike, smelled the air burning when it crashed somewhere in the town, was stunned by the enormous wave of thunder that followed.

The servant held the parchment board in front of the baron, who signed in large, looping child's letters; Allystaire took the pen and, despite the clumsiness of his gauntlets, signed in a quick, neat scrawl. The choiron inspected the parchment, eyed them both. To Allystaire he said, "You signed without title or surname?"

"I signed with the only name that cannot be taken from me."

"Very well." The priest pointed Allystaire toward the chair on the right of the judge's chair. "Take your place, Allystaire."

Treading with heavy steel-clad stamps and lightly jingling spurs, Allystaire ascended the gallows platform and strode over to the chair, but did not sit.

"Let those who bring accusation come forth." Symod's rich and powerful voice rolled over the courtyard. It demanded attention, and more. It demanded obedience.

The Baron of Bend, once again walking with the support of a liveried servant on either side, struggled up the steps to fall heavily into the other chair. Wheezing, he called out, "I come before this assize to formally accuse that man," he said, pointing to Allystaire, "of Assault from Ambush, of Murder, of Theft, and of Failing to Pay Legal Duty."

"What do you seek?"

Another deep, heaving wheeze of breath. "I seek my lost revenues restored," he shouted, his jowls wobbling and beginning to tinge with red. "I seek him punished to the fullest extent."

Symod, sinking into his seat, turned to face Allystaire, his every movement stately and grand. "And how do you answer?"

"To his first charges, I do not, until he provides evidence of them. For his last, I say there was no legal duty. He is claiming a right to taxes on the sale of slaves, and such is not legal here or in any neighboring barony."

"I decide what is legal in Bend! And you owed taxes when you came through the gate which you did not pay!" The baron's jowls were shading to purple now, and the rain began to fall more steadily. The wind picked up the baron's voice and blew it away, so that Allystaire had to strain to hear.

Smiling coolly, Allystaire replied, "If I owed any taxes on property I brought into Bend—and again I question your legal right to claim such—it is moot, because I paid a gold link to your guardsmen upon entering."

The choiron listened to Allystaire and dimmed his eyes for a moment; he nodded and turned his level green gaze on the baron. "He speaks the truth of this. If he paid a gold link, what more tax could he possibly owe?"

"I collected no gold link from him! There would be records! The value of his animals alone…"

"I told you he spoke the truth," the choiron said, his voice cutting through the baron's words like an axe into a tree stump. "If you have no record that is none of his doing."

"Last I saw of that link, your men were fighting over it in the dirt," Allystaire offered, with a mocking mildness of expression.

"Let us address the other charges. I see little headway to be made with this one," Symod intoned.

"Very well," the baron said, his face cooling, even paling a bit. "May we present men who will give evidence?"

"You may. So long as they know that if they lie to me, I will press a heavy sentence upon them and upon any who fed them lies," the choiron warned.

The baron gestured to one of his servants, who ran at a sprint for the house that served as a keep. He quickly returned with four people, one of whom walked with a pronounced limp. They tromped over to the baron's side, arraying themselves on the platform behind his chair. Allystaire recognized the limping man as the survivor of the warehouse. He hesitated to put weight on the leg he'd been knifed in and so stood awkwardly, hunched over.

The other three, two men and a woman, he did not recognize, but the patched homespun they wore added another touch of incongruity to this already mad scene. They looked as though they wished they could hide behind the baron's chair, literally.

"First on my behalf and his own, Choiron Symod, is Rugard of Bend." The limping reaver hobbled forward, his face uncertain.

"If you are not giving evidence you must stand and leave the platform, my lord," the choiron said, waving his right hand dismissively. The baron staggered to his feet and dismounted the steps, sinking into his own armchair, the feet of which began to sink into the ground as the intensifying rain stirred and churned the dust.

Rugard looked hopefully at the empty chair and sank into it with visible relief when the Sea Dragon's priest waved a hand at it. He sighed audibly, then tried to recover some dignity by straightening his posture and pointing at Allystaire. "That man's a coward who'll backstab a man, and a murderer!"

"I have not asked you a question yet, Rugard of Bend. I have not even formally admitted you to the assize. BE SILENT." For the first time, Allystaire heard the choiron bellow with all the force of his voice; he felt the urge toward silence bearing down upon him like a strong hand clasped over his mouth.

Rugard parted his lips as if to protest or apologize, but no sound came out; he worked his jaw, moved his lips and his tongue, and still nothing. His face paled, and he slowly closed his mouth, his eyes drifting, almost sheepishly, to the planks at his feet.

"Now. Do you, Rugard of Bend, attest upon the wrath of the Sea Dragon, that all testimony you give here today will be truthful? Swear."

He nodded and timidly opened his mouth, managing a ragged whisper. "I swear."

The choiron nodded and, after a pause, gestured toward Rugard. "Now. You say this man—" the beringed hand, heavy robe draping over the wrist, swung toward Allystaire "—is a coward, a backstabber, and a murderer. Why do you say this?"

"He bust into our place, our warehouse, while we was finishin' the business he paid us fer, and started attackin' wi' hammer and sword till me mates was dead or near enough."

Symod tilted his head quizzically. "I have a question for the Accused," he said, turning slowly to Allystaire. "What does he mean, business you paid them for?"

Allystaire cleared his throat. "I had thought to secure the release of the folk they had enslaved by bargaining for them as though I meant to buy them."

"If you had paid and could take receipt, why did you then attack?"

Allystaire took in a small breath and licked his lips before answering. "The realization—actually, the fact was pointed out to me by another—that in so doing I had given them precisely the profit they wanted, and freed them to attack more helpless folk."

"Profit is not a crime," the choiron pointed out, turning his hand palm up, as if weighing something. "Braech is the Lord of Trade and Accords."

"Slavery, marauding, murder, and rape are crimes, and profiting by them must surely be crimes as well," Allystaire said quietly, but fervently.

"Are you some force of law in these parts," Symod asked, "to go passing sentence and punishment upon criminals, then?" Rugard made some noise of protest until the choiron demanded silence by extending his hand towards the man, palm out.

Allystaire thought for a moment, then shook his head lightly. "No. But I am no blackguard. Any man who would see such crimes done, or profit by them, surely is."

Symod smiled carefully again, considering Allystaire with his narrow green gaze. "Once again you speak of knowing who and what you are…and are not. I suspect we shall hear more before we are done." He stared a moment more, then turned back to Rugard. "How many in your band?"

"What, my lord?" Rugard was caught off guard. *Probably can't count that high*, Allystaire thought, but kept the notion to himself.

"How many men in your band? Do not make me repeat myself again."

"Right near a dozen, m'lord."

"A dozen men," Symod said, slowly, as if savoring the words with twisted lips. "And you call this man a coward for assaulting the lot of you by himself?"

Rugard's pale cheeks flushed darkly. "He took us by surprise, is all. If 'tweren't for his backstabbin' we'd've 'ad him."

Symod chuckled drily as the rain became a steady pound and began to gather in his hair and stream down his face. Allystaire heard it pinging off his armor as his hair slickened with it, saw the eddying dust begin to give way to mud. Another peal of thunder rolled over Bend, as more lightning played over the wide mouth of the Ash.

"From ambush, then. How did he do it?"

"I can't speak t'it 'xactly m'lord, I wasn't at the front but I know'd 'e'd've never got past me mates that way, and those folk—"

Symod cut him off and rose from his chair, his face a mask of cold fury. "I did not allow you to come before the assize to repeat what someone else told you, only to tell what *you saw.* All I hear from you is cowardice and hearsay and a petty need for vengeance against a man who bested you. Since you came before the judgment of Braech, you will receive his justice as well." He pointed one sharp finger at the man and spat the words, "Scourge that man out of the gates of this place."

An uproar swelled from all quarters. The Baron of Bend sputtered himself purple, unable to summon the strength to stand. Rugard blanched and nearly fell from his chair in wordless shock. The folk clustered behind the wounded reaver shrank as if flinching from a blow.

"No." Allystaire surprised even himself by speaking up. "If you want him dead, Choiron, give him a weapon and me room to swing."

"Do not attempt to gainsay me in my assize!" Symod swung the weight of his rage upon Allystaire as lightning flashed and thunder cracked once again, now directly overhead. "I am the Court and you are but the Accused. Be silent!"

Once again Allystaire felt that powerful weight pressing on his mouth, but he struggled through it. The effort of merely pushing words past his lips felt like dragging a warhorse up a hill. "No," he pressed on. "He would die rotting with the wounds of a scourge on his back. I offer him something clean."

The choiron's rage drained in shock. For a moment, his poise nearly faltered, but he quickly recovered himself with another small, flat smile. "*No.* Besides, why should you protest this man's death, since he is, as you have said, a murderer and rapist, a reaver and blackguard?" He waved forward the liveried men who were hesitantly climbing the platform; they seized Rugard, whose wounded leg went out from under him, and he was dragged away, blubbering.

He's a coward and getting a coward's death, Allystaire observed. *A death he did little to earn*, he countered himself. *And less to stave off.* No counter-thought followed. Aloud, though, he replied, "I do not protest his death, only the manner of it. If it is true that I passed sentence on his fellow slavers, at least I carried it out myself. Will your hand wield the scourge, Choiron?"

Symod's jaw tensed and his eyes flashed, widening even as rain streamed into them. He turned from Allystaire, seated himself again, and pointed at the baron. "Your other witnesses had best be relevant, Baron Tallenhaft Windspar of Bend, or this assize may well find against you. Call the next."

"If it please you, Lord Choiron, I have two to call together. Enoc and Fraim, both fishermen and citizens of Bend."

The two remaining men advanced cautiously, clearly cowed by the priest. They both knelt reflexively and lowered their rain-soaked heads. "Do you, Enoc and Fraim, both of Bend, attest upon the wrath of the Sea Dragon, that all testimony you give here today will be truthful? Swear."

"I swear m'lord," the men responded weakly. They stood again, and Allystaire could see, even from several feet away, the yellowing of one man's eyes. *The sots Idgen Marte spoke of.*

"Describe to me what you saw, then."

The taller of the two, and older if the grey in his hair was any guide, cleared his throat and opened a gap-filled mouth. "We was takin' refreshment in a taproom on the Street o' Sashes, m'lord," he began, air whistling through his teeth at *refreshment* and *Sashes*. "When we saw that man stride across the street, armed as 'e is now, and when some guardsman answered, that man right there, 'e made to follow 'im inside."

The other man, shorter and paunchy in squalid and oft-patched canvas pants, nodded emphatically. "Then when the guardsman's back was turned, 'e goes and draws a weapon. And 'e waits till just the moment 'e, the guardsman, is turnin' round, and 'e clobbers him good. Beautiful shot, it 'twere. 'spect it brained him right there. Then just as easy as y'please, 'im," he pointed at Allystaire this time, "walks o'er the corpse bleedin' and brainin' onto the ground as calm as y'please, like 'tweren't no more'n guttin' a fish."

Symod nodded slowly, turning toward Allystaire again. "Is this true? Did you attack this gate guard by ambush and deceit?"

Your word against two men who haven't fished in anything but their own vomit in years, he thought. But there was the matter of being Godsworn. *I have broken enough oaths in this life; I do not mean to add to the pile.* Finally, he nodded slowly. "Aye. I brained him much as they say." A pause. "Had I not, he would have roused the crew and I would have worsened my already bad odds."

"Then you admit to the crime you are accused of?"

Allystaire shook his head. "I admit to the method they describe. I maintain that it cannot be a crime to kill a man engaged in making slaves of poor folk."

Symod smiled coldly. "Were you some kind of legal scholar, hrm? Is that why you were Castellan of Wind's Jaw Keep? For your great knowledge of the law of the land?"

"No. Though I am educated enough to know that there is no law in any of these parts upholding slavery, and that if he claims to make one," Allystaire went on, pointing one gauntleted finger at the baron, "it holds no weight because he is *not* a legitimate *baron*. Not in a legal sense."

At that, the man who styled himself Baron of Bend rose from his seat with a roar and took one step, his delicately shod foot slipping up to the ankle into the sudden whorls of mud. With the help of sodden servants, he was able to extricate his foot, but the elegant slipper was a total loss. He was never able to utter a word.

Symod rolled his eyes and continued to ignore the witnesses who stood, soaking, hats in hand, a few feet away from his dais. "Perhaps not in a legal sense, but tell me, Sir Allystaire, what makes a legitimate baron?"

Allystaire wearily shrugged his shoulders with a heavy clank. "I do not care to debate politics with you, Choiron. We are here for an assize."

"And it is for that reason that you will answer any question I put to you," Symod replied coldly, eyes narrowing again.

"As you will. What legitimizes a baron is when enough men call him that and do his bidding on the back of it. When he has enough spears or swords or bows to make his command mean something. He has those things only because, I suspect, Baron Delondeur is busy pressing the borders he shares with Barons Innadan and Telmawr, so he looks the other way, lets this patch of misery run itself so long as it pays regular tribute. When it stops, or when he is no longer looking east or south," Allystaire said, turning from the choiron to the baron in his dripping finery, "he will devour you like a bear snapping a fish from a stream, and you will just be another pile of shit in his tracks."

The Baron of Bend was too stunned to respond, but the choiron roared with laughter, throwing back his head and letting the rain fall upon him; the lashing wind boomed his laughter over the courtyard. "Oh…oh I can see you have met Baron Delondeur, Sir Allystaire. Indeed." He turned back to the two wet fishermen before him. "Have the two of you anything more to say?"

"We're tellin' the truth m'lord" stumbled over "We ain't lyin' yer emm'nence"—in truth, Allystaire couldn't tell and didn't care which of the men said what.

The priest turned again to Allystaire. "Have you anything else to say to their accusation, which you have confirmed is true?"

"Only that the reaver courted his own ruin by taking slaves. Whether he died looking at me or looking away from me made little matter to me at the time." A pause. "He was armed," Allystaire added, tilting his head speculatively. "But he was slow."

Symod snorted with mild laughter.

Meanwhile, the baron had come to resemble a wet, bulging sack of offal rotting on the now-ruined cushions of his chair, which had sunk a further two inches into the gathering muck.

Only one witness remained, a woman. She had little grey in her brown hair, but the lines on her sun-browned face were deep and hard; the combination made it hard to measure her age. She stood unmoving and uncomplaining in the driving rain, and didn't seem to be following all the talk that floated around her. Symod dismissed the other two with a wave and then cleared his throat imperiously. She looked up and shuffled forward slowly, not meeting his gaze.

"And your name?" Symod's powerful voice oozed condescension.

"Yolande, yer worship," the woman answered. Her voice was distant.

"And you are here because?"

"Morrys was m'husband," she replied, then turned her face toward Allystaire. The driving rain filled the many lines on her face with a constant stream of water. "Morrys was the man you, ah, *brained*, was yer word, m'lord. The man on the gate."

"Morrys, then. Did you know he was a slaver?" Symod sat straighter, utterly unbothered by the rain.

The woman shrugged, returning her gaze to the boards at her feet. "I 'spected 'e was up t'nothin' good. Told me 'e was just a sword-a-hire and after divvyin' the la'est loot 'e wanted to take a southerly ship."

Allystaire felt his guts twist a bit; they twisted more when the woman reached into a pouch on her belt and fumbled with slick fingers before pulling out a small piece of blue stone. *My lapis*, one small, gem-loving part of him couldn't help but think.

"He gimme this, said 'twere more t'come in silver, mebbe gold. I guess this is yours, m'lord," she said, holding it toward Allystaire. "I 'spect yu'll be wantin' it back."

The choiron chuckled deeply. "Indeed, Yolande, I believe that is part of the gemmary that Allystaire used for buying slaves. Slaves your husband helped take." He waved a hand to dismiss her, and stood, gathering his rain-slicked robes about him, though the sealskin he wore kept him dryer than the rest of them. "Profit from slaving is ill-gained," he declaimed, turning the weight of his gaze and voice on the woman, "and no one has any right to keep it nor to tax it. Give it back." Moving with surprising haste, Yolande scrambled over and deposited the small bit of gemstone, crudely broken off the larger hunk, into Allystaire's gauntlet and scurried away.

"I am ready to declare my judgment," Symod said, his voice seemingly amplified by a peal of thunder behind it. "Sir Allystaire acted boldly, and the Sea Dragon ever rewards boldness! These false charges you have brought, Baron Tallenhaft Windspar of Bend, are dismissed. Allystaire emerges clean, in this, his victory. Remember well your Oaths to take no vengeance upon the other. Sir Allystaire, would you ask any restitution?"

Allystaire's gaze was fixed on the shrinking huddle that was Yolande, already creeping off the stage. He shook his head curtly, and then looked to the choiron. "Am I dismissed, then? Is this mummer's dance done?"

Symod smiled again, and the rain slackened. "Not quite. I have said that Braech favors boldness, Sir Allystaire, and you are bold indeed. His favor would ever be upon the man who takes on a dozen, knowing that his cause or his benefit is at stake, and emerges stronger. I told you that ere we finished this day you might better know yourself, and I tell you that this storm that has blessed us today is a sign of even greater favor from the Sea Dragon!"

The choiron descended his dais and bid Allystaire to join him in the center of the platform. "Braech Wave-father extends to you His hand. He would see your boldness in His service." Symod smiled widely, all those around them forgotten, the absurdity of the tiny courtyard and its toy walls seeming to melt away. Allystaire felt a thrum of power in the air, something he could taste, like salt, only he tasted with his whole body.

The choiron drew closer, laying a hand on Allystaire's shoulder; his voice dropped, but it still resonated with power. "You have left all that you knew, and all that you were, and all that you had. And yet before you now lies the chance to be so much more. You need but kneel and swear your service. The Sea Dragon listens. There have long been bold warriors in His service, and power is granted to those who are truly willing to live their lives in His name."

Allystaire stared cautiously at Symod for a moment, then at the retreating back of Yolande. He cleared his throat and fixed his blue eyes on the choiron's sea-green. "Then I hope he hears me when I say that I will have no part of any god who sides always with the strong and favors only the victor." He shrugged Symod's hand off his shoulder, but he felt the buzzing current of power move to a higher pitch, a more threatening one, its edge thinning to a blade. He took half a step forward.

"The favor of Braech is not lightly turned away," Symod seethed, sliding to stay in front of the armored man.

"Neither am I," Allystaire replied, his tone answering Symod's. "Where was your Sea Dragon's favor for the folk of Thornhurst who were driven from their homes to be sold as slaves? Where is his favor when he is given glory by men who sack towns and burn villages? The bold and the strong need no more favor; they have Fortune's." He tilted his head and smiled mockingly. "Mayhap your god is but bearing *Her* upon his back. A misbegotten pair, and I say *to the Cold* with the both of them, along with any other god who gives meat to the rich and dirt to the poor, who rewards the strong and damns the weak. Now get out of my way." Each of his last four words was punctuated by a half step forward that pushed Symod to the very edge of the platform; he had no choice but to move or fall backwards.

The choiron stepped aside carefully. As Allystaire hopped down and began to stalk off, he raged at his back. "You will regret this, you crusading *fool*! Braech's favor denied is quick to become Braech's wrath!"

Allystaire ignored him and bellowed, "*Ardent!* To me!" The broad, muscled, grey horse stood placidly in the rain; it lifted its head and cantered easily to Allystaire's side. Behind him, the sun poked through the thunderheads and the rain died into a spitting patter.

He swung into the saddle and with a flick of the reins, crossed the courtyard to the gate, riding through it and out onto the street, leaving Baron Tallenhaft Windspar of Bend, his laughable pretense of a castle, the coldly raging priest of Braech, and the afternoon sun behind him.

On the street, he spotted a huddled figure and rode to her side, extending a hand toward her and saying, as gently as he could manage in his anger, "Come with me."

CHAPTER 13

The Widow and the Knight

She'd had a bad week of it. Morrys coming home had been a bright spot, for a bit. But in the weeks he'd been out his cough had gotten worse and the strength had gone out of him. It wouldn't be long before it left him altogether—hadn't she always told him he'd die on the road or on the water? Maybe this way he'd die at home and that would be something.

Then just two nights ago he'd come in with that hunk of blue gemstone, proud of it like a boy with his first catch, and he'd given it to her and promised there'd be more, that their luck was finally turning and maybe he could buy a boat.

She'd heard all of that before, and watched him drink and dice any number of boats away, but she let it go and smiled and went about mending nets and sails and whatever other scraps people brought her because she didn't know how to spend a piece of blue rock like she did copper links.

And then he hadn't come home, but that wasn't unexpected, really. When Rugard had limped to her door with some watchmen, that was something else. She hadn't met any of Morrys's crew before; he'd always said they weren't for mixed company. This big rough man talked a lot, and fast, but couldn't stand on his own and seemed too eager to tell her that Morrys was dead, that some angry lord had done for him the way you do a pike that's flopping around in the air, clubbed him in the head till his brains were done for.

Done fer 'tweren't a far road for Morrys's brains to travel, she'd thought, but hadn't said. Then she'd gone along with the watch because she learned a long time ago, when Baron Delondeur's men had razed the little fishing village she'd grown up in on the other side of the Ash, that you did what the men with the swords and the horses and the bows did, or they killed you. And Yolande was a survivor.

She'd survive this, too. Maybe she couldn't find another man—too many bright mornings on the water with the sun beating up into her face had seen to her looks—but her hands had a few years with the needle in them yet.

And now another man with a sword was telling her what to do. He'd ridden up on his big horse like some knight out of a story. Except knights in stories, she remembered, wore bright armor and plumed helms and carried flaming swords. They didn't have broken noses or cold bleak eyes. Knights in stories didn't wear ugly grey armor or ride broad squat horses that looked as like to bite her as soon as carry her. But she swung up behind him on the saddle and held on, and the horse moved with clean purpose. It was like trying to ride on the stern of a squat, broad-beamed boat.

She thought she could just about smell the knight's anger, though. It was something clean and pure and cold, like snow melt in a rain barrel.

Yolande thought that just maybe that kind of anger was something like the knights in stories.

She was frightened, but she didn't think this lord meant to kill her, and soon enough they were near the quays. He swung down out of the saddle and stared up at her, his broken nose flaring in the ugliest way; in the sudden and dazzling sunlight of the afternoon that the nearby Ash flung back at them, she could see dozens of tiny scars around his eyes, cheeks, and the nose that splayed to the left.

"Have you any possessions you need to fetch?" His voice was a deep calm well with something older and stronger than rock underneath of it. She was convinced now that she was right to be afraid of this man.

But maybe not afraid for herself.

"Fetch? Why? Where'm I goin'?"

"Wherever the Cold you want. But you are going today."

Yolande blinked, startled by the blunt phrase, and shook her head. "I've spent two-score years, or near enough, on one side or t'other o'the Ash and I don't mean t'leave it."

The man shook his head, his mop of thick dark hair brushing the back of the steel plate shirt he wore. "You do not have to leave the Ash," he said, forcing himself to speak more quietly. "Yet you *must* leave Bend. Understand this. Things went poorly for your beloved baron back there, and while an Oath to Braech may keep him away from me, in his anger he will look for others to hurt." He raised a gauntleted finger and pointed it at her. "You seem a likely target."

"I 'aven't any money and no goods the likes of him'd want," Yolande protested. The pile of nets sitting on her table in her shanty were on her mind. They weren't going to mend themselves and there were still many turns of light tonight.

The big, homely man shook his head. "It will not be money he wants. It will be blood. If he cannot have mine, he will have someone's." He reached behind his steel plate and pulled out a purse and pressed it into her hands. "This has three gold links, more than a score of silver, and a bit of copper. Take it, buy a place on a ship, go wherever you want, but go now. Today."

The purse weighed heavy in her hand and heavier in her mind, and she already knew she'd never dreamed of having this much wealth. "Why're ya givin' this to me, m'lord?"

"I am not even sure I know. Payment for the lapis. Payment for the life you have had to lead. Your husband may have been a slaver, but you were not. No reason for you to die for his choices."

"Did you really kill Morrys? Why?" She couldn't avoid sounding plaintive; so much weight in her hand now and no Morrys to see it, to share it.

"He was a reaver, a bandit, and a slaver." The man's voice was hard and so was his face; there wasn't a hint of sorrow anywhere on it. "I am sorry for where it has left you. But I am not sorry that I did it."

"Y're a hard man, ya are," Yolande accused, lifting the purse as if she meant to hurl it in his face, but this purse was more nets that she could ever mend— she knew she'd never hurl it. "A hard man."

"Someone ought to be when it comes to slavers. If there were a hundred Morryses taking slaves I would kill every one of them if I could, and if it made a hundred widows like you mayhap I would beggar myself giving them all a new life," the man said, all in a rush. His face remained as hard as the stones under her feet. Then, softer, a little of that stoniness fading, he said, "But I killed one Morrys and made one widow who will die if she does not leave this place. Let me set that right."

Finally, as she knew she would because somehow here was still a man with a sword telling her what to do, even if it was take a great huge pile of silver, she nodded. But she added, reflexively, "Can't leave today. Will have to wait till the morrow."

"Oh you people and your freezing tides," the man muttered, rolling his eyes skyward and throwing out his hands impatiently. And, she thought, revealing that he knew nothing of rivers or ships.

"Why can a gods-cursed ship not just *sail* when the men on it have a mind?" He held up a hand to her and cradled his head in the other, shaking it, then said, "Go. Talk to captains. Find a ship, decide where to go, pack what you want and I will see you onto it. The sooner I put my back to this place the better."

Yolande knew when a man's patience was near an end. It was a line she'd walked with Morrys for twenty years, though even in his cups he'd never raised a hand to her. She didn't think this man would, either, but she wasn't about to test him. She gave a rough curtsy and hurried away.

Her shanty wasn't far from the quays; it couldn't be if she wanted to get the mending business. She gathered up her sewing kit, a little store of copper she'd managed to save, a few things she'd knitted, a muffler, and a warmer cloak, and wrapped it all up in the quilt that had been on her bed since she'd wed Morrys a score of years ago. Then she dropped the packet of tea she'd just bought into a pocket in her cloak. No use wasting it. She bustled back to the quays.

Soon, maybe a hair under a full turn, she'd booked passage down river into the bay and beyond into Londray. A city that big on that much water, surely she could get mending work. Maybe better than mending work. It had only cost a handful of silver. *Only!* A handful of silver was more than she had ever had.

After that she was back to the quays to look for that big homely lord and his broken nose. Yolande was half-certain he'd be gone, ridden off impatiently. She found him standing in the exact same spot, one hand resting on the head of that big black-headed hammer, the other holding the reins of his horse. They were of a piece, those two—huge in the shoulders and bigger than they were tall, homely, mean, and menacing. The crowd gave them a wide berth.

She took a few steps toward him, and suddenly a cloud passed away from the afternoon sun, and its rays reflected off the water and lit him in a kind of golden fire. In that moment she truly thought she was looking at the hero of some minstrel's story, a legend walking the sad streets of Bend, his armor dazzlingly bright, his right arm a blinding white thunderbolt. His face was still stern, it was still angry, but it was an anger that looked at the world, found it lacking, and was waiting for the moment to set it right. She felt an urge to run away, and just as sudden and strong, an urge to run toward him and ask what he would have her do. She wanted to ask his forgiveness and his protection and his blessing, all at once.

In the end she did none of that. She walked toward him, calmly, carefully. With the first measured step, the blaze disappeared. He was just a man in armor again, standing and waiting while the crowd moved around him. Yolande gave her head a shake; fool notions filled a dazed head too easily. Yes, it had been a long, hard week.

CHAPTER 14

Ordination

By the time the haggard fishwife had approached him again, Allystaire had had quite enough of the quays. The smell was repulsive, hanging in the air like a filthy curtain, and the people were abhorrent. So far as he could tell, the primary trades were not fishing or sailing so much as cheating, robbing, swindling, and whoring. In the time he stood there he had stopped counting whores and started on panders. He got up to a dozen and a bit of itchy bloodlust, his hand closing under the head of the hammer, before he stopped himself. *Since when did whoring bother you anyway?* He chewed on the inside of his lip as he considered one, a swaggering brute with heavy shoulders, a long knife on his belt digging into his paunch. He saw the way the two thin, frightened women that stood behind him twitched at his every word, forced themselves to laugh at his jibes, and walked in clear fright of him. It was then, with his hand starting to lift the hammer free of its own volition, that he realized the answer to his own question.

It is not the women that bother me, he thought. *It is the men forcing them into it.* He slid the hammer back into place and shook his head. *Get out of this place without shedding more blood.*

By then, Yolande had returned, approaching him hesitantly, as if she were still fearful of him.

"Found me a ship. Gonna take it to Londray and see wha' I can find there. Mebbe go on t' Keersvast in time," the woman drawled slowly.

Nodding, he said, "Take me to the ship."

When they reached the ship of choice, Allystaire realized that he'd anticipated a much smaller vessel; this one was bigger than most of the others in view. The finer points of seamanship eluded him; water was wet and you needed a good wind or a lot of strong backs on oars—that summed up most of what he knew. But the ship didn't look likely to sink and appeared in good trim and boasted a curious carving of a northern troll on the front. "The bow?" he wondered aloud; Yolande stared at him a moment but said nothing.

She approached the ship and called out something he couldn't make out to the men on board; one of them strolled down the gangplank in a ridiculous rolling walk. Allystaire grudgingly admitted to himself that bare-chested and barefooted looked a lot more comfortable in the day's heat than the three stone of steel he wore.

The rolling walker was bald-headed but heavily bearded and browned by the sun. A small whistle or pipe gleamed lightly against his skin, held around his neck by a whip-thong.

"Are you the captain," Allystaire asked brusquely.

"No m'lord. I'm the bosun."

Allystaire squinted and thought a moment. "That something like a bannerman or a sergeant? You keep things running while the officers swan about?"

The man laughed, an overdone gesture with a thrown-back head. "Aye, m'lord, you've the right of it, y' do."

"Good. This woman, I understand, has booked a passage on your vessel at considerable cost. I want you to understand this and understand very well, and realize that I have no malice toward honest men such as yourself," Allystaire said. He leaned forward then, filling this bosun's vision with his broken-nosed, scarred face. "When she reaches Londray she will send me a message; if I do not receive that message it had best be because this boat, and all the men on it, are on the bottom of the bay. If they are not, they will be. Do you understand?"

The bosun bristled a bit, and his hands curled into fists. "Not every man on this piece of water is a pirate, m'lord. We say we'll take a passenger somewhere, we do it." His back straightened, his chin lifted, and he looked evenly at Allystaire as if ready for a fight.

Allystaire considered the man's posture, his expression, studied him closely with narrowed eyes. Then he nodded and extended a gauntleted hand. *Sweet Fortune. This one is like every good bannerman I've ever known.* The bosun took his hand, and they shook. "Take her aboard straightaway, if you please, bann… bosun. There are men in this city who mean her harm."

He nodded, with a curt, "M'lord," and extended a hand to help Yolande up the gangplank, which she slapped away, then strolled halfway up the flexing board with ease. She stopped and turned toward Allystaire.

"Why? Why're ya doin' this after y'widowed me?"

"I told you. I am doing it *because* I widowed you."

She shrugged and nimbly scooted up the ramp. Allystaire turned and mounted his horse and rode straight for the gates of Bend.

No crowd gathered for long between him and the gates. Ardent's hooves rang sharply off the irregularly spaced cobbles with a martial cadence. *Feels rather more like riding* to *a battle than* from *one*, Allystaire mused. He didn't quite let Ardent have his head the way the destrier would've liked for fear of crushing anyone who strayed into the street. Even so, some of the slower moving folk that found themselves out in Bend's afternoon sunlight were scampering for the sides of the road, certain that they would have been trampled had they not cleared the road.

Without a glance back, Allystaire headed through the timber palisade gate, a part of him hoping that one of the guards of Bend would bar his way. As he trotted past, his hand remained wrapped around the haft of his hammer, just beneath the head, preparing to lift it free. Neither guard, in mismatched armor and carrying spears, stepped away from his post. He put the distance of a long bowshot between himself and the walls before he tugged the reins and drew Ardent to a slow walk.

He slipped easily from the saddle and removed his gauntlets, his hands clammy with sweat from the heat of the day. He ran a bare hand along the horse's equally wet neck. "Should have thought more on fodder and water for you, old friend," he murmured, as he felt the ripple of muscle as the horse walked. "Ardent," he said, trying the word out carefully. The horse whickered softly.

"Amazing how quickly that name is working," he snorted. The snort turned into laughter—a long, rolling, almost manic sound that crashed back at him from rows of sun-baked trees lining the road. When his laughter subsided and the last echoes reached his ears, he walked on for several moments in silence.

"I expect Idgen Marte might do what she can to keep the passage of the wagons hidden. May not be much. In the end even I ought to be able to track them, I think."

He got no answer from Ardent or the trees, so he walked on in relative silence for a long while, sorting through his thoughts. In time he began to chide himself. *You've made your whereabouts known to Baron Oyrwyn, emptied your purse, and made an enemy of a choiron of the Sea Dragon who actually seems to command real powers. Anything else?*

Allystaire walked and thought a moment before answering aloud. "I killed some reavers. World is always better with fewer of them. Saved a village worth of folk."

His mind didn't miss a beat. *And what'll they do the next time reavers come along? Needn't even be reavers if Delondeur ever decides to shut Bend down; you said it yourself. Are you going to stay and protect them? Be lord of some fishermen and pig farmers and corn millers?*

"No different than being lord of peat diggers," Allystaire responded, but the words came out hollow and flat. This back-and-forth with himself went on for turns of walking, punctuated with regular stops to allow Ardent to graze and Allystaire to fill water skins and change out of his armor. It was later in the day, but the sun still filled the surrounding forest with soft golden light that went unnoticed as he argued and remonstrated with himself.

"Poor girl. Mind is addled now. What was I thinking chasing Leah off? Idgen Marte was right. I did face ten men, by myself, and lived…" He stopped and shook his head. "Allystaire, you old fool. You are going as crazy as Garth always said you were."

He walked but a dozen paces more, looking to a clearing at his left, when a voice, a voice he knew and yet did not, said his name. "Allystaire." It was a woman's voice, but it carried a note of command in it. He turned, stepped around the front of Ardent, gaping at what he saw.

Underneath a large oak stood a woman, glowing like a soft clean lantern, like a window catching the noonday sun on a cloudless day.

"Allystaire," she said again, and his boots crunched on the stones as he drew, as he was drawn, closer. She was nude, he saw, but something about her nakedness gave her power. He looked only at her face for as long as he could stand, but eventually his eyes were drawn to the rest of her. Long, thick blond hair fell down her back. At least he assumed it was blond, for the glow that emanated from her made it hard to judge. Her body was the epitome of womanly beauty and perfection in symmetry and proportion. Finally, he drew his eyes back to her face.

It was Mol's face. And Leah's. And the fishwife's. And countless others. Audreyn's, his mother's, Dorinne's. Perhaps every woman he had ever known, all in one both old and young, beautiful, powerful, somehow terrible. She did not shift or change; there was something timeless, utterly unchanging about her and yet, she was all of the women he had known, and many more besides.

He could not hold his gaze upon her for long. He barely met her eyes, had an impression of them being golden orbs without pupil or iris. Before he knew it he was dropping hard to his knees a few yards away, and he did not know why.

"Allystaire; do you know who I am?" Her mouth did not appear to move, but the words sounded in his ears all the same.

"No," he said, quietly. He lifted his face back to her, and for the first time in days he felt more fear than anger as he tried to look directly at her.

"I am someone this world had forgotten, or who had forgotten this world. It is difficult to say which."

She was suddenly standing directly in front of him. He hadn't seen her move.

"I remember now. The world must remember, and you will be the instrument that makes it, my Allystaire. My servant and prophet, revelator and paladin." Her hands settled onto his shoulders; through the heavy riding leathers they felt like a fire that burned without pain; it thrilled through his arms, to his core, and down his spine. He drew a breath that caught and burned his lungs. He could not have spoken to protest if he had wanted to. There was no acceptance or denial on his part. There was Power, in front of him, touching him, and making of him what it would.

"Stand, Paladin." He stood, quickly, no pain in his knees or back slowing him. "Give me your left hand." With stunned slowness he lifted it, and she took it in her hands.

Direct contact between her flesh, if flesh it was, and his, almost sent him back to his knees in shock, but her hands held him in place.

"These days I have tested you, Allystaire, and each challenge I placed before you, each foe I sent you to vanquish, you overcame." The Goddess, for Allystaire now knew that was what She was, without thinking it and without saying it, was speaking now with Her lips instead of Her mind. That comforted him somehow, but did not soften the power of Her voice.

"The first time, you saw the work of evil men and you rode toward it when most would ride away. The cries of the child that woke me were carried to your ear by *My* will." She smiled; the sight of it was like a lover's hand caressing his entire body all at once. "And when you heard them you ran to her. You brought aid and comfort to a girl who had no means to repay you. Most knights of this world would have left her, but you did not. You brought succor and hope to her, and of her hope you made a truth; you found her kin, you kept an oath, and you freed her people."

She raised the palm of his hand to her mouth and pressed her lips to it; he let out a strangled gasp.

"With this hand, you will bring Hope back to this world. With this hand, you will mend flesh, heal the sick, refresh the weary and comfort the dying. You cannot—you will not attempt—to reach into Death's demesne, and not every affliction will fall to this Gift, but with it you will do the work I have too long neglected."

His left hand fell back to his side, his body taut like a drawn bowstring. Her voice rang like a harp in the hall of some wise king out of story.

"Give me your right hand."

Allystaire did as he was bid, lifting his right hand to Hers. Nothing in him could possibly have resisted.

"When you found the evil men, the rabid dogs of men, who had burned and killed, raped and enslaved, you fought them and you killed them. You did so with no thought of plunder or glory, no hope of reward, and no trace of cowardice. You raised your hand for the weak and not for yourself. The weak are my people, and now, they are yours as well."

Once again She raised his hand to Her mouth, and once again She kissed him, but instead of kissing the palm, Her lips brushed the flesh of his wrist, and

Her teeth followed. A cry died against his teeth. She lifted her mouth free, and he looked to his wrist. No blood flowed from it. Instead it felt as though something invisible, but bright and powerful, flowed into it. He felt it join with his blood and flow through him, imagined he could feel it sinking into his bones and his muscles, settling, waiting to be called forth.

"With this hand, you will bring Justice back to this world. Raise it in a righteous cause, and your wrath will be terrible to behold. In the defense of the innocent, the weak, the helpless, your strength will be a thing out of legend. Raise your hand with thoughts of winning glory and riches, and battle will turn against you." For a blazing instant, the pain in his arm sang like the clearest trumpet call ever sounded—then was gone.

She released his hand and raised hers to his cheeks. Before he could gather wits enough to understand, she was kissing him, full on the lips, and the kiss was not chaste. It filled his bones for a moment with a flash of fire. When the kiss ended, he would have fallen, but she held him up as easily as he might have an infant.

"You spoke the truth when most men would have lied, and you saw the course it took you to the end. With clear sight and mind, you faced the consequences of your actions. When none were imposed upon you, you took it upon yourself to set right the life of a lone widow."

Her hands stroked his throat, fingertips moving as if drawing runes across it; he felt something settle into his skin, through it, to the workings of his throat. He wanted to cry out, to sing, to scream, and he could not. "From this day no lie may pass your lips, but no man or woman may, by sorcery or trickery, speak falsely to you if you Compel them. That is my final Gift to you today, and the one you may rue the most in the end." She stepped away, and he faltered, his mind overwhelmed.

"Sleep, my Paladin. Nothing will disturb your rest this night; it may be the last easy rest you ever have. We will speak again." Then she was gone.

For Allystaire, it was as if brightest noontide had suddenly turned to moonless, starless night, and he fell forward and knew no more.

* * *

He was pulling himself from the grass into a nearly panicked fighting stance, hands groping for a weapon, before he even realized he had woken. He shook his head and cleared his eyes to find himself in a clean and ordered campsite. A fire was laid in a circle of stones, Ardent picketed to a nearby oak, and his saddle and tack were neatly piled beside him along with his armor and arms. He wore only his riding breeches.

Slowly, certain things dawned on him. "My back does not hurt," he murmured. "Nor does my knee." He reached back with a hand to massage the small of his back, his fingers finding and tracing the scar of an arrow that took him halfway between spine and kidney more than half a score of years before. "It always hurts when I sleep on the ground."

"What happened? Have I been dreaming?" He bent and rooted among his saddlebags, his hands pushing clothes aside till he pulled out three leather purses. One was limp as a sock; the other two had but small bulges along their bottoms.

"No. No I have not," he said, dropping them to the grass with a touch of disgust. "I did not," he repeated, gaining strength from the words. He looked up, lifting his eyes above the treetops to the clouds that shrouded the morning sun. He had slept unusually late. A gleam of sunlight found his eye, causing him to turn away quickly from the sting. "Point taken." He stood up straight, rolled his neck around his shoulders with a deep breath. "What do I call you then," he spoke aloud, raising his voice to the trees, the sky, the sun beyond. "Goddess? Mother? Have you a name?"

He received no answer, but he nodded anyway and began to pack his camp. On a clean, flat rock by the fire he found a loaf of bread, a slab of cheese, and a steaming mug of tea. He nodded again, saying, "Mother it is, I suppose."

Allystaire knelt down and tore off a hunk of bread. *Probably ensorcelled. Or you're still dreaming.* He eyed the brown loaf in his hands and said aloud, "This bread is no dream. Neither was She." His words rang with certainty; he breathed in the warm morning air like a condemned man set free and tore into the bread. It tasted good, was still faintly warm, and took some chewing. The cheese was cold and firm enough for his teeth to leave marks in.

The tea was so strong he nearly gagged and spat. Instead he set his jaw and cheeks and slurped it down in two great scorching gulps. He ate at a deliberate pace though, neither slowly nor quickly, but methodically, till the food was gone.

His meal finished, he rose, dressed, doused the fire, packed his arms and bags, saddled the horse, and rode off into a mid-morning silence broken only by Ardent's hooves and the occasional bird, not even by his own voice, aloud or in his mind.

CHAPTER 15

The First Miracle

"They have made more progress than I had hoped," Allystaire said aloud to Ardent, as he led the horse down the beaten track of fresh wheel ruts. "Rain must not have fallen as heavily here." It was dusk, and on a slight rise above a turn in the road he saw the two wagons in an L-shape, smoke of a fire rising behind them.

Slowly, he led the horse up the rise, expecting a sentry, particularly Idgen Marte or Renard, to spot his approach and greet him. None did so. He paused, but only to free his hammer and let go Ardent's reins, wrapping both hands around the iron-banded wood. The destrier followed him easily up the rise, and the two of them made enough noise to rouse the camp. A greasy weight settled on the bottom of his stomach as he cleared the wagons and found the several dozen folk of Thornhurst gathered around, Idgen Marte standing in their middle and speaking, Renard standing at her side, holding his spear uncertainly. Allystaire stopped beyond the circle to listen.

"I know how to bind wounds," she was saying, "and to sew them. Not how to mend bones." Her voice was even and her posture steady, balanced, graceful. "I can do naught for your lad but ease his way," she added clearly, but carefully, choosing her words slowly.

A murmur ran through the crowd; Allystaire heard sobs, unease, grumbling. He shook his head and stepped forward, sliding his hammer back onto its iron loop with a distinctive *thunk*. The slick weight in his stomach dissolved and flowed lightly up and into him; he felt it gathering like a storm in his breast. "Where is the lad?" His voice cut through the chatter like a horn cutting the stillness before battle to signal the advance. "Take me to him."

All of them turned slowly to stare at him; only Idgen Marte and Renard actually moved. The crowd didn't part until Allystaire growled, "Now! Take me to the boy!"

That got them moving, scrambling out of his way to clear a path, while Idgen Marte pointed with her chin to the back of one of the wagons. Allystaire quickly hauled himself inside and knelt down; before him on the bed of the wagon lay a small form covered in a rough blanket. The wool stuck wetly to his misshapen legs.

"He was capering around in front of the wagons, tripped and fell right under the wheel," Idgen Marte told Allystaire as she strolled up to the wagon behind him. "Rolled right over his legs before we could stop the horses." She leaned against the back of the wagon, looking haggard. "Have we anything to worry about behind us?"

Allystaire shook his head faintly, replying, "Not soon, I think," in a faraway tone. In his mind he thought on the Goddess's words of the night before, as he flexed his left hand.

With this hand, you will mend flesh, heal the sick, refresh the weary, and comfort the dying, She had told him, and the memory of Her lips upon his palm burned as he felt something gathering in his hand. He held it like a fist, as if trapping something, and lowered his hand to touch the child's sweaty brow. The boy whimpered and thrashed. Likely, he'd been given as much wine as he could hold to keep him asleep.

Allystaire spread his hand till it half-covered the boy's head and face and pushed his senses through his skin. "Heal the sick, mend flesh," he murmured. "This boy is not dying," he added through gritted teeth. He felt something moving, some wave of intense feeling move from his chest and through his arm, down into his fingers.

"Why are you...what in the Cold are you doing?" Idgen Marte faltered in confusion and shock. Allystaire threw aside the blanket with his right hand and stuck his hand on the boy's broken, misshapen knees. Something moved in him; something moved *through* him—an intense love, a boundless well of compassion, and a sorrow that called tears to his eyes.

Beneath his firm grip, the boy writhed and screamed. And then his bones began to meld as the healing flowed. The lad's scream became a strangled gasp, and Allystaire clutched at the side of the wagon to keep himself upright as the torrent poured through him, as the child's legs mended and straightened and finally *snapped* into place. His cries died as his flesh knit itself like a curtain suddenly closed. His eyes opened and he scrambled up out of his makeshift bed. Allystaire slumped to the floor of the wagon, supporting himself on knees and fists, streaming sweat. Idgen Marte, eyes wide in her dark face, backed half a step from the wagon's edge, staring at him.

"What did you do? What have you become?"

Allystaire lifted his eyes from the wooden planks and turned his sweat-streaked face toward her. "She called me…*paladin*." The last word somehow lifted him, in triumph, and he heaved one last great breath as he sat on his haunches, nodding in slow certainty. "A paladin."

Idgen Marte's mouth worked soundlessly for a moment, and her head shook slowly. Finally, she whispered, "I knew there was…so you're a…a paladin…" She finally laughed, nervously, "So you've come to believe you're a story too, eh? You've cracked?"

Allystaire said nothing, his lips bent in a faint, crooked smile. He stepped down from the wagon, suddenly clutching the tailgate as his head spun for a moment. Then he reached up, gesturing with his hand for the lad to come to him. The child stood nervously, so Allystaire lifted him clear of the wagon, setting him down lightly upon his feet. The torn, bloodstained tatters of his trousers fluttered around the boy's whole, healed legs. He looked up at Allystaire with calm but worshipful eyes.

"Come now, Idgen Marte. You witnessed what I…" There, Allystaire paused and shook his head. "No. Not what I did. What was done through me. You saw." He looked down at the boy and patted his shoulder. "What is your name, lad?"

"Gram, m'lord," he replied, the same awed but still expression on his small, thin face.

Allystaire turned to face Idgen Marte again; his faint smile still lacked mirth, but there was something less grim in it, now, something with a promise of more than fury and death. "Stay here with Idgen Marte for a moment, Gram." The boy nodded lightly at the warrior and wandered back toward the wagons to stand, trusting, at Idgen Marte's side.

"What're you planning to do," Idgen Marte asked, as one of her hands settled on Gram's shoulders.

"Thought I would make a bit of a speech."

He rounded the wagon and left the two of them behind, walking into the circle of light cast by the flames, seeming brighter now that dark had overtaken dusk.

"Good people of Thornhurst," Allystaire half-shouted, drawing their attention to him; they stopped whatever tasks they'd set to, returned from wherever they'd scrambled but moments before. "I come to you this eve with a message." He paused, waiting for their eyes to turn to him; he felt more than saw, for many sat too far from the flames to be more than shapes.

"A message of hope from someone who has heard your suffering and come to answer your cries." He turned toward Idgen Marte and Gram and waved a hand. "Come here, Gram."

As Gram walked over into the circle of light, a gasp ran through the crowd. A man and woman, the former hobbling and with a fresh scattering of bruises on his face, pushed their way through the crowd and swept the lad into their arms. Gram remained quiet. The man handed him off to the woman and turned to Allystaire.

"What've you done?" His tone was shocked and his jaw sagging.

"I told you; I bring you hope," Allystaire said quietly. He turned to the crowd and raised one of his hands, palm out. "How many of you are godly folk, who fear Braech, are careful never to curse Fortune? Eh? How many of you listen to Urdaran and turn away from your toil and your burdens in this life?"

No hands raised. Allystaire lowered his, nodding slowly.

"I do not blame you. When does Fortune ever turn her wheel toward such as you?" There were a few rumbles in the small crowd. "Braech would praise the courage and cunning of men who stole your goods, or your very lives, with fire and sword." Deathly silence greeted that. Allystaire thought he saw a brief flash of heat lightning on the far, dark horizon. "Urdaran offers you no solace or respite, only empty bellies and vacant eyes.

But I bring you hope. I bring you a Goddess who woke to the cries of the least of you, and who brought her weeping to my ears so that I might save her." He turned to Gram, still wrapped placidly in his mother's arms. "And now for second time, this Goddess has given me a chance to save one of your children. It is because of Her—the Mother—that this boy walks again."

Gram wriggled away from his mother's arms and came forward to Allystaire, saying, "When y'healed me, m'lord, I thought I heard a lady's voice singin'. And something very warm-like, hotter than the hearthstones after a day's fire."

A dozen folk stood, shouting questions; Allystaire raised his hands to calm them, and finally Gram's father spoke above the rest.

"Is this a trick? How do we know y'aren't in some sort o'game here?"

"That's not fair, Chals," another man shouted from back in the crowd. "Yer boy's bones was showin' and he was done fer. There still blood on his trews? Was e'rywhere on the wheel and soakin' into the road. If he's walkin', 'twere magic and no trick."

Allystaire raised his voice above them all, his battle voice, but he issued no commands. "I do not lie to you, Thornhurst. I *cannot*," he added, surprising himself. "I near beggared myself, and I killed men—which I do not do lightly—to save you. And even as I saved you, I did not understand why." He smiled as he spoke, his hands raising, wrists pointing upwards. "But now I do. The Mother was Calling me."

"Does She call us?" Gram and his family fell back into the crowd as the shouting began again. "What are we to do? Do we give homage?" Similar questions filled the night air till Allystaire once again called for silence.

He let his eyes trail into the darkness where Idgen Marte stood by the wagon, then back to the village folk. "As for worship…" He paused, shrugged. "I do not know. But together, we will learn, as Thornhurst is rebuilt."

"Why you? Why not me?" A younger, male voice singled itself out, but the speaker did not push forward. Renard, standing a bit apart from the crowd, turned as if to locate the speaker.

Allystaire struggled for an answer. All that the Goddess had told him the night before sprang to his mind, but before he could answer, Idgen Marte called out, "This Goddess has sent you a paladin, boy. A holy knight of legend." With her casual, graceful saunter, she emerged into the light. "What more ought any of you to ask tonight? I saw a miracle. A thing of tales, in front of my eyes, and now all of you see the same," she pointed toward Gram, "as that lad lives. Celebrate that and leave off questioning for one night."

In his head, Allystaire heard Idgen Marte's words as if plucked out upon a harp, and he felt a swell as of voices shaping a note, and in his mind he heard Her voice. *Others will be Called, my Paladin. These are my people now, and yours.*

The music slowly ebbed. Around him, the folk of Thornhurst, singly and then in groups, sank to one knee, lowering their faces. Allystaire shook his head, opened his mouth, then stopped, as Her voice sounded again. *Remember well that you belong to them.* Then, carefully, he too bent a knee and lowered his head, and on a hilltop where walked a lad who should have died, they—Paladin, warrior, soldier, villagers—felt something birth itself into the world in the still summer night.

* * *

When he awoke early the next morning, sitting upright against a wagon wheel, the resurgence of pain in his knee and his back led Allystaire to wonder, briefly, if the previous day had been an elaborate flight of fancy. *She promised a restful night,* he reminded himself, *not freedom from pain.* The tang of the old wounds was all the sharper for a day's respite, and as he levered himself to his feet, he heard the usual sharp cracks from his joints. His hammer had lain at his right hand throughout the night, and now he bent, wincing, to pick it up and slide it into its spot at his hip.

He stretched his arms wide, yawning, then turned east to watch the sky slowly lighten. He heard quiet footsteps behind him, but did not turn around; he simply waited.

"Tell me. All of it." Idgen Marte's voice was soft and almost pleading.

Somehow, Allystaire was unable, or unwilling, to turn from the sunrise and the way it so slowly, but so inevitably, rolled back the dark. "I think She was guiding my steps from…well, from the day I rode into Thornhurst," he said, frowning, as the woman stepped to his side and followed his eyes toward the horizon.

Idgen Marte didn't respond, but she turned her eyes to him, watching, waiting; he could feel her impatience in the way she rocked forward on her toes, the way her long frame seemed coiled and taut.

Finally he turned from the sun and faced her. "At the assize, even before the assize, I could *feel* the power that radiated from the choiron. I felt the power granted him by the Sea Dragon. I saw him bend his will against people when they spoke. He tried to silence me, and he failed." He swallowed, turned away from Idgen Marte's intense brown eyes, and resumed watching the glinting daybreak. "He found in my favor. Told me I had been bold and cunning, that Braech favored me. That Braech wanted my service." He heard Idgen Marte gasp, and he turned back to her, holding up a hand. "I told him what I thought of a god whose favor was ever for the victorious. He dismissed the baron's claims, but there was a woman. A widow of one of the reavers."

Idgen Marte smiled knowingly, shaking her head. "How much silver did you give her?"

"Most of it," Allystaire admitted, shrugging heavily. He laughed faintly. "I thought I left Oyrwyn with gold enough to last me a year of good living. Surely enough time to start earning more. Nigh on a month and the bulk is gone."

Idgen Marte poked him with a knife-edged hand, sharply, in the side of the ribs, where his boiled leather vest didn't protect him. "You've no idea how to tell a story, do you? On with it."

He flinched away from her playful, but still painful strike, and rubbed lightly at the spot she'd hit. "Fine, fine. I had put the widow on a boat and given her enough silver to buy a boat of her own, I think," he continued. "I know less about boats than I do farming," he grumbled. Idgen Marte glared and he picked up the story again quickly. "I rode out of Bend. It was no trouble to follow the tracks of the wagons. And then She was there." He paused, searched for words, and found none, but went on anyway; Idgen Marte's eyes were rapt. "She told me that she had tested me. Mol, the villagers, the slavers, the widow, all of it. And then She bestowed upon me three…gifts. Three…powers? I do not know what to call them."

Allystaire looked down at his hands, spread his fingers wide; both hands were calloused, scarred, rough and heavy, with swollen knuckles and large fingers, some of them crooked. "You saw the first of them last night. The lad. Healing him." He held up his left hand, turned the palm toward himself and studied his skin. It looked much the same as it had done for years.

"And the others?"

He slowly shook his head. "I suspect you will see them." Allystaire felt keenly for a moment that some other sense was appraising the warrior in front of him, using his eyes. A presence was weighing and judging her.

Idgen Marte laughed lightly, tossing her long dark braid. "Now *that* is story-telling. Drama." Her mirth faded quickly, though, and she studied his face. "In the stories I heard, paladins were men of fair face and fairer voice. Refined and courteous. Parthalian, for instance. The stories say he was so beautiful to look upon that no maid could refuse him, yet in his honor, he never asked. There's nothing about being broken-nosed and linkless, with all the wit and charm of a hunting hound."

"You forgot old and stoop-backed."

"See? You're hardly some fair and flawless knight out of minstrel song."

Allystaire snorted. "I have known many knights. Too many. Those who remain fair do so because they die young. Some have glib tongues or cunning minds, but no more than other men."

"Allystaire," Idgen Marte said, stepping closer to him and wrapping her arms around his neck in an embrace that was half sisterly, half back-pounding warrior's embrace. And she did pound his back, twice, with a firm fist. "If any true paladin ever walked this world, I think he probably looked like you." She stepped back, laughing at the confused flush in his cheeks. "More important, he felt like you," she added, poking him, not too lightly, in the shoulder that had been skewered by a slaver's sword not long before.

"You told me I was terrifying, not two days ago," Allystaire replied, doubtfully.

"You are," she said, flashing that faint and knowing smile. "And that's precisely part of what I meant. But I think the villagers have all realized, or will soon, that they aren't the sort of folk who need fear you."

Idgen Marte turned and walked off, leaving Allystaire alone with the first real light of dawn greeting his eyes. He blinked against it for a moment, then followed the woman toward the blanket-huddled shapes of the villagers and began to rouse them. He was gentler than Idgen Marte, who didn't quite resort to kicks, but wasn't shy about threatening them.

Renard soon joined her, his rumbling voice booming over the unseasonable morning cool. *Watching two of nature's own sergeants at work is a beautiful thing*, Allystaire reflected. Soon the Thornhurst folk, down to the youngest, were in various stages of preparation—building up fires, fetching cookpots, tending to horses. He soon realized that the best he could do was stay out of their way. *Bit like commanding men again*, he thought. *Two men, anyway, and a whole gaggle of camp followers.* He winced, not for the first or last time, at his own thoughts, then went to tend to his horses.

The previous night, he had picketed Ardent with the palfrey and the mule, and as he walked to the treeline where they stood, Allystaire paused when he saw a small figure moving among his horses: Mol. He took a few steps toward her and must've given himself away, for she spun to face him. In the pale light, under the boughs of trees, her face was half in shadow, and yet the pools of her eyes seemed a slightly brighter darkness within it.

"Mol." He said her name quietly as he stopped in his tracks. The girl stared at him for a moment.

"I was talkin' to Ardent," she said, matter-of-factly. "He was waitin' for you to learn his name. Says it took ya too long, but then he seems t'think y'aren't very keen."

Allystaire smiled uneasily. "Says all that, does he?"

"Thinks it," the girl responded with a shrug. She turned and started patting the horse's flank.

Allystaire took another couple of steps toward the girl and the animals. "Mol, did you hear me talk last night?"

"I could hear it. The Mother told me y'were t'heal the boy."

"She talks to you?"

"Betimes," Mol replied, turning back to him. "I wish she did all the time. Her voice is the best singin' in the brightest day," she added wistfully. "I think She came t'me after the reavers left and I was alone. And there are some times I don't remember rightly. I remember bein' angry, so angry at you, but not why, but She told me ya'd set it right." She trailed off, struggling for words. She bit her lips and continued to stroke the grey horse that stood placidly above her and finally said, "And ya did."

"Has She told you what we are to do next?"

Mol shook her head quickly. "Ya'll figure it out. Y'have so far."

Allystaire's eyes sank to the ground, and he sighed deeply. "Guidance, Mol. I know how to give orders to knights and soldiers, not how to…" He quieted as the girl walked to him and took his hand between both of hers.

"Have faith. In yourself as well as Her." Something in Mol's voice had changed, from one moment to the next, as soon as she had taken Allystaire's hand. Her demeanor had grown serious, her face calm in a way that didn't seem at all like the child he'd come to know on the road.

"Faith is not one of my few virtues," Allystaire protested. "You noted that yourself, once."

Mol fixed him with a large-eyed stare, and said, "Remember that She had faith in you before you did in Her."

She dropped his hand and padded away quietly without a backward glance. Allystaire fed and saddled and packed his horses and mule. "Time you had a break, I suppose," he murmured to Ardent, as he tied a lead to his halter, as well as one to the mule's, and gathered the reins of the palfrey. The destrier tossed his head in protest and pulled against the lead. Allystaire tugged it gently and started to mount the palfrey, but the smaller bay pulled away from him.

He tried again, and once more the riding horse shied away, leaving him with one foot in the stirrup and one bouncing in the dry grass. Finally he planted his foot and hopped away. Destrier and palfrey both stopped, staring at him with big liquid eyes.

"A conspiracy," he murmured. Begrudgingly he untied the rope lead from Ardent and affixed it to the palfrey's halter, then led his animals down the hill and to the road, where the small caravan was slowly gathering, Idgen Marte at its head and Renard at the back. Allystaire tied the palfrey and the mule to a wagon and slid up onto Ardent's saddle. It took him only the briefest moment to realize that all eyes were fixed on him; he sat straight in the saddle, looked to Idgen Marte, and gave a simple nod of command. She raised a hand—whips cracked, wheels creaked, and the wagons began to roll.

The pace they set was plodding and careful, but steady, covering much more slowly the very terrain Allystaire and Mol had ridden over but a few days before. The cooling calm of the post-storm air was gone, burned away by summer's oppressive heat, and once more moisture was thickening the air and worsening the heat. Patches of grass along the dusty, beaten track were browning. In most cases, though, the villagers, even the children, bore the heat well.

Allystaire relaxed his senses, sitting easily atop Ardent, reins in hand. He reflected on the past few days, turning over the events. *How much did She guide me? Or Mol, for that matter?* He thought over Mol's words, her constant questions, her insight. Her words from the dawn came back to him; *Remember that She had faith in you before you did in Her.* He grunted, smiling in spite of himself, and looked back at the horse plodding along behind him. "Have you faith in me as well?" Ardent didn't answer. *If he had then I would know for sure I had gone mad.*

It wasn't until well after noon—he, Idgen Marte, and Renard insisted on no pauses for a midday meal, so everyone ate bread and dried fish as they walked—that he realized that a crowd of folk, mostly the younger, had clumped around him.

He halted, suddenly focusing on their faces; they were browning again, now in their second day back in the open sun, and their eyes followed him with a kind of fearful awe. *They look like a pack of pups waiting for a good word from the kennel master,* he thought.

"No time to stand about gawping," he said gently, gesturing toward the dusty wagon track with one hand. "There are many miles yet to go." A few of the younger children dashed away, but one of the knot of villagers, an older woman, spoke up.

"This lot was sayin' that in the stories, s'good luck to touch one what's been touched by a god," the woman said, her voice wavering a bit. "'Specially paladins."

"And where have they been hearing stories about saints or god-touched folk or paladins?"

"Well, they 'aven't. Been no time fer stories since we left that rotten town. But the woman, Idgen Marte, she told some of the little ones that. They been sayin' it all day."

Allystaire groaned inwardly and started tromping forward again, his boots clouding dust behind him. "Did she now? Well, I have never been good luck before, and besides, the Mother is not Fortune; do not mistake her for that fickle and inconstant deity." *Fickle and inconstant deity? Am I a freezing theologian now? Am I setting dogma?* He had the sense of being smiled at, a knowing and puissant smile in an ancient face observing him distantly. *I suppose I am.*

"Better luck, I would say," Allystaire went on, as a few of the crowd closed in, "is having a paladin with you on the road home, ready to help you rebuild your village. It is not luck you need now; it is hard work and the willingness to do it." *And luck, that they can get any crops in, or find any game, or that some winter stores are already set by…*

That seemed to satisfy them, and they dispersed back among the larger crowd that walked between the wagons.

* * *

In the evening, with a gasp of sunshine left, Allystaire had drawn them into a camp much like the one of the night before—well off the road, up a slight rise and against the treeline, the wagons drawn into an L-shape with a gap between them. Rather, he had suggested they stop, and Idgen Marte and Renard had directed the making of the campsite. He tended to his own horses and watched Idgen Marte and Renard organize the cooking and distribution of food; the stores that the reavers had bought or pilfered as they prepared for their next expedition had been neatly liberated by Idgen Marte when she'd followed Allystaire the day he rescued Mol's kinfolk.

He drew aside Idgen Marta and Renard with a glance and a jerk of his chin. "If ever I have to move an army," he said, "remind me to make one of you Quartermaster and the other Chief Bannerman."

"Which one gets paid more," Idgen Marte asked, without missing a beat.

"The one who does not tell folk to rub against me like I am some kind of talisman."

"Beggin' your pardon, m'lord, but *are* you lucky?" Renard took half a step forward, a large and gnarled hand reaching out toward Allystaire, before he let out a guffaw. "Just takin' the piss, m'lord, if I may. Being out among these folk has me feelin' like a man again, instead of some useless toy soldier."

"Well, Renard, I have a man's work in mind tomorrow." Allystaire's face was somber in the shadows of oncoming dusk. "I imagine we shall make Thornhurst tomorrow, but something grim awaits these folk—a great pile of their kinfolk burned to ash and bone upon their green. I doubt they have forgotten it, but likely they have not precisely remembered it, either. I mean to gather up men who can hold shovels and take them on ahead in the morning. Find them for me, aye?"

Renard nodded; he only just stopped short of clicking his heels before he trotted off.

"Women and children shouldn't have to see it, hrm? These people aren't as weak as all that." Idgen Marte smirked at him.

"I never said they were weak. But I suspect they are used to burying their dead one at a time," Allystaire replied, his jaw tightening a little.

"Fair enough," Idgen Marte allowed, still smirking. "But what are we poor women to do if something should assault the caravan while our brave, strong paladin is away?"

"Pray for the poor bastard before you skewer him," Allystaire retorted, grinning in spite of himself. He reflected a moment and asked, "What are your thoughts on gods and prayer?"

"Scared, mostly," she replied. "That choiron, for instance. A right cold one, and with real power put into his hands. Urdaran's priests, when they aren't frauds, which is rare, are useless. Might as well be eunuchs. If I ever went into a temple, it was Fortune's." She hooked her thumbs into her swordbelt. "Life of a sword-at-hire, I suppose. Take any edge."

"And the Mother?"

Idgen Marte grew quiet, brown eyes sliding toward the dusk-shadowed grass and dust at their feet. She kicked at a tuft with the toe of her boot. "I know what I saw in the wagon last eve. And I know I've heard tell of priests or magi could do that if conditions were right."

"Idgen Marte, look at me," Allystaire said softly. She raised her calm, wide, knowing brown eyes to his. "I am what I told you I am. And you know the truth of it. You feel Her yourself, or you soon will, I think. I need to know if you are with me. Beyond all stories, links, or coy answers." He extended his right hand, the same one she'd taken in contract but a few nights ago, though it felt like a lifetime had passed.

She considered a moment, but she took his forearm with her warm, rough hand and nodded once, curtly. "I am."

For Allystaire, the moment felt heavy, but comforting, like sliding his arm through the straps of a shield made to fit his height, weight, and reach. He pumped her arm once, nodded. "Good. Now, I suppose I ought to go set some more dogma."

"Just don't write anything down," Idgen Marte suggested, in a helpful tone. "Then no one can examine any contradictions later."

Allystaire laughed a little and paused to inhale deeply before setting his shoulders and walking toward the central-most cookfire. A few seconds later, all eyes were turned to him. *Just like giving orders to soldiers. Only these folk are not about to die.* "I thought perhaps I should speak a bit more about the Mother," he began, as soon as their chatter had died down. "I do not mean to bore you with sermons or hound you with teachings. But I want to say something bluntly: the next few days will be hard. You will have to rebuild and bury not only many of your kith and kin, but much of the lives you knew." He waited for his words to sink in.

"I need you to understand that the Mother will be with you. With us," he continued. Yet She will do no work for you; She will make no needful task vanish with a puff of magic." He turned slightly and raised a hand toward the last bit of sunlight left in the western sky. "The sun is not always above you; it does not always warm your back or light your way. But you know it will always return. I think the Mother is like the sun in this regard; She will see to it that we have what we need, and occasionally more. It was fitting last eve that we prayed to Her as the sun set. I think we should do so again, if you would."

He turned back to them and raised a warning hand. "First rule, if we must have rules: the Mother compels no man, woman, or child to worship Her. Come to Her freely or not at all. Try to bring a man to Her by coercing him, or bribing him, or forcing him, and his will be no true faith. Nor will yours. If you would pray with me, then let us do so. If you would not, I will speak no ill to you or of you."

With that, he knelt, peering through his brows to watch who else knelt— Mol and Gram wormed their way through the crowd, as children will, and a gaggle of other youngsters followed them; they all knelt around him. Idgen Marte, Timmar, and Gram's parents knelt, followed by a veritable wave of kneeling, and if any of the folk in the small caravan remained standing, they did so in silence and shadow, where Allystaire could not see them.

CHAPTER 16

The Last Reaver

"Allystaire. Wake up." Renard's voice had a rough timbre that sawed sleep into pieces, like a bad knife cutting into a stale loaf. Allystaire's mind sprang to wakefulness, his body feeling a bit sawn as well. The hooded lantern dangling from Renard's hand did him no favors; in the pitch darkness its light was far too bright for just-woken eyes.

"What is it?" He winced as he pushed himself to stand and took up his hammer.

"Someone sneakin' into the camp. Idgen Marte caught him. He was armed."

"Is he still alive?" Allystaire asked, half-fearing the answer.

"Dirtied a bit maybe, but alive. We're not sure what he was after, but men don't skulk about with knives and darkened faces for no reason."

"Everyone needs a hobby, Renard," Allystaire quipped, as he followed the tall, bearded soldier to one of the dampened fire pits. His eyes had adjusted, and Renard let a little more light from his lantern. A man lay sprawled on the ground, his hands bound behind him, feet knotted together with rope, his face blackened with ash and clay. Idgen Marte stood above him; her silhouette and the short, heavily curved bow in her hand were unmistakable in the darkness.

Allystaire walked up to him, just out of lunging reach, and went on one knee to get a close look; he made sure to drop the head of his hammer, conspicuously, into the dirt not far from the man's knee, and to wrap his hand around the haft as he studied the intruder.

Behind the darkened face, Allystaire could see fear masquerading as anger, and he realized that the man in front of them was a beardless youth. Tall for his age, but too young, Allystaire thought, for dark business.

"What is your name?"

The young man paused, licked his dry lips, eyes darting side to side. "Gerold."

Allystaire knew—with a certainty akin to the way he knew the feel of his own hammer or how to take Ardent into a charge—that the young man lied. He considered this odd certainty for a moment, thinking over the Goddess's words to him. He studied the youth's face and focused his will upon him. He felt something gather like a hammer blow that stopped just above the lad's head, then dissipated and flowed into him, and Allystaire could then feel a connection between them, like a cord joining their minds. He tugged on it.

"What is your name?"

"Norbert," the lad answered, seeming startled by the sound of his own voice.

Allystaire focused more intently, narrowing his eyes in concentration. "Why were you sneaking into our camp?"

His eyes wide with alarm, the lad answered fast, "I thought I could kill you. For killin' my crew."

"You were one of the reavers then, who razed Thornhurst?" Allystaire heard the sound of a bowstring being drawn, of creaking wood. Idgen Marte had nocked an arrow and now trained it on the bound form. "We are not murderers," he hissed at her. She lowered the bow and let up on the string, but the arrow remained nocked. "Why were you with those slavers?"

"I had just joined 'em; I weren't really a part of the…the job. I was lookin' after the horses. Captain left me and another new fella out here w' some spare mounts and supplies, said we were t'watch fer pursuit and meet back in the warehouse in three days. Other fella lost 'is nerve and ran but I went into Bend only to find it all in an uproar, everyone on about how the crew were killed by some mad knight, and I been followin' this caravan since last eve." As the youth spoke, his face grew more and more pale, more strained; his eyes bugged out, the whites of them huge in his face.

Allystaire looked up at Idgen Marte's shadowed face, and she shook her head very slightly; the young man had managed to stay hidden from all of them until tonight. He tried to push himself away from Allystaire, his face set in a mask of terror, but he couldn't go far before brushing up against the stones of the firepit.

"What've ya done t'me? I'll not say more," the lad all but whimpered, turning his face away. Suddenly he seemed very much a child.

"I have two more questions, and you *will* answer them if you want to live to see the dawn," Allystaire said quietly, leaning forward and reaching out for Norbert's jaw, turning the lad's face toward his with carefully exerted pressure. Norbert could turn to face him, or his jaw could break. He turned, albeit slowly.

"You will find, Norbert, that you cannot lie to me. My first question is this: did you kill any of the folk in Thornhurst?" Allystaire released his jaw, and the lad worked it as though it hurt.

"I didn't, m'lord, I didn't," he said, all in a rush. "I cared for the horses and was just learnin' the rest."

"Good. And my second question: why had you joined with the reavers?" Once again, he mentally gave the cord that linked them a hard, sharp tug.

The lad swallowed a few times, looking hard at Allystaire, breathing heavily. Finally, he said, "I watched my da and his die with bent backs from cuttin' peat up in Oyrwyn. I couldn't face it, m'lord. Gods help me, I couldn't. Thought joinin' a warband were better, even if it meant I died younger'n them, even if the band were brigands. I knowed they were, m'lord, I did. But I took a long look at the bog and decided that brigands looked better."

Allystaire nodded slowly. He stood, picking up his hammer, but making sure the heavy iron head dangled more or less at Norbert's eye level. "We have a volunteer for the morrow, Renard."

"M'lord? That wise?"

"The more hands, the lighter the work, no?"

"Is this because he's from the freezin' moors?" Idgen Marte snapped, slipping the nocked arrow back into the quiver at her hip.

"It might be," Allystaire said. "He spoke truly when he said he killed no one in Thornhurst."

"How do you know?" He could feel her anger, hotter and brighter than the fire in Renard's lantern. Renard took a careful step away from them.

"I told you, Idgen Marte, that you would see the Goddess's other Gifts in time. Did I not?"

That gave pause; the spark of her anger dimmed, but did not extinguish. "He should hang," she insisted, though a little uncertainly.

"He may yet. But not tonight. All of you, get some sleep. I will take the remainder of the evening watch. It should not be very long."

She was still angry, but Idgen Marte knew he'd brook no further argument; she and Renard retreated, leaving Allystaire alone with the hog-tied, would-be reaver.

"I don't suppose you'd untie my hands, m'lord, so I might sleep?" Norbert ventured quietly.

"If I do, will you try to work your feet free and do a runner?

"Yes." A pause. "Dammit!"

The rest of the night passed in silence, Allystaire wearily walking the perimeter of the camp until dawn.

* * *

Allystaire, Renard, Norbert, Timmar, and a half-dozen other village men left the camp as the first grey light of daybreak fell over it. Most of the men shot dark looks at the newcomer and grumbled when Allystaire fastened a rope around Norbert's neck and tied it off on Ardent's pommel.

Rubbing the horse's neck, and reasoning that he wouldn't stand being left behind anyway, Allystaire said loud enough for all to hear, "Ardent, if the man on the end of the rope tries to run, snap his neck." The horse whinnied in agreement.

Norbert paled, and he wasn't the only one. "Uncanny animal," Allystaire heard one of the village men mutter. *Let them all think so*, Allystaire thought. When he caught Renard's eye, he winked lightly; the soldier's beard parted with a small and secret smile. He cut Norbert's legs free, so he could walk, and then the group of ten men set off at a brisk pace. They bore shovels and mattocks, more fruits of the slavers outfitting themselves at Allystaire's expense. Only Renard and Allystaire carried weapons; the former his spear and the latter his hammer, and both had opted for leathers instead of armor.

They reached the outskirts of Thornhurst not long after the sun had crested the treetops to the east, but Allystaire could smell it long before the road turned and opened on the first buildings—the huge stink of fire, the appallingly familiar-seeming scent of charred flesh, like a great outdoor cooking pit, but wrong in a way that weighed heavily on the mind as well as the stomach.

Help them, Mother, he suddenly prayed, inwardly. *They have never seen the like before. Give them the strength to bear this task. May they never face another akin to it.* He could see their steps falter, slow, and then stop, the telltale tinge of bile growing in their cheeks. "Renard," he said suddenly, "the vinegar."

The bearded man nodded and swung a sack off one shoulder. "Gather round now lads, in a line and quick." The men snapped to the note of authority in Renard's voice; he handed each of them a large square of cloth, then produced an earthenware jug.

"Fold 'em like you would to keep the dust out of your mouth and nose in a bad summer. Come on now." Farmers all, they needed no instruction, and soon each held a folded rag. "Hold 'em out!" He thumbed open the jug, its cork hanging by a length of string, and poured generous measures of vinegar over each man's rag, then one for himself, and all except Norbert and Allystaire tied a soaking rag over mouth and nose.

"The smell will still sting, men, but the rags will help. Plenty of vinegar if they dry out," Allystaire told them. "What we do here today will sting in other ways," he went on, more quietly, "but it needs doing. You have all buried friends and kin before. Think of this the same way—gone to their last rest. Gone to the Mother. As the sun warms the earth they rest in, so will She keep them in the next world," he finished, before he even knew what he was saying.

Her words came back to him, floating across his mind like a well-loved and remembered song. *Prophet and revelator.*

"Do I get one o'them rags, m'lord?" Norbert asked, his ash-and-clay-darkened face running with rivulets of sweat, his voice jerking Allystaire out of his sudden and brief reverie.

"No," he said simply, coldly, and some of the village men turned away quickly. Despite their hidden faces, he could see the ripple of fear that ran through their bodies at the sound of his chilled voice.

"Please m'lord—" Norbert's words were cut off as Allystaire turned to him and wrapped his hand hard around the lad's jaw, holding his mouth open; only a whimpering breath came out as Allystaire leaned forward.

"You will breathe every bit of this miasma. You will smell every bit of charred flesh and you will look at every single burnt bone. Every one. Do you hear me?" Allystaire leaned closer until his forehead was nearly touching the smaller man's, his face suddenly white with anger, his voice like a blade being inched from its sheath. "You will see every bit of the *job* your crew did. Do you hear me?"

Norbert nodded feebly, as much as he was able, air creaking in his throat, a tear leaking from one eye and cutting a line through the muck on his face. Allystaire let go and stepped away; the angry red imprints of his fingers stood out like welts on Norbert's neck and jaw, having cut quickly through the ash.

"What about you, m'lord?" Renard asked quietly, as the two of them led men and horses into the village.

"No." Allystaire turned a baleful stare back at the would-be reaver and said, "Men like him need to know that some of us will endure the worst they can do." Inwardly, though, he wished for one, and celebrated his choice not to eat so much as a morsel of bread that morning. Then, clearing his throat for more than one purpose, he said, "Timmar! Pick us a likely spot to dig and have men pace off the ground. Mark it with the rope."

The villagers stopped, all of them, to stare at the pile of bones on their charred green. "I thought you lot were told to pick a spot," Renard suddenly boomed, and the men hopped away as if stung, turning their backs to the green and scattering across the ruined village.

Allystaire nodded approvingly at him. "Going to have to keep them moving," he told Renard. "Keep them working. If we let them pause and think on it, it will go badly for them."

Smiling faintly, Renard replied, "All due respect m'lord, don't go teachin' your chief bannerman how to motivate his labor party eh?" Allystaire chuckled, then jerked a thumb over his shoulder toward Norbert. Renard nodded and drew a short, sharp knife from his belt and walked over to the lad, who quailed and took two steps as if to run, only to stop short when Ardent let out a loud whinny and tensed backwards, preparing to rear.

"That was uncanny," Allystaire quietly echoed the farmers' earlier reaction, not a little surprised. Renard cut the boy's hands free and untied the rope about his neck. Immediately the boy set to rubbing at the raw red ring in his flesh, but Allystaire walked toward him, holding out a shovel.

"Peat bog lad like you knows his way around a shovel." Allystaire raised it so that the sunlight glinted off its sharp, new edge. "You probably know, Norbert, in a pinch a shovel can be a poor man's axe. Or a hammer. Plenty of ways to kill a man with a good sharp spade." He lowered it, held it by the haft, and held the rounded wooden end out to the boy.

"If you so much as think on using this like a weapon, I will take it away from you, and I will show you each and every way. Remember, boy. You can dig, or you can hang. I am likely the only man here who wants to see you dig."

* * *

As it turned out, Norbert did indeed know how to use a shovel. Allystaire and Renard were both handy with a mattock, and the villagers all knew a hard day's work. In the first turn or so they kept pausing to gaze off in the direction of the village and the stink that followed them, but with the vinegar to hand, regular water, and Allystaire and Renard to encourage or to drive them as needed, soon enough they were stuck into the task.

Timmar had chosen a place just out of sight of the village green itself, where the road wound down into the Ash valley that Thornhurst rested in. It lay a little lower than the ground around it and looked like a well-shaded spot in the afternoon, with a lightly wooded hill rising just above it. The villagers took the lead in deciding all manners of length, width, and depth, but Allystaire worked a mattock faster than any of them, cutting up loose chunks of sod, then hunks of dirt, for the others to shovel into a pile.

With Ardent grazing nearby, unconcerned at the growing piles of dirt around the edges of the pit that now stood above the men's knees, Allystaire and Renard worked side by side. Finally, his shirt drenched from the morning heat, Allystaire stripped it off and tossed it carelessly onto the grass above, then set back to working. He swung the mattock mechanically, with very little grace, driving the thin point into the dirt beneath his feet, then twisting the wooden haft in his hands to bring the wider head in and pull up clumps and rocks. He swung several more times before he realized some of the men nearest to him were staring.

"What is it, lads?" he asked, grounding the mattock on the flat of the head and leaning on the bottom of the handle with one hand. "Something wrong?"

"Weren't you wounded, m'lord?" One of the men nearby pointed toward Allystaire's left side.

He looked down and inspected Idgen Marte's stitches, which were even and neat, but the flesh around them was indistinguishable from the rest. Gently, he tugged at one of the tiny bits of thread with a fingernail, and it pulled free without pain; the rest followed with little resistance. While there was the typical neat row of scar left behind, the wound was closed. *Too fast.* Allystaire pondered this a moment, then let the thread fall from his fingers and drop to the ground.

"Was it a Gift from the Mother?" Another man, resting a booted foot on a shovel, peered closely at Allystaire's bare chest, and added bluntly, "Ya've a lot o'scars m'lord."

"All fighting men have scars excepting the ones who die the first time out. Enough gawping. If you need a break, fall out, otherwise back to your tasks." Renard didn't shout, but the futility of negotiation or discussion was implied. The men returned to their task, and two who had been resting hopped back in and set to.

Despite their toil, the pit was far from deep enough by noon, and Allystaire heard the sound of hoofbeats pounding up the road from the village. He pulled himself up in time to see Idgen Marte sliding off the back of her courser, strands of brown hair plastered to her forehead by the heat.

"For all of our sakes put a shirt on, you scarred fool," she started in, the instant he hove into view. "You'll fright the children and womenfolk into ill… hang on." She suddenly strode close and bent toward his left shoulder, poking at it, then looking back at him quizzically. "My stitches don't pull out." She frowned up at him, the corners of her mouth pulling at her scar. "And that oughtn't be healed yet." She straightened up and asked softly, "Did you use Her Gift on yourself?"

Allystaire shook his head, dropping the mattock at his feet. "Not at all. Have not felt a twinge in it since before the assize, anyway." *Could I do that?* he found himself wondering. "Mayhap She urged me on a bit. I have always been quick to mend, regardless."

"Nobody's that quick to mend without magic," Idgen Marte insisted. "Tell me the truth."

Allystaire half-smiled and said, "I have no choice but to do exactly that, I think."

Idgen Marte stared hard at him, then poked again at his fresh, pink stitch scar with one finger. "You'll explain that to me later." She wiped her finger on her trousers. "In the meantime, the wagons are pulled up just out of sight of the village. Best not to let them all into it yet."

"Going to be nigh evening before we've got this properly dug, m'lord," Renard called up from near the pit.

"You'll want to finish in one day," Idgen Marte said, where none of the digging men could hear. "This lot've got their nerve up for this and it'll—"

Allystaire cut her off with the wave of a hand. "I know." Clearing his throat, he called out, "Break for lunch, men. See Renard for a bit of special ration." The erstwhile gate guard was already pulling a large stoneware jug from his rucksack, along with a series of small cups. Food was produced and spread about.

"Idgen Marte," Allystaire said, turning back to her. "See if you cannot get a few of the folk to check on some of the outlying farms in the valley." He paused. "I assume there are some, anyway. Probably animals that need rounding up and tending to, and the villagers will be glad to have them. And if any of them have hand carts or barrows, bring them along." He looked back at the pit and suddenly shouted, "I said the men could break for lunch, not *you*, boy."

Norbert leaped to his feet, arms and legs all a blur with his shovel.

Idgen Marte watched the skinny young man for a moment. "Y'should've killed that one," she said hotly.

"Mercy is a kind of strength, betimes." As Allystaire heard himself speaking the words, he wondered why they sounded familiar. In a sudden flash, he recalled the darkened streets of Bend; of guardsmen lying upon it wounded, but alive; and of those same words coming to him unbidden. Quickly, he added, "You heard Norbert's words to me last night; he did not lie. He may die here yet, but until I decide otherwise, he will work."

"And what gave you the right to decide that, *my lord*?" Idgen Marte managed to compress a lifetime's worth of scorn into those two words.

Biting off the angry response that sprang to mind, Allystaire thought a moment, chewing on his bottom lip. "What would the pale and perfect paladins in your precious stories have done? Would Sir Parthalian have slit the boy's throat?

Would Reddyn the Redoubtable have pounded his head to pudding with a hammer while Norbert was tied and helpless before him?"

Idgen Marte stared at him, her lips in a thin line, her scar livid and white. "No," she finally, grudgingly, conceded.

"Nor shall I. The Goddess did not choose me to make me a murderer, or even a headsman. I may well kill men for Her, but only those who deserve it." He thought of Her teeth digging into the flesh of his arm, the words She had spoken to him: *Terrible to behold,* She had said. *A thing out of legend.* A tiny spot of fear pricked his stomach.

He pressed on. "I am not convinced that our young idiot does deserve it. You heard what he said—the brigands looked better than the bog. Well, I have seen the bog, Idgen Marte, and you have not. I cannot fault a man for making that choice if he has not yet drawn blood, and you and I both know the only blood Norbert has drawn is from his dinner or his own hand."

The warrior laughed a little, and some of the tension drained from her face and neck, the healthy brown glow of her skin once again relegating her scars to a curiosity of her handsome face. "Y'might be right. Get back to digging. I'll bring some goat carts or the like." She made to leave, then turned back, and pointed to a length of twisted white flesh along his ribcage. "What in the name of the Seven Stones did that?"

"A lance. Aldacren Keep, in Barony Telmawr."

"Tourney? Accident in the lists?"

"One of my first real fights. Knights armored and horsed, arrayed against each other, with the footmen and the bowmen standing around hoping we would settle it on our own." Allystaire snorted. "We never did. The real work always comes down to them." Shovels and mattocks began to bite earth and ring against rock behind them once more. "Now get going."

"Fine," Idgen Marte replied, with the sigh of the aggrieved and with a bit of her knowing smile resting once more upon her features. "You shall owe me the rest of that story tonight."

"If you insist."

"Cover your hide unless you want to owe me the story for each and every scar," she called, as she pulled herself into the saddle and turned her lean courser.

"What makes you think you see them all, eh?" he called back, and for a moment, felt certain he had finally gotten the last word, until the smallest afternoon breeze carried her ringing laugh to his ears. He returned to the dig with a sigh.

* * *

Two or three turns later, when Allystaire heard Idgen Marte's courser returning, he didn't even wait for her news. "Norbert. You are done digging, for now." In truth, most of them were; the pit might be deep enough, more than three feet down into the earth now, wider and longer than any houses in the village. *Won't hurt to deepen it a bit more. Lot of bones on that green.*

Norbert nearly collapsed against the now almost waist-high edge of the pit. "Thank you m'lord," he gasped in exhaustion. The men working on either side of him paused, leaning on their tools, watching him with unconcealed disgust. Their hands curled around the wooden shafts of their tools, but Allystaire was already walking to the edge of the soon-to-be-grave and reaching down to grab a handful of sweat-soaked homespun.

"I said you were done digging, not done working. "Allystaire hauled him bodily out of the pit and set him on his stumbling feet with a light shove. "Timmar, and any two more of you who have something left of your strength, come with us." The sputtering boy turned to try out a glare, but quickly thought better of it. Allystaire retrieved his shirt and tugged it back over his shoulders.

Idgen Marte was down off her horse, allowing it to nose on the browning grass by the side of the track. "Folk are out rounding up animals. Found some cattle, some goats. There are two carts, one small and one larger." She looked back over her shoulder, then to the grave the men had spent most of the day digging. "Going to take more than one trip to empty that green," she added, more quietly.

"The sun is with us for turns yet," Allystaire replied, feigning a brightness of tone. "And I mean to put these folk to rest before it sets."

With somewhat forced confidence, Allystaire quickly strode down the track and back into the village, the men he'd called for following him, none with quicker steps than Norbert. He led them straight to the village green. "Norbert, await me. The rest of you, get those carts sorted and ready to haul." He indicated the rickety wooden constructions Idgen Marte had retrieved. Dung carts, from the look of them, but no smell from them could penetrate the rotten miasma that had hung over the village for days. "You," Allystaire said, facing Norbert. "Come with me."

He walked the boy right to the edge of the green, waited till they were side by side, then gave the lad a gentle shove on the shoulder toward the broken pyre of charred bones. "Begin gathering the bones."

Norbert halted and turned toward Allystaire, shaking his head, tears in his eyes. "No m'lord, please. An' you are a merciful man, or you'd've hung me. Don't make me gather the bones, m'lord. I can't," he blubbered, cringing as Allystaire stepped toward him. "Ya said I needed to dig, and I dug. How long will ya drive me like a dog?"

Instead of seizing him, Allystaire laid a steady hand on his shoulder. "If you were a dog, lad, you would have no choice in what you had done and I should not treat you half so hard," he said softly, though not altogether comfortingly. "And you will work until I tell you to stop. That is the way of it. That or a quick drop." He paused, and then added coldly, loud enough to be overheard, "I know how to tie the rope right, Norbert. When I commanded men, if I needed to sentence one—a coward, a rapist, a spy—I saw to it myself. There is rope in the wagons and stout trees a short walk in any direction." He paused, waiting for that to sink in. "Pick the direction you wish to walk, lad."

Norbert made for the pile of bones on the green.

Idgen Marte sidled up next to Allystaire, hissing in his ear. "What do ya—"

Allystaire silenced her with a look. "I mean to effect a rough justice here," he whispered. "Mayhap not as rough as you think. Wait."

A few of the men motioned as if to join Norbert in the pile of bones, but Allystaire stopped them with a wave; the rest stayed with the carts, and Allystaire stood at the edge of the browned and blackened grass, watching as the tall, thin youth began gathering up armfuls of bones. Some clattered through his hands and a few fell to pieces as he picked them up, charred through in thin places. He started at the edges, filling his arms and walking back to the smaller cart, filling it.

Timmar wandered to Allystaire, spat in the dirt, and said, "Beggin y'r pardon m'lord, those're our folk. M'sister's husband is out there, and m'friends. We should be doin' this."

Allystaire turned to him, his face calm and impassive. "Wait," he murmured, then slowly turned back to watch Norbert. Soon there was a path trodden through the grass, and a rounded edge of charred grass had been revealed.

As they waited, they formed a grim tableau: Allystaire watching with arms folded over his chest, the village men increasingly nervous and muttering amongst themselves, Ardent and Idgen Marte's courser listlessly whickering and nosing for grass. Norbert made one trip after another until he had nearly filled the smaller cart.

Finally, stopping to pick up a charred skull, Norbert fell to his knees, sobbing.

Nodding slightly as he felt the release of the collective tension, Allystaire walked across the green with slow, measured steps till he was at the youth's side and could hear his tear-choked, halting murmurs. Mostly it was blubbering nonsense, but he heard the grief in the boy's repeated, halting apologies, hunched over the bone with his head in his arms. Allystaire knelt by his side and took the crying lad into his arms. Norbert slumped against him, still sobbing, and they remained that way for a long moment.

"I'm sorry m'lord. Sorry. I'm so sorry, m'lord I…"

Allystaire let Norbert carry on sobbing his abject regret for a time, till finally he started to tug the boy to his feet.

"Stop blubbering and stand up." Allystaire drew back with a hand on his thin shoulder. "You did not do this, lad. But you stood by and *saw it done*. You saw it done and *did nothing*. You are not the first to witness a horror such as this unfold, and you will hardly be the last. Yet your own part in it you will have to understand…and atone for. Do you hear me?"

Wiping his mouth with the back of his sleeve, the boy nodded his large, narrow head several times. "I hear you, m'lord."

Allystaire nodded almost solemnly, then waved the rest of the men onto the green. "Help us work, lad. You will eat tonight, and sleep, in safety and without bonds. Tomorrow we will discuss the rest of what you owe. Aye?"

The boy nodded again and, his tears dried, set back to work, sniffling occasionally. The other men joined him, tugging their linen masks once more around their faces. With paladin, farmers, and former-would-be reaver working together, the pile of bones diminished. Sensing the end of their task heaving into sight, they worked with renewed energy, trotting the carts in teams, and soon the green was emptied, leaving behind a large blackened scar.

"Nearly the dinner turn, m'lord," Renard pointed out, as Allystaire came trundling up to the pit, dragging the last cartload behind him.

"Then any man who wishes to may quit to eat," Allystaire replied, panting heavily as he set the cart down. "I intend to see the work done."

"Any man?" Timmar asked with a note of scorn in his voice as he began unloading the cart, turning an eye on Norbert.

"Any man," Allystaire repeated, stopping in his tracks and straightening his aching back and spreading his shoulders a bit. He fixed his eyes on Tim in a mild challenge; the villager soon looked away, his lips pressed firmly together, his stubbled jaw taut.

When the last bones were unloaded, Allystaire took a moment to gather himself and watch the crew that had dug. Many watched him, too, as if waiting for further instruction even as they grabbed shovels, but a few followed Norbert with their eyes. The gangly lad was conscious of their stares, and uneasy, but he reached for a shovel all the same. Suddenly he was sprawling on the ground, a stocky, square built villager standing above him, gripping the shovel the boy had been about to pick up.

"Eh? Want this, do ya?" The man proffered the wooden haft toward the fallen Norbert, as if to help him up, then jabbed it sharply at him, poking the end into his ribs. "Maybe you want the other end." He started to reverse his grip. Two other men began to close in, and Norbert scrambled backward on all fours, away from the pit, his eyes wide in fear. The man lunged forward as if to bring the shovel down, but the wooden haft thumped solidly into Renard's outstretched hand.

Allystaire was two steps away with a fire in his eyes when he saw the brawny, bearded man jump out of the pit and catch the swung shovel with an easy hand. His jaw tight, he drew closer, watching silently.

"Allystaire said any man who wanted could have a rest. Why don't you take one, Henri?" Renard pulled the shovel free from the man's hand, hard enough and fast enough that the villager staggered back a few steps.

"I don't recall this one bein' a man," Henri snapped back at Renard. He made a grab for the shovel, and Renard, Allystaire could see, subtly shifted his hands. When Henri pulled, Renard relaxed his grip so the shovel's haft swung forward and smacked the villager on the side of the head with a thud.

Henri let out a surprised yelp and leapt forward toward Renard, who, with a sergeant's instinct for when enough was enough, simply extended his fist to meet the man's charge. Henri hit the ground in a heap. Norbert had scrambled to his feet and looked ready to bolt in any direction that didn't lead to violence, but a glance at Allystaire stayed his feet. The two villagers who'd been closing in on the downed boy suddenly turned for Renard with a roar; the bearded soldier raised his fists defensively and said calmly, "Don't try it lads."

"ENOUGH!" Allystaire's bellow rang out, a huge animal roar reverberating in the still summer air. All the would-be combatants turned suddenly, white-faced, toward him. He stalked forward and seized a handful of Henri's shirt, hauling the man to his feet. "You. You are done. Go back to the wagons and help the women. If they will have you." He shoved the man, who looked defiant, even with the purple bruise blossoming on his cheek.

Allystaire had started to turn away, but, feeling eyes upon him, swiftly rounded back upon the stubborn villager, his face pale with anger. "Well?"

"M'lord, it's not right!"

Allystaire stepped toward him, a seething impatience roiling inside him. *Peasants*, he thought, only to find himself filled with a brief moment of self-loathing. "Another word—even one—from your mouth, and I will organize a proper fistfight for you. Three falls with Renard. Now go," he said, spitting the final syllable between clenched teeth. Reluctant, but silent, Henri tromped away.

"And the rest of you," Allystaire roared, turning around, "any more such nonsense and it will be three falls with *me*, clear?" He turned an angry eye on Renard; the bearded man nodded simply, a chastened red spot growing high on his cheeks.

"Back to work and quick," Allystaire snapped. "Fine example for your departed kinfolk."

Norbert, meanwhile, had edged back to the pit to resume pitching in.

* * *

Before dark the grave was covered, if unevenly, and most of the sod patted more or less back into place. The green was free of bones, if not clear of ash, and the folk of Thornhurst, after the longest week of their lives, finally returned home. Most of the nearby buildings were unusable, but Idgen Marte's group had created manageable lengths of fence with posts and rope, and this held a small herd of cows; another, smaller pen held goats. They had dug a large firepit, and the flames now smoked and guttered while carrying a sweet scent into the air.

Idgen Marte squatted by the fire, feeding long, dried stalks of weeds into the pit in bundles; a large pile of the stuff, freshly cut, sat next to her.

"Holy grass," she explained, as Allystaire walked up behind her. "Leastways it is to the elves such as live south. Burn it on feast days. Lucky for you I found it growing here. About as far north as it grows."

"Not sure luck has aught to do with any of this," Allystaire muttered, as he knelt down, keeping one eye on Norbert. For his part the lad was doing a poor job of trying to stay close to Allystaire without looking like he wanted to stay close to Allystaire; he fidgeted nervously from a few yards away, constantly looking over his shoulder. "I think the lad will work out," he offered, quietly, to the warrior squatting beside him.

"If this lot don't hang him first. Or stone him, or press him, or simply slit his throat," Idgen Marte retorted, her cheerful tone mocking him.

"They will do none of those," Allystaire said sternly. "Nor will you."

She tossed another handful of weeds into the blaze and watched it begin to smolder. "No, I won't. But the others will take some close watching." She shifted her feet underneath her and sat back on the grass, one hand planted behind her, and turned to look at him. She shook her head a bit and said quietly, "They'll come to hate you, y'know. That you've saved them, brought them a Goddess, and showed them a miracle—that'll do, for a time. But if you stay here too long, you'll only show them how much they lack. All that they can never be."

"Mayhap," Allystaire replied just as softly. "If it comes to that, I will only stay as long as I must. See the place rebuilt, wait to see what, if anything, our friend the Baron of Bend sends up the road after us. For now, though, they will listen and learn whatever I might teach."

Idgen Marte narrowed her eyes and flattened her lips. She said, "You're planning to preach in the morning, aren't you?"

"No," Allystaire said, rising to his feet and dusting the seat of his trousers with a hand. "I mean to preach now. In the morning I have to invent funeral rites." He turned and offered his hand down to help Idgen Marte up. With a snort and roll of eyes she popped to her feet and batted aside his hand, albeit playfully.

"What can I do in order to miss the sermon?"

"Find me a building with four walls, a roof, and a door we can bar from the outside," Allystaire replied smoothly.

Idgen Marte glared at him. "You were waiting for that one, weren't you?"

"Of course. Now, off you go," Allystaire said brightly, smiling.

For once, the warrior had no retort, no last word. She simply trotted off. Allystaire felt a brief flush of victory.

* * *

The preaching Allystaire did that night was minimal, mostly summed up with the phrase that had come to him often the past few days: Sometimes, mercy is strength. He didn't reference Norbert as he spoke, or look at him or at the men who'd attacked him. The bulk of the folk had listened quietly, but he had seen some restless figures in the back muttering to each other. *Trouble*, he told himself, *but I cannot say they have no right to their anger.*

As the folk were milling around after another quiet moment of kneeling prayer at sunset, Allystaire waited for Idgen Marte to return. When she did, he caught her eye and nodded toward the loitering Norbert; she took his meaning immediately, corralled the boy by an arm, and led him off.

Allystaire watched the crowd, noting those whose gaze seemed to follow the pair. After a few moments, he stood and gathered a large parcel of food—dried fish; thick, garlicky sausage; bread; and a small pot of fragrant root stew one of the village women had made. Pausing only to make sure that Renard was among the crowd, spotting his beard and the spear the man carried like an over-sized walking stick, he nodded in silent assent to his own thoughts and tried to saunter casually in the direction Idgen Marte had led Norbert. Soon he found what appeared to be a small curing shed outside of a farmhouse that had seemed to be spared the worst of the devastation; two tall figures stood silhouetted in the dying light outside of it.

The smell of the food Allystaire brought with him must have attracted their attention, for they suddenly turned toward him. Idgen Marte came forward to take some of the bundle of food out of his crooked left arm, while Norbert simply stood by and watched hopefully. Allystaire set down a rough bit of cloth on the ground and he and Idgen Marte spread the food upon it; to Norbert he gave two small dried fish and an oval loaf of brown bread, but as he held it out, pointed toward the curing shed with one outstretched finger.

"In there lad," he said, holding out the food toward the boy's slightly trembling hands. "You will eat and sleep there."

Norbert took the fish and bread and held them carefully, turning a half step toward the open door of the shed before saying, "They mean t'kill me, m'lord. They'll see me hang t'night! Surely you can see that."

"Aye," Allystaire nodded, his voice calm, but not unkind. "They do. And I can."

"Have I not done all y'asked?" Norbert's voice was slightly plaintive, nasal.

"I am not finished asking." Allystaire paused a moment to let Norbert ponder that, but more whinging appeared to be imminent, so he raised a hand to stop the boy from speaking and went on, "If you will pause and think—a skill I am not yet convinced you possess—you will realize that I do not mean to let you hang tonight. Now, off you go to the shed. Eat and rest."

Nodding along to a murmured string of thanks, Norbert retreated into the shed; Allystaire shut the door behind him and turned back to Idgen Marte, who was already well stuck into the meal he had brought. Slowly, with a straight and carefully held back, he lowered himself to the ground.

"Rough day cutting turf, eh," Idgen Marte asked mockingly, around a steaming mouthful of tuber and gravy.

"No other kind," Allystaire grunted. They ate for a time with no sounds other than their chewing and that of the night around them—crickets, the wind, the occasional owl.

"They do mean t'hang him, ya know. And I'm not sure they haven't got it right."

"I did not ask you," Allystaire pointed out. He glanced toward Idgen Marte, but her form was indistinct in the fireless dark, so he turned to stare into the night. "It might be justice to hang him. I know that."

"And yet…"

"And yet I do not think it would be the *Mother's* justice," Allystaire said, quiet but firm. "He fell in with bad men, yes, but *he is not one*. Not yet. He would have become one, yes. Yet now? Now I have as much a chance to save him as I did to save Mol. Surely I am not the only one who sees that?"

For a long moment, his words were met with a silence that was eventually broken by distant birdsong. Finally, Idgen Marte heaved a sigh and murmured, "You really are what you're claiming to be, aren't you." He could see her hold up her hands to forestall him. "I know, I know. You think I should already believe. Well, Allystaire, I want to believe, and in the main, I do."

"Then what is—"

"Three days ago I didn't know if paladins were real, or just legends. Even the stories of holy knights in this part of the world? Centuries old. Why now? Why here? Why…" She trailed off, gesturing vaguely at him with one hand.

"Why me?" Allystaire chuckled lightly. He bit down on a hunk of sausage to give himself time to think. After chewing a while, he said, "Now and here? I suspect because enough folk cried out for it. The other, I cannot answer." He paused; the Goddess's voice, telling him, *Others will be Called,* played on his thoughts, but he said nothing of it. "Not in one night, anyway."

"You're meaning to stay here all the night, your back against that door, guarding a boy who meant to be a reaver because you think if you don't, it'll mean his life, aren't you?"

"That is remarkably, ah, similar to my plan of engagement, aye," he answered delicately.

Idgen Marte laughed lightly, all the sigh and anger and wariness gone out of her voice. Her laugh, Allystaire realized, was more musical than her voice, somehow overcoming the rasp that cut through her words.

"Am I amusing?"

"In your way; you just answered my question, is all." She stood, and he slowly followed suit, turning to face her. "You won't watch him alone. Renard can mind the camp. I'll string a hammock in a tree. Take my bow."

"No bow," Allystaire said, "unless you have fowling arrows with blunt heads. No one is going to die here tonight, if I can help it."

"I don't carry arrows that can't kill a man," Idgen Marte said flatly. "And I won't see you die here because some dirt eater gets lucky and brains you with a mallet. 'sides, if I have t' feather one, I'll take him in the leg and you can heal him. Problem solved."

Sighing, Allystaire relented with a wave of his hand. "I am too tired to argue, and I want a turn or two of sleep before they come with the rope."

Idgen Marte was already trotting away. Allystaire put his ear to the door of the curing shed, and heard the smooth, regular breathing and occasional dry snore of Norbert asleep. He sat down, back to the wall, laid his hammer across his knees, and drifted into the light, nearly-waking sleep he had known for a score of years.

When approaching steps woke him, the slender moon had moved a good distance in the sky. Better than two turns, he guessed. They were four, and they made no effort to hide their approach. With a sigh, Allystaire slowly levered himself up to his feet, grasping the hammer by its iron head and using the point at the end of the haft to drive creaking knees upright. Perhaps, in truth, he stood a bit more slowly, with a bit more show of pain, than necessary. *A warrior might move fast, but never in haste.* The stern, rolling voice of old Baron Oyrwyn echoed in his head.

"Goodmen," Allystaire called out to them, as he settled the hammer into his belt and crossed his arms over his chest, "there is neither jakes nor midden dug this way, and it is far too early to be up after the day's tasks, even for good farming folk." His voice was jovial, friendly. "So what brings you here?"

One of the four stepped forward, a thick, knobbled wooden stick clutched in one hand. It was Henri. "We want that freezin' reaver lad. He 'angs. T'night."

With a sigh, Allystaire shook his head and shuffled his feet slightly. "Afraid not, Henri. Now go back to the wagons—all of you—and find your beds."

"Enough orderin' us about like yer our lord," one of the men in the back, whose name Allystaire couldn't recall, exclaimed. He brandished a rope and a shuttered lantern. "'angin' such as 'im is justice."

"Aye," Allystaire said, with a sharp nod. "It might be. Braech's justice. Fortune's justice. A lord's justice. But it is not the Mother's justice." Repeating that phrase filled him with a quiet certainty that he was right; he felt that radiant, unearthly smile again, if only for a fleeting second.

"I want Thornhurst's justice," Henri shouted, taking a step closer and raising his stick uncertainly. "I want justice for my sons, who died with bolts in their necks!" His voice climbed as he spoke, trembled with ready tears.

"And the men who did that are already dead, Henri," Allystaire said, quietly. "Killing this lad will not add one link to the price they paid. Nor will it cut a copper shaving from the cost laid upon you."

Henri took another half step closer, close enough for Allystaire to see the tears on his stubbled cheeks and the stick raised a bit higher.

"Stop," Allystaire said coldly. "Stop now, because if you try to hit me with that stick, I will take it away and break it over your head. Stop because I do not want to hurt any of you, but if you doubt that I will do so, to defend an unarmed, sleeping boy, think back on what that warehouse looked like after I set you free. Stop because the Mother calls me to defend him now, as I did you, then." His heart pounded at the front of his ribcage, his body tense with the fear that his words would not convince, and he would have to hurt them.

"Stop, turn around, and go back to sleep with this promise: he will do more good for Thornhurst alive than he would dead. He will pay everything he owes, like the dead men on that floor did. The Mother's justice may not always be as swift or as final as it was then, but I will be damned if I shall not see it done, no matter what form it takes."

The other three men dropped their weapons, such as they were—a mallet, the rope, a long skinning knife—and melted into the night. Henri stood before Allystaire, trembling in anger; finally, the stick fell from nerveless fingers, and the man pitched onto his knees, weeping openly.

"Where was 'er justice then, m'lord," he moaned. "Where was She? Where were you?"

A day's ride north of your valley and hoping not to see Garth's great black charger on the road behind me, Allystaire immediately thought, once again chastising himself inwardly with a sharp frown. He knelt next to Henri and put a hand upon the farmer's shoulder.

"She told me, Henri, that She had forgotten this world. Or that it had forgotten Her. I cannot explain the past, and I cannot bring back your sons any more than I can roll back the ocean or cleave down a mountain. I can tell you this: She hears your cries. She will hear the cry of every father like you, and those cries will not be borne forever."

Henri knelt on the grass and rocked slowly back and forth, shaking his head, tears spilling from his shut eyes. *What good am I, then?* Allystaire was shamed by his thought, but he had no answer, so he knelt in the grass with his arm around a man he was sure was older than he was, and waited. *At least I did not have to kill him.*

As Henri's sobs slowed and he collected himself, Allystaire stood and helped the farmer up with a proffered hand. Henri refused to look at him, staring straight at the dark ground as he spoke.

"M'sorry m'lord. I 'ad no right t'gainsay you. Or t'threaten. Please fergive me," he mumbled, embarrassed and apologetic.

"Henri, I have been lax in this, but it is time for you folk to stop calling me *lord*," Allystaire replied, quietly. "And since I am no lord, I will not order men silenced." *And you were as much threat to me as a mouse is to a tomcat.* He took a deep breath and clapped the other man on the shoulder.

"Yet mark this and mark it well; I will do the Mother's will as clear as I may see it, no matter who—foe, friend, neighbor, or stranger—opposes me. Aye? It is not my forgiveness you need ask, in the end. If you knelt last night, it is Hers."

Henri looked up, and even in the meager light of the quarter moon, puzzlement was plain upon his rounded peasant face. "'Ow d'I do that?"

"Ask," Allystaire replied with a certainty that startled himself. "We are all, I think, as children to Her. When you were a lad, could you not simply ask your own mother's forgiveness for your mischief?"

"Not 'less I wanted a ladle aside m'head," Henri answered, after chewing his bottom lip for a moment.

"I could fetch a ladle if it would help," Allystaire said flatly.

"You couldna hit harder than me mum did," Henri stubbornly insisted.

Sighing, Allystaire took half a step back and pinched the bridge of his nose for a moment. "Just ask, Henri. Ask Her. Kneel and pray. Beg of Her some task, if you must. But for the Mother's own love, head for your blankets and go back to sleep, aye? The turn is late."

Perhaps Allystaire's small prayer was answered, for the grizzled farmer cracked a yawn as he nodded; Allystaire fought back his own yawn, and Henri took a few steps away before turning back to him. "You won't tell no one about this, will ya?"

After a moment's pause, Allystaire replied, "Only if I must. I will not hold it over you; that I can promise."

Henri nodded, and Allystaire struggled to read his face. As the farmer walked off, Allystaire stood listening to the sound of boot steps until he could hear no more; then he settled himself against the door of the shed and slept again, lightly, till dawn.

CHAPTER 17

Serving in Grief

Allystaire awoke to the rattling of the door behind him as Norbert pounded upon it from within. Yawning, he stood and rapped back with a sharp blow of his fist. "I wake, lad, I wake. What is it?"

"I need the jakes, m'lord," came Norbert's voice from within, frantically.

"Fine, fine." Shaking his head, Allystaire unbarred the door and stood aside; Norbert trotted out and looked, blinking, from side to side.

"Where—"

"Find a tree, boy, and be quick. And do not get out of my sight," Allystaire called out to Norbert's suddenly retreating back. Cursing and stamping the feeling into complaining limbs, Allystaire trotted after him, but pulled up when he saw the boy stop in front of a large oak and start fumbling with his clothes.

When he was done, Allystaire waited as the boy turned toward him, then had to choke down his surprise as he saw Idgen Marte emerge from the thickly leaved branches of the tree Norbert had just pissed on. He saw her carefully climb down and jump a few feet from the base of the tree in distaste, her hair knotted and carrying more than one or two twigs, her clothes disheveled, unstrung bow in hand. Quickly, he turned away and started walking, silently counting in his head, reaching exactly four when Norbert caught up with him.

"M'lord, will I be free to go now? I did the work you—"

Allystaire turned on him and gave him a baleful stare, his eyes widened in sudden fury. He said nothing, only stared, and kept boring his gaze on the gangly lad until Norbert quailed and apologized in a tiny voice.

Turning back away from him, Allystaire walked again, waiting three steps before he said, "I have decided I will not hang you. Not after the trouble I have gone in order to keep you alive." Behind him, Norbert commenced a chorus of thank-yous. Allystaire turned and cut him off with another glare. When silence was restored to the warm, early morning, he said, "What I will do is much worse."

Soon enough, Allystaire, Norbert, and Idgen Marte had made their way back to the camped wagons, where all the village folk stirred; they were cooking, waking later sleepers, seeing to animals, milking the meager herd and flock that had been rounded up, and carrying out other domestic tasks that seemed like the work of mad arcanists to Allystaire. He sent Norbert off toward Renard to be fed, then walked off, alone, toward the mass grave that had been dug the day before.

The ground was uneven in places and showed the marks of shovel and mattock. Allystaire had seen to it that stakes were placed at each corner, so they could skirt the grave itself, and he walked around to the head of it, facing east over the rising ground of the lip of the river valley, and knelt, fixing his eyes as close to the sun as he could manage.

"Mother," he began, then almost immediately faltered, grasping for words that would not come. He started again after a few deep breaths.

"Mother, if these are our people, what do I say to them this morn? What can I do for their grief in the face of this enormity? I killed the men who did it. They deserved it, and they have neither my pity nor my grief. Yet their deaths healed nothing."

"'Tis not healin' we need, only a way forward," put in a quiet voice behind him, which Allystaire didn't have to turn toward in order to recognize. "We'll heal on our own, wi' time. Just set our feet on the right road." He heard quiet footsteps on the grass and turned to look at Mol; while he knelt, she was roughly at eye level with him, and she lay a hand upon his shoulder. "Ya din't kill those men t'heal anythin'. Be a trap t'start thinkin' that way."

Nodding distractedly, Allystaire looked to the ground in front of him for a moment, then stood, patting Mol on the shoulder as he did. "Go and gather them, Mol. Words need to be said over this grave. Tell them I need half a turn."

She nodded and rushed off, running without apparent worry across the grave, passing Idgen Marte on her way. Similarly, the warrior walked heedlessly over the burial site, blinking sleep out of her eyes, carrying a mess of ropes over one shoulder, and clutching her bow and swordbelt together in one hand. "How're the funeral rites coming?"

"Be better if people did not keep treading all over the grave," Allystaire remarked.

She snorted. "Foolish northern superstition, that. We don't even dig graves where I come from." Then she cracked a yawn, holding a hand for his patience. "Do funerals happen before or after breakfast?"

"Before. Now, come help me fetch some stones. Large and flat."

"Markers?"

Allystaire shook his head as he turned. "Too many bodies to mark them all. I mean to make an altar, such as I can." With fair precision, he sought out the spot where he'd made a campfire a lifetime ago, on the day he'd found Mol shivering in the inn's cold well.

Reaching out with the sheathed tip of her sword, Idgen Marte tapped the ring of stones he'd put together. "Stones. Large and flat." She gestured with her free hand from him to the stones and began belting her sword back around her waist.

Allystaire squatted and hauled one up easily, then stood to hold it toward her; Idgen Marte's only response was to cock an eyebrow and tilt her head.

Allystaire gestured toward her with the stone, as if to hand it off, and she held up her hands by her shoulders, palms out, shaking her head. "I don't haul rocks. Nor water nor coal. Nor do I split wood, plough fields, tend to animals, wash pots, sweep floors, beat rugs, or clean hearths. You want the rocks, old man, you carry 'em. Only rocks I'm carrying best be small, shiny, and for preference, set in gold."

Sighing, Allystaire squatted down and gathered up as many of the stones in his arms as he could, then stood straight, with visible strain, and began walking with short, jerking steps back toward the pit. "Little honest labor would not hurt you," he grunted, waddling.

"'Honest' and 'labor' are both *ugly* words. They hurt me here," Idgen Marte protested, touching her chest lightly. "Only labor I'll do with my hands is with bowstring or hilt."

It took Allystaire three trips to gather all the stones, and though Idgen Marte walked with him, true to herself, she didn't carry so much as a single one. When he finally had the entire ring, Allystaire busied himself with arranging them into a crude pile; finished, it didn't stand much higher than his hip, but its surface was flat and mostly even.

Wiping sweat from his eyes, he glared at Idgen Marte and knelt, reaching out to the pile of stones and retreating into himself. *Mother,* he thought, *I do not know if it is temples you want. I do know that these folk will want something of you when I am gone. Faith without an object will wither. Let them make a place here, a temple in your name; make this its center. Let it mark forever the graves of those I could not save.*

When Allystaire opened his eyes, for they had closed as he prayed, Idgen Marte was kneeling on the opposite side of him, one hand reaching tentatively out toward the small pile of stones. When her hand joined his upon it, her finger-tips lightly brushing the opposite side, he felt a jolt run through him. From the way she jumped, so did Idgen Marte. He flattened the whole of his hand, splaying his fingers, over the stone. It felt warm. He heard a very faint cracking sound.

Idgen Marte had opened her eyes, her fingers still just lightly brushing the stone. "Look," she said, jumping to her feet; Allystaire slowly pushed himself up and took a step back.

The pile of rock before them, while still only a few feet in height, was no longer made of individual stones. Instead, they had fused, somehow, into one unbroken whole. The edges not regular, the top not even, but a single block of grey stone nonetheless.

"Let it mark forever the graves of those I could not save," Idgen Marte murmured; she looked from the altar to Allystaire, attempting her usual smirk, and failing. "Why that? Why make it a reminder of what's past?"

Allystaire thought on this for a moment, letting his fingers trail over the top of the still-warm stone. "Memory matters." He paused, then, unable to contain himself, adding, "I did not say that out loud, you know. I was praying, aye, but silent. You heard my thoughts."

Snorting, Idgen Marte said, "I am no sorceress able to pluck thought from your mind."

"I did not say that you were, or that you could. Yet you did hear the prayer, because She let you hear it. Do not try to deny it," he added sternly, as she opened her mouth to protest.

"So what if She did?"

"Must I also point out that the stone fused only when we both touched it?" Allystaire smiled knowingly. "She is not done with you, Idgen Marte. You know this. Sooner, rather than later, She will Call to you, and you will have no choice but to answer."

Tightening her lips into a thin line, Idgen Marte searched in vain for a response, but the folk of Thornhurst had begun to gather around, and Allystaire simply smiled at her as he moved forward to address them.

Instinctively, they avoided the grave, except for Mol, who dashed across it to join him once more. She labored to carry a large stone, but she smiled as brightly as the morning air around her. "She spoke t'me," she said, her voice a note of pure joy. "Told me t'bring a rock. Er, She weren't real clear on why, she just told me…" Mol held up the rock at the end of her skinny arms, toward Allystaire, her mouth twisting from bright smile to slight confusion.

Pointing to the altar behind him, Allystaire smiled back at her. "Go set it there, and come back and join me." The girl bounced off, and Allystaire took a deep breath, cleared his throat, and boomed to the gathered villagers.

"Neighbors." He paused, shaking his head. "Friends? Are we friends, good folk? I am afraid that many of you fear me. To some of you, mayhap I am just another man in a steel suit, with arms and a will to see things done his own way. Mayhap I have acted too much in that manner. I am sorry for frightening you." He found that his hands were clasped behind him, his bearing instinctively military. He dropped his hands to his sides and went on.

"Understand this: folk like you have naught to fear from me, or from any servant of the Mother. I serve Her by serving you." He paused to let that sink in, then added, "This does not mean I am going to start fetching your ale or drawing your water." There were a few chuckles in the crowd, and some lightened faces. Allystaire decided that was a victory and moved on.

"Today, I have asked you here so that I may serve you in grief." Another pause. "In front of you, as you well know, is where we laid your murdered kin to rest yesterday. Today we are here to say farewell to them, to let them move to the mild summer and the warm winter of the next world. The Mother will find them there, as She found you here, and gather them to Her care."

He waited, watching the crowd; many faces began to fall, eyes to cloud and well. "I do not know what your custom is for moments like this. Where I hail from, we speak words of praise and, if need be, blame, over our fallen kin before we move on. If any of you wish to speak, come forward."

Allystaire waited; the crowd in front of him hesitated, but then he felt Mol brush past him. He expected her voice to be small, but it carried powerfully in the otherwise quiet morning.

"Slavers killed my father, I 'spect," she said, digging her bare toes into the grass and folding her hands in front of her. "I din't see it happen, but he weren't with ya when y'were rescued. Was him who set me into the cold well when he saw thin's goin' wrong. Did it quick and made cert no one saw 'im do't. Saved me, I thin'." She paused, wiped her hand under her eyes, and added, "He always let me listen t'the stories minstrels or peddlers would bring to the inn, e'en when I was s'posed to be asleep." Her voice thickened with tears; many in the crowd lowered their heads, eyes shut tightly. Quickly, biting off the words, she finished with, "And he made the best beer fer forty mile in any direction."

That said, she turned and ran to Allystaire, pressing her face against him and sobbing; he knelt to embrace her and could feel her small body shuddering with days of grief suddenly unleashed all at once. He stood, still holding her, and looked to the crowd.

One by one at first, then forming a line, the folk of Thornhurst came forward and spoke of their sons, their fathers, uncles, and nephews. Their wives, daughters, nieces, and mothers. It took the best part of three turns with the sun beating down on them and sweat streaming from all of their faces. Allystaire felt it pooling on the small of his back and down his arms.

Allystaire was sure, when it was over, that everyone had spoken, save Norbert, Idgen Marte, and Renard. Even Henri came forward to speak, shakily, about his sons, Matthar and Kev. Mol had gone to join her uncle Tim when they came forward, so Allystaire simply stood back, listening.

By the end of it, clouds had drifted in front of the sun, and a breeze had begun to blow across them, soft, yet potent. It took with it the worst of the heat and dried the sweat and tears on their cheeks.

When the last speaker had finished, Allystaire came forward again.

"The Goddess has listened to every word you said here today. She has come to know the kin that you lost, as have I," Allystaire began.

"Mol," he said, waving a hand toward the girl. "Come here please." Mol disentangled herself from her mother and her uncle and dashed over to him again. Allystaire turned and walked to the altar, gesturing for other folk to come closer, if they wished. Some few, including Gram and Henri, crowded around.

"Do you see this? This is the beginning of Her place among you. A temple, if you would," Allystaire explained, gesturing toward the altar of stone, upon which sat the rounded one Mol had brought. "Put your hand upon it, Mol." He looked to the silently loitering Idgen Marte who, grudgingly, placed her own fingers upon it. Once again he retreated into himself, thinking of the Goddess's words to him, of the touch of Her hand upon his, and thought again—*Let it mark forever the graves of those I could not save. Let it be a sign to Your people that their cries will never again go unheard.*

Once again he heard a cracking sound, louder this time, and felt a thrumming vibration pass through the stone, and suddenly his hand was pushed upward by nearly a foot. Idgen Marte and Mol jumped back, and the crowd gasped.

Before them now stood a larger stone altar; instead of a solid block, a flat oval stood on three short, rough columns. It was all of a piece—light grey, smooth, utterly featureless.

Around it, folk suddenly knelt. Allystaire did the same, sharing a smile with Idgen Marte and Mol.

The sun broke free of its cloud cover and shone on them, rays bright against the surface of the altar. The stone flashed a brief red-gold, then was grey again.

Allystaire thought he heard a single piece of a song, just a few notes, then all was still, and he pushed himself back to his feet, his knees protesting all this up and down.

"It is in joy that I would serve you now. Let us, together, make this altar worthy of Her. As we rebuild this village, on this spot, let us raise a chapel. Use it to meet, to pray, to celebrate, and to mourn. Shall we?"

The villagers looked from him to each other, eyes wide.

Henri was the first to speak, growling out a rough, "Aye!" with his eyes slantwise toward the ground. Around the rangy farmer echoed a chorus of *ayes* and a general, if subdued, agreement.

Nodding, Allystaire continued. "Very well. In that case, we have a bit more to do. Norbert!" His voice resounded sharply through the air. "Come forward."

The tall youth, loitering far back of the crowd with Renard close at hand, did as he was bid, though not without trepidation. He was careful to skirt the grave, and the crowd that had gathered around the altar parted, but reluctantly. Murmurs ran darkly among the villagers as he passed.

"Norbert," Allystaire said, "you have admitted to knowingly joining the brigands that sacked this town and tried to enslave these people."

"Aye, m'lord, but—"

"But nothing!" Allystaire's voice rang like a hammer on hot steel. "You joined them, and while your hand held neither blade nor torch, you stood by while men you traveled with murdered and burned and raped. And worse, from this evil you stood to profit. All this is true, aye?"

Swallowing hard, Norbert nodded and muttered a single, shamed, "Aye."

"Then your life is forfeit." He paused to let that sink in, then added, "Unless you are willing to come forward now and beg the Mother's forgiveness. She is merciful; yet you may find Her mercy a bitter draught." Allystaire stood aside and indicated the rough altar with one hand.

Gulping again, Norbert took a few faltering steps forward and knelt in front of the altar. For a moment he simply stared at it, then he cried out in a loud, pained voice. "No. NO!" He raised his hands to cover his eyes, and Allystaire knew that whatever the lad was seeing, it was not the altar, not the grass, not the foothills beyond them to the north and east. Norbert slowly sank into a huddle on the grass, much as he had done on the green amidst the pile of bones the day before.

Allystaire felt a pang of guilt for making the boy relive his misdeeds yet again. As he looked down at Mol, who watched Norbert with curious detachment, he thought back on her words about her father.

His guilt burned away like mist under the rising sun.

Finally, Norbert simply sprawled in front of the altar, sobbing and clutching his head with his hands. Allystaire stepped forward and hauled him up.

"You have asked. Now are you ready to hear what you must do to earn Her forgiveness, and that of the folk around you?"

The lad nodded limply, his face a mess of tears and grass.

"Very well. As I said, your life is forfeit. For a year and a day, you will serve this village with the labor of your hands. Your bed and your board will be found for you, but in exchange, from morning till sunset, you will refuse them *nothing*. You are everyone's farmhand; you are everyone's peat digger, hod carrier, woodcutter, and shepherd. Every waking minute of your life belongs to this village. Refuse a task at your peril. And—*look at me, Norbert*," Allystaire suddenly bellowed, for Norbert's glazed gaze had fallen to the ground. He glanced back up with fresh tears filling his eyes.

Allystaire seized his collar and pulled his face close. "Mother help you, lad, if you try to run away, and you had best hope I am dead. For then, at least, you must wait till the next life for me to find you. And I will." He took a deep breath. "Do you accept?"

Norbert nodded frantically in the affirmative. "I do, m'lord. I do. People, all of you, I do. Anything. Anything you ask."

Just what did you show him, Mother? Allystaire found himself wondering. "Good. And people of Thornhurst; remember that mercy may be a kind of strength. The boy's labor is yours, *but not his life*, nor his thoughts. He will eat and sleep as well as you, for without food and rest, what work can he do? Do you all understand?" More general assent was murmured. Allystaire let Norbert go, and stepped away from him, inhaling a lungful of air with which to shout.

"Then for the Mother's sake, go and eat. Sing and play and tell tales, the lot of you. A great deal of work remains, but it will keep. Take the day to remember your kin in happiness. Get drunk, if you have a taste for it! But remember that we—all of us—must be ready to put our backs to it tomorrow, aye?"

Amid roars of laughing approval that met the exhortation to inebriation, the crowd melted away, leaving Allystaire, Mol, and Idgen Marte alone with the transformed altar that the three of them, together in prayer, had raised out of unworked stone.

CHAPTER 18

A Strength Out of Legend

The late summer sun was, if anything, more brutal than that of midsummer. The gentle hill upon which the altar sat was baking, much of the grass parched and browning.

So was the pair sparring upon it.

Allystaire carefully circled, his long, heavy sword held in a cross-body guard, the tip above his left shoulder, blade canted slightly forwards, the pommel near his right hip. He moved his weight from one foot to the other as he stepped side to side; suddenly he lunged forward, swinging the blade in a high-line, horizontal cut.

With neat economy of motion, Idgen Marte squatted under the sweep and lunged forward with her own sword, striking him twice—once just below each kneecap. The second blow sent him down to one knee, cursing, laying his sword down alongside himself.

"The knees?" Allystaire spat into the dirt their circling feet had stirred into small dustclouds moments before.

"Y'don't get to ask an opponent not to hit you somewhere when it counts," she noted.

Glaring up at her under knitted brows, Allystaire rumbled, "I do not need lessons for a squire."

"Then stop fighting like one," Idgen Marte retorted, poking him in the shoulder sharply with the tip of her sword.

Allystaire swatted ineffectually with his bare hand, missing completely as she drew it back.

"Trying to get your fingers cut off?"

Allystaire reached for his weapon, wrapping his fingers casually around it more than a foot up the blade, which was covered in a sleeve of grooved pieces of wood Idgen Marte had supplied, exactly like her own.

"Do not patronize me. I was fighting battles when you still wore dresses." He rose stiffly to his feet, picking up his sword with one hand on the hilt and one along the lower, dull part of the blade.

Idgen Marte's face blazed with anger, the scar down her chin taut and white as she set her jaw and charged at him. Allystaire suddenly dropped his right foot back and held out his sword, holding it like a spearman set for a charge, grinning very faintly.

The grin faded as Idgen Marte dropped to the ground, sliding with one foot forward, driving her boot sharply into his thigh as momentum carried her on her back, until she crashed against him and sent him sprawling. She popped back to her feet and laid the wooden covering of her blade against his neck, smiling crookedly.

"Did you really think that would work?"

"For a moment." He batted her weapon aside and stood, gathering up his own sword and turning to find its scabbard.

"You're lucky, you know," Idgen Marte called after him, as she began untying the knots that held the wooden slats over the edge of her weapon. "I was aiming for your balls."

"I have been kicked in the crook before," Allystaire snorted. "It hurts, but so does getting kicked anywhere. Got to learn to deal with pain."

"Or learn how not to get hit." Idgen Marte belted her sword back around her hips.

Allystaire buckled his back around his torso and once again set the comforting weight of his hammer in the loop on his belt. "Still not going to spar me with this?" he asked, rapping a knuckle solidly against the dull black head.

"Not on a beggar's life," she snorted. "No way to take the sting out of that, and I like my bones right where they are." Then, pausing and cocking one hip out, placing a fist thoughtfully upon it, she asked, "Why d'ya even carry a sword, anyway?"

A shrug. "It is expected. Knights carry swords. Most also carry something else—a mace or a flail or an axe. You never want to die for lack of being able to fight back. Yet most of them want to be swordsmen, so they spend all their time on it. The sword is elegant, versatile; glory is won with its point and legends are made with its edge. More teachers to learn from."

"So then why the hammer?"

He looked down at it, running his hand over the rough metal. "The hammer makes no false promise of glory or nobility. You know precisely what it does, and precisely what the man swinging it in anger means to do. And, I suppose," he added, "after the battle you could…" He shrugged vaguely. "Carpenter something with it, too."

Idgen Marte snorted and started walking back toward the village that was slowly rising again behind them; they had been swinging and smacking at each other in a treeless field beyond the grave and its attendant altar they had built three weeks before.

"You've never carpentered anything."

"Not true," Allystaire countered. "I have hammered some wood in my day."

"Like what?" Idgen Marte turned to face him, doubt written openly on her sneering, sun-browned face.

"Catapults. Siege towers—"

"Those hardly count," she said, cutting him off.

"I made a table once, a camp table, had some help from a real carpenter to help get the folding bits right. Built it out of the remnants of a smashed tower, in fact. Broke, though."

"How?"

A bit red-faced, Allystaire turned his eyes from hers. "I threw a man down on top of it."

Idgen Marte laughed too hard at that answer to follow up with another question.

"He disobeyed my orders during a battle," Allystaire went on, still slightly flushed. "And got good men killed for it. I should have had him hung. Or at least whipped."

"Instead you ruined a perfectly good camp table. Who was he?"

"Someone too important to throw through a camp table," Allystaire said, stomping away.

Idgen Marte trotted to catch up with him, her long, dark braid bouncing along her back. "How many of these cryptic stories are you going to start without finishing? How many d'ya have?"

Without turning, Allystaire shrugged and said simply, "A lifetime's worth."

"Well, how many is that?"

Allystaire turned back to face her. "I do not know. Is every campaign a story? Every battle? Every skirmish? Every death? What about all the times in between, eh? The marching and riding, the discipline, the bad food, the diseases that strike men down like a bowler at pins? Are they stories, too? What about the horrible things that happen when a town or a castle falls? Are rape and looting and burning and murder all stories, too?"

Idgen Marte frowned, then shook her head. "I've seen all that, too. I'm not some fool boy with a spear in one hand and his cock in the other, y'know."

"Then why ask me for stories if you have seen it all?"

Idgen Marte frowned harder. As she often did, she reached out faster than he could stop and poked him in the shoulder. "Swapping stories are what makes what we've done worthwhile, y'big dumb cow slaughterer," she said, jutting her chin toward the hammer on his belt. "If you can make a story of it, it can't have been so bad, aye? So at least tell me this: Who was the man who got thrown through a camp table?"

Allystaire looked off for a few moments toward the rim of hills, easily visible in the clear afternoon light. "Well, *now* he is the Baron Oyrwyn." He paused a beat. "And it was not thrown, exactly, more like a good hard shove." Another pause. "With both hands. And possibly some emphasis once he hit the table."

Idgen Marte blinked once, startled, then recovered her faint, practiced smirk. "You threw your liege lord's heir through a table? "

Allystaire raised a cautionary finger. "In point of fact, he was not the heir at the time, just the Old Baron's natural son, gone to the wars to learn the trade."

"Some day," Idgen Marte said, tapping his arm this time rather than poking him, "probably in winter when the snow is piled up past the door and there's naught else t'do, we are havin' a sit-down, and you are telling me every piece of all this. I tire of just hearin' bits."

"On my first campaign I was fifteen summers old. My last was not quite a year ago. Score-and-one years make a lot of stories, and some I mean to keep."

"That is why I'll ply you with ale. Brandy if I have to."

Snorting, Allystaire said, "You would get further with wine."

Idgen Marte opened her mouth to retort, but one of the village boys came pounding up to them, chest heaving, and paused to suck in air and try to speak at the same time.

"Calm, lad. Calm. What ails you?" Allystaire felt the hair on the back of his neck stand, his heart slow down, and a ball of lead take shape in his stomach. He felt himself instinctively straightening up, his feet spreading and weight shifting. He glanced to Idgen Marte and saw her doing the same.

The boy gasped a few more times and finally managed, "Men…men, m'lord. armored. Armed. Comin' from the other side o'the road. We was mendin' fences and saw 'em—"

"How many?"

The lad held up his right hand, all fingers splayed. "At least so, m'lord. P'raps more."

"That is a good lad. Now run back to the village and find Renard. Then gather up all the younger children and go wherever he tells you. Run!"

With another quick, deep breath the boy gathered himself and loped off with the boundless energy of excited youth. Allystaire turned to Idgen Marte. "Horse. Bow. See if anyone can get Ardent saddled for me. If I draw my hammer, waste no time."

Idgen Marte hurried off at a steady, ground-eating pace, her legs swinging in long arcs from her hip, sword and braid bounding along behind her. Allystaire began a steady trot, but slowed to a walk as soon as he came in sight of the village green. *Best to be seen calm.* Despite his slow gait, Allystaire's mind raced. *I have my hammer. Sword. Shield is leaning against the saddlebags. The ones with my armor in them.* "Could be nothing," he reminded himself. "Just men passing through."

As he passed by the green and saw the people of Thornhurst start to flow toward him, then behind him, he began to feel their fear—the fear that it was all happening again. He heard the buzz of their talk, heard his name, heard *Paladin* and *Mother* whispered in voices that craved, but lacked, certainty.

He saw Renard—spear in hand, sword on belt, leathern coat sewn with scales—and felt a surge of confidence; he wasn't alone in facing whoever was heading their way. And Idgen Marte was somewhere nearby readying herself for battle, if it came to that. If he couldn't see her, he reasoned, so much the better.

A small, painfully bright spark suddenly blossomed in his chest, in his head, in his skin, in and around him all at once. *There is* nowhere *that you are alone, my Allystaire,* murmured that soft and musical voice. This time, though, its warmth felt less like comfortable sunlight and more like roaring, consuming flame.

He strode up the road with his hands by his sides, arms swinging lightly, eyes peering ahead. Scarcely threescore yards from the green he spotted them; five armored shapes on horseback.

He stopped, set his feet, and waited for the shields to pick themselves out; the lead rider wore blackened armor, a masked helm. *Red goblet upon blue circle on half silver.* "Casamir," he growled, hands itching for his hammer. Flame roared in his ears. Briefly, he remembered their recent meeting in the Sign of the Stone Wall. *I should have killed him then*, he thought, as he recalled Casamir's gloating face, his dark, delighted eyes, the way he backed out of the room smirking, hands held wide and away from his weapons.

His eyes quickly took in the rest; two he did not know, but the fourth and fifth were all too familiar. *Skoval*, he thought, seeing three yellow diamonds descending a red field. And lastly, his heart sank at a dark, gated tower upon a silver field, though he knew the man from his black-enameled scaled armor. The giant black horse he rode was nearly matched in size to Ardent.

"Garth," he murmured, the fire in his head dimming for a moment. He lowered his head and took a deep breath. "I do not want to have to kill you," he whispered. *Please, Mother*, he briefly prayed. *Please don't let it come to that.*

The five knights arrayed themselves, poorly, he noted, with Casamir and one of the unknowns, simple blue and yellow checks on his shield, in the front. The lancers were farthest back, at the edges, and Garth anchoring the space between them.

Casamir removed his helm mostly so that he could smirk, a hateful expression on a hateful man's face, even with sweat streaming down from the dark widow's peak on his forehead. "Go on and reach for your hammer, pisspot. Do it and make an end of this."

Allystaire saw movement among the line, let his eyes flicker. Garth had likewise removed his helm, letting the braid of his long blond hair free. His skin was paler even than Allystaire's, and his eyes so light a green as to seem nearly white; his features were surprisingly fine, almost delicate, and his looks belied by the heavy scaled armor he wore, the heavy longaxe resting across his pommel. "We're ordered to bring you to Wind's Jaw, Allystaire."

"On what charges," Allystaire's voice rang out sharply, "and on what authority? We are not in Oyrwyn."

"Writs of Exile and Divestiture were pronounced upon you weeks ago," Garth said. "You've no legal standing to contest us; you can only hope for Gilrayan Oyrwyn's mercy. As to what barony we are in?" Garth shrugged. "I don't see Lionel Delondeur here to protest."

Garth stepped his horse a few paces closer. Even at a distance, Allystaire thought he could read sorrow in the pale man's features as he added, "And there are six of us, and one of you. Unarmored, these are bad odds. Even for you."

"I only see five," Allystaire replied, with a boldness he did not precisely feel, fire in his limbs or not. "One of you has been afraid of me since he was twelve summers old," he said, turning his eyes to Casamir and offering a cold smile before looking back to Garth. "And you and Skoval, I taught. Are you quite sure that I taught you everything I knew? Is this how you want to find out?"

"Enough prattling," Casamir sulked. "We *are* six…and what d'ya know…" At that moment, a sixth horse trotted out of the treeline bearing two riders. One was another armored form, the other smaller and struggling, with a mailed arm around its neck. As they drew closer, Allystaire saw that the smaller person was Gram. "No need t'risk anythin'. Hold your hands up. Jarmir, the fetters. Garth, take his arms. I'll want to put that stupid laborer's tool on my wall."

The sixth mounted, armored man, another Allystaire did not know, drew close enough for Allystaire to see the fear in Gram's eyes as he struggled against the ironclad arm that held him in place. Allystaire's lips pulled back in a growl as he saw steel bared—a dagger drawn by the knight and held against the boy's stomach.

Allystaire turned to Garth, who had dismounted, and shook his head, his voice low and rough and promising violence. "This is not what I taught you,

Lord of Highgate. This is not knightly." The other knight—yellow and blue checks—had also dismounted and held a pair of bar-and-cuff fetters, open, dangling from a hand.

Garth flushed, but retorted sharply, "Neither was leaving your sister to face the baron's rage."

Allystaire's anger leapt within him, but he turned to face Casamir as the knights came within lunging distance of him. "Let the boy go. Let him go and I will come, peacefully."

From behind him, Allystaire heard the sharp intake of breath. He hadn't realized that a crowd had formed not twenty paces away, and he could only hear them now, couldn't spare the time to turn around, could only hear the choked sob at his words, the murmur of growing fear.

Casamir nodded magnanimously to the other warrior, who shoved Gram casually off his saddle. The boy landed hard on his side, yelping in pain, but hopped back up and began to edge away.

Allystaire held his hands up, palms out, arms straight up from his shoulders. He felt Garth approach him from the side, felt steel-gloved hands tug at the buckle of his sword, felt its weight come free from his shoulders. He didn't look at the pale, sharp-cheeked man; he kept his eyes focused on Casamir.

Jarmir seized his left hand and snapped the cuff around, slid the bar home, then reached for his other hand. Allystaire, rage and fury going cold within him, let him seize it and begin to snap a bar closed around it. Some brief instinct in him made him join his hands closer together, made him wrap the fingers of his right hand around the fetter on his left wrist. With the heightened senses that came over a man as battle was joined, he felt every grain of the rough iron. When his hammer came free and the second cuff closed, he saw Casamir gesture casually to one of the lancers and say, "Ride the brat down."

The knight hesitated, looking to Casamir, lance tip wavering in the air.

At the very moment Casamir uttered those words, Allystaire felt a surge of strength and purpose within him unlike any he had ever known.

His right fist tightened around the cuff on his arm, and he pulled. The iron—stout, thick, well-made—parted like wet paper, and a chain with a heavy weight at the end now dangled from his right wrist. He snapped his leg out in a kick at Garth's knee, even as he drew the fetters back in a swing. The blonde knight collapsed in a heap, his leg suddenly buckling beneath him. Allystaire had no time to worry at the condition of his erstwhile friend and student, nor even to marvel at the song of strength that suffused his limbs.

The heavy chain felt like the kind of long grass he might have, as a child, picked up and whipped in the air in the summer, to hear the sound it made.

The chain in his hand *whistled* as he swung.

It met the helm Jarmir wore, bronze fittings on steel, and tore through it, taking off the top layer of the knight's skull as it clove straight through him. He collapsed in a heap of clattering metal suddenly dark with gore.

Time seemed slow around Allystaire; his heart thudded in his chest, and he heard the Goddess's words in his ear again: *Terrible to behold.*

Allystaire bent and scooped up the hammer that had fallen from Garth's stunned fingers, the chain still dangling from his right wrist. He fixed his eyes on Casamir, whose wide-eyed face had suddenly gone white, and whose hands were scrabbling to fill themselves with sword and shield. Allystaire ran straight for him, the song of the Goddess's voice filling his mind, Her bright fury filling his limbs.

The hammer was a feather in his hands. He raised it; Casamir finally tore forth his sword and dug spur into the flanks of his horse, which came charging toward Allystaire. Allystaire smiled, stopped, waited, waited…then stepped to his right and swung his free left hand, grabbing a goodly handful of Casamir's belt and yanking him from the saddle. The man hit the ground with a resounding clang, and Allystaire was already swinging his hammer down into the middle of Casamir's blackened cuirass. Whipped with the heightened power that flowed through Allystaire's arms, the hammer caved in the armor and the chest of the man wearing it. Another blow, then a third, then Casamir struggling and screaming an awful, wet sound that soon quavered and died.

When Allystaire heard the sickening metal 'ting' of the breast and back-plates meeting in the middle, he straightened up from Casamir's ruined body. *A thing out of legend.* The Goddess's whisper shivered down his bones.

Allystaire looked up in time to see the lancer who'd been ordered to ride Gram down lower his lance, then give his charger the heel. The lancer bore a foot of razor steel and was unarmored.

In the face of the shining fury that sang in Allystaire's limbs, this seemed a small matter. He pulled the hammer back over his head in a two-handed grip and hurled it forward. Till now, throwing his hammer had always been a desperate move. He dimly recalled throwing it at a crossbowman a month and a lifetime ago. Then, the hammer was heavier and thrown more slowly. Now, it did not roll end over end—it flew straight through the air like an arrow fired from some mad giant's bow.

When the hammer hit the mounted man head-on, it knocked him backwards from the saddle. Shield and lance fell from nerveless fingers as the man collapsed almost bonelessly from the back of his saddle. The horse reared up a few feet in front of Allystaire, but he ignored it, already turning to the rest of the battlefield.

The horse upon which Gram had been held was upended, trapping its rider beneath it and thrashing in pain. Fletchings sprouted from several spots along its flank. Suddenly Idgen Marte dashed from the trees, bow in hand, hair streaming behind her. In a flash her sword was out and the horse's throat cut; its thrashing quickly ceased.

The rider, though, had sprung clear and rolled to his feet. Nimble, even in armor, he came up with his knife in one hand and his sword in the other.

Idgen Marte stood between him and the fleeing Gram, her long curved blade and her bow—useless with an enemy so close—filling her hands. The armored man, feeling he was at an advantage against an unarmored woman, stepped forward almost contemptuously, brandishing his sword in an overhand arc.

Allystaire had thought Idgen Marte was fast when he had sparred with her. He saw now that she had been holding back.

Almost from the moment the armored man raised his arm, she had pivoted on one heel, stepped behind him, and slashed across the back of his knee with his sword. Mail links and leather straps flew free. Even as she slashed downwards with her blade, she slipped her curved bowstave between his legs and twisted, sending him toppling to the ground, face first.

Before Allystaire had taken even half a dozen steps, the fight ended with her planting a foot on the knight's back and laying the tip of her blade to the back of his neck. He left his blades on the grass and lifted his empty hands, yelling that he yielded. Allystaire quickly turned back to his own part of the field.

Garth still lay prone upon the grass, clutching at the knee Allystaire had kicked. A crowd of villagers still lingered some yards back along the road. Skoval had thrown down his shield and lance, and sat atop his horse with his hands up. "Down off the horse, Skoval. On your knees." He didn't turn back to see if Skoval had obeyed, because he saw Renard, spear in hand, parting the crowd and coming onto the scene. Allystaire walked to the inert body of the lancer, his chest caved in with the impact of the top of the hammer, and found that he had to set his foot against the plate armor he wore to tug the hammer free. It finally popped loose with a wrenching sound, leaving a horrible rent in the steel beneath it.

Idgen Marte had kicked the sword and knife away from the man she'd unhorsed and defeated, slipped her bow onto her back, and kicked the man back to his feet. He limped, but he moved, her unwavering sword at the back of his neck apparently providing a powerful inducement.

Allystaire turned toward Garth, his hammer dangling from his hand. The pale blonde man struggled to back away, scrabbling on his hands and one foot, keeping the other, oddly bent leg—the one Allystaire had kicked—as motionless as he could. "Stay put or I will break the other one," Allystaire warned. Garth stopped, panting harshly.

"What *are* you, Allystaire?" His chest heaved, his eyes blinked in fear. "What have you done? What devil's bargain have you made?"

"I will show you precisely what bargain I have made, Garth." He slipped the hammer back onto his belt and knelt next to the knight's broken leg. Roughly, he seized hold of Garth's head with a sweaty hand, seeking to weave a rope of connection as he had done with Norbert.

"If that boy had been murdered," Allystaire asked, through gritted teeth, eyes shut, "cut down by a man you were riding with, *what would you have done?*" He tightened his grip, both on Garth's forehead and the grip of his senses on the other man's mind.

In rapid, heavy words, Garth spat out an answer. "He would've died on the way back to Wind's Jaw. He would have died, or I would have."

"And what of Casamir? What of me?"

"I…*agh!* I don't know. *I don't know*," Garth screamed, writhing under the paladin's dual grip. Allystaire released him, and Garth fell back to the ground, panting and sweating harder than before.

"You get to live." Allystaire reached down to Garth's knee, roughly seizing his broken leg, wrapping his right hand around the joint. When he pushed his senses, he could feel the shape of the joint, feel the way the long bone of the shin was snapped; he concentrated intently, pulled again from that deep well he found within himself, drew up sorrow from memories of past friendship, and poured it into the man's broken bone. It snapped suddenly together, whole, and Allystaire immediately withdrew his hand.

He stood, offered his hand down to the fair-haired and fairer-skinned knight, and pulled him, shocked, to his feet. "You will limp a while, yet you can walk now." He paused, waited for the blonde knight to set his weight disbe-lievingly upon his leg, all the while boring his blue eyes into Garth's pale green. "That is the bargain I made. It was with no devil." Then, letting go scornfully, he warned, "Stay put. I am not done with you."

Allystaire turned on somewhat weakening feet toward Skoval, who knelt with Renard's spearpoint held mere inches from his throat. "And *you*." Con-tempt and anger warred for control of Allystaire's voice as he stalked forward, his hammer still gripped in his right hand, growing steadily heavier. "Take off your helm."

Skoval did as he was told. Beneath it he was brown-haired, with rounded cheeks and a hairline well up his forehead. His large, morose brown eyes were ringed by heavy circles, and the large mustache and whiskers he wore gave his entire face a hangdog look.

"I'm sorry, m'lord Allystaire," he rumbled, slowly, his voice a rock rolling slowly against other rocks. "We were only doin' what we were ord—"

His voice cut off quickly as Allystaire leant over him, clamping his hand hard around the man's jaw. "You were going to say that you were doing what you were ordered, yes? That you are a loyal Oyrwyn man and the Baron of Oyr-wyn sent you here for me. I. Do. Not. Care." With each word Allystaire's fingers gripped tighter, till Skoval let out a sharp gasp of pain and tried to pull back.

"M'lord!" Renard hissed. "He's yielded!" Allystaire turned his glare on Re-nard, but the bearded soldier, spear held scant inches from Skoval's throat, met him stare for stare. "He's yielded. Think on your own words t'them. This is not knightly."

Allystaire's fingers unclamped, and he stepped back, flexing his hand into a fist and then straightening it, then back into a fist, several times, breathing deeply. He stalked away, eventually lowering his hand to his side and slipping the hammer back onto his belt; suddenly, Allystaire realized he was working very hard to keep his hands from trembling, and his legs upright. "Round up their horses," he called out. "Disarm them, strip them, bind them, gag them, and toss them onto the green. We will deal with them on the morrow." He bent down to retrieve his sword, then as soon as he picked it up, leaned on it for support.

Allystaire walked off clutching his sheathed sword in nearly nerveless hands. He had almost made it past the crowd of villagers, when, with a sudden exhalation, he fell to the dirt in a boneless heap. The village folk were too cowed or too slow to react quickly enough to catch him.

CHAPTER 19

The Cost

Allystaire awoke to some of the most intense pain he had ever felt. He was more than a little familiar with the ache that inevitably followed a battle, but this was like the ache of a dozen battles, a score, a hundred, all rolled into one and topped with a good dose of being hammered upon by a gravekmir with a grudge.

He let out a moaning sigh, struggling even to open his eyes. When he did, he saw, for a moment, nothing, then tiny pricks of twinkling light appeared, and he realized he was looking at the night sky. Beneath him was soft, cool grass, and something was folded underneath his head for a pillow.

"D'you always pass out at the end of a fight? Damned inconvenient." Idgen Marte's mocking voice from somewhere nearby. "This time, though, you aren't even cut, so I can't begin to guess why. Just a case of the fainting vapors?"

He tried to respond but, for a few moments, all he could summon was another moan. His muscles were stretched beyond all reason and sore beyond the telling, and he could not summon the will to speak, much less move, so he could only lie there and listen to Idgen Marte's mocking laughter, which fortunately died quickly.

He heard the noise of movement, and then she walked into the field of his vision, a tall and irregular shadow that blocked the stars. "Are you wounded? You aren't allowed to die on us now…"

With heroic force of will, Allystaire raised his hand and waved it dismissively before dropping it back to the grass. "No," he croaked, "I am not." Then, swallowing hard, he said, "Is there water? Food?" He was suddenly, painfully, famished.

"And wine," Idgen Marte replied. Her shadow moved away; there came the sound of more movement, then a bottle was pressed to his lips and cool liquid began to burble down his throat. He coughed a bit, but swallowed most, then somehow found the strength to raise himself with an elbow into a half-sitting position. His torso and right arm protested the most.

Idgen Marte knelt next to him and helped him stay upright. In the darkness it was hard to be certain, but he imagined there was genuine concern upon her features. "We carried you out toward the altar. We thought—and, well, Mol told us—that's where you'd need to be."

Allystaire thought on this for a moment, then nodded. "Suppose so," he murmured. He moved his head weakly atop his neck till he spotted the squat, square shadow that must've been the altar. "Help me up."

Long, hard arms looped behind his back and under his shoulder, and Idgen Marte squatted to get her legs beneath her; suddenly he was drawn upward, even as he heard her gasp at the shock of his near-dead weight. Upright, he was able to take a bit of the burden on his own feet, and with hobbling steps and her support, he made it to the altar and fell forward upon it, hoping his weight would keep him there.

Mother, he thought, and in his head his voice was as weak as his arms; *Mother, is this some punishment? Have I displeased you so quickly?*

There was no answer. Allystaire thought over the battle, thought about ripping the shackles off his arms, about the lightness of his hammer and the way it cut the very air itself. He thought back to the way he had crushed Casamir's chest until both sides of his armor met flatly together.

At that he felt a small rush of triumph, though mingled with fear. Once again, words came back to him, unbidden this time, and remembered instead of whispered. *Terrible to behold.*

"I think," Allystaire said, as he pushed himself off the altar, then haltingly turned around so that he leaned, instead of lay, upon it, "that this is the price I pay. That my arms are not made to do…" He paused. "To do the things they did. This may be the price of Her Gift."

"So every time ya fight, you're goin' to collapse? Price seems a bit high."

Allystaire ran his hands along the stone beneath them, felt it warm against his skin. He stood like that for a long moment, silent, praying only so far as to open his mind to the Goddess. He said nothing; he asked for nothing. Whether it was the altar, the moment of prayer, or just his own will, he found the strength to push himself back to his feet, and the weary soreness that suffused his limbs receded by the smallest of degrees.

"Not every time I fight, no," he said, standing at last on steady legs. "Until Casamir ordered his man to ride Gram down, I had no plan. I suppose I was going to go with them and attempt to talk sense into Garth and Skoval. But the instant he threatened the boy…" Allystaire shrugged, grunting as he still felt twinges of pain in his shoulders. "Then the Goddess gave me strength. She told me it would be terrible. That was Her word—terrible."

"Well it was freezin' terrible for sure," Idgen Marte agreed, and Allystaire imagined the grimace twisting the scar near the corner of her mouth. "Three men vomited trying to pull Casamir out of his armor. He had to be washed out with buckets of water. And you took the top of that other lout's head clean off. Brain and bone all over the grass." She shook her head. "When this village lives again, when traders come through, and peddlers and minstrels… have you any idea of the stories they'll carry to the rest of the world? It'll spread like a fire. The Holy Knight who strides the world like a giant, who strikes men down with his hammer the size of a tree, who crushes men with his bare hands."

She stepped closer to him, and in the dim star and moonlight of the evening he could finally see her face, read the note of fear in it. "I thought you were going to kill that Skoval with your bare hands. Tear his jaw off and crush his skull with it."

Allystaire chuckled uneasily, but shook his head. "No. The Goddess's strength had left me by then. Gram was safe; the fight was over. Yet his protest, that he was only doing what was ordered…" He felt his hands curling into fists and closed his eyes, took deep breaths till he calmed.

"So how exactly do you know them? And what in the Cold d'you plan to *do* with them?"

"Casamir, I grew up with. We were squires in Oyrwyn together, under the Old Baron, Gerard Oyrwyn, and rivals from the moment he realized I was a better hand at everything than he. The lance, the horse, the *mêlée*—there was little he could do that I was not better at, and I was not always the best, either," Allystaire said. "There was always something dark in him. Swung his practice blades at the youngest pages a little too hard. Serving women left his chambers bruised. He was always able to make himself useful enough, though, to be tolerated. He was brave, but it was a cunning bravery; good enough in a fight, but you never wanted to show him your back. And always an eye for his own pocket and his own name. I would have thought the Young Baron would have found use for him, and he did, for a while. But even he has limits, I suppose."

"The pigs could have use for him if y'like," Idgen Marte said wryly.

Allystaire let that pass, a brief flash of unease in his stomach at the thought quickly replaced by rumbles of hunger. "I thought you said you brought food?" He watched her walk a few steps away and bend to the ground, then continued. "Garth and Skoval, I trained. Good men. Loyal, brave; Garth was the kind you would trust with his own command. There was a time when we would have stood at each other's backs against anything." He sighed and dropped his hands to his sides. "That time was not as long ago as it feels. Just a few months, really," he added quietly.

"Skoval, on the other hand, has the mind of a dim mongrel dog; if you had the charge of him, he wanted to make you happy. There was never an evil thought in his mind." He paused. "Never a thought one way or another, yet a good and guileless man, in truth."

Idgen Marte leant over, holding toward him a flat, mostly stale trencher filled with a cold joint, cheese, and cold pease pottage with a wooden spoon stuck into it. He seized the spoon and attacked the green, vinegary mush, making the bulk of it disappear in a few mouthfuls.

She let him eat for a few moments before asking, "And what do you mean to do with them?"

"Goddess help me, I have not the faintest idea. Well, the one whose name I do not know…the one who took Gram. Him, I am going to speak to in the morning." He paused in his meal. "How is Gram? Was he hurt?"

"Not badly. A bruise and a scratch and I made sure the latter was clean. Don't change the subject. What of the other two?"

"I do not know." Allystaire shrugged, even as he began gnawing at the meat he held in fingers slick with chilly grease.

"We could ransom them," Idgen Marte suggested. "Be a good way to lay in some weight."

"The Young Baron would never pay," Allystaire replied. "If he learned that we held them, he would just send more men. More than we could stop." He kept at the meat, attacking the bone steadily, devouring the flesh with a hunger he had rarely known. It seemed hardly sufficient, once it was gone and the cheese besides. After considering it a moment, he held the trencher to his teeth and crunched down upon it, grinding the hard bits of bread between his teeth and letting his spit soften others. Soon, it too was gone.

Idgen Marte laughed a little at his sudden display of gluttony, having been quiet while she watched in mild astonishment. "Send them on their way, then, with a warning to leave Thornhurst well enough alone."

"Be kinder if we just slit their throats, I suspect. Gilrayan Oyrwyn insists on his own way, no matter the consequences." Allystaire waved away any further questions, cracked a yawn, and said, "No more talk tonight. Let us deal with them in the morning."

"The bodies will be ripe in the morning," Idgen Marte argued. "We didn't dress 'em. Nobody had the stomach."

Allystaire handed her the spoon and cracked a cavernous yawn. "Morning."

"Fine, fine," she relented, slipping the spoon into a pocket. "Where are you sleeping tonight, what with no fugitives to guard?"

Allystaire grunted lightly. "Remind me to check on Norbert in the morning." Then, gesturing to the field the altar sat in, he said, "I doubt I can make it too far away from here." He paused. "Feels right, anyway." He yawned yet again. "Feels soon, too."

"Think it'll be safe, out here alone?"

Allystaire tapped a hand against the altar he still leaned against. "Not alone." She had turned to leave when he cleared his throat. "You did a good thing today, Idgen Marte."

"I do good things every day, Allystaire."

"You stood between a man in armor and a frightened boy who could work all the years of his life and never afford to hire someone of your skill. Two months ago, would you have imagined yourself doing that?"

"That knight was as dangerous to me as a mouse is to a hunting pard," she snorted.

"And yet you could not have known that when you stood against him. Goodnight."

"I had his measure," she muttered. Idgen Marte strolled away, her figure slowly blending in with the shadows cast by the moon, before disappearing into the night.

Allystaire found a cool spot on the grass and collapsed. He slept, but no more deeply than he had before his life had begun anew just a few short weeks before.

CHAPTER 20

The Shadow Ordained

When Allystaire awoke, summer sunlight was already hammering the ground relentlessly, covering everything in an almost palpable haze. He was soaked in sweat, and his body still bore the heavy ache of the night before. The pain was more tolerable, if only just. Blinking as he pushed himself up, he felt an irritation on his right wrist and reached to scratch it, grimacing as his fingers met the rough iron of the manacle still dangling from his wrist.

He laughed. "How in Cold am I getting *that* off?" He shook his head in answer to his own question, then stood, gathering his hammer, and began to shuffle back along the road toward the village. Before he reached it he could smell the cookfires and hear the rustle of the camping folk coming to life. When he reached the edge of the spread of blankets, bedrolls, and lean-tos they'd slept among, the morning was suddenly silenced but for the lazy calling of birds, which sounded just as tired of the heat as anyone.

The silence abounded because the entire village, as one, had turned to stop and stare at Allystaire. He sighed, his head and shoulders slumping. *Do we have to do this again?*

With a deep breath, he lifted his head and walked on amongst them as if none stared. He held up his right hand, the fetter dangling from the end of its thick-linked iron chain. "Before lunch, someone get an anvil and a fire. I want this off. First, though, I need breakfast." He thought a moment, as everyone stood still and remained silent. "And perhaps prayer afterward, if anyone wishes to join me." They stood like rabbits that thought they'd spotted a hunter. He sighed, wondering, *Am I always going to have to order them?* He waved his hands impatiently. "To it, folk. You have lives to lead. A town to finish rebuilding. *On with it.*"

They scurried away in a sudden burst of motion and energy, but for the most part they stayed silent. Allystaire sighed and watched them scatter.

"Too used to taking orders, ya know. They'll never be able t'look at you as aught but their lord."

"Am I bound to have you answer every unvoiced thought I have from now until my death?" Allystaire turned to find Idgen Marte standing a few feet behind him.

"If you're lucky enough, I suppose."

Allystaire snorted and went in search of food, finding small dried fish and hard rolls in sacks in the wagon. He ate quickly, hardly tasting. Idgen Marte lingered nearby. "I need Renard and the three prisoners." He thought a moment and added, "And rope."

"Gonna hang 'em?"

"Might like to make them think so. First I want to talk to them alone. Without spectacle." Allystaire gestured to the dirt track leading west. "Out where we confronted them yesterday."

"I said *they'll* look at you as their lord, not me."

"I do not know where you put them. And I need a moment alone." He pointed a finger in the direction of the sun, though it was obscured in the haze. He turned his head slightly to the side, and added, "Please."

She nodded and turned away, began eating up the ground with the usual long strides of her legs. He turned off the track and wandered into the trees that lined it, until he came to the site of yesterday's battle. Sod was torn, earth was disturbed, dark stains still marred the track, and the body of the horse Idgen Marte had brought down with her bow still lay in the grass. A fox darted away as he approached, its muzzle darkened.

"Wish she had not had to kill the horse," he murmured to no one. "Still, probably the best she could do at the moment." He wandered away from the large, pungent remains, tamping down the anger that it had been foolishly left out in the grass.

Allystaire turned his mind from this and looked more or less in the direction of the sun. "Mother," he began aloud, then foundered. He cleared his throat and started fresh.

"Mother. I would know that it is Your justice that is done this morning. If I am inclined to mercy, let it not be merely because these men were once my friends. Let it be because they deserve it. If I am inclined to wrath, let it again be because they deserve it."

It wasn't long before he was joined by Renard, who ushered Garth, Skoval, and the unknown knight who had held a knife at a boy's ribs. The last walked with a splint tied around the leg Idgen Marte had cut out from under him. He was of medium height, standing a bit shorter than Allystaire but with a similar kind of bulk that came from years of bearing arms and armor. He had coal-black hair, a rough black beard, ruddy cheeks, and a bulbous nose. Idgen Marte walked alongside him, supporting him with one hand wrapped tightly around his arm.

"All three of you may sit." Allystaire held out his hand and Idgen Marte tossed him a coil of rope, which he unwound and began to knot. Garth and Skoval remained standing, but the third man collapsed to the ground with a grunt and a sigh.

"The two of you," Allystaire said, pointing with the rope toward Skoval and Garth, "know me." He paused, staring at them for a moment, narrowing his dark blue eyes at them. "Perhaps it is better to say that you *knew* me." His hands continued to work the rope, and he saw their eyes growing wide. "Who in the Cold are you?"

"Miles," the man answered, his voice cracking. "Sir Miles of Coldbourne Moor."

Allystaire laughed, a short, harsh sound. "Did not take the bastard long, did it?"

"You didn't leave him much choice," Garth spat back at him, his pale cheeks flushing with anger. "I'd never known you to be a coward, Ally. Not till a month ago."

"What was my choice, Garth? I left because it was me or him, and I could not betray the Old Baron by killing his son, bastard or no. I promised the old man I would serve his son as I did him. I tried. I failed. I broke that oath. I could not betray the father by killing the son."

"You left your own sister behind," Garth shot back, his face even redder now. "To be disinherited."

"I asked Audreyn to come with me. She refused. She stayed *for you*. Whatever else the Young Baron is, I thought there was enough of his father in him to keep him from seeking revenge on her."

Garth drew in a deep breath. Behind the sitting knights, Allystaire saw Idgen Marte turn to Renard and mouth the word, *Sister?* She turned back to watch Allystaire with narrowed eyes.

"Why did you not come to me? You could've hidden with my folk, waited for it to blow away." Garth sighed, some of his anger melting away. "You had friends at Wind's Jaw, and Coldbourne, and Highgate." He looked down at the grass under him, then back up at Allystaire, his eyes carrying in them a fresh hurt. "Had you called, Ally, we would've come. Had you asked, we would've moved against him. We would've made you baron. Still would."

Everyone in the shade of the trees suddenly and collectively drew breath. Allystaire felt intensely the pull of Garth's words and could picture, for a moment, the battle they could summon. He saw Wind's Jaw keep with a new flag snapping above it in the mountain air: gold sunburst on a brilliant blue field.

"Of the major liege lords, at least two would rise for you," Garth said urgently, fueling the fantasy. "Highgate would be yours. Coldbourne, of course. The Horned Towers would stand with Gilrayan, but at least a dozen of the lesser knights would rise for you. Skoval. Curtes. Mauntell. Downys.

The soldiers and the levies know you as the best captain they ever had, to say nothing of the warbands. You think they've forgotten?"

Skoval nodded approvingly; Miles cleared his throat and added, "I'd step aside and give you Coldbourne back, m'lord. I'd be your man."

"No man knows better than you where and how to fight in the high country," Skoval put in, and Allystaire was momentarily silent and still, though stunned into noting, *That might be the most sensible—mayhap the only sensible— remark I have ever heard him utter.*

The thought came to him again; he knew every approach to Wind's Jaw, and every angle the defenders inside it could and couldn't use, how to bring the engines up and where to aim them. Men would rise; he saw that now, an army at his back marching up the eastern trails with the rising sun at their backs and the pennant he imagined, brilliant blue and bright burnished gold, flapping above them.

"Take Oyrwyn, and Harlach would be ours in two years. You conquered nearly half the place as it is. Then we can turn to Delondeur," Garth murmured.

Allystaire turned his eyes from the grass, from the visions he conjured in it, toward the light of the morning filtering through the leaves. He smiled faintly as the words of the Goddess filled his head once more.

He saw the banner he imagined in tatters, flapping above a gutted castle. Bodies strewn everywhere. Ravens flying unchecked among the carnage.

Garth rose halfway to his feet, a hopeful smile breaking out on his face.

Suddenly, Allystaire laughed. He crossed the grass toward Garth and reached down as if to take the man's hand. The pale knight smiled more widely and started to stand, when Allystaire cuffed him sharply on the back of the head.

"Raise your hand with thoughts of winning glory or riches and battle will turn against you," Allystaire said, his voice quiet, his face still slightly dreamlike, as if still seeing a vision. "That is what She told me, Garth. Part of it." He shook his head, bringing his eyes back into focus and his harsh, rough features into sharp awareness once more.

"Glory, titles, men flocking to my banner? I wasted too much of my life seeking that, Garth. *Wasted*," he repeated, putting scornful emphasis into the words. "I am barred from them now. No. You will not entice me with this. I do not know if I have a home, or ever will again. Yet I know it is not in Oyrwyn, at Coldbourne, or at Wind's Jaw."

Startled, sprawling back to the grass, Garth looked up in shock and pushed himself to his knees. "Who is this *she* you speak of?" He tossed a glance over his shoulder toward Idgen Marte. "Her?"

Idgen Marte and Renard burst out in laughter, hers a shade too husky to be musical, his rolling and harsh, like rocks crashing against each other.

"No, Garth. The She I speak of…we have been calling Her the Mother."

"Your mother's dead, Allystaire. My father helped you carry her casket from Coldbourne Hall to your family's tomb."

"I did not say *my* mother. I said *the* Mother, Garth. Open your ears if you will not your eyes." Allystaire squatted down in front of the paler man and fixed him with a dark blue stare. "Garth. Think over the battle yesterday, if battle we can even call it. I broke your leg—your armored leg—with a kick from a riding boot. How does it feel now?"

Garth swallowed hard, and, perhaps unconsciously, edged away from Allystaire, blinking a few times. "Itches."

"Itches the way a wound does for a few days after it is well and truly mended, aye?"

After a moment's hesitation, Garth nodded.

"How do you think I did that?"

"Sorcery of some kind."

Allystaire shook his head, smiling ruefully, the way one might when trying to explain something to a child determined not to learn. "It is not sorcery. It is a Gift of the Mother. The power of a Goddess in my hands."

Garth looked away, his fair skin flushed. "You've finally cracked. I always knew you would. What exactly do you fancy yourself to be?"

Allystaire only stared at him.

"He is a *paladin*, you tit. A holy knight. A hammer in the hand of an angry Goddess." Idgen Marte's voice rang out impatiently and she strode forward till she was standing above the blonde knight, her face taut with bottled rage, long white scars livid against her dark skin in a way that Allystaire had never seen.

"I've witnessed him perform more miracles in the last week than any song cycle attributes to Arentenius and his Argent Blade, and you've been on the receiving end of three. He snapped your leg like a child would a twig, then he compelled the truth of you, and then he healed you. If you cannot acknowledge the truth of that, then you aren't just a freezin' idiot, you're a liar and a coward. And if you doubt his word again I will give you your sword back and we'll find out just how well you can dance on a leg that should still be broken." Her hand strayed dangerously to the hilt of her sword.

"Stay your hand," Allystaire said, quietly but firmly. He straightened up and placed his hand lightly on her arm, and he felt the smile of the Mother in his mind and words he had thought when he had first met Idgen Marte, an old lifetime ago: *I like this one.* He knew, of a certainty now, that those words had not been his thought, or at least not his alone, on that night in the tavern. The Mother had reached out to her as surely as to him. "We will speak after this. Alone," he said, and gave her the gentlest push against her arm, indicating that she should step back.

She stepped back, dropped her hands, and took deep breaths, nodding. Allystaire saw her turn her face toward the morning sun, and he smiled before turning back to Garth.

"Tell me how things stand, truly, back…" He paused, stopped himself from saying home, and said, "back in Oyrwyn. Tell me no lies, and I may let you head back with the corpses and a warning."

Swallowing once, Garth suddenly blurted, "I married her, Allystaire."

Allystaire blinked in shock as he stepped away. "What?"

"Before the news of your flight had spread, before the Writs were published. We found a priestess of Fortune and had her say the words in front of three witnesses." He swallowed hard, and pressed on. "I know you weren't there to grant leave, but it seemed prudent."

Allystaire absorbed this slowly, then nodded. "Audreyn's life was always her own; her pledge was her own to give." He paused, found the other man's pale eyes, held them a moment. "For whatever it matters now, Garth, I would always have said yes."

Garth nodded, and for a moment an old bond seemed to kindle between them, the easy, unspoken companionship of men who'd faced danger together, knew it, and saw no need to cheapen it with words.

It quickly passed as Garth cleared his throat and went on.

"The Young Baron is as bad as ever. Maybe worse. I keep waiting for his father's blood to show true, and then he raises up blades-at-hire and thieves if they say what he wants to hear." He jerked his chin toward Miles, who grimaced and fidgeted uncomfortably on the grass.

"'Ey! I'm as much a knight as any of you. Granted title by Baron Oyrwyn hisself," Miles protested. "I earned it fair."

"Did you?" Allystaire tilted his head toward Miles, and let the rope he'd been knotting dangle from his hands as a noose. "Under the Old Baron, being a knight meant more than wearing a suit of steel and knowing how to swing a sword, Sir Miles. It meant being educated. Can you name all of the fourteen original baronies, Sir Miles?"

The man chewed at his lips in the midst of his dark black beard, eyes darting side to side. Allystaire chuckled and went on.

"Are you lettered, Sir Miles? Can you read and write your own dispatches and ciphers if commanding men in the field? Did you spend your months with the Old Baron's dwarf chirurgeon, learning the ways to treat a wound, how to end a man's life painlessly, where the blood flows strongest in the body?" Allystaire waved a hand to forestall any answer. "Sorry, that last is a trick, for old Michar is dead a half score years and more. A shame, though. His training, his knowledge, the medicine he alone knew, saved more Oyrwyn lives than all the steel and stone in Wind's Jaw. Saved mine, more than once."

Allystaire cinched the noose a little more tightly and looked closely at the man.

"Do you know the history of the barony you serve, Sir Miles? Or your fief? Coldbourne Moor has been the seat of no fewer than six different families. And that is just as far back as Oyrwyn's archives reach. Could be many more."

Miles shook his head, his eyes flitting from the noose to Allystaire's face and back again.

Allystaire nodded slowly, his manner that of a scholar imparting a lesson to a dim charge. "It has been seen as something of a cursed fief. No family holds it long; often it is granted to a successful retainer or a landless knight who does sterling service to the baron. Often it has been simply a second holding for a family of greater means. My grandfather was awarded Coldbourne Hall for his service at the start of the Succession Strife. He was not much more than a soldier, but apparently a damned good one, for it earned him not only knighthood, but land and title. I do not know where he came from, but my father suspected that he had begun life as a laborer, perhaps even on the bogs of Coldbourne itself."

Casually, Allystaire draped the rope over one shoulder and squatted painfully to one knee, in order to look Miles eye to eye, meanwhile continuing the lecture.

"My father broke the 'curse', as it were, by actually living long enough as Lord of Coldbourne Hall to have children. Heirs. Three generations of the same family. Had not been done for well past five-score years by then."

"Now. Miles, Lord of Coldbourne Hall and the Moors; do you have a family? Children?"

Miles swallowed hard, his eyes wide and rolling in his head. "I…I had a son, m'lord. Bastard son. Down in Londray. Or I did. Been a few years."

Allystaire nodded faintly. "How old?"

With a shrug, he replied, "Half a score years by now?"

"Gram—the lad whose life you threatened yesterday—is roughly that age. A defenseless child with no part in any squabble between the Young Baron and me. Casamir ordered you to kill him. Would you have done?"

"Would I have done…m'lord?" Miles swallowed again, edging back. He did not get very far before Allystaire clamped a hand on his shoulder, holding him still.

"You put a knife to the boy's ribs, Lord Coldbourne. You used a child as a hostage, threatened his life, to get me to surrender in a ploy to curry favor with a baron in whose service you have been for perhaps a fortnight, who thinks so little of you he has not bothered to give you the proper arms upon your shield. Now answer my question, Miles." Allystaire's voice was a calm even rumble, but as he leant closer, it evoked the deadly whisper of steel.

"Do not attempt to lie. You will find that you cannot." His hand tightened on the man's shoulder and then clasped the back of his neck, fingers digging roughly into the flesh and the bone beneath. "Would you have killed the lad?"

Miles's mouth worked soundlessly for a moment, then, finally, he croaked, "Yes."

"Why?"

"What d'I care, he lives or dies?"

"You have killed children before? Women? And would do so again?"

Once again his mouth opened and closed and no sound came out. The man clamped his mouth shut, closed his eyes, shaking with the force of the effort. He threw all his weight against Allystaire's hand and fell back upon the ground, pale, trembling, sweating.

Allystaire stepped back, his eyes dark with fury. Miles blubbered on the ground, eyes still tightly shut. "Warlock. Sorcerer. Forced me…forced me t'say I…it's a lie!" The man sat up and started to push to his feet as if to run.

Allystaire casually backhanded Miles across the mouth, sending him sprawling back onto the grass. "I cannot force you to say something that is not true."

He pressed his lips into a flat line and said, "Garth. Skoval. Help Sir Miles of Coldbourne Moor to his feet."

The other two prisoners stood with the abrupt attentiveness of men used to obeying. They bent to seize Miles with their still bound hands and managed to force him to sit up, if not stand. Allystaire stepped in front of him and began to settle the noose over his neck. "This will go poorly for you if you insist on staying on the ground, Sir Miles," he murmured, with grave formality. "You would have committed a murder, and you are a murderer, many times over I suspect. Yesterday, a knight in armor on horseback—you used the weapons of your station to threaten a child and terrify poor folk. You are not the first man to do that. You will not be the last. But today, you will hang for it."

Garth and Skoval both paled, and the paler knight licked his lips and spoke. "Allystaire, you've no legal—"

Allystaire turned his hard and pitiless blue eyes on his brother-in-law. "I did not ask your legal opinion, Lord Garth of Highgate."

"I cannot allow—"

"Who speaks next, *hangs* next," Allystaire roared. "You will not try to tell me that this man deserves less than death for his crimes yesterday, or the many that lie behind it."

"You won't hang me, Allystaire," Garth said. "And he may deserve it, but he is knighted by a baron's hand. He cannot be hanged like a common bandit."

"He is the commonest of bandits," Allystaire spat back. "One with a title, and the wealth and arms that position brings." He cinched the noose tightly around Miles's neck, and tucked his hands under the man's arms, dragging him up to his feet. "Stand up and die like a man."

Desperately, tears streaming down his cheeks, Miles sobbed, "Ransom, m'lord! The baron will—"

"Do you think I would trade justice for links? No." Allystaire turned back to Skoval and Garth. "Get your shoulders under him. Lift him up. You remember how." Flicking his glance back to Miles, he added, "It will be quick. I promise you that."

He took the end of the rope that coiled around his arm, loosed it, and threw as much as he could over the nearest, stoutest tree branch that stood the right height—just under twice his own length—above the ground. He pulled the slack through, then braced it by wrapping it around his back and tying a quick sliding knot with the end, setting his feet into the ground and digging in. "Renard, Idgen Marte."

Renard set down his spear, and both of them came over to assist him in holding the rope taut. "Do you wish a prayer, Sir Miles? Do you wish to discuss disposition of your remains? Or to speak some final words?"

"Freeze you and your whore Goddess, you freezing warlock," Miles shrieked, struggling against the grip of Skoval and Garth, uselessly.

With a slight, cold shrug, Allystaire said, "In the next life, Sir Miles, should you meet the Mother, I should recommend not calling her that." Then, without any further warning, he tensed his shoulders, yelled, "DROP!" to Skoval and Garth, and dug in his heels.

Skoval and Garth both fell to their knees, each seizing one of the man's trouser legs, and pulling hard. Miles, still screaming curses, went silent after a *crack* so sharp it startled birds from the nearby trees. The rope dug into Allystaire's shoulders and back, a thin line of fire, and Idgen Marte and Renard braced him as the dead weight tried to pull him forward, his feet digging into the ground. He hauled back on the rope, silently counting in his head till he reached a score. When he did, he slowly stepped forward, lowering the rope until Miles's body hit the ground, lifeless and still, neck unnaturally bent.

The two surviving knights of Oyrwyn scrambled back to their feet in shock, faces blanched. "Fortune freeze me, Allystaire, I thought you were trying to scare us," Garth said, trembling a bit.

Allystaire fixed a hard stare on them. He unlooped the rope from around his shoulder and began unknotting it, staring evenly, not blinking. "He wanted killing. If you cannot see that, you are not quite the man I thought you were."

Garth swallowed and turned his eyes away.

Skoval cleared his throat. "Allystaire, you always were a hard one. This isn't the first man you've hanged. Cold, it isn't the first man we've helped you hang. He was different, though, he was a—"

"He was a what? A lord? A brother of battle? A knight?" Allystaire spat these words while he finished unknotting the rope, throwing it aside in disgust. "He was a murderer, and would have been again. Did you not hear his own words? Did you not see what he did?"

"To men of station, it isn't done, Allystaire," Garth protested, his voice mild, tone reasonable. He opened his mouth to say more, but Allystaire suddenly advanced on him, radiating a frozen anger.

"It is now," he said, almost whispering. "Think on the actions of your dead comrades and on what happened to them. You saw the power the Goddess has given me and you saw where evil led them." He smiled, though as often seemed to the case, the expression did not touch his eyes. "You will carry the news of what you saw, and its proof; you may take the bodies of your fellow Oyrwyn knights—what is left of them—back to the Young Baron, and tell him exactly what you saw." He waited a moment, and then added more audibly, "Add this warning: by the time he can find me again, I will not be alone. He will have two servants of the Mother to contend with, and together, we will grant him as many dead knights as he wishes. If ever a man in his service sets foot in this village and harms a single being within it, or any other under the Mother's protection, I will lead a crusade against Oyrwyn the likes of which he cannot imagine. And should it take the rest of my life, I will take Wind's Jaw apart until no stone stands on another, till no stick of wood remains unburnt. Do you understand?"

"Wind's Jaw was your home once," Garth replied, quietly defiant.

"Not anymore," Allystaire replied flatly. "Now answer my question: do you understand the message I have given you?"

Garth and Skoval nodded mutely.

"Good. If I ever see the pair of you again I hope we are not across the field. Should we be, I shall not look for you. But know that if either of you becomes the kind of man Casamir or Miles was, then no old bonds of battle or new bonds of marriage will shield you. Now go."

He turned his glance to Renard, who had watched quietly, and said, "Fetch their horses. And two more, to bear the bodies. Their arms and armor are to be returned to them, as well as Casamir's, and the helm of the knight I slew with this—" he raised his arm from which the shackle still dangled "—to serve as proof of the Mother's wrath." He dropped his arm and continued, "The remaining horses, arms and armor, and any links the dead men carried, are forfeit. Payment for disrupting the peace of this place. Cut them free so they can deal with this." He nudged Miles's limp body with the toe of his boot.

Renard drew a knife and slipped it through the thongs bound around Garth's and Skoval's wrists. Allystaire nodded to Idgen Marte, indicating that she should follow. She nodded, watching him curiously, then did as he bid. They passed through the village, most of the folk busy at one task or another—cutting wood or hauling rock to rebuild various walls, mostly, or rethatching the roofs of buildings that still stood. The pair continued down the track toward the field where the altar stood.

Sensing their destination, Idgen Marte said, "Now if this is about morning prayers, I already—"

Allystaire turned to her with a quiet, lightly mocking smile. "Will you, for once, stop talking, and simply *look*?"

They rounded the final bend to the Temple Field, as Allystaire was beginning to think of it, and he pointed. Where the heavy rays of morning sunlight struck the altar, a sudden brilliant intensity of light gathered, and a glowing form, so bright it hurt to look at, and yet so inviting they could not turn away, suddenly coalesced.

Allystaire heard Idgen Marte draw in a sharp breath, almost choking on it.

"So it only takes a Goddess to silence you." Allystaire took her arm with his hand and said, "You shall not get the last word with Her, either."

They approached the incandescent Goddess, who stood drawing a finger over the stone altar they had raised, as if writing upon it. They could see traces of smoke rising up from the surface as Her hand moved upon it.

The Mother raised her face to them, and both fell to their knees after but one glimpse of Her face, old and young, wise and maidenly, beautiful and powerful, all at once. "My children," Her voice sounded in their ears like enormous drumbeats, shaking their entire bodies. "You pleased me with this work." Allystaire glanced up to see her touching the altar. "Though it remains undone. Others are needed to complete it. Arm, Shadow, and Voice—these are but three. The Will and the Wit remain. It falls to you to find them, and to do it before autumn becomes winter."

Suddenly She was standing in front of them; there was no sense that She had walked. One moment She was yards away, behind the altar; now it was as if the world had simply shifted about Her.

One hand settled on Allystaire's head. "My Allystaire, your anger in my service could undo you. I implore you to remember *love and mercy*." He looked up, eyes suddenly stinging with hot tears at this mildest reproach, to see the painful sunlight of Her gentle, sad smile. "The men you killed in hotter blood, I do not grieve. Yet this very morn, in My Light…could that man have been saved? Now you will never know. I do not rebuke your choice, my Knight; I would not have chosen a man of less conviction. Yet I ask that you think on it."

She turned to Idgen Marte, and Allystaire dropped his face, eyes tightly shut, squeezing back the wetness in their corners. He heard the Mother say, "This day has been long in coming, my Shadow." And then no more, as her voice sounded in his head and, he knew, his alone. *Leave us, my Knight. This moment is for no one else to see.*

With enormous reluctance weighing on his shoulders, Allystaire rose; he saw Idgen Marte still kneeling, her eyes closed, and the Goddess then lifting her to her feet as She had once done to him, saw Idgen Marte shudder and heard her sob, then saw her fall against the radiant form that held her up. Then, heeding his Goddess's words, he turned away from a moment he was not meant to see, and walked back to Thornhurst, wondering if he had hanged a man who deserved to live, or suffered to live a man who should have died.

CHAPTER 21

Arm, Shadow, and Voice

The bright thrumming music of the Goddess faded from his head, but not until Allystaire found himself standing sweat-soaked before an anvil in the still un-repaired remains of what had been Thornhurst's smithy, though not much of one, Allystaire thought ruefully. *Enough to shoe a horse and bang out a plow or some other infernal farm implement,* he mused. He had a hammer, a prybar, and a chisel, and he realized that he must've been popping links off the chain on his wrist one by one, for he was down to the cuff.

"Damn stupid way to do it. One of those dead bastards probably had a key somewhere on him anyway." He slipped the thin edge of the bar through the cuff, against the back of his wrist, placed his hand against the side of the anvil, and pulled the bar toward himself. It took some doing, and despite the anvil, it seemed to come within spitting distance of breaking his wrist, but eventually the fetter gave way. He started to toss it to the ground, but stopped himself. After a moment's reflection he bent down and picked up the links he had broken, stuffing them in a pocket and moving back out into the late morning sunlight.

In his field of vision, Thornhurst took shape; the sounds of hammers and adzes competed with penned up sheep and clucking chickens. He found Idgen Marte sitting on a rock outside the smithy, nodding lightly to the hum of a voice Allystaire could hear but not quite see. When he took another step, he saw Mol kneeling next to her, speaking. He didn't strain to hear; both stood as he approached.

"We're three now. 'Tis one closer t'what we're meant t'be," Mol said, making this authoritative announcement with a portentous gravity that would've been unusual from any other lass of her age and size.

Idgen Marte smiled gently and reached down as if to tousle Mol's hair, but the look the girl fixed upon her did not brook that kind of nonsense; the warrior dropped her hands casually to her waist as if she'd meant to all along.

"She said something to that effect," Allystaire replied. "Arm, Shadow, and Voice." As he said this, he pointed to himself, Idgen Marte, and Mol in turn. "Are we in accord?"

"Does it matter," Idgen Marte wondered, and for once, her tone lacked acid.

"We do, and it does. We three of us should go see yer friends off, Allystaire," Mol declared.

"How do you know about—"

Mol turned her large, dark eyes to him, cutting his question short. "Right."

The three of them ambled off toward the grove where Miles had hanged; it didn't take long to find Renard and his spear shepherding Skoval and Garth and four horses. Two of the horses had tightly wrapped bundles bound to their saddles.

Allystaire pointed to one. "Casamir?"

"And Jarmir, Ifhans, and Miles," Garth answered dourly. "Or such pieces of them as will be necessary to identify them for the baron and their kin." The pale knight swallowed once and said, "It was an ugly way for knights to die. Even Casamir."

"Then they found fitting ends, for they were ugly men," Allystaire replied.

"You didn't know Jarmir or Ifhans," Garth began, only to pause as Allystaire waved away his words.

"They stood by while a ten-year-old child was held at knifepoint. They let a child be threatened to secure their own surety and favor. That is all I needed to know. You make sure you tell the Young Baron how they died."

"When it comes to Casamir and Miles, I agree with you, Allystaire," Garth replied. "Yet I remember my old arms-master and teacher telling me that a man who was badly led was not always to blame for his own deeds. I remember a man who cautioned me against absolutes."

"That man made excuses for those who were useful to him, or were his friends," Allystaire replied quietly. "Or at the whim of his misplaced loyalty."

"You were like a son to the Old Baron, Allystaire. The son he wished he'd had. Can you truly call that misplaced?"

Allystaire was silent a moment, then finally shook his head. "No. No, I do not think I can."

Garth nodded, then pulled his helm back over his head, its scales clinking lightly as they settled over his long hair. He pulled himself up into the saddle. Allystaire quickly checked to see that Garth's longaxe and Skoval's sword had been tied into their sheaths, the knots cinched tightly around their horse's pommels.

"You don't believe in the Mother, do you?" Mol stepped forward, her young voice carrying a heavy weight beneath it.

The blond knight shook his head from side to side, looking curiously at the small girl who approached his horse.

"Why not? Ya've seen her miracles."

"I have seen the work of sorcery before. Fortune grant I never do again."

Mol tilted her head to the side, as if listening to some sound audible to only her, then nodded. "You believe, yer just not ready t'admit it yet. Think on it as y'ride."

Allystaire stepped up to Garth's horse and hooked his fingers through the halter. "I spoke to Miles of this; the other men who died, had they family? Widows, children?"

Garth shrugged, setting the havelock of scales that lay along the back of his neck jingling against the pauldrons of his armor. "Jarmir and Ifhans, I do not think so. None that I know of. As for Casamir, there are probably bastards about."

"If there are any, the price of their fathers' lives should be paid. I would not look to the Young Baron to do that; can I depend on you?"

Sighing reluctantly, Garth nodded. "The good a father does may buy the son loyalty, but the ill a father did should not buy him spite," he said in a tired voice, as if repeating something he'd memorized.

Allystaire nodded and let go the halter of Garth's destrier, a black horse of similar size and, Allystaire knew, temperament to Ardent. "Good. In that case, there is a casket of valuables buried underneath a linden tree outside Cold-bourne Hall; the one I scolded Audreyn for climbing too high in when she was a child. She will know it. Gemmary, mostly; some plate."

Garth blinked, turning in the saddle to look down at Allystaire, leather and metal creaking as he moved. "Thought you'd have taken it all with you."

"Seemed unbrotherly, as half of it belonged rightly to Audreyn. I suppose all of it did, technically."

"What do you want me to do with it?"

"What I just told you. Pay the life price if the baron will not. Give the rest to Audreyn." Allystaire patted the neck of Garth's great black horse, which barely acknowledged him. "Go with the Goddess. Think about what you saw and heard. And try to convince the Young Baron not to send more men after me. I will make it cost more than it is worth."

"Haven't you any words for your sister, then? Or is it all warnings and worry for other men's sons?"

"There is nothing Audreyn needs to hear from me. We spoke before I left."

"Doesn't mean there isn't more you could say," Garth countered. He shook his head, sighed heavily, and added, "You're one of the bravest men I ever knew, Ally. Always were. Yet when it comes to your own family, you remain a coward." He jerked his reins to turn his horse and gave it a quick, light jab with his spur, and it galloped off.

Skoval sighed, stepping his horse over to the two horses bearing bodies, gathering up their reins. He looked back at Allystaire. "I'm no man of wit nor learning, Ally," he rumbled, his voice slow and ponderous, "yet I know what I saw on the field yesterday. I've not had much truck with gods or goddesses, but somethin' has put power in your hands. Not sorcery. 'Twere it some foul bargain, I expect 'twouldn't happen the way it did. From where I sat you were saving a lad's life, n'then you healed a man you'd hurt. Doesn't seem like devilry to me. Y'can count on me to tell folk the plain truth of what I saw, if they'll listen."

Allystaire reached up to take Skoval's hand at the wrist and give his arm a pump. "Mayhap I should have listened more, Skoval. You are a good man. Better, I think, than I gave you credit for in years past. Goddess go with you."

When Allystaire uttered the small but sincere benediction and let go of Skoval's hand, he felt some tiny tingle pass between them, and some small note of the Mother's music sounded in his head. The big, sad, mustached knight nodded, gathered up the reins of his dead comrade's horses, and rode off after Garth at a calmer pace.

Renard shouldered his spear and wandered over, and the four of them watched as Skoval trotted out of sight. Renard spat into the weeds and wondered aloud, "Y'sure you want to let them leave, Allystaire? May not be the wisest course."

"Wise or not, it is the course I have chosen. Enough blood spilled over my past. And," Allystaire added, smiling lightly, "I think we may have made a pair of converts. One for sure."

"I felt it," Mol added, nodding decisively.

Idgen Marte cleared her throat almost delicately, then said, hoarsely, "As did I."

The four of them stood like that for a moment, watching the woods, watching the sunlight slowly fill the copse, listening to the distant sounds of the village, the ring of tools and the chatter of industrious work. Renard snapped them back to life with a grunt. "Enough gawking, I expect. Plenty of work t'be done, plenty of light left. Off we go, eh?"

Allystaire laughed lightly. "You are the Mother's own sergeant, Renard." He clapped the man companionably on the shoulder. Mol reached up and took the bearded soldier's free hand in hers, and Idgen Marte chuckled subtly.

"We will catch up with you," Allystaire called, though Mol had already led Renard away, his spear parting the leaves and branches above them. They were soon out of sight.

Idgen Marte stood fixed in the same spot, squinting at a beam of sunlight. Allystaire took a step forward and laid a hand on her shoulder. For a moment, she slumped her shoulders and leaned back against his hand, but quickly straightened and turned to face him. "She doesn't leave much room for argument, does She?"

"None," Allystaire replied.

"Then why choose me? Why not choose anyone and impose Her will? Isn't that what She did?"

"I do not think so. You earned Her attention with your faith. Now She is returning it."

"You're telling me a Goddess has faith in *me*?"

"Should she not? Since we came together, Idgen Marte, have you made the choices you expected yourself to make? Do you think Mol talked you into coming out to that warehouse by yourself? Was it an accident that you arrived in time to save me from bleeding to death? Would you, a year ago, six months—Cold, even six weeks ago—have decided to follow a half-crazed beggar knight who talks to himself and takes on a dozen men at once without a plan and who, most importantly, cannot afford to pay you?"

"You're saying all this was fated, are ya? Has She been pulling strings since we met?"

Allystaire shook his head, his eyes closing for a moment as he thought. When he opened them again, he said, "No. I think that She tested you, as She did me. You have had several chances to walk away, aye? And most would have left you with more links in your purse and fewer people depending upon you."

"I followed ya for the story; stories usually have great piles of treasure. Heaps of gold, gemmary, ancient weapons, and the like—"

"I do not think this story ends with our getting rich," Allystaire offered mildly.

"I could probably beat the Pale Knight and his Hound Man back to that linden tree you talked about," she muttered.

"My grandmother planted linden trees everywhere there was a bare patch of grass around Coldbourne Hall. You would never find it," Allystaire said, smiling broadly.

"You're lying."

Allystaire's smile widened until it encompassed his entire face, the expression incongruous with his oft-broken nose. "I cannot."

Idgen Marte cursed and spat on the grass, looking down at her boots for a moment before squinting back up at him. "We're going t'be leaving soon," she said.

"Clarify *we*."

"The two of us, I think. Mol is too young for the road, and besides, she is not meant to leave Thornhurst. A temple will rise here, and it will be hers to guide."

"Will the villagers mind her words once we are gone?" Allystaire asked doubtfully.

"I think they will with Renard standing behind her," Idgen Marte said. "He isn't meant to leave either."

"Where are we going, and what are we waiting for?"

Idgen Marte frowned, shook her head, and stuck her hands uncomfortably on her belt. "The answer to either question is *I don't know*. She told me to wait for a sign. *He will see*. That is all She said. I suppose *he* is *you*."

"Then we wait for a sign."

"If it helps, I think I know why we have to leave."

"Well?"

"The Wit, or the Will. Both. Whoever they are. We're to search them out."

"The Wit and the Will," Allystaire murmured, thinking the words over, gaze drifting to the trees. Then he looked back toward Idgen Marte, tilting his head to the side. "Why the Shadow?"

She merely smiled slightly and said enigmatically, "You'll see."

CHAPTER 22

A Storm

Days passed, became weeks, and summer slowly began to burn itself out. Summer and winter were the longest seasons by far in the baronies, and this summer seemed determined to drag on and erase as much of autumn as it could. The business of throwing up walls and thatching roofs was made all the more miserable by the relentless heat. After three solid weeks of work, with scores of the trees that had surrounded Thornhurst now stumps, none of the folk were any longer sleeping outdoors except by choice. The wagons that had been their prisons, then briefly their homes, were tucked away inside a barn; cows were milked once again; hearth fires lit; crops and gardens repaired and tended. Life slowly returned to a kind of normalcy.

Rough stone walls began to take shape surrounding the altar field. Early afternoons, with thunderheads often looming above, usually found Allystaire stacking stones alongside a handful of village folk. Different Thornhursters came each day, when they could find an escape from their own work, to help build the temple Allystaire had preached of nearly a month before. Mol always appeared with them; she had early on insisted on certain elements of the building, especially the space within. Allystaire had envisioned something much smaller than what was now being laid out.

This afternoon found Mol standing in front of the altar, arguing insistently with the local stonemason, Giraud.

"E'rywhere I tell ya, Giraud, including in the roof," she insisted. For a lass of ten summers, there was a remarkable dearth of pouting or temper. She did not put hands on hips or stomp her feet. She was simply implacable.

"'It ain't possible, lass," the large, heavy-shouldered man insisted, tugging on his thick brown beard. "I dunno how t'do what you're askin'."

With a sigh, Allystaire set down the pile of stones he was hauling and stepped over the wall, which rose almost to his waist, his boots sinking a bit into the hay-strewn floor.

"In the first place m'not askin'," Mol was saying calmly, carefully, when Allystaire came up behind Giraud, who was even broader than the paladin.

"Giraud, neighbor, let me save you the trouble. If Mol is insisting it must be a particular way, it must," he said gently. "You may not know how to leave windows and gaps for the light where she is telling you, but it is not simply Mol who is speaking, eh?" Allystaire pressed his lips together and tilted his head forward a bit, hoping to impress his meaning on the other man.

"I can't build somethin' I dunno how t'build," Giraud replied, exasperated, his hands thrown into the air in frustration.

"I did not know how to do anything the Mother has asked of me, until the moment I did it. Faith, Giraud. Right now, faith means doing what the lass says." He dropped his voice a bit, glanced at a satisfied Mol nodding her head and walking off to go oversee something else, and added, "Trust me, goodman. You will do what she says in the end no matter how you argue."

The large, dour-faced but gentle man closed his eyes, murmured, "Faith," and went back to overseeing the afternoon's construction.

Allystaire clapped him on the shoulder and followed after the girl. "Mol… what was that about?"

She turned and said, "Light. What else would it be?"

"What do you mean, 'light'?"

She sighed, very faintly, and explained in careful tones. "She wants *light*. In the mornin', at midday, at sunset."

"Then perhaps we should be building in the mountains and not in a valley."

Mol smiled brightly, and for a moment looked like any excitable child of ten summers. "We could build another one, there'd be time 'fore winter—"

Allystaire stopped her. "Mol. If the Mother herself tells me to go climb a mountain and build a temple there, I will, and by myself if need be. Short of that, let us finish this one first, aye?"

She deflated, just a little, a child with an idea discarded, but soon brightened and wandered off on bare feet to instruct someone else.

Allystaire hauled a few more piles of stone from the stocks that had been gathered over the past weeks, but soon drifted from the temple and wandered back into the village, his steps carrying him into the mostly rebuilt inn he had burst into his first time in the village center.

Idgen Marte was already there, with the place to herself, a large flagon of what Allystaire knew to be a rather sour beer, and two cups. She filled one and slid it toward him.

"See anything yet?"

"Naught but stone and dust."

"Storm seems likely. It'll be the most entertaining thing since the hang—"

Allystaire cut her off with a look and a curled fist on the bar. She held up a conciliatory hand and went back to drinking. Allystaire took a painful first swallow, tried to splash the liquid past his tongue and down his dry throat. After swallowing, he said, "You have a point."

"I have at least three."

He snorted, tried to quickly toss down more of his beer, only to grimace when it found his tongue despite his best efforts. "Tell me again what She said."

Idgen Marte groaned and, for a moment, dropped her head into her arms. "I've told you every day since She told me. You know what She said. We're to wait for the sign. *He will see.* That's all She told me about how long we need t'remain here. The sign will tell us where t'go."

Allystaire raised his cup, set it down empty with his teeth clenched in near pain. "We are doing the Mother's work. It will rarely be pleasant, and not always exciting."

"We're in the way, Allystaire," Idgen Marte protested. "Well on our way to being useless mouths. If this drags into winter then we're stuck here till the spring thaw."

"We are only just getting into autumn now. Why so worried about winter?"

"You've lived all your life in a place where people swear by the Cold and you wonder why a southerner like me is concerned about winter? It's too long by half. And your autumns are plenty cold enough for me."

"We are where we are supposed to be," Allystaire insisted. He reached for the flagon and poured a second cupful, then drained it quickly. "If you are so desperate for something exciting, why not a bit of sparring?"

"I can only smack you around so much before growing bored, old man," Idgen Marte replied, already uncoiling off the bench she'd sat on, "but if you insist." She reached for her swordbelt buckled against the wall, and the two of them headed for the door.

They stepped outside and had taken perhaps five steps from the door when the thunderheads finally cracked above them and rain began pouring in sheets. Allystaire stopped and laughed, turning his head up to the rain. Idgen Marte did the same, and the two of them headed back inside.

"Build up the fire," Allystaire told her. "The folk will all crowd in here soon enough. I will start fetching up beer." He took the flagon they hadn't quite emptied and knelt, pulling open the cold well, and dipped the flagon to fill it. He set it upon the bar, reached up onto the shelves for another pair of the crude earthen vessels, filled them, and reached for another. While fumbling around on the shelf above him, his fingers brushed against something with a different texture than the typical pottery of the inn's flagons and jars; it was cool and hard. He stood and peered into the shelf, pulling forward a thick, squat, darkened glass bottle. It was covered in dust; when he blew it off with a quick breath, he discovered a faded sigil stamped upon it.

He turned to Idgen Marte with a wide grin tugging at his features. "Brandy. From the south of Innadan. Most of the best wine in this part of—"

She cut him off with a wave of her hand, then reached for the bottle. "If it won't taste like this green beer the reavers provisioned us with, hand it over with all due haste."

Allystaire carefully placed the bottle on the bar in front of her. She snatched it and stared at it, frowning, turning it side to side. "How in the Cold d'ya drink out of this thing?"

"You do not." Allystaire lifted the bottle, still holding it carefully. "This… this was meant for a very wealthy man. Or woman. You break the neck of it off. With a sword, if you are feeling showy, I suppose. Then carefully pour out the contents and drink it all at once. By intent, the bottle is ruined."

As he spoke, the door banged open and the first clutch of rain-drenched villagers began pouring in. Instinctively, Allystaire ducked low, tucking the bottle of brandy underneath the bar, by his feet. Idgen Marte finally hopped off her stool and went to the hearth, most of its stones still black with soot that would never wash away, and began poking at the logs with an iron bar, causing the fire to spit and flare.

Some of the village folk directed themselves instantly to the bar, and Allystaire began handing over flagons with good cheer, while palpably concerned about the bottle resting by his boot. Soon a crowd filled the inn, and the fire was pouring smoke and heat into the place, and Allystaire was busy hauling ale up from the cold well and filling jars and flagons—before he knew it, Mol was standing barefoot on the bar and drinking beer from a small cup he hadn't given her and couldn't reach to snatch away. Idgen Marte was sitting with Renard and occasionally looking back at Allystaire with pleading eyes. Thunder cracked and rain pelted the newly patched roof, forcing its way through the thatch in spatters. Allystaire gave a minute shake of his head and Idgen Marte turned to survey the crowd with a sigh and her lips pressed into a thin line.

Suddenly, as Allystaire handed over yet another cup of small beer, Idgen Marte stood and made for the door, flinging it open and stepping into the storm, with a discreet wave for him to follow. He glanced down at the bottle, started to kneel, thought better of it, and came around the bar, edging his way through the crowd; the sweat he wiped from his forehead was enough excuse, and he wouldn't have been heard among the hubbub of people suddenly enjoying an afternoon free from worry and full of free drink.

He stepped outside and found Idgen Marte standing in the flimsy shelter of the overhang of the inn's thatch. The thunderstorm would, surely, break the heat and cool the evening when it passed, but the rain-filled air was still muggy and hot, the wind like a breath of steam. And yet the swordswoman shivered as Allystaire approached.

Unsure of how to approach, he decided on a light tone and said, "What? Do you need a brandy *that* badly?"

She scowled at him, the scar by her lip livid against her brown skin. "I'm no trembling sot. I thought of something and it frightened me, and I don't know why." She looked off into the storm, then turned her face back on him accusingly. "I don't frighten easy, but…"

"What? What could it possibly be?" Allystaire spread his hands wide, palms up, eyes and brow furrowed in confusion.

"Look back inside. Almost the entire village—everyone we rescued, and a few stragglers that lived far out in the valley, or fled to the hills—is in that common room. *Look.*"

Allystaire ducked his head back in and began counting up the people, noting the names: Mol, Timmar, Gram and his parents, Giraud, Henri, the latter actually sitting at a table with Norbert. Leah sat at a corner table with Renard. His gaze started to move on, then slid back to the two of them, alone in a dim corner. Despite himself, Allystaire smiled, and thought, *You sly old soldier. Good for you.* He moved on, trying to see what could've scared Idgen Marte. Seeing nothing amiss, he ducked back outside.

"Well?" she insisted defiantly, arms crossed over her chest.

"I saw nothing but folk happy to have a day free of labor, storm or no."

"Allystaire, who took them from this village and why?"

"Reavers, to make slaves of them."

"And so, think like a slaver," she went on, raising a hand to lead him on like a tutor with a reluctant student. "Whom do you take from a village like this? Whom do you leave behind?"

"You take the younger women, obviously," Allystaire said after a moment's pause, his jaw tightening a bit as he spoke. "You take the grown men. Not the elderly, but those used to work. They grew up around here, they will be used to hopping at the sound of orders. I suppose you take the children."

"Right. All of which they did; and not so very many young men, because…"

"Their blood is hotter. Most of them probably were killed first. Probably by plan."

Idgen Marte nodded again, folded her hands together under her chin as she fixed him with a stare. "Whom do you not take? Of all the folk in a village like this, which have the least profit in 'em, if you're the sort who thinks that way?"

Allystaire thought back to the laughing, stylish captain in his fine green brigantine, felt a dull, satisfied ache for a moment in the knuckles of his right hand. "The older women, I suppose. Panders will not buy them, and no one is likely to make oarsmen of them."

"And there's nearly a score survived the taking, most of 'em sitting in that common room right now with their children," Idgen Marte replied.

Allystaire tilted his head to the side. "And this frightens you because?"

She stepped forward and slapped him on the shoulder with an impossibly fast hand. "You said yourself that the reaver captain was dangerous, that it wasn't his first time. So what does it mean?"

He shook his head slowly, and she smacked him again, her eyes widening as she said, "It means someone wanted to buy them, Allystaire. *Someone wanted to buy women*—not maidens, not comely lasses, but farmwives. That's not what scares me though. What scares me is I can't think of a good freezin' reason why, but someone has."

As Idgen Marte spoke, a sudden shiver went down Allystaire's back, matching hers from when he'd stepped outside, and it was nothing to do with the hot, wet air or the rain or the lightning that flashed on the green. "Goddess," he murmured, blinking for a moment and staring at the rain before turning to her. "Why does that thought frighten us?"

"I don't know," Idgen Marte replied. She waited a moment, then tightened her jaw and exhaled sharply. "I do mean to find out. We haven't asked these folk what their captivity was like. And you didn't leave any Cold-be-damned slavers alive to ask *them*, so we'll have to ask—"

As she was speaking, another flash of lightning illuminated the village green, and Allystaire suddenly made out the forms of three robed, hooded figures struggling down the track. They were thin, and the one in front, shorter than the others, held a long stick behind him that the other two held onto. Allystaire grabbed Idgen Marte by the arm and ran down off the steps of the inn and into the rain.

He caught up with them in moments, Idgen Marte a few steps behind, and yelled over the din of thunder. "Come, there is shelter this way, and fire. It is dangerous to be out in this."

The three figures all turned toward the sound of his voice. The one in the front was barely out of boyhood; the other two, one a young man and one a grey-bearded elder, turned eyeless faces to him in silent supplication, and Al-lystaire felt his stomach quail. *Blind monks*, he thought, before the boy started to speak, his words lost to the rain and wind.

CHAPTER 23

He Will See

The three Urdarites sat together at a table dragged so close to the hearth it was in danger from sparking cinders. The village folk gave them a wide berth, with benches, stools, and tables drawn tightly against the walls. The silence was nearly complete, broken only by hissing logs and the occasional slurp of beer or creak of bench.

Allystaire and Idgen Marte stood on either side of the bar, with Mol sitting at the far end with her legs drawn up beneath her, staring with murderous intensity at the cluster of sopping, grey-robed men at the other end of the room.

The youngest of the three Urdarites, whose intact green eyes were large with fear, clung to the edge of their table as though he wanted to climb underneath of it. His robe hitched above his ankles as he sat, exposing his poorly shod feet, his shoes really little more than cloth wrappers held on with leather thongs.

The eldest, whose grey robe had a thin line of silk edging its hem and hood, sat closest to the fire. His face was deeply lined, and a patchy beard covered his cheeks. His face was turned directly to the fire, and he wore a contented, vacant, smile.

The third was a grown man, older than the boy who guided them but much younger than the older man. He clutched onto his walking stick like it was a totem, and curled his body around it, his face pointed at the floor. Occasionally the older priest spoke to him in quiet tones, but the younger monk ignored him, just as he ignored everything else.

After several minutes of warming himself, the elder monk turned carefully around on his stool so that his back was to the fire, cleared his throat, and addressed the room in a ponderous voice. "Good afternoon, my children. Thank you for the use of your roof and your fire," he began, spreading his hands on the surface of the table, his gnarled fingertips digging into the recently worked wood. "Why do none of you speak? Has it been so long since our Order visited your hamlet that you fear to approach? Do not hesitate; Urdaran's inward gaze has much to teach such as you."

That's got the feel of a practiced speech, Allystaire thought. Even as he was thinking over the monk's words, Idgen Marte had darted away from the bar and snatched the back of Mol's shirt, for the girl had hopped down off the bar and started for the table of Urdarites, a frighteningly determined look upon her face. Idgen Marte hauled her back to the bar and leveled a wide-eyed gaze at Allystaire, who then realized that everyone, down to the boy who had led the Urdaran priests into the village, was staring at him.

"Freeze it all," he murmured, audible only to himself, and took a deep breath. He knelt down and retrieved the bottle he'd stashed beneath the bar, and with a look at Idgen Marte, sharply rapped the neck of it against the bar; it cracked with a heavy *thunk*, and another gentle rap was enough to knock it free. He poured a generous measure of it into a wine cup and left the bottle on the bar, pointed to it, then murmured softly to Idgen Marte, "*Save me some.*"

He walked with heavy steps, magnified by the silence in the room, his movements followed by every eye and by two eyeless faces. He picked up a stool as he walked, set it near the table, and sat down, placing the cup of brandy on the center of the table. The grey-robed boy stared at him with saucer eyes, trembling a little. Allystaire thought of smiling, thought *That'll be sure to send him running*, and settled for saying, "Relax, lad. No one here means you any harm."

This didn't seem to have much of a calming effect, so Allystaire turned himself to the elder priest, who was smiling at him benevolently, if a touch theatrically, from underneath his shriveled, empty eye sockets. "What is the name of this village, and what is your name, my son?" His question was delivered in the same ponderous, quavering tone.

"This village is Thornhurst. My name is Allystaire."

"Ah, an uncommon name. And your voice does not seem to have the local flavor to it. A bit north of here, and educated, I suspect, yes? Where are you from, my son?"

This old man is tiresome. Allystaire cleared his throat and said, "Where I am from or whether I am educated does not matter very much."

The old priest fumblingly reached out for Allystaire's wrist and seized it in a surprisingly strong, if thin-fingered grip. "The Inward Eye sees all in the end, my son. Do not seek to hide even trivial things."

With his jaw suddenly tense, Allystaire reached over with his free hand and plucked the Urdarite priest's hand from his wrist with gentle but irresistible force.

The old monk recoiled as if stung; the young boy gasped audibly, then whispered, "'It's forbidden t'touch Urdaran's anointed, m'lord."

"Forbidden by whom?" Allystaire's casual response caught the boy off guard; he simply bobbed his jaw up and down soundlessly a few times. Carefully, Allystaire set the old man's hand down near the brandy cup and said, "Have a drink, Urdaran's anointed. Rest yourselves. We will bring some food." He turned to the village folk crowded around the walls and waved a hand at them; a few of them pushed off the walls or stood up from their benches and milled around, desultory looks on their faces. He cleared his throat again, and added, "We will not allow anyone to find the hospitality of Thornhurst lacking."

Finally, he turned and snapped his fingers at some of the dawdling villagers, and two walked purposefully toward the bar and the pantry beyond it; soon enough they emerged with bread, cheese, and dried fish. They brought it near, but stopped just short of the table. With a frustrated grunt, Allystaire stepped toward them, grabbed the food in his hands, and laid it out on the table, once again making sure it was close enough to the arms of the blind monks for them to feel its presence.

The elderly priest slowly turned his wrinkled, ruined face toward Allystaire and cleared his throat. "You are not happy for us to be among you, my son. This much is plain to my ears. We should speak, perhaps, in less crowded quarters, of what has drawn us here?"

Quietly flexing one of his fists and frowning, Allystaire said, "Perhaps."

With a frown deepening the wrinkles of his face, the old eyeless monk said, "Why so angry? Have we offended? Should we move on? 'Twould not be the first night Urdaran's faithful servants were cast out of a place for fear of what they might see. We sleep most nights upon rocks and tree roots, in wind and rain and heat, with the danger of animals and the night about us; we learn not to mind such things. But the fear of a village which has turned its eyes outward, against that we cannot defend ourselves. It is a shame when Urdaran's children turn against his anointed, but so it often is."

Allystaire heard a muffled yelp from the back of the room and then a light thud as the door shut; Idgen Marte disappeared out the front door, half dragging Mol by the hand.

The young monk quailed in fear; the other monk continued to hunch miserably over his staff, hood pulled tightly over his head. With the skin of his jaw tightened, Allystaire leant over their table with one fist planted on its surface. "No one here is going to harm you, old man, nor your guide, nor your fellow *anointed*. With my word upon it, you are as safe here as you would be in the fastness of your own blind god's loveless embrace. Remember this, though, when we speak again." Allystaire leant down a bit more, while the old monk sat in shocked stillness. "I am not your son. Urdaran has no children in this village, save the three of you. We can speak on why that is and what has drawn you here later. Now, I must confer with my comrades." He turned and swiftly headed for the door, stopping only to point at Timmar and murmur, "Find beds for them, and more food and drink if they want it."

With that, he stomped out the door, letting the wind bang it against the jamb as he stepped outside. Mol and Idgen Marte were standing just a few feet away from the door. The rain had lessened considerably, and the air bore a cool promise of autumn. He stopped in front of his fellow servants of the Goddess and hooked his thumbs on his belt.

"Well. What do we do?" he asked.

"Drive 'em off. They aren't needed here." Mol had her arms crossed over her chest and her face set in hard determination. *I know that look*, he thought, and when Idgen Marte caught his eye he realized she knew it too, and she shook her head slightly.

"Mol, whatever else they might be, they are two blind men and a child. Do they bear some power from their god? Perhaps. Remember what I told you when first I spoke of such as them? They mean to ignore the world. Urdaran teaches that we should all look inward, to our own minds, to seek…" Here, Allystaire paused, groping for a word, and finally waving a hand in disgust. "I do not know what they seek. Regardless, I perceive no threat."

"Cold, lass, I think even old Allystaire could take them without fainting away at the end of the scuffle," Idgen Marte suggested with a light laugh.

Mol scowled, digging her arms more tightly around her thin form. "I don't think they can hurt the folk. It's the Mother I'm thinkin' of. Can't they hurt Her, hurt what the folk think of Her?" She shivered very lightly. "Our faith is new. Theirs is old. So is their god. What d'we do if they start preachin'?" She shook her head and toed the dirt at her feet.

"If they start preaching, I suspect we do the same. Mayhap louder. Yet I will not take action, or encourage anyone to do so, against an old blind man because he serves a different god than we do. That is not the Mother's way."

As Allystaire said this, he realized that all three of them knew the truth of his words before he had really uttered them. "We will keep Her people by showing them all of the Mother's ways—not merely Her wrath, Her love, Her compassion, or hope, but also Her patience. The night before we came back to Thornhurst, I set our first rule, do you remember? Come to Her freely, or come not at all." He paused a moment. "If folk must come to the Mother on their own, then they must be allowed to leave Her if they wish. I do not think they will. Now," Allystaire reached back and gently pushed open the door to the inn; "Are you going to come be sociable? We have guests."

A bit reluctantly, but with her aggression melted away, Mol rushed past him into the inn; Idgen Marte paused to murmur a question.

"Is their arrival an accident? Didn't the eldest one say something about—"

"He did. I can tell you already that this one is theatrical. He may be making it all up."

Idgen Marte muttered as she passed him, "Plenty of folks are gonna say that about *us*, ya know."

Allystaire sighed heavily and turned back into the inn, drawing the door behind him. After the cool of the outdoors, the air inside seemed oppressively hot, filled with too many bodies and too much woodsmoke. He noted, happily, that while most of the villagers had gone on with their drinking, a few, at least, had stopped to make some small talk with the Urdarites. All three of them were eating and drinking, the young guide most animatedly. Even the second priest, who had simply curled around his stick, was limply shoving food under his pulled down hood. As Allystaire watched, he lifted his head with the lightest of motions to whisper something at the eldest priest, whose every gesture seemed calculated—slow, grand, and designed to draw attention.

We lost a fine minstrel when you decided to cut out your eyes, Allystaire thought, chuckling lightly at his own thought. He approached the Urdaran's table, once more drawing over a free chair and sitting himself down.

"Fathers," he began, his voice deliberately calm, "we can give you beds and food. Stay as long as you wish. And we will ask nothing in return."

The elderly monk smiled, the expression strangely incongruous on his mutilated face. "I knew wisdom and kindness would prevail, my son."

"Let me amend myself," Allystaire said, working hard to keep his voice calm. "I ask nothing except that you recall that I am not your son. No one here is."

The smile quickly became a frown. "Every man is Urdaran's child, even those who worship Fortune or Braech or—"

"Father, if you must preach, do not preach to me," Allystaire said evenly, as the fingers of his right hand curled faintly in the suggestion of a fist.

The old priest, still smiling theatrically, opened his mouth as if to respond, but was stopped short when the other hooded, eyeless monk reached out a hand, having uncurled from his private misery, and drew the older monk toward him. Allystaire could not see much of the younger man's face, but what he did see appeared pale and drawn, with flesh drawn taut across sharp bones. He whispered to the older priest, words which to Allystaire remained annoying susurration. The older priest shook his head as if in disbelief, then turned a blank face toward Allystaire, then back to the younger man.

Though unable to make out words, Allystaire was certain he recognized dismissal of an underling's ideas when he saw it, and this thought was confirmed when the younger priest burst out with, "It is, damn it all! Why will you not listen?" Then the hooded man suddenly stood, fumbling with his stick and his free hand to get around the stool he'd been sitting on. He stumbled forward haphazardly, quickly tripping over the chair their sighted guide sat upon.

Allystaire was up in a flash, reaching out and grabbing the blind Urdarite monk with sure hands. The man felt feverish, heat emanating off him even through his robes, and Allystaire felt a small, almost threatening shock. He helped the man upright, holding him in place till the boy recovered from his surprise and stood to help the priest back to his seat.

"Calm yourself, Rede," the old monk was saying. "Sit. Settle your mind and focus your inward eye…" The younger Urdarite only laughed bitterly, and without humor.

Can't have been blind very long, Allystaire mused. He lowered his head slightly to get a look at the man's face beneath his hood.

Indeed, the younger Urdarite must have been feverish, for his face was not only pale, but streaming with sweat, the sheen of it coating his cheeks, mouth, and jaw. A crude strip of bandage was bound around his eyes; the edges of the sockets that Allystaire could see were raw, red, and cracked. A thin trail of pus led down his cheek from the corner of his left eye.

"This man's wounds are untended. He is ill," Allystaire announced loudly and with his accustomed ring of authority. A half-dozen villagers, including Norbert, leapt to their feet and were standing around him in a cluster almost as soon as the words were out of his mouth. Allystaire leant closer to the monk and sniffed the air. His mouth curled when he smelled the sickening rot that could mean only one thing.

"Rede? That is your name, yes?" The monk nodded, and Allystaire went on. "Your wounds are putrescent. I can help you if—"

Allystaire's words were cut off by the stentorian rumble of the older Urdarite. "Absolutely not! Urdaran forbids any intervention in the choosing of his priests. Childe Rede will pass this test, or he will move on to Urdaran's endless embrace."

Allystaire found himself leveling a hard, angry stare at the old monk for a moment before suddenly laughing bitterly at the futility of such a gesture. He said to Rede, who had gone still in his grasp.

"Rede, how long since they maimed you?"

"Three days," Rede mumbled, the words coming out in a hoarse whisper.

"If you do not wish to die, come with me. I can help, if you will trust me." The monk nodded eagerly, his hood slipping further over his sweat-slicked face. Allystaire took one feverish wrist in his own hand and led the monk toward the door, waving his free hand at Idgen Marte and Mol as he neared the bar. "The temple. Go." Both of them filed out ahead of him, Mol holding the door open before scampering off after the leg-swinging gait of the tall swordswoman.

"No! I forbid this! All of you stay put! It isn't done!" The older priest was not giving in.

"You do not give orders here, father," Allystaire replied curtly, as he stalked purposefully from the inn, leading Rede behind him.

Allystaire heard shouting and commotion in the inn behind him but ignored it; he also heard a crowd stomping after him. Without bothering to look back, he called out, "If that other monk wishes to follow us, show him the way." The storm had blown away completely, and the relatively cool breeze was a welcome change from the stuffy interior of the inn.

Rede's steps were halting and slow; finally in frustration, Allystaire stopped, bent slightly, and lifted the monk, slinging him carefully over his shoulder. Rede cried out wordlessly, and in spite of struggling in protest, he seemed weightless upon Allystaire's broad shoulder.

"Apologies, Rede. I assume your wish to live will allow you to bear the next few minutes in discomfort."

"What temple are you bringing me to?" Rede moaned, as he bounced upon Allystaire's shoulder.

Catching himself just before saying *you will see*, Allystaire replied, "A new temple." And as he spoke, the field and the low stone walls surrounding the altar came into view. Rede's limp and fevered form couldn't have weighed more than eight stone, Allystaire guessed. He was able to vault the low wall with little difficulty, and when he reached the center of the still-rising temple, he laid the feverish man against the altar. Idgen Marte and Mol already waited, both of them looking to him expectantly.

Allystaire turned quickly to them. "Hands on the altar. Pray." He bent and started carefully peeling away the bandage; it took layers of skin with it, and Rede futilely raised his hands up as if to push Allystaire's away. With a grimace, he ripped the bandage free, tearing pieces of the skin hanging loosely around the Urdarite's eye sockets. Trickles of blood and a fresh torrent of pus leaked from the wounds.

Whether Rede had been blinded with a blade, hot iron, fingers, or some horrible tool meant to scoop out eyes and damage the flesh around them, Allystaire couldn't quite say. Perhaps it was some combination of all four. But the man's eyes were a ruin, the flesh swollen and torn, one socket gleaming wetly.

Idgen Marte looked on uncertainly, one hand on the altar; Mol had placed both hands upon it and closed her eyes, her face blank and somehow beatific. Allystaire glanced at them and told Idgen Marte again, "Pray! *Please!*"

Then he turned back to Rede, whose hands now lay feebly at his side, his sightless face turned toward a small ray of sun pushing through the last of the thunderheads. Allystaire placed the palm of his left hand across the monk's maimed eyes, kneeling, placing the other upon the altar.

Mother, please. Please, Allystaire thought, as he reached into the place he'd reached twice before; there was the sensation of dipping his hand into a well to draw forth water, but by the time he brought it to the surface, it had slipped through cupped fingers, leaving behind only drops that dried upon his skin as soon as he felt them. He tried again, and it was as though his hands had punched into cold stone instead of descending into water. He almost drew back, had the sensation of pain spreading along his knuckles, but he pressed harder against the monk, gritting his teeth. He reached again—again, stone.

"Rede," he gasped, in a sudden flare of insight, "did you do this willingly? Did you give your eyes to Urdaran in mad devotion?"

The young priest twisted and writhed under his grip, screaming raggedly, his voice a hoarse animal cry of pain.

"Answer me! You must!"

"No! They told me I had a Gift, that the Inward Eye would reveal secrets to me. Portents and omens. Gave me no choice!"

Allystaire felt Idgen Marte's and Mol's hands settle upon his shoulder; he spared a glance for them. They had shuffled closer, but both kept one hand on the altar and one upon him.

"Do you want that Gift? If you wish it *gone*, speak now! *Now*, man, or I cannot save you!"

With a weak, tearless sob, Rede nodded his head beneath Allystaire's hand. "They took my eyes! Why? I begged them not to. I want to live, but not in this darkness, not with this great…thing…in my head…"

Allystaire closed his eyes and whispered, "Please, Mother. This man is yours; his suffering makes him so. Please."

Idgen Marte and Mol's fingers curled tightly into his shoulders; he reached once more into the well of love, of forgiveness, of bright sorrowful compassion; but now the well had become a stream, a lake, and his hands brought forth a wave of it and poured it over Rede's eyes and face. A cascade of warm power poured from the paladin's hand; the Goddess's love roared in his ears like a wind. Allystaire felt the man writhing again, heard him scream in agony that tailed off into a whimper. Allystaire fell backwards, the strength drained from his limbs, but he saw Rede shift against the altar and lift his sweat-soaked head and blink against the sudden burst of sun through the dead and drifting storm.

Blink—and shield his eyes.

Allystaire sat on the hay-strewn dirt, stunned. Idgen Marte and Mol both collapsed against the altar, but Idgen Marte lifted her face, and with the familiar twisted grin he hadn't seen in days, uttered three careful, quiet words.

"He will see."

He smiled back at her, the truth of her words landing snugly in his gut. He pushed himself to his feet, unsteadily, with one hand braced against the altar for support. Rede covered his face with his hands and breathed deeply; slowly he parted his fingers, but shut them quickly, covering his eyes from the resurgent late afternoon sun. Allystaire bent and helped the man to his feet.

"Move your hands," he said, gently. "This light is of She who healed you. It cannot hurt you." He reached up and firmly, but lightly pushed Rede's hands away from his face. The monk blinked a few times, his eyes watering and bleary, but whole, brown, and healthy. He turned his gaze from Allystaire to the walls around them, to the crowd of villagers that was slowly gathering, to the sun above them, then to the altar. He turned around, placed his hands upon the stone, staring intently, tracing his fingers upon it.

"There's…writing here…glowing…I can't…" Rede leant far forward over the smooth-grained stone, his legs quivering beneath him so intensely that Allystaire prepared to catch him should he fall. The monk became fixated upon whatever he saw. Allystaire saw only the smooth stone surface, but his mind returned to the weeks before, when the Goddess had come to them, and he remembered her finger moving upon the stone in tracery.

"Stay this madness! Childe Rede, return to me and let us leave this place of sin behind us!"

Allystaire, Idgen Marte, Mol, and the village folk all turned to the old monk, who was being led up the path by his guide, each holding one end of the old man's stick.

"You have allowed them to pollute you, Rede! You have allowed worldliness and concern for the self to pollute your Inward Gaze—"

The old priest was cut off with a loud *thwack* as he walked straight into the back of his stunned, silent boy, who'd dropped the stick and was staring open-mouthed at Rede. It took a moment for the youth to remember his charge, and to turn and right the old man before they could both tumble in a heap, but almost instantly the lad turned back to Rede, who looked up from the altar with a wide, unsettling smile upon his face.

That is a mad grin if I have ever seen one, Allystaire thought suddenly. *I do not like the feel of it.*

"Begone from here, you wretched old beggar," Rede called with surprising vehemence, stumbling away from the altar with halting steps. "You aren't—"

He was cut off as the youth started shouting, and as Allystaire stepped behind him and half-seized him, half-propped him up.

"He has eyes, Father! *Eyes!* Great Urdaran! Eyes!"

"What are you babbling about? The only eyes he has are those which Urdaran will grant him, to peer into the secrets of the mind, to—"

"No, Father, he has his eyes. The ones he was born with," Allystaire said, still propping up the rictus-grinning Rede with one arm. "What you and your God took from him, my Goddess has returned."

"Goddess? Fortune worshippers, eh? An unusual faith for *peasants*." The monk spat the word like a curse. "You *lie*," he raged, striking the dirt with his stick like a club, bending his knobbled knees beneath his dark robes. "Fortune grants no such powers. Nothing is given to Her servants but tricks of the eye and the mind, the will to peddle influence with the rich, and the accumulation of the filth of life!"

"It is no trick, and I am neither a peasant nor a servant of Fortune."

"Sorcery then! Sorcery most foul!" He raised his arms theatrically and, with a new tack, addressed the crowd that he could not see but could doubtless sense. "People! Good folk! If you have a sorcerer in your midst, he is a most foul being and must be destroyed! Fetch wood and oil and *seize him*!"

He got as far as *seize* before his words were overrun with a chorus of buzzing, angry calls and shouts. The monk drew in a deep breath, preparing to shout above the din, but Allystaire raised a hand, and the villagers fell silent.

"I think you will find your orders to burn me for a warlock poorly received, Father," the paladin said, working hard, and not entirely successfully, to keep a hint of mockery from his words.

"Then you have turned their very minds to your own ends!"

"Enough, Gaumm. Enough." Rede's voice was weary, but firm, and he took halting, careful steps away from Allystaire to approach the old priest. He patted the youth on the shoulder, who still watched him with shocked eyes and slack jaw. "The man who addressed you, this Allystaire, is no sorcerer, and you know it." He gripped the old Urdarite's shoulder; the monk tried to push away, but couldn't. Rede's hand was white-knuckled, his eyes shining large in his face. "You know now why we came. What I told you in the inn is still true. We came seeking him. This Allystaire," he said. "And the woman, and the child," he added, "who joined him, somehow, in healing me. This is what we felt in the world; a Goddess waking! A paladin striding the world! Search inwardly, as you always told me to do, and you will know." He turned to the ground and drew a deep breath, and Allystaire thought he looked like nothing so much as an impersonation of Gaumm.

"I have felt Her and seen Her cleansing light!"

Something in Rede's voice twisted the word *cleansing* in a way that sent chills down Allystaire's spine. *I do not like the sound of that word in his mouth*, he thought. Hairs rose on the back of his neck, and he turned to Idgen Marte, whose eyes were wide and whose cheeks were taut, and Mol, whose equally wide eyes were staring daggers at the recently healed man.

"It filled me! It drove the disease from my body and granted me back my eyes with the power of Her purity, Her white-hot flame against the cold void of Urdaran—" Rede's eyes were wide and unblinking, his voice rising to a pitch as fevered as his skin had been a few moments ago.

"Enough, Rede," Allystaire called, quickly and in his authoritative captain's voice. "The Goddess healed you with Love, not flame. With Compassion. We will speak of it later." He stepped down the track after Rede, stopping in front of Gaumm and the youth.

"Father, I still mean what I said. None here will harm you. You may stay as long as you wish and be provisioned."

"No!" The monk raised his hands in a warding sign against evil, fingers crossed in intricate patterns, and spat to the side. "We will tarry here not another moment! Come, boy! Lead me from this wretched place."

The boy looked up at the priest and reflexively reached out for the end of the man's stick, but his eyes flitted from Rede to Allystaire, settling on the latter.

"Are you a paladin, m'lord?" His whisper was feather-soft, his eyes wide in awe.

Smiling despite himself, Allystaire nodded. "Aye. And my name is Allystaire, not *my lord*."

The lad nodded, dodging a poorly aimed cuff from the priest behind him, who then swung his stick weakly and thumped it against the lad's shoulder.

"I want t'stay with you!" he burst out to Allystaire. "I'd rather be your squire than an old man's dogsbody!"

"What is your name, lad?" Allystaire frowned faintly.

"Isaak."

"Isaak, you have promised to aid Father Gaumm, yes? You are pledged to him?"

The lad nodded quickly. Behind him, the Urdarite monk began tapping in front of him with his stick, doddering off without guidance, using his stick to find the edges of the track.

"Then with him you must go. He is your responsibility; pledges like that may not be broken lightly. Return Father Gaumm to a refuge, a place of safety—a temple or a keep where he is welcome—and think on your future. If you wish to come to the worship of the Goddess…well, I cannot promise to make you a squire, but none who come to Her willing will be turned away. Do you understand?"

Isaak swallowed and nodded sadly, but turned away and quickly caught up with the old monk, seizing the end of his stick and leading him at a faster, but still sedate, pace. He threw a look back over his shoulder, grimacing, and Allystaire offered him a gentle, encouraging nod.

Rede all but ignored them, having returned to studying the altar.

"I take it that you have abandoned Urdaran's service, then," Allystaire called out to him, turning from the sight of Isaak leading Gaumm away in the last of the afternoon's light. Rede laughed bitterly but did not yet answer, so absorbed was he in the study of the altar.

An idea suddenly occurred to Allystaire, and he yelled, "Norbert!" The tall and no longer quite as gangly youth bounded up to Allystaire, who ordered, "Back to the inn; get together some food. Jar of wine or two. Then back here on the double and run it off to them," he said waving a hand toward the young boy and the old monk, who were making slow progress. "They do not seem likely to get far."

Before Allystaire had even finished speaking, Norbert was running off at full gallop. *Turned into quite the runner, that one,* Allystaire noted to himself. He turned back toward Rede and the altar. Idgen Marte and Mol had recovered; the former peered over the robed man's shoulder to see what he stared at, while the latter stood up on the tips of her toes, fingers on the altar. Rede turned and swatted at one of her hands, snorting.

"Away from here, child."

"You've no right to tell me—" Mol's protest was cut short as Rede turned and smacked her hand again, louder this time, loud enough for everyone to hear.

"'Tis no place for lasses sticking their noses."

He didn't finish his sentence, because faster than Allystaire could've followed, Idgen Marte lashed out with a straight, short punch that drove her knuckles behind Rede's right ear. He gasped in pain and fell forward, clutching at the back of his head.

Idgen Marte was drawing her arm back for another blow when Allystaire's bellow cut across the field.

"*Hold!* No one does violence in the temple of the Mother except at greatest need!" He felt, as he said them, the rightness of his words. *Add it to a list of rules before you leave,* he thought, immediately wondering if the thought had been his alone. He began taking short, slow, deliberate steps back up the field to the temple, giving himself time to think.

Idgen Marte dropped her hand but glared menacingly at the loudly protesting former Urdarite, then turned the full force of her anger toward, if not on,
Allystaire himself. "How dare he," she snarled.

Rede finally hauled himself back to his feet and turned his shocked, aggrieved features toward Allystaire. "Who are they to even be here, Paladin? Why
is the Goddess's holy place trampled by all of these…" He trailed off as Allystaire
closed in on him and loomed over him, his mouth set in a tight, grim line.

"These what? Poor folk? They are Her people. As for them," Allystaire nodded toward Idgen Marte and Mol, "they are, as am I, Her servants." Rede looked
back over his shoulder and flushed, though whether in anger or embarrassment,
Allystaire couldn't say.

Rede sputtered, "Servants? But they are…they're not…"

"Think carefully on your next word, friend Rede. Whatever it is you are
about to say that they are or are not, understand that the Goddess has spoken
to them, called them, chosen them; She has identified them as Her Voice and
Her Shadow. That is who they are."

The flushing in his cheeks spread to his neck, and Rede bowed his head.
"I am sorry, Paladin. I was—in my haste and delirium over the Goddess's healing—I must…" He gestured to the altar.

"Whatever it is you see on the altar, Rede, study it. Copy it. Draw it. Are
you lettered?"

Rede cleared his throat. "I was, until. Well I suppose I am again. Still. At
that. Usually the acolyte who serves as a guide will—"

"Good," Allystaire said, trampling over what he sensed was a lecture about to
be delivered. "Idgen Marte, Mol, would you please go fetch ink, parchment, and
a pen? You will find them all among my things."

Warrior and girl-priestess nodded and walked off. Rede continued to stare
at the altar stone, and Allystaire asked, "What do you see?"

"I am not entirely sure. Runes that I do not recognize, though mayhap
someone else will. A kind of small drawing, I think. Of what, I don't know."

Allystaire nodded, looked down at the altar, seeing only bare grey stone.
"How do you see them?"

Rede thought for a moment on this, and said, "Have you ever stared too
long at a light, and then turned your gaze to shadow? Or even looked at the

sun?"Allystaire nodded, and Rede went on, "Like the glow in your eyes then. Only it doesn't move when I move my gaze. It is just…there."

"Fading?"

"Not at all."

"Good. Then you can take a moment to tell me why you and your companions came to Thornhurst."

As Allystaire spoke, a pounding of feet on the track signaled Norbert's arrival, and just as quickly he was galloping up the road and over a slight rise, a large sack slung over one shoulder, a leather strap holding two thick clay jars dangling from a hand. "Norbert," Allystaire called out as the lad ran past, "see if you cannot talk them into staying. Insist that they are welcome here." Norbert might have waved an acknowledgement on his way past; it was hard to say.

"The Urdarites felt something come into the world," Rede said. "Some power. They wanted to know it, to quell it, or to seize it if they must."

"And you said it is the Goddess they felt?"

"And you," Rede pointed a long, slightly dirty finger at Allystaire's chest. "The sensing of something, some power, has been sporadic. A splash in a great pool weeks ago. Other ripples, some mild, some great bursts of power, since."

"How do they feel these things?"

Rede looked up from the altar and shivered, shutting his eyes and curling his arms for a moment around his thin torso. "With the Inward Eye. When an Urdarite gives up his eyes, something replaces them," he said, tapping the middle of his forehead. "You cannot see, yet it…it shows you things. It judges. It—I didn't like it," he suddenly said, turning away and shuddering again.

"Why would you come seeking us out?" Allystaire's eyes narrowed as he studied Rede. Now, able to look at the man instead of the dying, blind monk, he took in his features. A beak of a nose set beneath wide, hungry eyes; gaunt cheeks; lank hair; and a manner that varied wildly between halting and darting made Rede somehow both pitiable and off-putting, even unnerving. "Does Urdaran not ask you to withdraw from the world?"

"Urdaran does," Rede answered darkly. "But that does not mean He, or His priesthood, wish to see new things arise. All of the Temples seek power in their own way. Braech has the water, the wind, and the rage of them made manifest in men; Fortune directs the streams of gold and silver. Urdaran moves to the fonts of power and obscures them. None of the Temples will permit a new power to arise and challenge it; they sponsor the Temples Minor and then absorb them…"

Suddenly Rede leaned hard against the altar, holding a hand to his temple. "I…speaking of these things. It is as though the Eye is still in my mind. It pains me."

"Then speak on them no longer," Allystaire replied. "I will have more questions for you later. For now, study the runes as long as you need." *If the Urdarites felt Her, felt my Gifts, Her power—who else has?*

His musings were driven off as Mol and Idgen Marte arrived with the requested writing tools, and Rede set down to the business of copying what he saw on the alter stone.

Allystaire drew Idgen Marte and Mol away from the alter—by now, most of the village folk had dispersed as well—to let Rede work. They watched from a short distance for some time as the light receded, till finally Allystaire tilted his head toward Idgen Marte and murmured, "The Wit, or the Will?"

"Neither freezin' one, I hope," she whispered.

"He isn't," Mol piped in, her voice a little distant.

"Isn't what?" Idgen Marte asked gently.

"The Wit *or* the Will," she replied, lifting her face to Idgen Marte and smiling dreamily. "He saw. Is seein', too. That's his part. Wit and Will are still out *there*." She indicated *there* with a grand sweep of her arm that Allystaire speculated incorporated most of Baronies Delondeur, Innadan, Oyrwyn, and probably across the Ash into Varshyne.

"That is a lot of 'there'," Allystaire said in a tired voice.

"You'll find 'em," Mol insisted brightly, reaching up to take Allystaire's massively-knuckled right hand with her little one, squeezing it. "Faith," she said.

"Faith," Allystaire repeated, nodding, and then Rede lifted up several sheets of hastily scribbled-upon, blotched parchment in triumph.

* * *

Some time later, Allystaire, Idgen Marte, Rede, Mol, and Renard sat around the table in the mostly restored village house that had been set aside for Allystaire and Idgen Marte's use. He'd protested at first, but the villagers insisted that he make use of it. He and Idgen Marte traded use of the bed and shared the rest of the house in most other ways. A small fire burned on the hearth and had been used to light lamps he kept dangling on chains from the roof timber.

The sheets of parchment were scattered across the small round table, its unfinished, still slightly rough surface obscured by Rede's papers. They took turns passing them from hand to hand, turning them about in what light they had. All except for Mol, who dozed lightly on her stool, head slumped on her chest.

"Not a word any of us can read. Not so much as a single rune or cipher," Allystaire said quietly, setting down the parchment he'd been examining. He sighed and rubbed the bridge of his nose with finger and thumb.

Renard stared listlessly at the fire behind them; Idgen Marte flicked a curled edge of parchment with her finger. Rede stared at the sheets before him with a frightening intensity.

"Surely the Goddess will lead us to an understanding. Surely She has not granted my sight back in futility. I must simply study them some more—"

Allystaire cut him off with a wave of his hand, and bent over the table, neatly shuffling the parchments into a straight-edged pile, then dropping a round, dry stone atop them. "We can study them in the morning when there is better light." He paused a moment, and almost absentmindedly added, "Her light." Then, tapping Renard on the shoulder, he pointed with his chin toward Rede. "Find a bed for him?"

Renard stood with a grunt, nodding the affirmative as he did. "Come along. There's space at the inn, I'm sure. Might be on a bench or a floor but it'll be a roof and blankets." Then Renard bent over and gathered Mol up in his arms. She didn't protest and barely stirred. Sleepily, she wrapped her arms around the soldier's broad neck and laid her head against him; her weight didn't seem to impede him, and he ducked out into the night, gesturing for Rede to follow.

The former Urdarite priest tugged on the sleeves of his rough monk's robe and said, "Could we find more fitting raiment tomorrow?"

Allystaire narrowed his eyes. "Fitting what?" *I don't like the sound of raiment.*

"Well, me. I cannot wear the robes of a god I no longer serve."

Idgen Marte stood, yawned widely, and said drily, "Surely we can find you some good work clothes."

Rede rubbed his hands together. "Work clothes? Not…vestments? Robes?"

Allystaire snorted a quick, mirthless laugh. "Two things you ought to know, Rede. First, everyone in Thornhurst works. Until this village thrives on its own again, no one loafs. Second, we do not have vestments, raiments, robes, chasubles, or surplices. Put that thought out of your head."

Rede's mouth fell open in quiet disbelief. "Yet if you are Her paladin and prophet, what is your badge of office? What do you wear to…"

Allystaire thought on this a moment, and then bent down and lifted his hammer from where it rested on the ground, sliding his hand up the haft to just under the head, and tapping the top of the sledge with his free hand. "This." Then he lifted it and pointed to the far wall, where his battered grey armor lay in as neat a pile as he could manage. "If need be, that."

Rede began to protest again, when Renard's voice carried quietly from outside the door. "Make me wait a moment longer, priest, and you'll be sleepin' in the mud."

"He isn't accustomed to waiting," Idgen Marte said, crossing her arms and tapping her boot once or twice on the floorboards.

Rede hurried to the door, stopping a moment to look back at them. He turned his drawn and pale face from one to the other and exclaimed, "Scandalous!" Then he whirled out the door with a dramatic flare of his mud-spattered robe.

Silence reigned a moment; outside crickets sang and an owl called, as Allystaire and Idgen Marte stared at each other. Finally, she held her hands out, palms up.

"Have you the faintest idea what that fool meant?"

Allystaire thought a moment, then cleared his throat and spoke, choosing his words delicately. "I believe good father Rede believes that we are, ah, sharing the bed, so to speak."

Idgen Marte laughed heartily for a moment, joined in by Allystaire, and both of them sat again.

"*Scandalous*? As if farm folk like this could be scandalized," Idgen Marte remarked incredulously.

"I do believe Urdaran has some ideas about how clergy comport themselves."

"Good thing I'm not clergy then."

"I think you probably are. We both are."

"Not like any clergy this world's known then."

"I think that is the point," Allystaire said, then considered, as he scratched the side of his nose. "What in the Cold are we going to do about him? I think he imagines he is Called, as we are."

"Imagines?" Idgen Marte waved a hand dismissively. "He *assumes* he has been. And more to the point," she leaned forward and dropped her voice, almost whispering, "what if he has been?"

Allystaire shook his head. "That I do not fear. The Mother would have come Herself, aye? As She did for me, and for you. And I think for Mol, when neither of us saw. Moreover, Mol said so."

Idgen Marte nodded, visibly relieved as she sat back. "If the Voice says it's so, it's so."

Allystaire nodded agreement, pushed himself to his feet, licked his forefinger and thumb, and started extinguishing lamp wicks; they hissed against his skin. "Aye. Time to sleep. The bed is yours."

Idgen Marte stood and headed for the doorway to the only other room of the tiny house. "You know, for what it's worth, the Mother didn't say anything about being chaste when She came for me."

"Nor me," Allystaire said, quietly. "I do not think that such is Her way."

Idgen Marte nodded, shouldering aside the blanket that covered the doorway and disappearing behind it.

Allystaire dimmed the rest of the lamps, felt his way in darkness to his hammer, grasped it in one hand, and then stumped over to the far wall. He put his back to it, sat down, laid the hammer at his side, and slept lightly, hindered along the way by the occasional thought of Leah or the Goddess or other women he had known. There was one face that kept swimming before his eyes, until he pushed it away firmly.

He dreamt of her, anyway, of dark auburn hair and fields of wildflowers.

CHAPTER 24

Serving in Joy

Allystaire woke quickly, as always, scarcely breaching the surface of consciousness before he snapped into full awareness. He had barely moved—his hand rested upon his hammer, his hips ached from sitting all night, his back and legs were sore, and a thin light slanted through the wooden walls of the small house. He rocked forward and came to his feet with a groan, picking up his hammer and tucking it snugly on his belt. He tottered over to the door and through it, letting it swing open behind him, and yawned in the sun. He stripped off his shirt and went to the rain barrel at the corner of the house, picked up and filled the small bucket that sat next to it, then bent forward and dumped it over the back of his head. He repeated this a few more times, washing his arms, back, chest, and head with the lukewarm water.

He was halfway through these mild ablutions when Idgen Marte stumbled out, blinking, a jar in one hand. She took a healthy swig, gargled, spat a mouthful of beer into the dirt. Her hair, for once, was unbraided and fell over her shoulders and halfway down her back in a thick dark wave. She wore a long, shapeless cotton shirt that came halfway to her knees, and no sword.

"You know," Allystaire said, his voice croaking with disuse, "without a weapon, and with your hair down, you almost look feminine. Best you do not let anyone else see you. They will be trying get you married and stuck in a kitchen."

She snorted, took another swig from the jar, and swallowed, then held it out toward him. "And without a shirt on you look like a shaved bear. Half-shaved, anyway. They'll be baiting you in a pit, they get a glimpse." He reached for the jar, and while he took a swig and sloshed it around his mouth, she pointed to the long and twisted scar on his ribcage. "You still owe me the rest of that story."

Allystaire lowered the jar and handed it back to her, empty, as he swallowed, then winced. "Ah, where was I with that?"

"Telmawr. Aldacren Keep. Knights, lances, banners, all that shit."

"Ah, yes. That. Well, after the first charge it all degenerates. Chaos. Murder everywhere. When you read about battles in books it talks about lines and ground and maneuvers. In reality, you do not see any of that. Not in the midst, anyway. That all changed for me later, but that day, it was kill the man in front of me and hope the one behind was a friend. All that chivalry? Yielding, letting an unhorsed knight recover himself? That, as you said, is shit."

Idgen Marte pushed a handful of hair out of her eyes and grinned.

Allystaire took a deep breath, exhaled, and said, "Well, after we had been at it for an turn or two, I was unhorsed. That is to say, my horse took a spear in the neck and I cleared the saddle before it could fall on me."

He paused, shrugged at the disbelief that was plain in Idgen Marte's mocking grin, and said, "This was near a score of years ago. I was young and spry."

"You weren't ever young."

"I was spry, anyway." He cleared his throat and went on, "Well anyway, as I was standing there wondering what to do without my horse, some knight in cloisonnéd plate tried to spit me upon his lance. Right flowery thing it was, too, with vines carved all the way up. Foolishness. At any rate, I tried to turn away, and the lance found me but did not quite spit me like the knight intended. I realized pretty quickly that it had torn me open, but shallowly and straight across the ribs."

"So what'd you do?"

"I used the fact that it was stuck between my body and my armor. Yanked the idiot right out of his saddle because he had the thing lashed to his freezing gauntlet, if you can credit it. The force splintered the wood, and I tugged free.

As Sir Cloisonné lay there like a fool, with one useless arm, I gave him a thorough clubbing with a spiked mace I carried in those days. Once blood started to ooze from his visor I caught on that the business was through. Good thing, too, because that foolish mace got bone-stuck."

Idgen Marte chewed her bottom lip for a moment. Allystaire, thinking he was done, retrieved his shirt and started to tug it back on.

"How'd ya survive? Still an ugly wound in the middle of a fight."

"Well," Allystaire said, drawing out the single syllable. "That was pretty much the end of the fight. The idiot in the cloisonnéd armor with the vine-carved lance turned out to be Baron Telmawr." He paused again, shrugged almost apologetically, and said, "Watching their baron brained took some of the fight out of the knights, and while it took a while for word to get out to their foot, some of the Old Baron's retinue saw what I had done and surged forward in triumph. I was hustled back to the camps and the chirurgeons and the praise of my liege."

"And the chirurgeons didn't manage to kill you?" Idgen Marte stretched her arms out to either side, till her back and shoulders crackled lightly. "Seven of every ten chirurgeons, physickers, alchemists, and healing-men I've met in this part of the world have been quacks out to poison anyone they can."

"You have not met dwarfish chirurgeons, then," Allystaire replied. "The Old Baron did not hold with quackery. In his host, chirurgeons knew how to set a bone, when to bleed a wound and when to sew it, when a man was lost, and how to send him off with a painless slice. Michar saw to all that, and more. They got me to his care right quick that day. First time that dwarf saved my life. Not the last. Gerard Oyrwyn always said that Michar cost more than any three knights put together, and that he was worth more than any ten. I cannot say he was wrong."

"You talk about Old Baron Oyrwyn like a boy talks about the grandfather he worshipped," Idgen Marte noted.

"I never met my grandfather," Allystaire said, shrugging as he smoothed wet hair back along his scalp. "By all accounts, he was a terror in the field and most everywhere else. Gerard Oyrwyn was better than that. Not a hero, true. He had a cunning mind and an eye to advance his family. Yet he wanted his knights to be something more than murderers in enameled steel."

"Why no paint on your armor, then?"

"I left the brightwork behind," Allystaire said. "Took the best armor, not the prettiest."

"Lot of men would say those were one and the same," Idgen Marte pointed out.

"Style," Allystaire said, "is for dead men."

She snorted again and turned back to the house. "Style is at least half of the point." He heard her mumbling something about 'northern barbarians' as she vanished into the darkness of the house.

The thin predawn light thickened as the sun rose. Allystaire gathered his shirt, went back into the house, and got himself shaved and was dressing when Idgen Marte emerged in her gusseted and studded arming jacket, leathers and riding boots, sword on one hip, quiver on the other, knives at the small of her back.

"Expecting a fight?" Allystaire had just settled his hammer on his belt, which was cinched around plain riding leathers for trousers and a clean shirt; no armor, no other arms.

"Expecting to be gone," she said, filling the last syllable with urgency. "It is time to go, Allystaire. Rede saw. It's what She told me we were waiting for."

"I agree, but we do not yet know where we are going."

"Pick a direction. Throw a handful of grass in the air," Idgen Marte suggested, throwing up her hands, exasperated. "Piss at the wind and follow the stream. Does it even matter where? We just need to *go*."

"We cannot just leave with no plan and no destination," Allystaire argued.

"I think I can help wi' that." They whirled to find Mol standing at the edge of the table, reaching carefully to pluck the sheets of parchment from the table. She rifled through, them, selected one, then padded, bare of foot, to the front door, pausing to look back at the two of them. "Well?"

They followed, Allystaire taking a moment to tug his boots on. Mol stopped just a few feet outside the door, in sight of the village green, which still bore a large, dark scar, but a smaller one than a few weeks ago. She held up the piece of parchment in her hand; instead of rows of handwriting, it had a few scattered marks. Mol held it steady, both hands above her head, and a ray of the rising sun caught it. Allystaire and Idgen Marte held their breath as they waited to see what the Mother's light would reveal. Allystaire thought the runes began to glow; Idgen Marte peered forward, craning her neck, expecting, perhaps, unseen letters to crawl across the page. They stood tense and anxious, jaws taut, fingers curling.

Nothing happened.

They waited a few moments more. Mol turned back to look at them, her face obscured by her upraised arms. Exasperated, she lowered the paper and turned around, frowning. "Can y'not see it?" She held it up again, not quite as boldly as before. She extended her arm in front of her like a frustrated scholar with an idiot for a pupil, then stabbed at the sheet with one finger. "Were y'expectin' the Mother to make the runes come alive for you? To spell out in mystic fires the course yer t'take?" She stabbed at it again. "Tis a map, y'great stupid…" She groped about a moment for a word and, finding none, exhorted them again, "Tis a map. This is Thornhurst." She pointed to a rune at the center.

She moved her finger along a line east and slightly north, if indeed it was a map, and pointed to the next mark. "Ashmill Bridge." Further east. "Birchvale." Her finger moved diagonally across the map, pointing to a large mark that would be far south and a good deal west of Thornhurst. "Londray." She traced her finger up from that point to a smaller rune that was closer, but still west. "Bend." She turned to face Allystaire, holding the sheet to him. "I dunno the names of the other places. But *you* do. These are where yer t'go, the two of ya."

"Where do we go first?" As Allystaire took the map, he started filling in the details the Goddess had not given it; the line of the Ash River, the High Road that struck north from Ashmill Bridge, the mountains rising on its western side, and rising and rising, and the road along with it, until it met with the southern reaches of Barony Oyrwyn. He filled in other towns as he looked—mostly in Delondeur, but a few over its border with Innadan and just over the very southern edge of Oyrwyn.

"Doesn't matter," Mol said. "However you mark it best, I expect. If ya've been to a place before…Bend and Thornhurst…ya'll know if y'need t'return or not."

Allystaire nodded, slowly, then handed the simple map to Idgen Marte. "Guess you got your wish. We leave today." He turned to Mol, looking somberly down at her, fearing her reaction.

She smiled up at him, trusting and bright, without a trace of sorrow. "Yer meant t'go, Allystaire," she said. "The Mother told me so. I'll go fetch Renard."

Allystaire watched the girl skip away. He took a deep breath; he felt free, a bit dizzy, but anxious to be in the saddle. Idgen Marte handed him back the parchment after studying it and said, "Best we head out of the valley. Find the Ash and make for those villages first, then the High Road, circle back down and end in Londray."

"How long do you figure?"

"Three months at least," Idgen Marte replied. "If we stopped a short time in each one, had no trouble, then came straight back for Thornhurst, mayhap we could beat the earliest snow."

"And the chances of having no trouble?"

She snorted. "Bloody freezin' small."

"What worked with a dozen pisspot slavers and fifty cowed villagers might not work in Londray. Cold, it might not work at Ashmill Bridge."

She grimaced, smacked his arm lightly. "Stop gatherin' worry." Her expression softened and she added, "She put Her faith in us, remember?"

"Aye," Allystaire said, and was silent for a moment, surveying the still mostly silent, rebuilt houses of Thornhurst. Behind their thin walls and hide-covered windows, village folk who had faced lives of slavery and horror were beginning another hard day. *Hard, mayhap,* he told himself, *but free. Free because of the Mother…and us.* He bit his lip and said, "A good start, I think. Yet only a start." He turned back to Idgen Marte and said, "Saddle the horses."

"Cold!" she exclaimed, her wide, crooked grin lighting her face again. "Been waitin' t'hear that for weeks." She dashed off, and Allystaire ducked back into the house. When he re-emerged, the sun had cleared the foothills and late summer light was bathing the valley in which Thornhurst rested. It glinted dully off the pitted and scarred surface of his grey armor, which clanked and clattered as he walked toward the village, saddlebags over one shoulder, sword belted on his back, his features set in scrunched consternation.

He headed for the village green, a walk of but a dozen yards or so from his door, and found a crowd gathered before the inn, with Mol, Renard, and Idgen Marte at their head. Both Ardent and Idgen Marte's courser were saddled nearby, and his mule was loaded with packs and bags. Rede loitered at the edge of the crowd, not part of it, but not quite apart from it, either.

Allystaire grimaced and opened his mouth as if to speak, but Mol stepped forward and raised her hand to stop him. A small knot of village folk came behind her, clustered together.

"We know yer leavin'," the girl said, bluntly. "Ya have to. We all knew this day was comin', and no one here will try t'stop ya. And I know what yer next words were t'be because yer still slow." She stepped to the side and looked over her shoulder at the knot of villagers behind her; it included Timmar, the stonemason Giraud, Henri, and Gram's parents. The mason held a large round bundle wrapped in canvas.

"When y'came among us…when y'rescued us, Allystaire," Timmar began, restlessly tugging at the edges of his shirt and hitching his pants before finally deciding to clasp his hands together behind his back. "When y'rescued us ya were careful t'always say ya weren't knight nor lord. Wouldn't let us call ya sir, or m'lord." He glanced up to Giraud as if awaiting help. The tall, dour-faced man cleared his throat and spoke in a deep, measured voice.

"'Twas plain to all of us you were a lord or a knight o'some kind e'en if ya didn't like to say so. And, well, Cold, yer the Mother's own paladin, Her Arm now. That means yer a knight no matter what some baron has to say about it. And, well…" Then he, too trailed off, and Allystaire stood and watched in mute incomprehension, before Henri finally spoke up.

"Cold, it ain't like he's the prettiest girl at the first fair dance ya'll were allowed at. Why're you so tongue-tied?" Henri shook his head at his townfolk and then turned his creased, smiling face to Allystaire. "All the knights in tales, and all those you killed on the road those weeks back, they all carried shields with, what're they…sigils and coats and heraldic whatnot on 'em. Yers was grey. We decided that grey weren't good enough."

"Don't worry, I told 'em what t'paint," Mol put in, quickly, as Tim and Henri unwrapped the canvas that surrounded Allystaire's shield, and boldly displayed its new design.

The design obeyed none of the standards of Heraldry as Allystaire knew them—no animals, no recognized symbols, no halfing or quartering—yet as soon as he saw it he knew it was right, knew it matched the glimpse he had when Garth's words of rebellion had briefly entranced him. A bright sky-blue field, dominated in its center by a huge, ten-pointed golden sunburst that was bigger than it ought to have been. Centered within it, not touching the top or bottom of the sunburst, was the outline of a simple maul, like the one worn on his belt, in a cooler and lighter shade of blue.

He smiled, and he felt, despite himself, an itch in his throat. *Shed a tear in front of them now and you're freezin' done for*, he thought. He strode forward, face blank, and accepted the shield with genuine, quiet gratitude. He took the old, familiar oak in both hands, studying its face closely for a moment before looking back up at the crowd.

"Who did the painting?" he murmured, just barely loud enough to be heard. "It is startling."

There was some shuffling in the crowd, and Henri reached to drape an arm around Norbert's neck and drag the reluctant youth forward.

"He did," Henri declared, astonishment and pride in his voice. "Just said he felt like he ought t'try, after a few of us had botched it. Had the steadiest hand by far."

Allystaire slung the shield from his left hand and put his right to use embracing the forearms of the men clustered around him. When Norbert's turn came, Allystaire pulled the blushing, scraggly-bearded youth closer and whispered, "By the time I return, you will be one of their own. Mark me."

Norbert nodded and stepped back into the crowd of villagers, blending into it as if he'd been among them all his life.

"Knights also have pennants," Mol put in, loud enough to be heard over the general din of shaking hands and backslaps and well wishes. "For the end o'the lance." The crowd let Allystaire disentangle himself and step back. Gram's mother came forward with a folded square of blue material in her hands and held it out to him, and Allystaire took it in his free hand and let it spill out. It was the same image, stitched rather than painted. *Where did they find the time*, he wondered, *or the material?*

"I have no lance," Allystaire said, suddenly and a bit stupidly, which drew a bit of a laugh from the gathered crowd.

"Well, that isn't quite true, m'lord" Renard put in, with a light, throat-clearing cough. "I, ah, took the liberty of keeping one before ya sent those Oyrwyn knights packing." Gram and another lad came around from the back of the crowd bearing a wooden pole nearly twice as long as the two of them if they laid down end to end, capped with a sharp steel point. They held it up on trembling arms, faces beaming with the solemnity of their task.

Allystaire's hands being full with shield and pennant, he fumbled for a moment before whistling. Ardent tugged his reins free of Idgen Marte's light grip and trotted over to his rider, and Allystaire slung the shield on the pommel and carefully tucked the pennant into his belt. Then he reached out and took the lance, lifting it easily with both hands, and slid it into the boot that descended from Ardent's saddle; it settled in perfectly. *Course it does*, he thought, *it was made to fit there; shaft-pole, point, and tack were all made at Wind's Jaw.*

"Now, Sir Allystaire, Paladin, and Arm of the Mother," Mol said, or rather intoned, her voice suddenly loud and clear and solemn, "you are attired for the task set to you." Her eyes were briefly distant, clouded, and she continued, "Carry, in word and in deed, the news of the Mother's awakening." She blinked several times, her eyes cleared, and she took a deep breath, smiling as Allystaire lifted his foot to Ardent's stirrup.

"One more thing, m'lord," Renard said, and Allystaire could have sworn the old soldier was blushing behind his thick beard. "Ah, if you would, before you go…as the Goddess's servant, if you'd…" He looked to his side and swallowed once, as Leah had suddenly appeared next to him, her cheeks glowing in the early day sun, her eyes beaming—but at Renard, not Allystaire. "We were hoping you'd marry us," the soldier finally stammered out.

Give yourself a moment to think on the words, he thought, but said, "Of course, Renard. I would be honored." He added in a booming voice, as he swung up into the saddle and flung his arm toward the Temple, "Come, we will all of us celebrate the first wedding at the Mother's Chapel. But first," he lifted his lance from its boot and held it down toward Gram, then shook the pennant free of its place on his belt, held it out, and tossed it to the lad's waiting hands. "If you would."

With surprisingly deft fingers, the lad quickly knotted the ends of the blue pennant around the wooden pole, just below the point. Allystaire half-bowed in the saddle in thanks, then held the lance high enough for the pennant to catch what little wind there was. He gave Ardent a brief nudge. Soon Idgen Marte was up on her courser to his right, and the two of them dashed off toward the temple with the crowd of villagers streaming behind them and the pennant snapping in the wind on the end of his lance.

The scene may have been bright and gay, but Allystaire sweated the entire ride, wondering just what a marriage ceremony ought to entail. *Think on what the priests of Urdaran, or Braech, or Fortune would say*, he thought, *then do the opposite.*

Idgen Marte swung easily out of her saddle and let her courser stray in the grass beyond the temple. In his armor, Allystaire was not so quick to dismount, and his boots left divots in the rain-softened ground. She offered him a sly, teasing smile, but left him to his thoughts as the crowd of villagers approached, Renard and Leah in the fore.

"Renard," Allystaire called, "for one day, set aside your weapons, eh?" The bearded man laughed and, with some hesitation, handed his spear to the excited crowd behind him. Allystaire turned his back to them and walked into the still-unfinished Temple. He stood behind the alter and prayed, *Give me the words, Mother. Please. They deserve it*, and traced his hands over the stone.

Then, all too soon, Renard and Leah were standing in front of him expectantly, with the villagers circling the hip-high walls. Mol had made her way to the front of the crowd; Idgen Marte lingered at its edges. Rede had managed to squeeze his way to the front.

Allystaire's armor clinked as his hands moved restlessly before settling on the altar in front of him, against which leaned his shield. "My friends; my brothers and sisters and children in worship of the Mother," he began, once the crowd had quieted, armor "I have served you in justice; I have served you in grief; I have served with you these several weeks in labor. Today, I am allowed to serve you in joy."

He paused to gauge their reaction; the crowd seemed to fairly buzz with the tension of waiting; Mol beamed an encouraging smile at him; Leah stared happily at Renard, who looked somewhat overwhelmed.

Allystaire leaned forward across the altar and gestured for the couple's hands; they each held one to him, and he placed them on the stone and gestured with his index fingers, till they comprehended and linked their free hands together.

"Leah, and Renard. If you would be wed in the sight of the Mother, promise but two things to each other: love, and service. Love and serve one another in day and in night, in joy and in grief, in plenty and in want. Know that in the Mother's eyes, love is the greatest and highest of ends. Failure to love is the deepest and darkest of sins. Do you swear, as I have said, your love and service to one another, and to the friends and family gathered here?"

They both nodded, waiting, and Allystaire cleared his throat in a prompt; Renard caught on and said, "I do swear my love and service." Leah, her eyes gleaming now with bright wetness, echoed him.

Allystaire smiled, waited, and the couple did the same. Then, clearing his throat and perhaps flushing a bit, the paladin said, "I presume you know what to do."

Renard was suddenly surprised as Leah's hands seized the collar of his shirt and pulled his bearded face to hers. They kissed passionately and for longer than Rede, at least, thought proper, or so Allystaire assumed given the former Urdarite's furious blush and thin-pressed, white-lipped mouth.

When their kiss broke, a wild cheer filled the air, and Renard swept Leah up in his arms and carried her with a joyous flair. Someone cried out, "Ale!" and another, "Wine!" and someone else, "Breakfast!" and the crowd bolted off in one great mass back to the green.

Idgen Marte cleared her throat, and Allystaire turned to her; their eyes met, and she jerked her chin toward their horses that roamed in the field beyond. He nodded very slightly and turned to face Mol and Rede, the only two left behind.

"Where are we going," Rede asked, suddenly and impatiently.

"*We* are going nowhere," Allystaire replied shortly. "I have not time to debate it with you, monk. I welcome you to the worship of the Mother and I hope it will see you well, but the journey Idgen Marte and I undertake today is for us alone."

Rede snorted indignantly, stood up, and stomped off.

"At least you get a day's respite from joining in the work," Allystaire couldn't resist calling after him. But by then, Mol had come and looked up at him with her large, dark eyes and her smile that were both so much older than she was, and the paladin knelt to embrace the young priestess. They spoke no words. Allystaire wrapped one arm around her back, and her arms clung around his neck. When he let go and stood, Mol turned and raced off, and he walked out of the temple and swung into Ardent's saddle, alongside Idgen Marte, who was already mounted.

Without a backward glance at Thornhurst and its joyful wedding celebration, they set off for the foothills to the north.

CHAPTER 25

Tales Scatter Like Leaves

"There was five of us. Five, and every man-jack knew his trade and kept 'is knife sharp."

The man was weasel-faced and pock-cheeked, and he sat at the bar in The Sign of the Boar and the Bushel, selling his story for the cheapest, newest white wine the tavern-keeper had, and as the turn grew later, the wine grew ever more watery. The tavern-keeper was a grim man who believed the worst of his custom and was usually proved right. Tending bar and shepherding drunks and trying to keep the stoop free of corpses will inure a man to all manner of tales and boasts, and though he had heard this story three times already, he found himself listening again as yet another drunk threw an extra copper link on the bar to encourage the teller.

"Five of us, and an easy mark. A farmer, y'know, some dirt-digger, an turn outta the gates and headin' back to whatever patch o' land he's been wastin' 'is life t'grow. N'we knows this racket, good work every harvest time. In they come wi' the fam'ly horse an' cart full o'…well, whate'er 'tis, melons or 'taters or cabbages. And a day or two later, out they comes with a less full cart, a purse full o'links if it's a good year they've had, maybe some brandy in the wagon, maybe some beer, few sides o' beef. Maybe they comes out w'the flamin' red skitters in their nethers if they been t'see Shary over there," the man said, pausing after this great outburst to prime the pump with half a cup of his wine, after raising his glass to a slightly bedraggled, none-too-fully-dressed woman at the back of the room who crowded near the hearth fire, small though it was.

She pulled her thin wrap tighter around her shoulders and looked from the fire to the bar as if trying to decide between her warmth and her curiosity; the tale won out.

"And usually, see, these stump-jumper types, they knows what to do and they usually hands over the money right quick and maybe whatever else we likes and then on their way. Well this farmer, see, he had some starch in him so we thought t'tickle 'is ribs with our knives, right?"

Shary rolled her eyes as she made her way carefully over to the bar; her movement was not without grace, but the way she avoided chairs and tables and hunched her shoulders spoke of a lot of time spent trying not to be noticed.

"Gonna tell us all about slittin' another poor man's throat, Gend?"

The man's pocked face suddenly grew deathly silent and deathly still, and he spoke very quietly, pronouncing each syllable with the care and import of a drunk.

"No, Shary. Lemme tell the story, aye?" He swallowed once, shook his head, downed the rest of his wine, and set down the mug. When another listener reached for his purse, Gend waved him away and looked at the rough, splintered surface of the bar he sat at, running an index finger along it. He pushed his empty mug away from him, sullenly.

"Well anyways this farmer was a younger fella and maybe 'e'd seen some fightin'. I dunno. I just know 'e had some vinegar and didn't take t'our askin'. So Tyl is just 'bout to cut 'im when we hear this voice behind us tellin' us t'stand down. That's all 'e said, *stand down*, but 'e said it like a man 'spectin' t'be obeyed. So we turns t'face 'im and 'e's this big ugly bastard. Not tall, but like t'fill up a room right enough."

Gend coughed for a moment, lifting his shirt to cover his mouth, then took a big gulp of air; the barman, Shary, and the other serious drinkers clustered around the bar hanging on his pause.

"Ugly, like I said. Nose been busted up, face too. And 'e's got some big bloody hammer just danglin' from 'is hand. I wouldn't e'en know what t'do with the thing. Knacker a bullock, I guess, or knock down a wall. And 'e says again, *stand down*, tells us t'get along, that our thievin' days are done…or, and I marked this well, 'e says, *You are either done thieving, or you are done living. Decide right now.* All fancy and somber like that. And Tyl just laughs at 'im and slips that hatchet he likes…hatchet he *liked* off 'is belt." Here, the taleteller paused and swallowed hard. "Tyl starts tossin' it, flippin' it end o'er end in the air and snatchin' the haft wi' his hand. Tyl tells the big ugly one, there's five o' us and one o'you, so what're ya gonna do? An' Tyl catches the hatchet and rears back like 'e means t'throw it as he's sayin', 'I'll put this in that pisspot farmer's head if you don't drop your hammer, fool. And the ugly bastard says, 'I take it that means you have decided.' And then 'is arm lifts an'…an' Tyl's freezin' head burst."

Gend lifted his gaze from the bar and swallowed hard, flicking his eyes from one listener to the other; the tavern keeper, despite knowing just how much wine he'd poured through the evening, would've sworn he was looking at a sober man at that moment.

"Bastard had thrown 'is hammer and it took Tyl's head. Took it *clean* off. Tyl's body just stood there for a moment and then crashed like a felled tree." Gend grabbed the front of his shirt and held it up to the flickering light cast by the lamps; they could see it spotted thickly with a dark stain. "Tyl's blood, n'his bone, n'his brain', all o'er me. An' the other three rush the big fella,', and I swear t'ya, 'e coulda killed all three o' them like crushin' a grape. Din't e'en bother t'draw the sword on 'is back. Put 'is elbow in Mern's face and broke 'is jaw, n'he punched Jorry s'hard i'the stomach the poor bastard started sickin' all o'er hisself. Klent, 'e lifted clean off the ground and threw back on top o'Tyl's body, like just for a bit of a laugh, ya know? And then 'e walks o'er t'me, n'm'just standin' there, me, blooded an' a good man wi' a knife, and 'e takes m'blade outta m'hand and…"Gend paused again and reached into a purse on his belt; out of it he pulled a curled ball of iron that may once have been a knife, but had been bent so thoroughly in on itself it was no more than scrap now. He set it deliberately and carefully on the bar, and the tavern keeper snatched it up to hold it to the light.

This was a new wrinkle in the story; Gend hadn't shown that bit of iron around before. "No man can bend a piece of iron like that with his hands. Snap it, mayhap, but simply twirl it 'round like that?" The tavern keeper tossed it back on the bar with a snort.

"I tell you 'e did, and if ya don't believe me, go find Jorry or Klent. Mern won't be talkin' none for a few months, I reckon. "Gend swallowed and then fingered his mug anxiously; a few links clicked onto the bar and the tavern keeper bent down to fetch the jug.

"And then 'e 'ands me the knife back and tells me t'show e'eryone I care ta. 'E leans that broad ugly face an' that bent-up nose right up against mine an' I can see…oh I can see somethin' hard in 'is eyes. I been t' war an' I been a thief an' I seen hard men an' I seen killers…I saw somethin' harder than any of 'em. Harder than all o' 'em put t'gether. Says 'is name's *Sir Al-us-stare*." Gend paused for a beat, and then said, "Called hisself a paladin, then. Sir Al-us-stare, paladin, Arm o'the Mother…whate'er that means. And then 'e told us t'run, and you mark me, I freezin' ran and I din't look back t'see what the lads did. And then I hear 'im chattin' all peaceable with that farmer lad, din't catch much. Somethin' about the Mother." He took a big gulp of wine then, nearly emptying the mug; his hand shook slightly and a bit of wine slopped over the edge, and he lifted it quickly to his mouth.

When he set it down, his face still pale, his hand still a little shaky, he added, "I think maybe I am done thievin'. I don' 'e'er wanna see those eyes again. Nor 'is freezin' hammer."

The drinker who'd been supplying Gend with wine tossed a broken copper link on the bar in derision. "A paladin, Gend? Ya've done better'n that before. My guess is, ya came inta some weight w'those lads, slit their throats and on the way o'er, heard some minstrel singin' o' paladins—Parthalian and that lot—and thought it a fine excuse."

Shary, meanwhile, had edged nearer to Gend and place a tentative hand on his arm. In the light spilling from the lantern and the rushlights clustered around the counter, her features came into better focus—fair but weathered skin, bedraggled blonde hair falling limply around her shoulders, wearing worldly wariness surely thicker than her shawl. A fresh, thin red line stood out vividly on her pale neck.

She cleared her throat tentatively and spoke, her voice not quite making it all the way out of her throat at her first few words. "Di…did you say the Mother? Arm of the Mother?"

The tavern keeper looked toward the woman, frowning, though not, it seemed, at her. He leant over the bar and pitched his voice low enough for her voice alone to hear. "Shary, lass, are you s'posed to be in here? Does Stehan know?"

She looked up at him, her eyes wide, shining in the darkness, and said loud enough for everyone to hear, "Stehan's dead."

"What?" The barman straightened up, missing a lamp hanging above his head by an inch or less. "Ya didn't kill him, didya? I won't be having the green-hats storming in here accusing me of harboring a murder—"

Shary cut off his sudden tirade with a quick shake of her head. "No, Hod, I didn't kill him, but I'm glad the bastard's dead." She looked back toward Gend, who was fiddling with the broken link tossed to him and staring ahead vacantly, and said, "I saw somethin'…somethin' odd this night too, Gend. And I heard the same thing. Well almost the same thing. About the Mother."

At the word *Mother*, Gend looked up at her, blinking away the vacancy in his eyes. "Eh? What of it?"

Shary licked her lips and glanced at Hod, then nodded toward a stool. Hod reached under the bar, pulled up a cup, filled it from a flagon, and handed it over. She took a quick sip of it, wiped her face with the back of her hand, and said, "Stehan was angry at us, at me and Filoma. We asked for warmer clothes; with fall comin' on, streets are gonna get chill. Or failin' that we asked him could we work indoors somewhere, like in a house or a tavern or the like, and he laughed at us. And then he got angry when Filoma said somethin' about leavin' maybe, n'he started askin' her where she got the weight t'talk like that. And when she didn't say anythin' he started hittin' her."

She paused then and had another sip from her cup, and set it down again. "She still din't say anythin'. Filoma's been hit a lot, by better than Stehan. And then he turns t'me and pulls out his knife and puts it against my cheek and tells Filoma if he don't tell him he'll cut me. He's usually bluffin'. Usually," she said, suddenly dropping her eyes to the bar and swallowing once, hard. Without looking up, she added, "He weren't bluffin' this time, but he started on my arm so custom wouldn't notice." She reached up and slipped down the shawl she'd been wearing; her upper arm had several thin red lines upon it.

She looked up, covered her arm again, reached for her cup and drained it with forced casualness. "He cut me up a little and Filoma tried to stop him—

she jumped at his arm and he smacked her away and then told her she better watch while he cut my throat open," she said, spitting out the words fast, and then turning wide-eyed to her audience and pointing a bitten fingernail at the thin line on her neck. "And he puts the knife to my throat and I suddenly see this shadow behind him that sorta…slides away from the side of the buildin', and suddenly it's no' a shadow, it's a woman. Tall and dark-skinned like I only seen on Concordat caravaners, and with a long scar here," she said, touching the left side of her chin. "And she has the knife out of Stehan's hand faster than I can follow, and he forgets all about me." Hod went to refill her cup but she put her hand over the top of it and shook him off, saying, "I'm not tellin' tales for drink. I'm tellin' somethin' I *saw*."

She turned back to Gend and the small crowd of drinkers who'd listened to his tale and said, "Well then he pulls out the lil' cosh he likes to carry on his belt, and takes a big swing at her, only she…she isn't there. And then she's behind him again but I n'er see 'er move. Then she takes that cosh away and hits him with it, once, twice," she mimicked the blows to either side of the head with one hand, "but not real hard. I think, this woman, I think she could've hit him a lot harder than she did then. And she tries tellin' him to stay down and back off and he can live through this. But then he calls out for Mathern. His bruiser, ya know, fat bastard, carries a mace, standin' just out the alley. And he tells this woman that she's in for it now, tells Mathern to splatter her brains all over the walls."

Shary gulped then, hard. Her eyes went huge with memory and awe. "Then I realized she's been…jus' playin' with Stehan. She draws her sword, long and curved like I never seen b'fore, and she has Mathern gutted almost before he knows what's happ'nin and then Stehan comes roarin' up after her wi' his knife again, or maybe he'd another, and she guts him too."

She licked her lips once, and ran her eyes over the crowd, then looked off toward the hearth, shivered a little and hugged her arms around herself. "I never saw anyone move so fast, and she weren't runnin', she weren't even hurryin'. She'd just be one place, and then another. She talked to us a little, after they were dead."

Shary paused then, thought for a moment, then shook her head and went on. "Talked to us a moment or two. Never said her name…when we asked, she said she was…said she was the Shadow of the Mother. Told us the Mother was…was a Goddess, like Fortune n'those, but new n'that…well lots o'stuff. Told us there was a temple t'Her risin' in a town out a ways…."

* * *

"Thornhurst, he said. Said all were welcome, but he had t'be goin', and Mother bless me n'mine." The farmer, a tall, broad and still young man carefully set himself down on the stool that faced the hearth, while his wife, her back to him, stirred something in a pot. "I thought I was dead or we were poor, Liss, and then…a paladin…a paladin outta stories. Can ya credit it?"

"Aye, Mich, I can," she said, turning around to face him with a slightly dazed expression. She'd listened to his story carefully, but as soon as he'd described the big, broken-nosed man she'd known just who he meant, could feel again that presence, that calm that he had, some great well of hope and sorrow all mixed up together and carried on his back. "He was here while you were away in Ashmill Bridge, Mich, not three days ago. Maris' and Nils' new baby— they hadn't named 'im yet—well, it looked like they were gonna bury him too, after their last. Poor thing couldn't breathe. And he rode into the village with all his armor and his arms and that woman behind him, strange lookin' one, south-erner I s'pose, didn't say a word, but he went right up to the house where the women were gatherin' t'try n'help poor Maris and he asked what was wrong?" The woman shook her head, smoothing out her apron with one hand, and sat down at the stool across from her husband, her eyes shining and huge as she reached across the table to one of his large hands.

"Well we thought he was jus' some lord, and we told 'im it was nothin' t'trouble such as him. But he got down off his horse and he took his helmet off, and I'll tell ya, Mich, he's not a comely man, with that broke nose and those hard eyes and those thin lips. There was somethin' frightenin' about him, yet…I knew I never needed t'fear him. "

"He asked again, real careful and slow like, and we told him there was a baby dyin'. And he just asked us to get out o'the way, and he went into 'er house and begged 'er pardon—him, with armor and horse, beggin' *her* pardon—for trackin' dust into 'er house. And he asked to hold the child, that's how he said it, only it was more a command, I think. "Let me hold the child," he said.

And she did, without thinkin'. And he unwrapped some of the swaddlin' and put his hand on the baby's bare flesh, and he closed his eyes and Mich, he said some words I din't hear and that baby took to cryin' so loud it startled all of us and then Maris was cryin', and he handed her the boy back and said t'call him *Balendin*, that was his name."

Mich absorbed this in stunned silence, finally saying, "Mayhap we should take a ride to Thornhurst, Liss…"

* * *

Lord Captain Luden Thryft was a busy man, and he damn well made sure everyone that came into contact with him knew it; his armor was carefully smudged, but not too smudged. His cloak was edged with mud and casually gathered at one shoulder. He constantly rattled his sword in its scabbard and paced around his spacious command tent so as to set his carefully gathered, pale-green cloak fluttering behind him. He had decided to make it a habit never to turn immediately when addressing reporting knights or bannerman; instead, in order to press upon them just how busy their newly elevated lord captain was, he'd continue with whatever he was doing prior—pouring wine, staring at a map, reading a book—while ordering them to report.

When he heard a horse barreling toward his tent, hooves pounding in the muck, he turned, cloak fanning out behind him, stamped to his feet in order to rattle his spurs and his swordbelt, and began carefully studying the empty space on a map showing the borders of Barony Delondeur with Barony Innadan, the eastern frontier of which he was now encamped near. Several wooden tokens representing Delondeur and Innadan troops lay scattered over the map; Thryft considered shifting some, but then decided he'd better leave them where they were. He heard the solid *thump* as the approaching rider dismounted behind him and heard his boots approach; he heard no jingle of spurs. He continued studying the map as he said, "Report, Bannerman."

"Sorry m'lord," came the reply, through heavy breathing, "Bannerman's dead. I'm just a chosen man."

Thryft looked up from the map upon the table, twisting his body to turn his face to the man. He was sweaty, mud-spattered, and pale. With careful deliberation, the captain straightened up to his full and considerable height. "Whose troop are you with?"

"Sir Goddard Bainsley, m'lord," the man replied, pushing the words out through his gasping breaths.

"And why is he not making this report, Chosen Man…?"

"Kyle, m'lord," the man said, suddenly wrapping an arm around himself as his breath heaved. "And Sir Goddard is bad hurt, m'lord. Bad hurt."

Thryft's hand fell to his sword and curled dramatically around its hilt. "You have made contact with the enemy, then? Where? Are we in danger of attack?"

The man shook his head, and finally seemed to have his breath under control. "I don't think so m'lord. It weren't no Innadan patrol…no patrol at all. Just two…two folk."

The captain pressed his lips into a thin line beneath his carefully manicured mustache and said, "Start at the beginning, Chosen Man Kyle. Quickly!"

"M'lord, we was on a press—"

"Recruitment!" Thryft suddenly spat, interrupting the man-at-arms.

"On a recruitment trip t'the border villages. We found a likely one, not been visited yet and we started, ah, we started offerin' Baron Delondeur's link around. There was ten of us. Sir Goddard, the bannerman, and eight men at arms, all've us horsed, blooded men, sir. Well we had some lads lined up, and their ma's and da's shunted aside 'cept for the men still young enough, and then this big voice behind us tells us t'clear off. I mark what he said well, m'lord, I can't forget it. 'Tis burned into m'mind, like. He says, *These folk will have none of your press gangs. Put this village at your back and trouble its people no more.* He spoke like a captain or a marshal, m'lord."

"One man? One man ordered you away from your appointed tasks?"

"I'm gettin' t'that m'lord, beg yer pardon," Kyle went on. "We turned on him. It was one man, on a horse, a great big grey destrier, a fine huge beast. And he was armored and armed like a knight. His shield was a blue field, somethin' on it in gold. I didn't see what. Well then Sir Goddard tells him to clear off or die, and this man shakes his head almost…almost sad like. He says, "I offer you one chance. Ride off and rejoin your army, or, better still, go freezing home." Sir Goddard says that loyal subjects of Baron Delondeur will do whatever he commands or be branded and scourged for traitors, and that not only will he press who he wants, he'll give their sisters and their sweethearts to his men and burn their frozen village to the ground. Well, the sunburst knight, he doesn't say another word."

Chosen Man Kyle took a long, dry swallow. He looked longingly at the flagon of wine on Lord Captain Thryft's table, pursing his lips. Quickly realizing the futility, he went on with his story, slightly hoarse.

"He gives his mount the spur and lowers his lance, and Sir Goddard, he does the same, doesn't miss a second. The bannerman tells us to ride the fool off if he survives Sir Goddard's charge, and 'tis then when the arrows start flyin'. Plucked our outriders from their saddles before we knew what was happenin'—"

"Arrows? What arrows? Was there a company of bowmen hidden in the village?"

"Far as I know, m'lord, there were but two. I'm gettin' to that…Sir Goddard and the other man, m'lord, they met with a clatter such as I've never heard—I have never seen a man flung as far off his horse as Sir Goddard, and he was a fair rider and a good hand with a lance. He clears fifteen paces easy in the air and lands with an 'orrible thump, and he screams, and you could just feel his bones shatterin', m'lord. Then it was all a mess. Arrows coming, m'lord, from two places, and then that big grey armored man was among us on his horse swingin' a hammer and he knew what he was about. Bannerman Teldin tried t'take 'im on and got his face smashed in and 'is neck broke. And then…the other one, the archer, m'lord she—"

Thryft's eyes widened. "She?"

"Aye, m'lord, she. She just appeared behind him, just standin' behind his horse, an' arrow nocked. It were sorcery of a kind, m'lord. Had to be! He spoke up again and said he demanded our surrender…in the name of *the Mother*, whoever that is. One of the lads made a move for 'im and the woman with the bow put an arrow through his hand, pinned it to his thigh. And then…" His face pale and his own eyes wide and fearful, his voice halting a moment. "Then, m'lord…then she disappeared again."

"This is too much to credit, Chosen Man Kyle," Thryft roared, pounding a fisted hand into his other palm. "Sorcery? A troop of *my men* driven off when they had the advantage five-to-one? How drunk *are* you, trooper?"

The man winced at his sudden demotion, and his face betrayed hurt. "M'lord, I'm as sober as the day I was born, and I rode straight through t'tell ya this, endangering m'horse. Sir Goddard is bein' borne in slow by the rest of the troop on account of his wounds. Only five of us left including him, m'lord. I can't imagine he'll survive the trip. He screamed every time we touched him or moved him. His…his arms were just hangin' limp, m'lord. Like the only thing keeping them to his body were his armor.

The captain crossed his arms over his mailed chest, slowly tapping the gloved fingers of his right hand on his left elbow. "A squadron of my best out-riders, half a score led by one of my finest knights, on a simple recruiting drive to a village full of *peasants*," Thryft practically spat the word, "who proceeded to defeat them?"

The soldier in front of him straightened up a bit stiffly at the captain's pronunciation of "peasants" and said, "The village folk had naught to do wi' it, m'lord. 'Twas the two…well, m'lord, I said sorcery, but he…they both said he was, well…" His voice trailed off, but he cleared his throat, rallied, and, looking straight at his captain, said, "a paladin."

"A paladin?" With theatric precision, Thryft raised one eyebrow at his soldier.

"Aye sir, so he said. When we had surrendered he took off his helm and… lectured us, like."

"So what did this paladin look like? Eight feet tall in gleaming argent armor, with a flaming sword and a face so fair half the village women threw themselves at him, and the other half wanted to? On a pure white steed as well, I suppose?"

"Er…no, m'lord. None o'that. Hard t'say how tall a man is when he's on horseback. A big mean lookin' grey destrier it was too, like I said. Be like ridin' on the top of a small mountain, I think. But he's probably no taller than you, m'lord. But he was a big man too, and when he got close, fierce lookin'. A man who'd seen some fightin'. Nose broke and all pushed to the side. And his armor was grey and rough looking. Sturdy enough, but no polish to it."

"And did this paladin have a name? Sir Splayed-snoot?"

"Said his name was Allystaire, m'lord. Sir Allystaire, Arm of the Mother."

The captain mused on this a moment, tapping his chin with the index finger of his right hand. "Broken nose, you said? Ugly man he was, and named Allystaire?" He glanced at the soldier, who nodded emphatically.

Lord Captain Thryft stood up, slapped his left hand against his thigh, and said, "Adjutant! Paper!"

"D'ya know him, m'lord?"

"I might," Thryft answered, "and if I do, he is no paladin, merely an exile who can't stay well lost." By this time, an aide-de-camp had produced paper, ink, and quill, and the captain was dashing off a quick note. "Courier! Courier!" he bellowed, even as he scribbled the last few lines, sprinkled the paper with sand, and then carefully folded it. He picked up a stick of green sealing wax, held it over a lantern that dangled from the beam till it melted, and sealed the folded letter with a heavy stamp that lay on his camp table. He thrust the letter into the waiting hands of the courier that had come at the lord captain's call.

As Thryft handed the letter over, he said, "With all due haste for the central camp; on to Londray if Baron Delondeur has made for Winter Quarters by the time you reach it. Kill a horse if you must." The courier nodded, saluted, and dashed off through the muddy, smoky camp at a steady trot, heading for a picket line.

* * *

Footsteps, though carefully trod, resounded loudly on the polished stone walkways of the temple. A careful tread was imperative, for the walkways along the floor were all just wide enough for one person to cross at a time, and extended a yard or so—it varied with tides—above a patch of rolling, lightly foaming sea water. There was only one figure crossing through the center of the temple now, a very tall woman walking beneath an enormous metal sculpture of a dragon; its surface was greening with age, and it stood on a massive plinth above the very center of the gleaming and slippery stone. The woman was clad in long sea-green robes, with a silver, gem-crusted amulet around her neck and a heavy, curved knife belted at her waist.

She paused briefly, contemplating the dragon as she passed beneath it. She clutched at her amulet and walked on, making no sign of obeisance. It did not do to show weakness before the state of the Sea Dragon Rampant, where legend held that Braech's worship had first come to the mainlaind— and where, rumor and superstition had it, the cowardly and the weak were 'fed,' as sacrifices, to the statue.

She soon passed out of the temple's central chamber and into a warren of tunnels and rooms behind it. Most of the building was projected onto the water on heavy, deeply sunken posts, and so the further back she walked, the more it felt as though she were swaying with the motion of the waves, though her gait had quickened now that the floor was a solid piece. She quickly found the door she sought, knocked, and opened it without waiting for a response.

Inside, the room looked much like an officer's cabin on a sailing vessel; most of the furniture was bolted into place and most movable objects were built with wide, flat bottoms. Behind a large table, upon which rested a double-sized writing desk, sat a man in blue robes whose height projected his salted-grey head far above the desk. He wore an amulet similar to the woman's, though of undoubtedly finer work and more weight of gems. In his hand was a quill; on the desk sat a bowl of sand, several cut-glass bottles of ink, and other accoutrements of his task. Several texts sat at his elbow, the top one of which was open. It was, the woman noted, bound in iron, and a heavy, open lock clanged gently against the table as the man's elbow brushed it.

She bowed lightly, inclining her body forward from the waist, but neither bending her neck nor dropping her eyes. "Choiron," she addressed the man.

"Marynth Evolyn," the tall, bearded man intoned, standing as he did so. "Why are my urgent studies disrupted?" Carefully, without apparent hurry, he slipped one long-fingered hand over the open text and closed it; the pages slipped together and the cover slapped loudly shut.

The woman, who was only a few inches short of the choiron in height, cleared her throat. "Reports have come to me, Choiron, reports of words that I thought would be of interest to you."

"What you think will be of interest to me is not likely to be," he replied, his face darkening, but his voice staying calm. "Speak quickly or continue to waste my time at your own peril, Marynth."

Clearing her throat, Evolyn reached into the sleeve of her robe and drew forth several rolled parchments, quickly drawing one open with a practiced motion of thumb and forefinger. "Are you quite certain, Choiron? Not even reports of heathens daring to call themselves paladins?" She let one paper snap closed, and unrolled another. "One apparently referring to himself as the *Arm of the Mother*? "

The choiron drew himself up to even fuller height, and squaring his shoulders. His eyes widened and his nostrils flared, "Where in the Sea Dragon's name have you heard…" His voice trailed off in ire.

Evolyn tilted her head to the side. "Braech is the Lord of Trade and Accords and overseeing such things are part of the duties you assigned me, Choiron; no one carries such tales farther or faster than gossiping merchants or yarn-spinning sailors, and all such folk belong to the Sea Dragon and seek out His Servants."

Symod recovered his calm and smiled, very faintly, nodding to the woman almost graciously. "Do go on, Marynth."

She smiled, spots of color appearing in her otherwise pale cheeks. "It appears that there are three of them…this 'Arm', whom my reports are calling, alternately, Alexander, Asdair, and—"

The choiron's face darkened dangerously and the Marynth's blush quickly faded as she took a half step backwards.

"Allystaire," he grated through clenched teeth. "So that was…" He took a deep breath, composed his face, and made a generous gesture with one hand. "Continue."

She nodded, took a ragged breath, and said, "Some unidentified woman who apparently travels with him. Accounts of her are much more varied and wild. And a third who appears entirely unconnected. Fewer tales of miracles and more of rousing preaching and calling to arms. He calls himself *Rede the Sighted, Eye of the Mother*."

* * *

"Coldbourne? What in the Greenest Cold is that old warhorse doing rousing *my* rabble?" The speaker stood in front of a small brazier that glowed with coals but gave off faint heat. He wore an arming coat with gleaming mail along the sleeves and a cloak of pale-green silk that would offer no protection against the weather.

The slightest hint of autumn chill snuck into the pavilion as its large front and back flaps were tied open. He was an old man, with a great grey beard that had once been blonde and a head that was fringed with a thin ring of hair that had lost most of its color, but he stood straight, with his shoulders back and his large, gnarled hands resting upon the swordbelt he wore. The blade it bore was too large, too heavy, and too well oiled to be mere ceremony. Upon his head sat a slim circlet of silver gleaming with the untarnished shine of newness, a roughly cut round emerald in its center.

"I cannot say, my Lord Baron," murmured the green-jacketed, lightly-armored courier who stood before him, his boots and clothing spattered with mud; he wavered slightly in his feet but snapped himself back to attention.

The baron caught this and said, "Green's sake man, sit, warm yourself. Wine!" He smacked a hand against his thigh as he called out the last word, and a servant scurried from the edge of the pavilion with a flagon, and another appeared with a tray of cups. The baron himself filled two and handed one to the soldier, who took it wide-eyed, and gratefully and started to mumble his thanks. The baron waved off the soldier's words and raised his own cup. "No bowing and scraping, man, not here…in the field we're all soldiers, eh? Share the hardships, the food, the victories, and the glory. Now, about this message." He held up the crumpled parchment in his other hand. "You know what it says?"

"I heard rumors, m'lord, and whispers, as I rode. Word of Sir Goddard Bainsely's death reached me on the roads and in the inns. Way I heard it, some giant ripped his arms off."

The baron snorted and waved the parchment dismissively. "Giants? This far south, lad? Nonsense. They stay up in the frozen places, contend with the elves and the wolves and the fur-clad savages. Too warm for 'em here. Besides, real giants, the true Gravekmir? They'd've left no bones of Sir Goddard Bainsely's to be sent back to the Salt Towers."

"As you say, m'lord. Even so, every tale shared that bit about his arms."

Baron Delondeur took a long sip of his wine and eyed the message again, holding it close to the light thrown by the brazier. "Yes. An account got to me by pigeon said much the same." He downed the rest of his wine and looked to a back, dark corner of the tent. "Finish your wine and go get yourself some food, lad," he said, his voice a bit distracted. "And here." He held his cup out—a servant darted forward to take it—then dug into a pouch on his belt and pulled free a small round wooden chit with something stamped upon it. "Take this to the paymasters. Means an extra week's wages. Find a bed, get a fresh horse, and back to your camp in the morning, aye?"

The soldier finished his wine in a deep gulp, splattering some across the would-be mustache scattered across his upper lip, and took the chit offered to him with a grateful, even obsequious sort of bow, mouthed his subservience, and disappeared into the twilight outside the tent.

"Go with him, all of you," the Baron snapped, once the soldier was out of earshot. A trio of servants that waited in the corners of the pavilion followed the soldier into the night.

Another figure glided out of the fourth corner of the pavilion, joining the baron at the brazier. He was robed in dark green, and his deep-set eyes, beneath a shaved head, were pools of shadow. Even in the darkness that began to gather with only the light of the brazier, his hands stood out. Ten tiny points of dark red light, one bright spot beneath the nail of each hand, blazed into the darkness of the tent. "It is what I told you would come to pass, Baron Delondeur," the man said. "Had you been willing to keep funding my haruspicy—"

"It was costing me a freezing fortune in links. And all the stops in between, so many mouths to silence and hands grasping for weight, Cold! Besides, sounds as though it's just three men."

"I disagree," the bald man said, his voice smooth, calm, and brooking no argument.

The baron was silent, and the bald man continued. "I think it is both less than three men, in the sense that such as you can understand, and far, far more. In any case I shall have to return to The Dunes. I will depart tonight. I will need silver."

The baron cleared his throat and nodded quickly. "You have the letters of mine that you need…"

"Indeed. Enjoy your little war, Baron…"

"It was my little war that I've hired you to help me fight!"

"And I shall. When I know my enemy. Until then, fight as you have been fighting this score of years and more. Move your toy soldiers around on the map and butcher some peasant boys. Bang at each other with your clever maces and your brilliant swords. It is, after all, going so very well for you." The man pulled gloves from inside one sleeve and tugged them over his hands; the tiny spots of red vanished, but the brightness of them seemed to remain in the baron's vision for a few seconds more. He turned and walked back toward the dark corner from whence he had come, and, as far as the baron knew, disappeared into it.

Not many turns later, the baron awoke with a start. The comely young bed warmer he'd had sent up was no longer at his side. A cold draft had blown across his face; his hands, fast for his age, reached for the sword that had lain at his bedside longer than most men lived.

It wasn't there. He sat up with a start, but stopped, as he suddenly felt a hand with long, graceful fingers and rough, swordsman's palms cover his mouth, and then the barest whisper of a blade pressed lightly against his throat.

"Hush, Baron. Hush," said a raspy-voiced woman. "Your little camp follower is well, though she and I had a talk, and I expect she won't ever be back. I'm not here to kill you, or even to scare you. Just to bring you a message from the man who is, how did I hear you put it…*rousing your rabble*?" The long, strong fingers uncoiled from around his mouth for a moment.

"Who are you and how did you—" The baron's grating voice stopped in a short choke as the tip of the knife suddenly pricked, very lightly, just under his chin, and the strong fingers covered his mouth again.

"I said hush. This isn't a social call. I've brought you a message. I am under orders not to hurt you if I can avoid it." Suddenly the woman's husky voice, after a chuckle, deepened in a slightly mocking tone. "There is a basic decency in him…we can try talking to him, he said, so that is what we're trying."

Her voice was arresting; something about it struck the baron as wrong, yet it had a quality that demanded attention. The knifepoint moved away from his throat, and the fingers released his mouth.

He stood up quickly, wincing at the pain that shot up his legs and into his back. He whirled around, looking for his attacker. "Where've you gone, you demonspawn?"

"Nowhere," said the woman's voice, right into his ear. He felt her lips, and her breath, and her tall form behind him, and he whirled around quickly again.

He saw nothing save the darkness of his tent. He heard the sounds of the camp beyond—horses, tents moving in the wind, fires crackling, the shifting of equipment, the talking and movements of men who couldn't or didn't sleep. But he saw only darkness.

"You aren't going to see me," the woman's voice said again, still in his ear. "Stop trying. Now be a good boy and take the message." Her arm reached around him and pressed a folded parchment into his hand. "And know three things, Baron Lionel Delondeur. First, I am no demonspawn, nor witch, nor sorceress nor devil's whore, nor any of the other names I've heard these many weeks. *I am the Shadow of a Goddess.* Second, none of your host saw me enter and none will see me leave, so think on how it'll make you look if you start talking about this. Third, if ever you do see me, it will be because the Mother has given me leave to kill you. Now read." With that, the presence behind him vanished. He didn't hear her leave, nor did he see any movement. His tent wasn't disturbed. The voice and the form that went with it were simply gone.

Not being one to waste time, the baron groped around in the dark and found his sword; he felt reassured holding it. Then he shuffled his way to the brazier and picked up a short rod hanging off of it, stirred up the coals till they flared, lit some small wooden sticks with them, and used them to start lighting lamps. Soaked in sweat that was quickly growing cold in the cool air, and bathed in the light of his many lamps, he opened the parchment and read:

Baron Delondeur,

I am writing to you because I believe from what I knew of you that there is, somewhere, some decency in you. All that old soldier rot you talk cannot be purely facade. I know you are wondering what an Oyrwyn exile is doing rooting around in your lands and filling your folk with far-fetched notions. I need you to understand that Oyrwyn has nothing to do with this. The Young Baron has, no doubt, published his Writ of Exile upon me. It is no ruse. I am no longer Lord of Coldbourne Moor, much less Castellan of Wind's Jaw. There is no army with me. If I have any friends left in Oyrwyn, I do not want them.

As for what I am now, any tales that have reached you may have grown in the telling, but there is a measure of truth in them. I bring the words and the anger of a Goddess with me, and She has an anger greater than any you can know. To be frank, Lionel, the Mother has plenty of reason to be angry. With you, with me, with the Young Baron, and with Harlach and Innadan and the rest. All the madness of the past forty years rests on our shoulders, and all the blood on our hands. Mine are as red as yours. I cannot clean them off now, but neither will I raise them in the name of glory to the few and dross to the rest. The rich man, the strong man, who grows richer or stronger on misery, is my enemy now.

There is misery in your barony that beggars description, in a town that calls itself Bend, at the bend of the Ash, just before it empties into the bay. How much you know about it is a question I am not asking you. Yet.

What I am telling you, Baron Delondeur, is that all the people that have suffered from this war, from the widows and the orphans to the legless heroes, are my people now. Mine and the Mother's. Keep them free of your squabbles. Find a way. Cling to that decency like a man on a storm-tossed sea clings to his rudder in the hopes that it'll see him out of the clouds and into the sun. The sun, Baron, belongs to the Mother. Find it, or be lost.

You know that I was never given to bluffing. Now I cannot lie even if I wished. I will ask you that question about Bend in person one day, Lionel. And your life may depend on the answers.

Yours,

Sir Allystaire, Arm of the Mother, formerly of Coldbourne Moor.

Baron Delondeur read and re-read the folded note four times. Each time the weight on his shoulders and the cold, sick steam in his stomach came closer to meeting each other in an explosion. Finally, he pushed himself to his feet, took another look at the letter, set his jaw, and held it into the brazier until it caught fire.

CHAPTER 26

The Alchemist on the Gallows

After several weeks spent on the roads, Allystaire, Idgen Marte, and their horses found themselves winding up a muddy track into a village nestled in the foothills along Delondeur's southern reaches. The Thasryach range rose above them to the north and the sun was declining towards the long Delondeur coast to their west. Twilight's shadows had just begun to swallow the lingering bronze light of a slightly cool autumn day. *Another ruined village. At least this one hasn't burned yet,* Allystaire thought, trudging past the first few sod houses, their low-slung roofs and hide-covered windows shutting out the world. He heard no shouts of children, no young men in the muddy, nearly empty fields surrounding the village.

"Surely three or four years ago their farms stretched a few miles back into the mouth of the valley," he said aloud, to himself, to his horses. Idgen Marte, riding behind him, had grown so used to hearing him mutter to himself that she no longer nagged him about it.

When they finally reached the center of the village, Allystaire guiding Ardent and their packhorse on leads, a grim scene lay before them: a hastily erected gallows that looked none too sturdy, surrounded by an angry crowd. Upon the gallows stood a dwarf with a rope around his neck. The crowd jeered at him while an old man standing behind him knotted the noose with gnarled hands. The dwarf was animatedly angry, his cheeks purpling with rage, but he couldn't speak, as rags had been stuffed into his mouth, and his thick shoulders were bent with the tension of the ropes binding his hands together. Instinctively, Allystaire let the leads in his hand fall to the ground, replacing them with the hammer from its iron loop on his belt.

As his heavy, determined tread carried him into the village square, he had the sense that Idgen Marte had slipped down off her courser, but he didn't bother to turn around and look; he knew he wouldn't see her. When he was perhaps twelve or fifteen yards from the gallows, he called out, "What in the Cold is going on here?" His voice rang like a bell above the general din of the jeering crowd; as one, they turned to stare at him.

The old man on top of the gallows paused in his work with the rope and sputtered, his cheeks darkening. "Nothin' m'lord, ah, nothin' for greatfolk like ya t'go concernin' yerself wi'."

Allystaire sighed and looked at his boots for a moment. With an indrawn breath and a gathering of his will, he looked back up and said, "I know what you see. You see the horses, the armor." He rapped a leather-clad, iron-studded knuckle against the breastplate he wore, tried a faint smile.

Nobody laughed or even returned his smile.

Nothing for it but to soldier on. "You see a lord, and think, I am here to tell you what to do. To eat your food, drink your beer, and corrupt your daughters. I promise you, none of that is true—but I did ask a question. Out of courtesy, I would like an answer."

Nobody spoke. The old man fiddled with the rope. The dwarf stared at Allystaire, his eyes bugging out and his jaw working around the rags stuffed into it, thoughtfully, almost, if a man facing the gallows can be thoughtful.

Allystaire pursed his lips and tried again. "My name is Allystaire. You appear to be, ah, passing a rather permanent sentence on yon dwarf." He lifted his hand from where it rested on the head of his hammer and pointed. "May I ask why?"

Half of the crowd remained silent; the other half tried to answer all at once. The specific answers were largely unintelligible, but Allystaire picked out the words 'thief', 'liar', and 'cheat' enough times that he concluded they provided the basic theme of the dwarf's crimes.

He raised his hands to quiet the mob, and—showing what he knew to be their conditioned response to armed men—they silenced themselves immediately. "Has he been sentenced by anyone? A magistrate, a justiciar? Has there been an assize?"

The silence lengthened till someone from the crowd called out roughly, "We ain't seen such as them in *years*. Got t'take matters in our own hands."

"I believe you when you say you have not seen a magistrate in years. I do. But if you are willing, I can offer you something fair. Something just."

"What? You come in wi' high talk that you're no lord nor knight an' 'ere you are, gonna tell us what t'do wi' a man who wronged us!" The old man on the gallows found his gumption and started tying the noose again, finishing it with a flourish and cinching it tightly around the dwarf's neck.

"I said that I was not here to harm you. I am not. I did not say that I am not a knight, for in fact, I am. But not of your baron, nor of any power you have yet known. And if you let me speak to that dwarf before you hang him, I can show you what I mean."

"How d'we know yer not 'is partner? How do we know you canna be bought?" The old man spat on the wood and gave the dwarf a hard shove on the shoulder, trying to position him over the trap; the dwarf hunkered down and refused to move, but, Allystaire knew, it was a strategy that was only going to work for so long. The old man picked up the long end of the rope and prepared to throw it over the bar. "Got a silver tongue, this'un, and likely a fair pot o'links in his goods, he'll buy you or he'll sell you somethin'…" The old man tossed the rope, and Allystaire's patience reached its end.

"*Stay your hand,*" he bellowed, the force of his voice surprising even himself. The horses whinnied and Ardent came trotting up to his right shoulder, snorting, ready for a fight. The villagers all took a step away from him. "I mean no harm to anyone here," Allystaire called out, "and that means the dwarf as well. I will know what he did. I will have the truth from him. And the rest of you will stand aside while I get it." With that he took a purposeful step toward the gallows.

The crowd parted before him, and Allystaire smoothly ascended the steps. He reached out a gauntleted hand for the rope. The old man, who, Allystaire saw now, was not as old as he'd thought, merely baked by a life in the sun and with a mouth less than half full of teeth, hesitated. Allystaire reached out and snatched the cordage.

Then, with a practiced ease that had the dwarf raising a heavily-browed eye up at him in mistrust, he slid the noose off and undid the knot. Tossing aside the rope, he reached out and pulled the rags free of the dwarf's mouth, unleashing a considerable quantity of dwarfish spit. *Thank the Mother for these gloves*, Allystaire thought.

The dwarf, like most of his kind, was burly in the shoulders, but the top of his head didn't come close to Allystaire's chin, yet his features were proportionate to his height. He wore no beard, but a heavy two-or-three day growth of stubble covered his fleshy cheeks. His head was shaved bald and gleaming, and his brows were thick but similarly bare. He worked his jaw and moved his tongue around inside his mouth, then rolled his neck around on his shoulders. When he spoke, his voice was hoarse and raw, but held a promise of deep, sonorous power.

"Don't suppose you'd untie me, son," he croaked at Allystaire.

Allystaire smirked very slightly to himself. He tugged a glove free and put his bare hand on the dwarf's shoulder, concentrating a bit. "And if I did untie you, what would you do?"

The dwarf said quickly, "Talk you out of hanging me, stall till you're all asleep, then find my wagon and my ponies and see how long into the night my ass can stand the buckboard on these artless mud tracks you people call roads." Then he stopped, stood up a little straighter, and eyed Allystaire, then shrugged his hand away while the crowd laughed and the old man smiled in gap-toothed triumph.

"How'd you do that, boy?" the dwarf croaked, narrowing his brows till they almost touched.

Allystaire let his hand fall to his side and ignored the question. "I think your hands can stay tied for now. How about you tell me your name?"

"Not till you answer my question," the dwarf insisted.

Allystaire reached out and put his hand on top of the dwarf's head, frowning in gentle apology. "Your name."

The dwarf struggled and clamped his lips together, then spat out, "Torvul."

"Torvul, these people accuse you of theft, of fraud, counterfeit, and deceit. How do you answer?"

Torvul snorted. "I sold them exactly what I told them I was selling. That they're as bright as the crops they raise isn't my crime."

"And what did you tell them you were selling?"

"Cures for what ails you," the dwarf said. "Cures and potions, distillations and tinctures for every complaint; alchemical concoctions of the finest ingredients and the most exotic extracts. Ancient dwarfish formulae and thousands of years of alchemical lore…" He began to fall into a cadence, his voice rising despite its raw condition.

The old man lifted up his hand to aim a huge beauty of a cuff at the dwarf's ear; Allystaire caught it on the downswing and gave it a light squeeze. The man winced and tried to tug back his hand; Allystaire did not let go. "The dwarf is telling the truth. Why is he on a gallows?"

"His cures only made us sicker, m'lord," the man protested, yanking his arm free with a great tug. "E'reyone who took one spent a day swoonin' and the next sickin' up and every new cure was worse. Like to near killed us all. We figured he were a witch or at least a thief, here to make us ill so's he could rob us blind."

Allystaire grasped the back of the dwarf's neck as he swung his gaze back down to the prisoner. "How do you answer?"

The dwarf's eyes shifted side to side a bit. "Well, ah…they are dwarfish cures, ya see. And I, ah…I have had some trouble with some equipment lately. And some formulae. But I had it worked out! I needed to compensate for elevation, you understand, and, ah, make some necessary substitutions for some ingredients that are beyond my reach just now."

Oh for the Mother's sake, he is no liar, just an incompetent, Allystaire found himself thinking. "Did you mean to steal anything?"

"Nothing here worth stealing, son. I've nicked and shaved and skimmed a bit in my time but never from custom…"

"Did you make restitution for the failed cures?"

The dwarf eyed Allystaire with the hardest, deepest-browed stare the paladin had ever seen. "Restitution?"

"Return their links."

The dwarf almost hissed. "Nobody died. I'm not paying any blood price for less!"

Allystaire turned to the would-be hangman. "Goodman. Would your folk accept their links back in lieu of a hanging?"

"Mayhap we could work out sommin' like 'at," the man replied, licking his chops thoughtfully.

"Then we shall. Untie him."

The dwarf opened his mouth to speak, and Allystaire raised a hand. "Better to lose some silver than lose your life."

"You haven't met many dwarfs, have you, boy?" Torvul groaned in audible pleasure as his bonds were cut free; he immediately lifted his hands and began to rub his wrists with surprisingly long and deft-looking fingers that bore innumerable small stains and scars. "Still. If I have to hang I'd rather it be in a decent place." He took a deep breath. "Londray, f'r instance. I could hang in Londray. Hangman likely knows his business there, been brought up in it like any trade. Or better, Keersvast. Yes. If you're going to hang me," the dwarf went on, nodding, "do it in a city, one with the stink of silver and the throb of life in it."

"I do not mean to hang anyone," Allystaire replied, adding almost absently, "today." The memory of hauling a rope over the edge of a tree limb outside Thornhurst and the snap of a man's neck came to him suddenly.

Torvul narrowed his wide, dark eyes and bored them into Allystaire's face for a moment. "You've the look of a hangman about you, I'd say. Maybe more like a justiciar that passes sentence and then grabs a sharp sword. Regardless, there'll be no hanging today, so if you'd be so kind as to move aside, I'll just bid farewell to the fine folk of…ah…er…" He turned his eyes toward the man who'd been fixing to hang him, and shrugged.

"Grenthorpe o'the Hills," the man answered, with a glob of spit that landed suspiciously close to the dwarf's boot.

"Right. A lovely name for a lovely place. Well, I'll just be looking for your links…" The dwarf began to shuffle with slow, painful looking steps to the stairs. "And thank you, Allystaire the Meddler."

The crowd had been watching in more or less a cowed silence ever since Allystaire's earlier outburst, but suddenly someone spoke up, "Ow do ya know e's tellin' the truth?"

"That is something you have a right to know," Allystaire said, turning to face the crowd. "Perhaps, these past weeks, stories have come to you by merchant or peddler or letters," he began. "Odd stories. Rumors. My name is Sir Allystaire, as I said, but I did not tell you whom I serve." He pause, cleared his throat, and said, "I bring to you the word of a Goddess—and She has Gifted me such that no one can speak untruths to me."

Having reached the bottom of the steps, Torvul turned to look back up at Allystaire, grimacing sourly. "*That's* your patter? That's the best you've got?"

The crowd, meanwhile, stood unmoved and silent for a long moment. Then one woman separated from the milling mass and walked forward. "We had, well, some tales come through a week ago, speakin' some silliness of a paladin. Are you tellin' us that's you?"

Allystaire turned a faint, smug smile at Torvul and descended the stairs to approach the woman. "Aye. I am Sir Allystaire, Arm of the—"

His formal self-introduction was unexpectedly cut off as the woman drew back her arm and slapped him with her open hand, her full weight behind the blow, her face suddenly exploding into tears.

"How *dare* you," she cried. "How freezing *dare* you come here now. Where were you a week ago?"

The smack of her hand against Allystaire's cheek resounded in the otherwise still and quiet morning and left a dark-red handprint against his rough, broad cheek. His hands stayed at his sides even as anger flashed in his eyes, and a cautious curiosity quickly replaced the anger. Finally, in as quiet a voice as his could be, he asked, "Why? What happened a week ago?"

"A priest! A priest who spoke of paladins and the Mother and a new temple to rise in Londray! And he had men with him and he said he was taking a tithe for *our new goddess*. And oh, those men o'his took what'er they wanted. Our food, our wine, our seed corn, and *our daughters, our sons*," the woman shrieked, and she leapt forth to hit Allystaire again; this time, he caught her hand gently but firmly in his.

"There is no other priest of the Mother," Allystaire said quietly. "No true priest. There are but three; two of them rode into your village today, and one is a girl of eleven summers in a village a hard two weeks' ride around the mountains." He lowered her arm with gentle but inexorable force and then slowly, carefully, removed his hand from hers. "Tell me what he called himself."

"The Eye of the Mother," the woman replied, speaking brokenly through her tears, "Rede the Sighted."

"I see." Allystaire's voice was as cold and smooth and deadly as a knife's blade edged in ice, and the look that came over his face made the poor woman in front of him take a half step back, her quieted half-sobs threatening to break open again.

Suddenly Idgen Marte was *there*, behind Allystaire's shoulder, and everyone started, including the dwarf, who made a pretty fair leap for a man who'd just been getting the feeling back in most of his limbs. The tall, dark-haired warrior stepped past Allystaire, putting herself between him and the woman who'd slapped him, deftly obscuring everyone's view of the volumes of murder and rage that Allystaire's face was speaking.

Idgen Marte placed one long-fingered hand on the woman's arm. "Sister," she murmured quietly, "tell me what happened. All of it. Just to me. No one else. We'll walk, and you'll tell me…" Gently, she lifted her hand and wrapped her arm around the woman's shoulders, turning her around and beginning to walk her away from the crowd, with a backward glance at Allystaire and a gesture with her chin to the rest of the crowd.

With a deeply indrawn breath, Allystaire turned to face them, winding down the boiling furnace that was brewing in his core. "Folk. Good people of Grenthorpe. You have been greatly wronged. There is no temple of the Mother in Londray. There is no Eye of the Mother. Rede is a sick, deranged man and a liar. And whatever it is he did, we will make it right. We will show you that the Mother and Her servants do not force anyone to Her fold." He took a deep breath and lowered his eyes to his boots, his leather-and-iron clad hands creaking as they curled into ineffectual fists. "I will make it right." He turned and began to stalk away, fuming; the crowd of villagers spoke amongst themselves in hushed tones.

Idgen Marte had trailed far out of earshot, her arm still around the other woman, who could be seen to be talking without pause for more than breath. The women made an incongruous pair—one tall, graceful in her arms and armor, the other shorter and stouter, but strong, too. Idgen Marte had to stoop to listen and shorten her stride to stay in step with the villager, but she did so without notable strain.

Meanwhile, Allystaire stalked off. Torvul swiveled his gaze between the villagers who'd been about to hang him and the stranger who stopped them, then took off at a fast pace after the paladin. When he caught up, he cleared his throat, pitched his raw but sonorous voice low. "You really think you are, don't you?"

Allystaire paused and turned to look down at him. "Really are what?"

"What you say you are," the dwarf said, his eyes narrowed. "I'm a cynical dwarf, me. I figured you were puttin' these folk on. But you *did* somethin', boy. You made me give voice to the truth of my thoughts." He frowned a bit, blew a heavy breath out over his top lip. "Nobody's made me do that since…well, longer than you've been alive, for sure." The dwarf lifted his eyes and tilted his head to one side. "So what is it?"

"What is what, dwarf?"

"What you did? Was it sorcery?"

"If you had any idea how much I tire of that question…"

"Still not an answer, is it."

"It is not sorcery," Allystaire replied curtly. "I do not think I am anything, dwarf. I am precisely what I have said. No more and no less. Now! Do you not have some links to gather?"

The dwarf snorted and crossed his arms over his chest. "Haven't got any. And even if I do, you can't—"

His patience at an end, Allystaire leaned down and roughly seized the dwarf's arm with one hand. "How much do you have and *where is it?*"

"Fourteen links gold, about half that weight in gold dust. Seventy links silver and twice that in thin bars. I haven't counted the copper but at a rough guess I'd say one hundred and twenty-two and a half. Also assorted gemmary I haven't appraised. Hidden here and there. A strongbox in the back of the wagon with a stuck lock I know how to jigger, false bottom in one of the feedbags, false caps on the wagon wheels…" The dwarf suddenly stopped short in his list as he jerked his hand out of Allystaire's grip with a surprising strength. He pursed his lips and said, "That's very interesting. You did it again. What *else* can you do?"

Suddenly, from behind Torvul, Idgen Marte's voice answered in an angry, purring, stage whisper, "Pray that you never find out, alchemist."

The dwarf leapt a foot in the air, spinning around and clutching his chest when he landed. "Sky! Don't frighten an old dwarf like that!"

"Get what you owe them and pay up," Allystaire ordered. "I need to have done with your foolishness and attend to this so-called *Rede the Sighted*."

"Why's he called 'the Sighted'?" Torvul asked, ever inquisitive, showing no sign of leaving.

"Do you never stop asking questions?" Allystaire growled.

"Not until I learn enough. Curious dwarf, me."

"Fine. This Rede was, until quite recently, an Urdarite priest."

Torvul's face wrinkled in disgust, his mouth sneering. "Fanatics, them. But wait—sighted?" He wrinkled a prominent brow. "Don't they put out their eyes to save the rest of us the trouble?"

"Aye. He calls himself the *Sighted* because I gave him his eyes back."

"That was a damn foolish thing to do."

"Smartest thing you have said yet, dwarf. Now go pay up." Allystaire fixed a hard stare on the dwarf's lined, wizened face, and Torvul threw up his hands in surrender.

"Aye, aye. You've got to tell a dwarf three times, you know. At least. But I'll be back with more questions." The dwarf walked off, watching Allystaire and Idgen Marte with piercing, curious eyes under his heavy brows, until the two turned away and began talking in low, angry voices.

"The village woman told me the whole story. Rede arrived here just over a week ago with a group of strong-arms; sounded like half a score, at least. He preached about the Mother, and Karinn—the woman—said it sounded good. Till he told them what they owed and took some of the younger folk hostage."

"Where was he headed? Where did he get half a score men? Why would he want hostages?"

She sighed, ticked off her answers with raised fingers. "I don't know. It wasn't with his natural charm. And he seems to think he's raising an army, to lead the Mother's Church to glory. Only he's not giving anyone a choice in joining."

Allystaire closed his eyes and pressed his gloved fingertips to his temples. "So where did he get the links to pay men to follow him?"

"I've no idea. What are we going to do about it?"

"We are going to find him. Then I am going to kill him."

Idgen Marte bit her lip and her dark brown eyes looked to the grass; she toed the ground with her foot for a moment, kicked it lightly, then looked back up. "I'm not sure that's the answer."

"Then we will keep asking new questions until it is," Allystaire replied hotly. "I give him back his eyes, and this is how he repays us? I made one rule. *One!* And he breaks it. Now the Mother is just another god who demands, represented by more men with weapons taking what they please."

"No," Idgen Marte said, shaking her head and peering carefully at him. "You didn't give him his eyes back. The Mother did."

Allystaire winced, and he heard Idgen Marte's words echoed in his head by another voice, chiding him gently but powerfully. He closed his eyes and nodded assent, whispering, "You are right."

"She meant for him to see. Had he not seen, we wouldn't be here. If you've healed someone with the Mother's Gift, is it right to kill him later, even if he betrays you? I'm not sure you can. Or should."

"We can think about that later. We must find him." Allystaire's eyes were shut, his hand rubbing lightly at his forehead.

"Agreed, but I need you to promise me something."

He lifted his head and dropped his hand to his side, swinging it carefully away from the head of his hammer; he fixed his eyes on hers and nodded slightly.

Idgen Marte nodded back and laid a hand, for a moment, on Allystaire's shoulder. "Let *me* decide if he needs to die. If he does, the Mother will—She will let me know. I think it would be wrong for you to kill a man the Mother just healed. Yes?"

He nodded again; Idgen Marte patted his shoulder with almost sisterly affection, and they took deep, heavy breaths. "We can't stay here," she said, after their brief pause, fixing her hands back to her swordbelt. "He's poisoned the waters for us. These folk won't be willing to hear us until that's accounted for."

"Aye. We will be off today. Need to purchase some supplies, I think."

"Nonsense," grated the dwarf's gravelly, attention-grabbing voice. While they'd been speaking, he had managed to creep up on them. "I'll cover all that." He hefted a thick, heavy leather purse with metal rings drawing the top of it closed, the rings themselves affixed with a miniscule mechanical lock.

"Very generous of you, Torvul," Allystaire replied. "We will be—"

The dwarf waved a hand dismissively. "Please, son. I live on the road. You think I can't guess your supply list? Besides, I didn't tell you my condition."

"Your condition is that you get to live another day, dwarf."

"Which is more than I can say for you if you go haring off after this Rede fella and his dozen hardcases," Torvul said. "Which could be a dozen and a half now, or two dozen, or two score for all you know."

"It would not be the first time I did just what you described."

Torvul snorted and tucked the purse almost delicately beneath one arm as he crossed his forearms over his belly. "Bragging is well and good for wenching, lad, but—"

"Dwarf, he does not lie. He cannot lie. When I met him, he was pursuing a dozen 'hardcases' by himself, and when he found them, he walked into their lair. None of them are still alive. He is." Idgen Marte crossed a few steps and leaned down till she was on eye level with Torvul. "And that was before the Goddess blessed him with Gifts."

Torvul stared up at the woman with quiet equanimity. "Generous lady, this goddess you talk about. My condition may not be as onerous as ya think. I want to help you find this Rede and his band. I owe these people somethin', I guess." He shrugged uncomfortably and rubbed the back of his neck. "My craft failed me. Failed them. I'm happy to take anyone's weight but I don't like makin' 'em sick. 'Less that's what they want, of course," he said, speculatively, his brow furrowing. "I have had the odd fat bastard of a lord ask for a regular emetic, and a couple of courtesans—"

"Enough," Allystaire said, halting the dwarf's musings. "What can you do that would be of help, dwarf?"

Torvul raised a finger to bid them wait. Then he dipped into a pocket and pulled free a small, stoppered glass vial and held it up to the light, revealing its yellowish liquid. "Drops of this in your eyes, your ears, and your nose, and you'll be trackin' 'em like a bloodhound and a hawk all at once. And it's just the start."

Allystaire and Idgen Marte exchanged glances and looked back to the dwarf. "How's it work," the swordswoman asked, reaching a tentative hand for the vial.

Torvul tched and the vial disappeared into a sleeve, or his pocket. "Not until you agree. And as for how it works…" He waved his free hand, the fingers jangling lightly in the air. "Magic."

"Alchemy?"

Torvul rolled his eyes and sighed a bit dramatically. "Yes, alchemy is a kind of magic. Sort of. Look. I haven't got the time, the books, or the patience to explain it to a couple of humans. It is a Dwarfish art that would take either of you a lifetime of study. So let me try it again." He made the same motion with his fingers while saying softly and dreamingly, "Ooh…magic."

"Why not just give it to us, then? Along with what else you think might be of use to us, and be on your way. After you have paid the village what you owe."

Torvul sighed, his brows drooping and eyes and broad, lined face affecting the aspect of a long-suffering martyr. "I don't suppose you're going to drop that bit. Buyer beware and all that. No guarantee stated or imp—"

When the dwarf lifted his gaze, his grey eyes met Allystaire's implacable blue, the paladin's face flat and impatient; the dwarf took an involuntary step back and exhaled flatly. "Hoo, boy you're a hard one, aren't you?" He stepped close to Allystaire, peered up at him closely for a long, still moment. "If you had thought I was guilty, that I'd deliberately poisoned these folk, say, or laid 'em all out to rob blind, you'd have hanged me, eh?"

Allystaire considered this a moment, and shook his head very slightly. "Not if you only meant to rob them. But I would have found a suitable justice."

"What about poison?"

"You would have danced your last but a few minutes ago."

"You've a robust approach to problem solving, lad. I like that." Torvul nodded and stepped back. "And I fancy the prospect of seeing it applied to this Rede."

Allystaire's mouth twisted sourly, and in his gut, muscles tightened as the dwarf's words stirred images of flattening Casamir's armor, of taking a man's head off with a flick of his wrist, of lifting a knife-wielding bandit into the air and thinking how it might just have been possible to bend the man until his back snapped. "It will be dangerous, old dwarf. We cannot promise to protect you if it comes to an open fight."

"Son, I've been on the road longer than you've been alive, and alone on it for five years. I have dealt with every kind of brigand, bandit, highwayman, road agent, city guard, warband, and pissant ne'er-do-well you can imagine and a dozen more you can't," the dwarf said, jabbing a finger in the air toward Allystaire to punctuate his points, "and I've bartered with, conned, snookered, hid from, outfoxed, run from, and killed more than my share. I don't need your protection. You might just need mine."

There was silence for a moment as the paladin and the warrior stared at the dwarf, then their gazes turned toward each other. "I like this one," Idgen Marte said, grinning in her lopsided way. Allystaire chuckled humorlessly and threw up his hands in defeat.

"Fine, alchemist. Get your wagon ready to leave within two turns." Then he frowned. "Pay the people first." The dwarf ambled off, waving a hand and muttering. Allystaire looked to the crowd that was still more or less milling around near the hastily erected gallows. "I should speak to that woman, Karinn—"

"No you shouldn't," Idgen Marte said abruptly and decisively.

Allystaire turned back toward her, his brow wrinkled curiously.

Idgen Marte frowned and said, "Just trust me. I learned what we needed to know. Her mind is at peace and will stay that way unless you stir it up. So leave it be."

"How?"

"The Mother gave you your Gifts. She gave me mine. Leave it be."

Allystaire nodded and raised a hand apologetically. "Right you are." Then he looked in the direction Torvul had headed and asked, "What do you think of this dwarf?"

"Just what I said. I like him."

"Then we had best go help him with his wagon and ponies."

It wasn't difficult to follow Torvul's path through the village, as the farm folk parted in his wake and seemed to stay away from where he had been, as though wary of illnesses that might travel with him, and his boots had made thick prints in the mud. They led to a barn, where Allystaire found the iron-wheeled dwarf wagon. He had seen dwarf wagons before, and the short, stout ponies that pulled them, and this would've been right at home among any of them. It was solidly made, with runes delicately carved in bands around all its sloping sides. It seemed spacious enough for a family of dwarfs to live in, and a small iron chimney stuck out from the back, from which a thin trail of smoke puffed.

Torvul popped his head out of the door that sat directly behind the driver's board, which Allystaire would've had to crawl through in order to enter. He had changed his clothes from the near rags he'd worn on the gallows; he now wore a thick, hooded leather jerkin that hung to his knees. Pockets bulged on its front, a series of pouches and purses affixed by small clips to rings that were sunk into the leather. Most of the pouches seemed cushioned, and, Allystaire surmised, held small bottles, while the gleam of metal tools stuck out of the tops of others. The arrangement offered the dwarf's hands and arms a wide range of motion.

Torvul hopped down, rather nimbly, Allystaire thought, for his age, and produced the same purse he'd shown them earlier. He dipped a hand into one of his pouches and drew forth a slim silvery tool. He inserted a thin hook at its end into the miniscule lock, twisted, and drew the lock free; it dangled from the end of the tool, which vanished back into the pouch. He opened the link purse, held it up to his nose, and inhaled deeply, then nodded and closed it in his hand. Only then did he notice, or at least acknowledge, Allystaire and Idgen Marte. He held up the leather bag of links. "This ought to do. With a bit of interest."

"Best count it," Idgen Marte suggested, resting her hands on her hips.

"I just did," Torvul said brightly. "They paid mostly in weight or bits, but I'm giving them back silver. Twelve links. And I suppose I've a bottle of *ikthamaunavit* I can spare."

"What do you mean you just counted? And what is ik…iktha…what is that bottle?"

Torvul laughed huskily. "*Ikthamaunavit*. Dwarfish spirits. The finest stuff. Put hair on your toes, as they say." The dwarf paused for a moment and tapped his chin thoughtfully. "Honestly I think in humans it takes the hair right off if you rub it on your skin. Excellent exfoliant and astringent, though—cleans a wound and makes the poor wounded bastard too drunk to care all at once."

After recovering from a brief, stunned silence, Allystaire said, "The links, what do you mean when you said you just counted them?"

"I smelled 'em."

"You smelled them?"

"Yes," the dwarf said, nodding seriously as he approached them and held the purse out. "Go on and count if you've a mind, but I know how much silver I sniffed."

"You can actually…"

Torvul rolled his eyes. "You are slow, lad. Did your Goddess's Gifts not bring you any wit? Eh? You could use some. Yes, to your question. I can smell ores and worked metals. Not all that uncommon for my folk."

"Please do tell us what silver smells like," Idgen Marte asked, smirking, while Allystaire stared uncomprehendingly.

"Earthy," the dwarf said, making his empty hand a fist. "A bit nutty. Like a good dark ale, the kind with acorns in, or maybe berries, if it's particularly pure."

"What about gold?"

"Like the smoothest spirit you'd ever hope t'taste. Like smoke clingin' to a woman's hair, like—"

"Please," Allystaire said, rubbing the bridge of his nose. "Please. You shall have all the time we spend riding in pursuit of Rede to discuss the aroma of metal. Let us get on with it."

Torvul looked at Allystaire, then back to Idgen Marte. "I take it you let him pretend to run things."

She shrugged. "Behind him is safer than in front of him. It's worked so far."

With a sigh, Allystaire turned and walked off, letting out a piercing whistle that was answered by a distant whinny.

As Allystaire retreated, Torvul muttered just loud enough for Idgen Marte to hear, "He what he says he is?" His brows knitted and his deepset eyes focused on the retreating man's broad back.

"Aye. And more. He's the Arm of the Mother. You'll see."

"What about you?"

"She called me Her Shadow."

"Eh? And what's that mean?"

Idgen Marte smiled broadly and began following in Allystaire's tracks. "You won't see," she said with a chuckle and slight shake of her head.

CHAPTER 27

A Potion for the Road

The villagers were appeased, at least temporarily, by Torvul's silver, so he and the paladin and Idgen Marte took their leave of Grenthorpe o'the Hills, with the former whistling brightly atop his wagon-seat and the latter in varying states. Idgen Marte seemed to have warmed to the dwarf; Allystaire had not, and rode ahead, palpably seething, so much so that Ardent whinnied and stomped and pulled against the reins.

"Is he always so cheerful?" Torvul asked, as he tended to his own reins with a light hand and a whip that tended to flick above the flanks of his ponies, rather than on them.

"Dwarf," Idgen Marte counseled, shaking her head from atop her courser as she maintained pace with the wagon, "you don't know the half of it."

"I don't recall the holy knights from any human stories and tales being full to the brim with rage all the time," he countered.

"He has his reasons."

"Maybe he should have a dwarfish brew or two."

Idgen Marte sighed and lifted her head to fix the dwarf with her brown eyes; he kept one eye on her and one on his team. "You do realize what he told you earlier, right? This man, Rede, was one of those blind priests of Urdaran. Through Allystaire, our Goddess gave him back his sight. She granted him as great a miracle of healing as in any tale you or I could name, and I can name them all. And now this Rede is taking the Mother's name for a pack of thugs, and strong-arming villages with it. How would that make *you* feel?"

"I'd mostly be curious about the profit to be made in healing like that, to be honest. Grenthorpe's the wrong place for that. You'll want a city for—"

"This isn't about links. If you don't understand that, you won't understand him. Us."

The dwarf clucked his tongue and raised a shaggy eyebrow speculatively. "Us, is it? More than mere comrades in arms?"

At that, Idgen Marte laughed, loud enough and harshly enough to draw Allystaire's attention; he turned Ardent around, the enormous destrier moving nimbly on the narrow, grass-grown track. He called back "What?" but Idgen Marte waved away his concern, and he turned his mount back to the front.

"You ask stupid questions, unless you really still think we're playing some kind of game."

"You might be. Could be a decent play, have this Rede fellow move on ahead of you, stir up trouble, you fix it, deliver people what they want and collect their adoration. And their donations, of course. Relieved folk are generous folk. If that's what's on, I want a sniff."

"And if it isn't?"

"Well then I suppose I'll figure out how he managed that trick of his. I've seen a fair lot of magic in my day. There's alchemy of course, and magic in the ring of the hammer, and magic in the chant of the loresinger, and magic to be sung from the stone. That's Dwarfish magic. Or it was. But then there's thaumaturgy and conjury, sorcery and witchery, and then there's the magic gods are known to grant. None of what I've seen can make a dwarf *tell the truth* when he's not got a mind to. Oh, a good sorcerer who knows how to muck about in the mind, he can make a body say whatever he wants it to, can just move the mouth like a puppet if he's deft enough. Yet I had a mind to lie and both times my thoughts just ran into a wall, and there I was telling him where I kept my weight." The dwarf chewed on the inside of his cheek a moment, hollowing a space above his jaw, then *harrumphed*. "That's a trick I mean to know about."

Idgen Marte gave a faint *harrumph* of her own and shook her head. "You're going to be disappointed."

"Hardly the first time, girl. Now…" Torvul gently tugged back on his reins. At his faintest tug the ponies drew to a stop, and he whistled sharply so that Allystaire turned to look back. The dwarf's forefinger and thumb fished the small bottle of yellowish liquid out of a pouch affixed to his jerkin and held it out to Idgen Marte. "Time for you to have your first taste of Dwarfish craft, eh?"

Allystaire trotted Ardent back to the wagon, the destrier restively pawing at the ground, pent-up energy showing in his bunched muscles. "Will this work better than what you sold the villagers, dwarf?"

"You wound me, Sir Allystaire," the Torvul replied, clutching dramatically at his chest. "Years of craftsmanship and study, decades of careful toil weighed against one failure? Is that fair, now? Is it?"

Allystaire sighed. "Fine. Give it over."

The dwarf leaned across his team to hand the potion over, but Idgen Marte reached out and snatched it first. "If it's going to sicken one of us, best it be me. That way you can heal me, eh?" She pressed her thumb deliberately and carefully through the plug of wax that corked the top of the bottle and carefully tipped some out on her forefinger.

"Eyes and ears and even nose if you like, girl," Torvul was saying. "A hawk and a hunting pard and a hound at scent all at once, you'll be."

Idgen Marte quickly swiped her damp forefinger across her eyes. She blinked a few times, settling the liquid in, then said, "Well it doesn't sicken me. Yet." She blinked again, then suddenly drew a sharp breath and raised a hand to shade her eyes. "Oh Cold. Oh gods it…" She walked her horse to the side and turned her gaze toward the gently rising trail that led further into the foothills, and gasped again sharply. "Oh Mother…oh Goddess, the things…it works. It works so well it's painful." She tipped more onto her finger and swiped it into her ears.

Meanwhile Torvul was chortling delightedly and rubbing the palms of his hands together, his elbows working like a scullion's. "What'd I tell you? Finest in this part of the world, I say! In this or any part!"

Allystaire walked Ardent closer to Idgen Marte and held out his hand; she carefully handed over the bottle, and he, with rather less precision, splashed some into his hand and rubbed it into his nostrils and then his eyes.

Suddenly the world changed. Everything stank, or not stank exactly, but the distinct odors of everything around him assaulted his nose immediately and vividly, each competing for his attention. The intense smell of horse was almost overpowering, and his eyes briefly watered. Then he knew his own sweat and the grime of his unwashed body after weeks in the saddle, then the tang of his armor and his arms, the sweat-soaked leather of his saddle. And then other scents—the ponies, Idgen Marte's horse, the many exotic, indefinable smells that emanated from Torvul and his wagon, spicy, sweet, bitter, too many to name.

Then, just as the world of scents exploded, so too did the visible world. At first his vision was simply filled, entirely, by the rise of Ardent's neck, and he lifted his head back, shying away from the sudden closeness of his mount. He swung his eyes to the horizon and could make out broken blades of grass dozens, scores of yards away, could see bent stalks moving in an almost imperceptible breeze.

"You can control it now," Torvul was saying. "Just think of looking far away, or of looking close. Think and it'll happen." The dwarf's deep, sonorous voice was soothing, guiding.

Allystaire tried to focus on a small, moving dot dozens of yards away. It turned out to be a dragonfly hovering just above the grass, its wings buzzing around its coruscating blue carapace. Despite his rage and the nature of their ride, he found himself smiling, if faintly. "You have made a wonder, Torvul," he said carefully, swinging his eyes back to the road and the hills beyond, looking for signs of movement, for signs of a camp. *With this, an army would never be caught unawares*, he mused.

"Don't I know it! Harder than old stone to make and keep current. Worth its weight in gold link, it is. Which, ah, if you'd see your way fit to, ahm," the dwarf cleared his throat, "offering a consideration. It is rather dear to make…"

Suddenly the distant sight Allystaire had was gone, his vision snapping back to its normal range and his eyes aching and burning. Gone, too, was the newly opened world of scent, his nostrils instead filled with an acrid, overpowering stench that nearly pulled him from the saddle in a fit of retching.

Idgen Marte, too, was suddenly clutching at her eyes and gagging at the bile rising in her throat, and she slipped out of the saddle and collapsed onto her knees on the road. Allystaire did the same, while Torvul stood in shocked silence for a minute, then muttered a string of low, guttural syllables that Allystaire couldn't have caught even if he hadn't been torn between burning eyes and rising gorge.

Still muttering unintelligibly, Torvul quickly flicked open the door of his wagon and reached back into it, pulling out a large corked skin, popping it, and tugging a clean folded cloth from a pouch on his belt. He quick-stepped off the wagon, pouring clear liquid onto the rag as he did, then carrying it to Idgen Marte, who, a bit weakly, tried to slap away his hands.

"Nothing but water. Just water!" shouted the red-faced dwarf, and she took the rag and began to swipe at her eyes and nose, broadly at first, then more carefully. He produced another rag, wetted it, and brought it to Allystaire, who took it in one fist, but then suddenly looked up, his eyes inflamed and watering, and seized the dwarf's forearm with his other hand.

"Are you a poisoner or merely a fool?" he shouted, swiping at his eyes with the rag and using the dwarf to lever himself back to his feet so that he loomed over the would-be alchemist, fuming as he daubed his eyes.

Torvul didn't protest as Allystaire yelled, nor did he answer. He simply offered the water flask and shuffled away. "I meant no harm," he finally said, rather limply. "Potion must've gone off."

"Just like the ones back in Grenthorpe. When was the last time any of your potions worked, dwarf?" Idgen Marte had pushed herself to her feet and, like Allystaire, her eyes were red-rimmed and she staggered a little, as though off balance.

"They've never failed me before," he insisted, practically spitting, turning away from the pair of them and aiming a kick at the dirt. "Shouldn't do any lasting harm," he added.

Once Allystaire and Idgen Marte's eyes were relatively clear, though still watering, they exchanged a brief glance and went back to blinking. "If your potions don't work, dwarf," Idgen Marte said, "what use are you?"

"They'll work," he said, reaching for indignant and finding only sullen. "When it matters. They'll work," he insisted. "They always have. Could be that bit was too old, had gone off. Been a bit since I've seen any of my folk to get the right essences."

"Excuses, dwarf," Allystaire said, swiping at his nose with the wet rag. "In the village you said you had to make do with different ingredients and, what was it, adjust for elevation? How long has it been since you have seen your folk to get these essences?"

Torvul thought on the question a moment, shrugged, said, "Two of your years, give or take."

"That potion was two years old? Freezing Cold, how long d'you expect them to last?" Idgen Marte's face was more shocked than angry, and she wrung the rag onto the road with one hand.

"As long as they damned well need to!"

"From where I am standing, that was not long enough," Allystaire snapped.

"Look, boy, potions are not all I bring t'yer fight," Torvul said, his tone assuaging, beseeching even. "I know these roads like I know my own backside. They're rough, a bit lumpy, but I know just the spot to scratch, eh?" He pressed on despite Idgen Marte's sudden chortle and Allystaire's puzzled, darkened face. "What I mean is, the likely hiding spots, I know 'em. The kind of men that work these roads. And I've been in a scrap, and the wagon's got a surprise or two. Just give me the chance," he almost pleaded.

For a moment, Allystaire almost felt pity for the old dwarf. Age and the ruin it had wrought on his face, his shoulders, his scarred and stained hands made it nearly pathetic for him to be standing in a roadway, begging to be allowed to follow like a dog. *He's an old fool*, Allystaire thought. *And so you called yourself on another road a few weeks' hard ride from here, on the trail of desperate men.*

"Fine, dwarf. Fine. But keep your potions in their bags unless you mean to poison our enemies."

Torvul opened his mouth as if to protest, thought better, merely nodded.

"So if you know the spot, where do we start scratching?"

Torvul pointed a single long finger in the direction of the hills, westward. "Plenty of old smuggler caves in there. Bring cargo by boat to the beach, with no tower, lighthouse, or guardpost twenty miles to north or south, walk it a day into the hills, stash it. Best way to bring goods into Delondeur, really."

"Then you are telling us that the hills are lousy with pirates?"

Torvul snorted. "Hardly. You people like playing at war with each other so much lately, no profit in piracy. Too likely you wind up chained to a galley oar, and nobody's got the links to spend on smuggled goods anyway."

"I would not call it *playing* at war, dwarf," Allystaire remarked coolly.

"No? Then what would you call it, spending twenty, thirty years fighting a war nobody can win over a crown nobody seems to want."

"I agree it is senseless; that does not make it any less serious for the men and women and children who suffer and die."

"Well it's you lot of barons and lords who're killing 'em, and I tell you what, one good Dwarfish Legion from the Homes'd sweep your knights and their toy soldiers aside and set all this business aright."

"Then where are the Dwarfish Legions now, alchemist? Misplaced them, have we? Forgot to bring them with us out of the tunnels?"

Torvul's face darkened and he practically shouted, "That's not for the likes of you to joke about—"

Idgen Marte suddenly and improbably slapped each of them hard on the back of the head, first Allystaire, then Torvul; Allystaire had learned to stop trying to follow her movements in moments like this. She was behind him, then behind the dwarf, and if he tried to stop and plot how she went from one place to the other as fast as she did, he felt a bit queasy. With the smacks delivered, she said, "Boys, you can measure your swords later if you must. Now, attend to what needs doing. That means finding that son-of-a-bitch, Rede. Aye?"

"Aye," they sullenly agreed, more or less in unison.

"Good. Now, have we a chance at finding them before dark, or should we rest?"

"I want to take them with light in the sky," Allystaire said, "if possible."

"Masterful grasp of tactics, that," Torvul muttered, not quite inaudibly.

Allystaire merely sighed and gave a low whistle; Ardent, who had, along with Idgen Marte's courser, drifted to the grassy side of the muddy road and begun grazing, ambled over and nudged Allystaire's shoulder with his nose.

"He has his reasons, dwarf," Idgen Marte said, quietly.

"You seem a sensible lass," Torvul said. "Mayhap you can talk him into a smarter approach. You don't attack a larger force in daylight."

"Maybe *you* do not, dwarf," Allystaire suddenly broke in, having mounted Ardent and walked the horse around to face Torvul and Idgen Marte, with the golden sunburst on his shield—a little dented from these weeks of wear and travel, but still vibrant—facing them. "Yet I want these men to know I am coming, to see me approach them openly with the Mother's sun blazing behind me, lighting my way. I want them to know I come amongst them unafraid, and that their ruin comes with me. Men like those make honest folk fear the dark. It is time they learn to fear the sun." Then, with a nudge of his knees, he turned Ardent and trotted off, leaving Idgen Marte smiling and Torvul scratching his expansive forehead in silence.

"And still, you doubt?" Idgen Marte murmured, turning her scarred grin at Torvul, shaking her head gently. "If you won't believe, dwarf, you'll just have to see."

* * *

They made camp as unobtrusively as they could, several dozens of yards off the road and much to Torvul's indignation, who protested the rough treatment of his team and wagon. The stands of slightly thinning and yellowing trees scattered along the road offered little protection but allowed a clear view of anyone moving on the road or approaching them, so they parked the wagon in front of a slight rise and made camp.

They were mostly silent as camp was made; Allystaire and Idgen Marte saw to the hitching, unsaddling, and care of Ardent and her courser, and the dwarf to his team. When this was done, Allystaire began the long and somewhat noisy process of removing his armor. Torvul leaned against one of his wagon wheels, arms crossed over his broad chest, tongue tucked into one side of his mouth, watching carefully. As Idgen Marte was helping him with the cuirass, the dwarf spoke up.

"I could make this a little easier," he said, lifting one hand and pointing at the pair of them. "Make it so it's a one-man job."

"It can be," Allystaire replied, "just takes longer that way."

"Point is it doesn't need to," the dwarf countered mildly. "You've got too many redundant straps. It doesn't need to cling to your body like a second skin. Keep it a bit loose, it'll shed a little more force."

Allystaire shook his head. "I knew men who believed that. Saw too many of them trip, catch on something." With some straps free, his breastplate was off, and he bent to unbuckle his greaves. "Saw one get his loosened gauntlet caught on his swordbelt. He was still trying to tug it free when he died."

Torvul shrugged noncommittally. "Fair enough."

When Allystaire was down to his gambeson, he quickly changed it for a shirt and vest. Idgen Marte rummaged in pile of saddlebags and found food—a hard loaf, cheese with a thick rind—and made a hasty meal. She and Allystaire drifted a few steps away from the dwarf, who suddenly found himself busy inside his wagon.

"D'ya want me to do anything besides find 'em?"

Allystaire shrugged, wincing as he did, and reaching up with his right hand to rub his left shoulder. "Use your judgment. If there is no risk to the folk they have taken, do what you like. If there is…"

Idgen Marte nodded, turned, and started to walk off, then stopped and looked back to him with a piece of her bottom lip stuck under her teeth. "This feels wrong. Rede is an idiot, but not…" she trailed off uncertainly.

Allystaire sighed and pressed his eyes closed a moment. "I thought that of him as well. Yet if he has gone mad, who can know?"

Idgen Marte gave a short, sharp shake of her head, her long braid a dancing shadow for a moment. "If he had gone mad, Renard and Mol never would've let him leave."

"He could have slunk away in the dark."

"Renard would've had him watched."

"You are not suggesting that anything has happened to—"

Idgen Marte shook her head again. "We'd know."

Allystaire chewed the inside of his cheek for a moment. "Trap?"

"I'm of a mind that it might be."

"Be cautious, then."

She smiled faintly and said, "Careful, yes. Cautious?" She turned and walked into the growing shadows of the trees; she did not slowly fade out of view, nor was she lost in the gloaming. One moment she was in his sight, the next she had simply vanished.

"How does she do that?" Torvul had exited his wagon and casually crept up on Allystaire. "And how does she expect to find 'em up in that warren of hills in one night? I'd expect it to take four, five days."

"The same way I made you tell the truth," Allystaire replied, tamping down his surprise at the dwarf's sudden appearance, pretending to adjust his vest as he turned around.

"Your *goddess*, then?"

"Aye," Allystaire replied, walking past the dwarf without eye contact.

"Look boy," Torvul said, stomping after him doggedly, "this is a lot for an old dwarf to take in. Maybe don't take it so hard if I don't buy what you're selling."

Allystaire stopped in his tracks and turned wearily toward the dwarf, his hands bunching into fists around his belt. "I am not selling anything. I have explained myself to you already and I do not mean to again. Doubts are yours to keep. Keep them quietly."

"I've a right to speak if I've a mind," Torvul insisted.

"Aye, surely you do," Allystaire said, adding smoothly, "and I had a right to ride on and let those folk hang you but I did not. Ask yourself—what profit have I made by it?"

Torvul thought on this a while, his eyes narrowed. "You could mean to murder me and steal my links, weight, and gemmary. You know about all of it."

"Why not let the villagers hang you and take it from them? Less trouble all around."

"I—"

"Would be hanging if not for me. If you feel you owe me anything for saving your neck from the hangman's noose, then by all the misery in the world, be silent with your doubts and your endless questions."

"You've a point there. Fair enough." Torvul cleared his throat, turned from Allystaire, and meandered slowly toward his wagon, disappearing inside it. He re-emerged holding a thick, well-shaped clay jug with a cork stopper plugging it, the cork held to the neck of the bottle with string. Allystaire was settling himself in front of the packs, with food akin to what Idgen Marte had eaten before vanishing. "What do you say to some Dwarfish beer?"

"Was it made by—"

"By me? 'Course it was. Be easy. No alchemy. Just brewing. Pure art, no magic, no chance it's gone off. I'd stake my life on it." As if to prove the point, he thumbed the cork from the bottle and took a long swallow, then offered the jug to the seated Allystaire.

"That being the case, then Cold, yes," he said, reaching for it and taking a long swig, sitting up straighter in startled shock at the first taste. He took another long pull, then sighed heavily. "That is proper beer. Have you any idea what passes for beer in the farmhouses around this barony?"

Torvul snorted as he took the bottle back and squatted down to one knee himself. "It's criminal. Why do you think I carry my own?" He took a hearty swig and again offered the bottle to Allystaire. "I've plenty in the wagon. And more is on the way; drink as much as you like."

Allystaire accepted the jug but took only a sip, explaining with a rueful shrug, "As much as I like and I would be of no use in the morning, I fear. I will enjoy what I can, though."

"Been travelin' that long, just the pair of you?"

"Since after high summer, but before its end."

"Sleeping hard every night?"

"Most," Allystaire said, treating himself to a smaller and more measured swig of beer and a satisfied sigh, as he handed it back. "We started with little silver and no gold and have not added to it on the way. A few nights we have been offered a hayloft or a shed. Twice, a pair of spare beds in a village inn. Once, a few weeks ago, the folk of a village the other side of the Thasryach insisted on giving us the best beds in the village."

"What'd you do to earn such a princely gift," Torvul wondered, grinning and not bothering to hide the faint hint of mockery in his voice. He began tilting the jug toward his lips.

"There was an infant, a boy child. His lungs were…" He searched for a word and settled on, "ill formed. The Mother's Gift put the breath back into them and filled them out, or, filled them up, mayhap? I do not know the words; I am no chirurgeon. Suffice to say, the child will live."

Torvul's arm paused in mid lift, a single drop of dark brown liquid hanging precariously from the tilted jug's lip. "You fixed a child's lungs? How?"

"I already said. A Gift, from the Goddess." He held up his left hand, palm inward.

"Your hand is a Gift from a Goddess?" Torvul carefully, slowly, set down the jug.

"I told you to leave off the doubting."

"Fine, fine." The dwarf had another swig of beer and set the half-empty clay vessel between them. "So when do you expect her back?"

"Idgen Marte? When she is done."

"No worries she'll be found out?"

At this, Allystaire only chuckled lightly, his eyes wrinkling, and shook his head. "No. None at all, in fact."

"Could have a lot of sentries out."

"They will not see her."

Torvul rubbed his creased forehead with thumb and forefinger and muttered, "Lot of confidence you have in her."

"Not confidence," Allystaire said, reaching for the jug. "Faith."

"Faith," Torvul repeated, his mouth stretched into a line.

"Aye, Faith," Allystaire repeated. He finished his swig and carefully thumbed the cork back into it as he set it down. "You could do with a bit of that yourself, I suspect." He slowly and heavily pulled himself to his feet and walked to the nearby pile of saddlebags and saddles that he and Idgen Marte had stripped from their mounts and pack animal. He drew his hammer to his side, settled down, stretched his legs, and crossed them at the ankle.

"You sleep like that?"

"Usually," Allystaire replied, letting his shoulders and his neck rest against the packs.

"Why?"

"A score of years playing at war will do this to a man, I suppose. Sleep well, alchemist. We will be up with the dawn, if not before."

Torvul cringed, standing and collecting his jug, cradling it against his belly in the crook of one arm. "Dawn?"

"Not a moment after."

The dwarf walked away grumbling in an odd and guttural language, glancing back once at the man who was already drifting into a quick and light sleep, while sitting nearly upright with a hammer under his right hand, as if he expected to jump up and go straight into a fight.

CHAPTER 28

Learning to Fear the Sun

Allystaire woke to Idgen Marte's hand resting lightly on his shoulder as she squatted beside him. He lifted his head, blinked his eyes once slowly, holding them closed as if savoring, for just a moment, the hint of sleep that remained. Then he opened them; even narrowed and weary, they missed little. "What did you find?"

"I didn't see Rede," Idgen Marte said. "I don't even know if he's giving the orders."

"Who is?"

She shook her head, a short but precise movement, a dim shadow against the darker blackness of the night; slowly, by degrees, starlight and a bright sliver of moon were beginning to make shapes clearer, and her face became more distinct. "I can't tell. No proper organization to the camp; it's a pigpen. The two guards I saw were sleeping and there seemed to be a fire for every two men. We could go tonight, right now, and scatter them."

"I meant what I—"

"—what you said. I know. You always do," Idgen Marte cut him off, an exasperated sigh trying to escape behind her words. She stood and said, "Dawn, then. I will lead us back to them." She strode toward a tree, then turned back. "Something was wrong. What, I don't know…but there was a scent. A wrong one."

"A scent?"

She nodded, her thick braid of hair bobbing. "Aye. Go back to sleep. Dawn?"

"Dawn."

By the time he answered, she was already climbing her way quickly and skillfully up a tree and settling into its branches. He settled back into his pile of saddlebags, shifted his tired legs and tried to ease the small knot of soreness that formed, every night, at the very base of his back. Despite that ember of pain, he eventually drifted back to sleep.

It seemed like only moments later he was opening his eyelids on the very first rays of light. The tiniest hint of chill in the air seemed likely to burn off soon. He stood, gathered up his hammer, and walked to the tree into which Idgen Marte had scampered. He gently kicked the trunk a few times with the toe of his boot, wincing as it pushed sensation back into his tingling, sleep-deadened foot. He heard muted curses from her perch in its branches and walked on to Torvul's wagon, where he pulled himself slowly up onto the board and rapped three times on the door. "Time we are away."

Grumbling and guttural croaking sounded from inside the wagon. Eventually the door opened, and Torvul's head and densely-knotted bare shoulders stuck out. "Not a civilized time to make war. Humans, always with the dawn."

"There is no civilized time for war," Allystaire said, his lips thinly pressed over his teeth. "Be ready in a quarter of a turn."

"Fine, fine." Torvul disappeared and his door slammed shut.

While he was out of sight, Idgen Marte helped Allystaire saddle Ardent and her dark brown courser, then helped him on with his full armor, sword, hammer. His shield he looped on his pommel, and lance he couched in the boot on the right-hand side of his saddle. She was already wearing her dark grey arming coat, but she slipped an iron-plated headband around her head, tugging it carefully into place above her eyes. When Torvul emerged, he was once again wearing his long hooded jerkin with its many loops and pouches and had produced a pair of weapons—a wide, broadly curved, but short stocked crossbow and a stout length of a hard-looking white wood, capped with heavy, rune-inscribed metal at the slightly thicker end. He laid these beside his driver's seat, then produced another earthenware jug of similar workmanship to the night before, only smaller.

"*Ikthamaunavit*," Torvul said, raising the bottle for them to see. "Not alchemy. Just distillation. Dwarfs have a bit before they go into a fight. Figured if we're keeping your hideous human turns we might as well keep one of my traditions." He flicked the cork out of it with his thumb and downed a generous belt before holding the bottle out.

Allystaire came over and took the small bottle, sniffed, suddenly wished he hadn't, and then swallowed a small measure anyway. The smell, harsh and unforgiving, was nothing like the taste, which was pure and smooth, hard and gleaming on the tongue like a sword in the hand or a morning in the mountains. He wanted more, and he stared for a moment at the dwarf in admiration, then handed the bottle over to Idgen Marte. She sniffed at it, wrinkled her nose, and took a swallow, immediately brightening.

"If I'm to die today, at least I'll die with a good drink. Many thanks, Torvul," she said, capping the bottle and tossing it back. He caught it, cradled it carefully, a smile like a proud father's on his face, and set the bottle by his feet.

"We'll save it for victory."

"Bright thinking," Idgen Marte remarked.

Allystaire, meanwhile, had started to retreat from himself, from conversation, from the camaraderie, watered by the dwarfish spirits, that was budding between them. When his helm settled over his hair, its cheekpieces resting against his skin, he had ceased to talk. He moved methodically, mounting Ardent, who pawed restlessly at the ground as he sensed his rider's fixations.

"About half a turn's ride. Then we walk," Idgen Marte said, pointing with her thrust chin westward. "The hills won't be kind to the horses nor the wagon.

Allystaire simply nodded and pointed west, and off they went, the horses trotting and the wagon rumbling.

* * *

Anghem was tired of the watch. It was boring, it was a little cold, but a man who takes the link must do what he's paid for. *Unless he can kill the bastard what gave 'im the links n'just take 'em all*, Anghem thought. It wasn't proper cold, though.

This wasn't the tundra or even the taiga, and Anghem missed the real weather, brought by the spirits of the sea and the wind to teach a man what he was.

He leaned listlessly against a tree—just because he had to do the job didn't mean he had to do it well—and waited for the rising sun, which he saw just beginning to lighten the eastern sky. The sun meant he could go back to the tents to eat and sleep. He wasn't sure which held more appeal, but he was thinking of both intently when he suddenly felt a blade across his neck, curved and so sharp that he felt it slicing stubble from his skin.

"Open your mouth, sailor, and I'll have your balls. Understand?"

Anghem nodded, the movement very stiff and controlled, made mostly with the chin.

"We're going to stand here and wait for my friend," continued the voice. He realized, sleepily, it was a woman; with a sudden flash of anger, he flattened his back against the tree to buy space, lowered his chin, and reached out to his left side, where the blade was held.

By the time his hands had floundered into empty space, the blade was back at his neck, held from the other side.

"Sailor, you couldn't catch me if you were sober and awake and hadn't shagged aught but a sheep for three months. You want to ever shag another poor ewe, you'll stand still and wait until…here he is," the husky voice said, and a sudden piercing ray of light stung Anghem's eyes as they were drawn to two approaching figures, one significantly taller than the other.

Soon the figures resolved into a large man, armored and imposing, and a beardless dwarf wearing some outlandish leather shirt strewn with pouches. The armor that the man wore over his chest, shoulders, upper arms, and legs was a drab, functional grey, but somehow the light seemed to attach to it—every time Anghem tried to focus on him, he had to shy away from the intruding brightness that dug sharply into his eyes.

Casually, without apparent worry over the axes at Anghem's belt, the man approached and reached out to wrap his gauntleted hand around Anghem's neck. The still unseen woman's blade slipped down to the very tip of his chest, above his mail shirt.

Anghem's hands started toward the haft of one of his weapons, and the dwarf suddenly lashed out with a heavy stick, smashing his fingers between it and his own weapon. Before he could even cry out, the armored man had wrapped his other hand around Anghem's mouth and clamped his jaw shut with a grip like an iron muzzle.

"You are working with Rede, who calls himself the Eye of the Mother?" The man's voice was deep and distant and, Anghem thought, strangely cold. For the first time in months, he found himself shivering. The fingers relaxed enough for Anghem to mumble, "Aye," his jaw almost numb, too dazed to wonder why he answered the question so easily.

"How did he hire you?"

"Wi' silver up in Londray, said he needed guards for the road, he was an iter…inter…itiner…a rovin' preacher."

"Where did he get silver," he heard the deep, but feminine voice growl from his right. He turned his eyes to try and catch a glimpse of her, but he saw only the shadow of the tree he sheltered against. Yet still he felt that sword against his neck.

"Got an answer for that?" The eyes that were peering at him had flicked to the right and then back.

Anghem simply replied, "Never thought t'ask. Work is work n'silver is silver."

"And what work have you been doing?"

"Roustin' the shit-diggers and dirt-clawers and tellin' 'em to listen smartly to Rede. The Mother's work, he calls it."

Before he knew it, the man's other gauntleted hand had balled into a fist; pain exploded over his right eye, a bright white bloom that was shocking in its suddenness.

"You know nothing of the Mother's work. Do not let me hear you say that again, or you will learn how much harder I can hit you," the man growled dangerously. "Have you harmed the folk of these villages? You or any of your band? Theft, rape, murder?"

"We take hostages an' if a few of 'em wind up in our beds it's o—" The armored man's right hand drew back but a few inches; Anghem had a brief instant of clarity, realizing that he no longer felt compelled to answer the questions put to him. The moment lasted until the iron studs that lined the armored man's leather gauntlet exploded into Anghem's temple and he knew no more.

The back of the guard's head bounced off the tree so hard that bark exploded in a shower of chips around him, and he sank into the ground in a boneless heap.

Allystaire knelt and pulled the axes free of the fellow's belt and tucked them into the back of his own. Torvul squatted by the fellow's head and held his hand out in front of his slack face. "Still breathing. Barely. Likely to have a scrambled skull when he wakes." The dwarf stood and spat into the grass. "That was just about the least useful questioning I've ever seen," he remarked to no one in particular.

Allystaire fixed his hard blue stare on Torvul and said, "There was nothing else I needed to hear from him. Ending the conversation probably saved his life."

Then the paladin turned and started stalking heavily in the direction of the camp proper, clanking as he went. Torvul found himself shivering in the wake of the indelible impact of Allystaire's voice and stare.

* * *

With Idgen Marte flitting in and out of his vision as she moved from tree to tree ahead of him, and Torvul puffing and trotting to keep up but still falling a few paces behind, Allystaire strode into the clearing in which Rede's mercenaries had made camp, with, as he had hoped, the sun rising behind him and its rays riding upon his pauldrons like shouldered spears.

He surveyed the clearing and found the camp within it poorly organized. Several scattered fires smoldered in front of tents organized haphazardly without an apparent central command and no clear lanes of movement. Weapons were, he noted, in abundance, carefully maintained, and easily reached, most piled carefully at the mouths of low-slung tents. A few figures moved, mostly squatting in front of guttering cookfires.

Allystaire paused more than a dozen long paces away from even the nearest man or tent, tugged his hammer free of its ring, and rapped the heavy black head lightly, three times, against the metal rim of his shield. The noise rang out across the otherwise still morning, and a dozen or so birds took flight from the nearest trees. He drew a deep breath and projected his voice as far and as wide as he could, beginning with a single syllable.

"REDE!" Allystaire's voice roared across the camp. The men jumped from their fires; tents were thrown open and men stumbled, blinking, into the morning light.

"REDE. If you make me call you a third time," he went on after his initial roar had died down, his voice still booming and filling the small, trampled clearing with its demand, "I will start killing your men. Come and speak to me now and we will avoid bloodshed."

His first bellow had been met with confused stares, but his second, boastful proclamation met with a smattering of laughter and a few hoots of derision. One man separated himself from the pack, tall and rangy, with bare arms and a thick coat of rings over a fur vest. Standing up from a cookfire and seizing a long hafted axe with a heavy, curved blade balanced by a spike behind and one atop, he advanced on Allystaire till it became clear that his full height put him more than a foot taller than the paladin. As he advanced closer and closer, Allystaire's gaze rose higher and higher until he realized that he was staring at a man nigh on two feet taller than himself.

"Giantkin," he heard Torvul pant from a few paces behind him.

"You horse-loving lords from the mountains on down, you always boast, and none of you have the arm to make good on it," the towering creature bellowed, spitting into the mud his boots churned. "Here is how a *Gravekling* boasts, horse-shagger." The giantkin, for so the dwarf had truly named him, planted the haft of an axe as long as Allystaire was tall into the dirt and continued, "I will split you like wood for the fire, an' you have the stones to face me!"

In answer, Allystaire only nodded and rapped the head of his hammer against the rim of his shield again. Then he dropped into a loose fighting stance, his left, shield-arm forward while his right hand gripped the hammer slightly behind, a good six inches of haft protruding from the bottom of his fist.

"This is a bad idea, boy. A rotten idea. No profit in fighting giantkin this way, a rotten idea all 'round," Torvul was saying, and Allystaire could hear him readying his crossbow, the telltale sound of the cord being yanked back.

"No," he said, simply, without taking his eyes off the approaching gravekling. There was madness in the giantkin's grey eyes and an unearthly wildness in the high slope of his head and the matted curls of beard that grew from just below his eyes to his neck. The giant axe whirled in his hands with deadly speed, his long, sinewy arms twirling the axe's head in the air and feinting with the spike.

Allystaire wasn't distracted by the spinning axe-head. Instead he kept his eyes on the gravekling's feet, and when one of them planted forward with weight and momentum, Allystaire lifted his shield and crouched beneath it, his eyes rising just in time to see the axe blade descend and crash into the face of his shield.

It was like being hit with a felled tree, and the impact sent numbing shocks up and down Allystaire's arm, but training and will kept it locked in place. For form's sake, he stepped up behind his shield and swung his hammer in a sharp, quick arc, but the giantkin harmlessly turned it aside with the haft of his axe.

"*Like wood*," the giantkin roared, and swung again, this time keeping the blade parallel to the ground, forcing Allystaire to catch it this time with the haft of his hammer, which he did, but he felt the haft-to-haft impact crackle along his weapon and feared he may have heard a tiny crack.

Rather than risk another blow with his hammer, the paladin lowered his shoulder behind his shield and bulled straight at the giantkin, aiming all of his mass and all the force he could muster into the giantkin's hips. Allystaire had, a time or two, sent small groups of stout armored men stumbling and falling to the ground with this ploy.

The gravekling let out a rush of breath and danced back a step or three, but stayed on his feet and brought the very bottom of his axe-haft down upon Allystaire's helmet, hard enough to dent it and stagger him. His vision blurred, Allystaire felt himself shoved backwards, and the ground rushed up at him. *Stay on your feet, stay on your feet, stay on your FEET*, his mind roared at him, but his feet ignored it and smashed together and he fell heavily to the ground, arms splaying to the sides. He felt his hammer tumble from his hand. He saw it bound away, dimly aware of Torvul cursing and yelling behind him as a crowd of other men in various states of dress, but armed, began to gather in a distant semicircle.

The giantkin roared in triumph and leaped upon Allystaire, bending over and seizing Allystaire by the neck with one massive, hairy-knuckled hand. "No boasting, no stones, and probably no cock either," he roared and lifted the paladin half off the ground. He slammed Allystaire's head against the turf, laughing, spit foaming at his lips. "I'm gonna think about this, about crushing your skull, when I go and take my fill o' that village lass in my tent again," he roared. "Your women might yell and curse and beg but with a gravekling is the only time they know a *man*."

His mind was fuzzy, his vision blurred, and his strength all but sapped, but when the gravekling spoke of the village lass in his tent, an image suddenly filled Allystaire's head of a bruised, terrified girl huddling in a pile of reeking blankets.

And then the girl's face became the Goddess's face and her sobs changed, became a thunderous wind in his mind. His limbs filled with the Mother's music, and he shivered in fear and delight. Fear at what he was about to do. Delight like a lover's touch long wished for.

Allystaire's eyes opened wide, his vision cleared. His right hand suddenly reached up from the grass to seize the giantkin's wrist, and closed into a fist around it. The gravekling's gloating roar turned into a scream of pain, and everyone watching the fight heard his bones crack and crumble.

Blood squeezed between Allystaire's clenched fingers like water wrung from a towel. He kept squeezing till the gravekling's powerful arm was a limp and shredded thing. The grinding and popping and the giant's unnatural roar forced his gorge into his throat.

His arm still clasped around the gravekling's ruined wrist, Allystaire swung his shield up into the huge face above him, pushing aside the hand that had pinned his shoulder with casual ease. The rim of his shield met the bearded cheek and caved in the side of the gravekling's face and he fell to the grass with a mighty thud. The paladin hopped to his feet, his body thrumming with the power of the Mother's Gift. He spared a brief downward glance to the gibbering, sobbing giantkin.

"May the Mother grant you mercy in the next world," he said almost calmly. "I have none for you here."

He lifted his heavy boot and stamped down onto and through the giant's skull, and the piteous, whining roar ceased. For a moment, eight foot of gravekling corpse twitched and writhed in the churned grass and then lay still. The sun broke upon the camp and lit the gold paint on Allystaire's shield, and the scene exploded into the chaos of battle and terror.

Most of the mercenaries stood in shocked silence for a moment, a stillness that Allystaire quickly broke. The song of the Goddess filled his limbs with a potent strength that burned like sunfire and begged for release, he let out a loud cry, crouched behind his shield, and simply charged at the nearest knot of them, swinging the round, iron-banded oak forward with a short, powerful burst. Men tumbled around him like pins knocked by a bowler, and Allystaire felt at least one arm, caught between his shield and the man himself, snap. There were screams he had no time for.

He turned, eyes searching for a weapon; rather than his hammer, his eyes settled on the long axe the giantkin had wielded against him. He shucked off his shield and bent, scooping the axe up in both hands. Meanwhile, he'd wasted precious seconds as a defense began to organize.

He saw a man, shirtless, having just roused himself, kneeling in front of his tent thirty yards away, a crossbow drawn and loaded. Allystaire realized the man knelt in a patch of shadow, and smiled to himself as he turned to face an onrushing attacker. Before the shirtless crossbowman fired, Idgen Marte was suddenly there, next to him. Almost delicately, she reached out and pushed the stock of his weapon, just as he fired. The bolt flew straight and true and into the back of one of the three men who'd found weapon and courage enough to charge Allystaire. The wounded man tumbled to the ground with a cry.

Meanwhile, as realization began to dawn on him, the crossbowman let out a strangled cry as he was expertly cut twice across the back, then a third time at his right elbow; bleeding, his arm dangled uselessly at his side and he fell, blubbering and begging mercy, to the ground. Idgen Marte's long curved blade rose for a moment, and then she crouched, stepped forward, and vanished from his sight. Deeper into the camp he heard cries of alarm and the sound of steel meeting flesh.

A warrior defiantly raising sword and shield to challenge Allystaire went quickly silent as the paladin, swinging the giantkin's axe with his hands gripping its last span, brought its heavy curve of blade down through the man's shield. It took off his hand at the wrist and cleaved through his collarbone and into his chest, and the man fell in a heap of gore. His companion, suddenly misliking the odds, stopped in his tracks and dropped his sword. Allystaire advanced grimly, without reaching for the sword on his back, and the man turned to flee.

The paladin seized him by the back of his jerkin and pulled him back. The other hand seized the seat of the man's pants and with no more trouble than a man might lift a small child, pulled the warrior off the ground, lifted him over his head, and hurled him toward the camp; he crashed into another mercenary standing by a pile of weapons and arming himself, and the pair of them, with a clatter of metal and cracking of bones, rolled into a tent.

"*Rede*," Allystaire called out, in a voice hoarse with rage, "end this madness. Come forth to me yourself and no one else needs to die."

Allystaire strode into the camp, ripping tents from their stakes and tossing them aside. Beneath each one huddled forms; two of them large, powerful, bearded men; some of them badly beaten young men; and two of them bruised, sobbing girls. One, he was sure, was the one from his vision; her wrists were closely bound in iron, the manacles joined by three stout links. With the strength of the Goddess still flooding his limbs, he knelt beside her and seized the chains. The girl wailed in fear but did not move, instead sitting tense and afraid. His hands wrapped around the cuffs and ripped them apart as easily as wet cloth. He slipped his glove off, wrapped his left hand around her wrists, and when he lifted it away, the deep red welts the cuffs had left vanished behind new, unbroken skin. Gasps—from the girl, from Torvul, and from beaten and surrendered men—filled the air.

Then, his face grim, his grey armor spattered with blood, the paladin stood and looked down at the girl and asked, his voice heavy, "Lass, will you tell me which one put these upon you?"

With a small, defiant lift to her chin, she pointed to one of the men Idgen Marte was now herding into the camp, the one whose arm Allystaire had snapped with his shield earlier. He gave a brief nod and stalked over to the man, the chain dangling from his hand. Idgen Marte, her eyes wide in her dark and sweat-streaked face, was shaking her head lightly side to side.

Allystaire shook his own head in response and held up the chain. As though it were argument enough, the swordswoman stepped aside.

Holding the chain up for them all to see, Allystaire, his voice hoarse but resonant, said, "These—when placed upon a man, a woman, a child, who has done no wrong, as a tool of rape, of murder, of theft and terror and horror—these should mean death."

He turned his livid countenance upon the man, who cradled his broken arm in front of him, and reached up with his free hand to toss off his helmet. The man, already in pain, looked upon the face of the paladin, saw the judgment there, and fell to his knees, a dark wet stain spreading across his trousers.

"Yet you," Allystaire said, looming over the man. "You do not get to die. You get to wear these for years until your death, unless mayhap you find a smithy who can remove them." The paladin seized the man's good hand and fit one cuff around it, then the other, wrapping his hands around the cuffs and squeezing. The man screamed and vomited and would have fallen forward had Allystaire not been gripping him; there were more gasps as bones cracked. When Allystaire lifted his own hand, the cuffs had been fastened so tightly around the man's wrists that their hinges, lock and pin, were simply gone. Each was a single, smooth, seamless band of metal, ground deeply into the man's skin.

"I'll die. I'll die from the pain m'lord," the man screamed, as Allystaire let go and he fell forward. Then, wrapping his left arm around the man's wrist, the paladin shook his head.

"No." With his left hand, he touched both of the man's arms, his eyes slipping closed, his face smoothed of its rage. When he lifted his hand away, the man was still pale, still breathing raggedly. He lifted his chained hands, piteously, eyes wide in disbelief.

"They still hurt, m'lord," he gasped.

"Aye," Allystaire replied coldly. "And they will. I did not lie when I said you would wear them for many years to come."

CHAPTER 29

The Shadow's Curse

As Allystaire bellowed into the camp and mercenaries fled all around him, a woman in long, sea-green robes sat for a moment, fearful and startled in a tent nestled in the hidden lip of a hill not two hundred paces away. She could hear his voice, a distant echo; moreover, she could practically feel the panic his strength had instilled in the men below.

She could feel the panic in her own body, too, in the heartbeat that crashed against her chest like storm-driven waves. The Marynth Evolyn was not a woman easily panicked, and she gathered herself more quickly than the hired rabble below her. The strong smell of salt and a feeling of cool dampness on her feet jarred her back from the edge of alarm. She sat upon a small, folding camp chair; a bowl of water had been resting upon her lap but had fallen and wet the hem of her robe and her boots. Visions had danced in that bowl until she had been frightened out of them. Frightened because the men whose eyes she peered out of died.

A guard to her side—a tall, hard-eyed man in green leather roughly the same color as her robe—bent to retrieve the bowl, but she stopped him. "Leave it."

"Are they all dead, Marynth?" The man's voice was hard, rasping, and respectful, without deferring overmuch. He stood, uncoiling to his full height, which was considerably above hers. A crossbow dangled from his right hand with an almost contemptuously competent touch. The entire weapon was elegantly carved to resemble a dragon: its wings the curve, its scaled belly the stock, its spear-pointed tail the butt, and the very front from which a bolt would fire, its open, toothy jaw. His fingers curled around it loosely, possessively.

"All those I can water-see," she replied, grimly. "That or pissed themselves so I can see no longer."

"Did you learn what was needed?"

"I learned, Ismaurgh, that a paladin walks this world. That is enough for one day."

"And now?"

"Now, you fool, we flee," the Marynth answered, and she felt her heart threatening to pound its drumbeat against her ribs once more.

* * *

With the mercenaries disarmed and the half-dozen captured village youth freed, Allystaire finally sank to his knees as the thrumming, sunlit music that fueled his strength drained out of him. He felt, almost more than heard, Idgen Marte's steps behind him, and a *thump* as something heavy was tossed onto the churned, blood-spattered grass, followed by a light, mournful whine. Torvul, meanwhile, kept a wary distance from the exhausted paladin, a hand resting on his crossbow.

With a deep breath and a gathering of his will, Allystaire stood upright—a movement protested in every muscle of his body—and turned to face Idgen Marte. The sound he'd heard was Rede, in a mud-spattered, grass-stained robe, being thrown to the grass.

"*You*," Allystaire practically spat, his voice raw and hoarse. "Account for yourself."

Rede huddled on the ground, refusing to look up, to meet Allystaire's gaze. When Idgen Marte toed him with her boot, he simply moaned.

"I will not waste time bandying words with you," Allystaire said, shaking his head and bending to one knee, inwardly grateful for the chance to relieve at least one painfully stiff joint. He stripped off his gloves and reached out to take the man's head between his hands; the former Urdarite slapped ineffectually at the paladin's blood-slicked armor, but inexorably his head was drawn to face Allystaire's.

"Where," Allystaire said, gritting his teeth and pushing his will through his weary arms, through his aching hands, into the mud-spattered man before him, "where did you get the money to hire these men? And why?"

Rede convulsed and cried out almost piteously, a cry that became a scream, and still Allystaire did not relent, though he felt a crackling, tingling energy between his hands and Rede's skin; it suddenly burst and danced up his arms, dissipating.

"A priestess of Braech," Rede said, "a woman. She brought me a letter from their choiron in Londray."

"What did this letter say?" Allystaire was able to relax now, and he felt the muscles of his body rebelling against even the slight effort needed to stay upright, but forcing the truth from Rede was, at least, no longer a struggle.

"It said that the Temple of Braech in Londray was prepared to recognize the Church of the Mother, under ME as her priest, if sufficient gold could be found to raise a temple there; with their recognition the priests of Fortune and the Urdarites would surely fall into line and the Mother's Church would not be relegated with the Temples Minor or the Elven Green."

"Why in this or any world would the Mother need Braech's recognition? And where did they find you? Surely Mol and Renard would have run them out of Thornhurst."

Rede's eyes flared suddenly and Allystaire looked at him without the haze of anger; he appeared thin and manic and feverish, though the skin under Allystaire's hands was cool.

"As they did *me*. All I asked was to preach and to lead! It was *mine*! No more than I was owed! The Mother *touched* me. She gave me sight and set weaker vessels like you and your whore and that ghastly child to test me so that my sight would become pure!" Rede raved and writhed in Allystaire's grip, spit foaming lightly at the corners of his mouth.

"You speak of what you are *owed*, Rede? About your *right* to lead? This proves beyond all doubt that you have no capacity to understand what serving the Mother means. She did indeed return your sight to you, as you say. And She gave you a task, a small one, but one that I could not do, nor could Idgen Marte, nor could Mol. And had you extended back to Her the faith She showed in you, then, perhaps, Rede, perhaps then you could have served. Preached. Even led. Perhaps, had you bowed your head and sought ways to serve—not so much Her as Her people—you might have become what you say you are." Allystaire felt the strength and the rage drain completely from him; the mud-and-grass-stained figure with his mad eyes, his pale skin, his knife-edged cheeks, his flesh burned away in his madness, became less hateful, and more worthy of pity.

Yet pity did not move the paladin to cease his questioning, though he did relax his hands, letting their tips press but lightly into the thin, drawn skin of Rede's skull.

"When did you leave Thornhurst?"

"Less than two weeks after you."

"And where did you go?"

"I preached in Bend and then between it and Londray. Baysend, Tark's Point. When I got to Londray, they were waiting for me."

"And where is their letter?"

"My tent."

"What did you preach in these towns?"

"The coming of the Mother! The time for the poor and the wretched to rise and be heard, to claim the justice so long denied them."

Rede had ceased to fight against Allystaire's questions, against the compulsion of the Goddess through Allystaire's hands. With a heavy sigh, Allystaire let go of him and stood. He looked down upon the man lying in the mud with anger, tempered just enough with pity.

"Rede, had you listened, one day you might have walked in this world as my brother in Her service. Instead, you have done evil in Her name. And that bears a price that must be paid."

Allystaire's eyes flitted to Idgen Marte, and his hand lifted to his sword. She rolled her bottom lip between her teeth and then suddenly shook her head and waved him off. She knelt over the robed figure and spoke in a rapid susurration.

"Rede, the Mother gave you back your eyes and She will not take back Her Gift. Nor will Her servants take your life. Yet Allystaire is right. A price must be paid." She reached down and laid the first and last fingers of her right hand upon his eyelids, pressing them closed. "Every day that ends without Her sun having seen you *serving* Her poor, Her weak, Her forgotten people—*serving* them, Rede—every day when you *do not do this,* you will spend that night remembering what it was to be blinded, and knowing what it would have been to live a life in darkness. Go now, and *serve,* and know that you have been given a reprieve, though you may deem it a dark mercy," she concluded, and both Allystaire and Torvul, along with all the assembled villagers and mercenaries, felt the quiet, enduring power that flowed out in her rushing words, even if they could not hear them. She stood and stepped away—for just a moment the morning sun bent around her, somehow limning her with shadow and light.

The former monk stood shakily, blinking warily at the sun and at the paladin and the shadow confronting him, and turned and began to stumble away raggedly.

"Rede," Idgen Marte called after him, and he stopped in his tracks, as if compelled by an unseen force. "When next you see me in this life, for good or for ill the Mother will retract this mercy. Remember that."

With a wordless yell, Rede resumed his stumbling departure. Torvul spat out a guttural, "Freeze. You mean to just let him go?" The dwarf dropped to his knee and raised his crossbow to his shoulder, moving one thumb up along the stick and flipping up a large-faceted crystal set in a ring of metal and attached with a hinge. His hand selected a bolt, but before he could load it, Idgen Marte was standing before him.

"The Mother gave me the task of judging him," she said; the tip of her sword dangled near the grass, the hilt held lightly and almost casually in her right hand. "And I did. Let him go."

The dwarf spat again, unleashed one of his unintelligible, guttural words, and stood, letting his crossbow dangle from the strap around his shoulder once more.

The three of them watched Rede break into a hobbled trot before they turned their attention to the cowed group of mercenaries and villagers who had sorted themselves; the former tending to their wounded and dead, the latter, roughly a half dozen, bruised and frightened and watching Allystaire and Idgen Marte in quiet awe.

Allystaire, running on the very last reserves of strength, waved Idgen Marte to him and said to Torvul, "If you can, see about food and water for these folk. There ought to be something in this camp."

Then he turned to the villagers, his eyes falling upon the bruised girl whose chains he had ripped off; her eyes, large and brown and scared, fixed upon him, and though he knew he was spattered with the gore of the men he'd killed, he approached her, trying to soften his face. She quailed at his approach, and he suddenly grunted as Idgen Marte's fingers, iron hard, poked him in a tiny crease not covered by armor on the back of his neck.

"You'll terrify her," she murmured, and edged past him, shoving him away with her free hand as she sheathed her sword with the other. "Watch the rabble." She drew the girl aside and spoke to her quietly; Allystaire strained to hear the words that passed between them, but could not, though he did see the fear written so plainly on the girl's face melt away, leaving her, if not serene, at least less troubled. Idgen Marte soon returned, leading the girl mutely behind her, and jabbed her finger once, then again, at two of the milling, frightened, and disarmed mercenaries. Allystaire saw her mouth the words, *Those two*, and he nodded, his face settling into a grimace once again.

Extending one leather-and-iron-clad finger, he pointed to them both— men whose ages were hard to guess, but younger than his, he was certain. One taller and fairer, the other shorter and heavier, both wore the mix of mail and leather common to their sort.

"You two. Come forward."

The two men stepped forward hesitantly; they did not move quickly enough for his liking, so Allystaire lunged forward and gripped one by the front of his collar and threw him forward, sending him stumbling and cursing toward the ground.

"Men like you, *dogs* like you, it is not enough to take the wealth or even the food common folk sweat for; you take their daughters or their sons."

The taller, fairer warrior, the one Allystaire had thrown forward, landed hard onto his hands and knees and tried to scramble back to his feet, until Allystaire's boot crunched into the small of his back, sending him back to the ground in pain with a yowl.

"Every man of you could die for a hundred crimes, I am sure. Yet forcing yourself upon bound folk who are little more than children is the crime you will die for today." His words were punctuated by the rasping hiss of the heavy, two-handed sword drawn from the long harness that crossed his back. He circled to the side of the man, planted his right foot on the ground near his head and the left onto his back, as, once more, the man tried to rise. "Have you a last word? Kin for word to be carried to?"

"This ain't lawful," the man yelled, struggling to rise, Allystaire's boot keeping him pinned to the ground. "I work for the Sea Dragon and 'ave 'is protection! I demand an assize."

"A waste of words," the paladin replied coldly. "It is justice, not the law, that compels me." He stepped down more firmly on the man's back and silenced his protests with one hard, downward swing of his heavy blade. Blood gushed into the grass and the mud, and Allystaire turned away, his sword held in both hands, a grim promise to the now panicking vanquished men.

The other warrior he'd singled out took off running, his squat and bulky form moving with surprising speed. This didn't avail him, though, as Idgen Marte sprang into motion the instant he did, and as the man reached the shadow of the treeline a score of yards away, she stood before him, her sword extended forward at the height of his neck, and he ran straight onto it, a foot or more of its gentle curve extending from the back of his neck. She stepped back, withdrawing her blade smoothly, and he fell.

"And you lot," Allystaire said, pointing to the gathered mercenaries; of the score that had occupied the camp when the Arm and the Shadow set upon it, less than a dozen survived, and now two fresh bodies were leaking dark blood into the ground. "You will walk, in pairs, in separate directions. You will take with you no weapons, no gold, no silver, but such water and bread as you can carry. And everywhere that you go, you will speak of what you saw today. Of your gravekling and your band bested by the Arm and the Shadow of the Mother—of two against a score. Of the two untouched and your score halved. Go now before I change my mind." Wearily raising his bloodstained sword, he added, "Any man who stands here still when a quarter of a turn has passed will be standing a head shorter."

CHAPTER 30

Bandying Words and Standing Watch

Some short time later found Allystaire and Idgen Marte leading the villagers, such mounts as the mercenaries had, and Torvul's wagon loaded with supplies and abandoned weapons back towards the road. The dwarf walked beside them as they led their own mounts, having given over the board of his wagon to the village girls. They'd walked in an awkward silence, Allystaire slow and pained and Idgen Marte impatiently; Torvul simply swung along beside them on his shorter, stouter, yet seemingly tireless legs. Finally, the dwarf broke the silence.

"What gives you the right to simply go lopping off heads after the fighting's done, oh mighty knight," he asked sardonically.

"It is naught to do with any right," Allystaire replied, exhaustion seeping through his words. "It has to do with justice."

"Seems to me justice is something for justiciars or magistrates or assizes."

Allystaire stopped and turned to face the dwarf, though he leaned a bit on Ardent's shoulder as he did. "The last assize I attended, dwarf, was headed by the same priest who hired those brutes and tried to establish a temple of the Mother he could put under his own thumb. He ordered that a man who came to give evidence be scourged from the town. Then he forced a woman I widowed to give me back a piece of a gem that was worth more than anything she owned. If that is justice, it is unknown to me. If taking the head of a man puts anyone in chains is not, then I am happy in my ignorance."

"I don't deny that the man had it comin'," Torvul said. "Just that there's a proper way—"

"The proper way to deal with a man like that is to put him in the freezin' ground," Idgen Marte snapped, spitting to one side of the track and giving the reins that rested in her hand a jerk, leading her horse away from them. "So long as it gets done, it's proper."

"You don't even need to think on it?" Torvul looked from her retreating figure back to Allystaire, who grabbed his own reins with a weary sigh and started trudging forward again. He was silent a moment as he pondered the dwarf's question; in the stillness of his mind and the enervation of his body, with the weight of his armor digging pain into his shoulders, the voice of the Goddess flashed across his thoughts. *I would not have chosen a man of less conviction.* The remembrance, if it was, or the reminder, as he hoped, sent a thrill through his limbs and renewed his energy a bit.

"No. I do not," Allystaire replied. "The Mother will not suffer such a man to live with those crimes on his hands. I would be no true paladin if I did otherwise." He walked on for another moment, and added, "Justice, I think, is less about the trappings—an assize, a court, a magistrate, oaths, and evidence—those are for the law. The law decides a fact, or creates one to suit its needs, and it says if this fact is true, however superficially, a man is punished accordingly. Justice looks at the harm done and the man who did it. Mayhap it considers what else he has done in the world, what else he is likely to do, what made him do what he did. The man whose head I took was a strong man, and in his strength he sought the suffering of others. Justice, for his particular crimes, meant death."

"You don't lack for confidence, I'll give you that."

"Faith is not mere confidence."

Torvul snorted and fiddled with some of the pouches clipped to his jerkin.

"Come now, alchemist," Allystaire said, turning and taking up his reins once more and slowly, painfully setting off down the path after Idgen Marte.

"After what you have seen today, will you still quibble and snort when I speak of faith?"

"That Rede fella had faith, too. And the Sea Dragon priests who supplied his weight have faith, of its own stripe. And so too does every dicer and player at cards when he invokes Fortune on his latest wager. What sets your faith apart, besides it allowing you to squeeze a giantkin's arm into slime and drag straight answers out of a crooked old dwarf? What about your faith means you get to decide that a man deserves death?"

"Spare me the rhetorical puzzles and the traps," Allystaire replied with a snort of his own. "The Goddess did not grant me these Gifts so that I would let them rest idle. I will not wring my hands and worry whether I should act or I should wait for the approval of a magistrate answering to a lord, who answers to a baron, who answers to no one."

"Who do you answer to?"

"The Goddess. Idgen Marte. Mol. Myself."

"Who the Cold is Mol?"

"The Voice of the Goddess. A lass of eleven summers. Going on a hundred."

"Still sounds like what a baron might say."

"Ask yourself what I have to gain by all this. What gold do I earn? What glory?" Allystaire spat into the track and slowly, carefully, hauled himself up into Ardent's saddle, the stallion snorting as if he sensed his rider's annoyance. "Enough. Enough, for good and all. I will bandy no more words with you. Where I find suffering, I will end it. Where I have come too late, I will make such amends as I am able. I can do nothing less." He turned the horse's head to face the rear of their short column, touched his heels to the destrier. With a gathering of thick muscles, Ardent clopped away, hooves loud even on the crude dirt track they followed, and soon the paladin was a fair distance from the dwarf.

Torvul grunted faintly and continued on, shaking his head lightly. "Could probably do more," he said, to no one in particular. Certainly none of the villagers took any notice of him—their bemused focus remained on Allystaire as he rode among them.

* * *

They camped halfway back to Grenthorpe on a relatively flat piece of land hidden from the road by a thick stand of trees; with Torvul's wagon set at an angle, their fire and camp were almost entirely hidden. The village youths fell quickly asleep while Idgen Marte, Allystaire, and Torvul spoke near the small fire, for which the dwarf had provided a metal brazier that concealed most of its light. From the road they were all but invisible; nevertheless, Idgen Marte kept rising to her feet and pacing and staring through the trees.

"Sit. Rest. No one is following us," Allystaire called quietly to her for the fourth time. "And if they are, we have all their weapons," he added, tossing a thumb toward Torvul's wagon. "What would they do if they found us?"

"Were I any o'them I'd've pissed myself lifeless after what you did to their gravekling," the dwarf offered. The jug of *ikthamaunavit* lay cradled in his arm. "Just psssssh," he said, waving a hand in front of his legs, which were stretched out in front of him and crossed at the ankles. "Till my kidneys popped."

"I am flattered," Allystaire replied, trying in vain not to grin a little. Then his attention moved back to the pacing Idgen Marte, and he called to her again, "Come back. Sit. What is bothering you so?"

With a heavy sigh, she turned back toward the small, sheltered fire and squatted in front of it, her scabbarded sword trailing in the dirt. "I don't like what Rede told us. Why would the priest of Braech take an interest in the Mother—so much so that they'd back them for a temple in Londray?"

"Never knew worshippers of the Sea Dragon to *scheme* so damned much," Allystaire agreed. "It is not usually their way; direct challenge is. They value conflict, yes, but also courage."

"None o'yer human gods make any sense. I mean they make more sense than those northern elves, what with tramping all over a land made of endless grey and white—if ice can be called white. Blue sometimes, maybe. Anyway, there ain't no freezin' *green* up there and yet it's all a religious elf'll talk of. Green this, Green that. And let me tell you," the dwarf said, sitting up straight, his voice dropping deeper as he raised one long finger to point to each of them in turn, "it's not a mistake that all those Green worshippers are up there where they can't be talking to decent folk. It's purposeful. Where they belong, freezing and starving."

Allystaire and Idgen Marte exchanged a quick glance, then turned to Torvul.

"What in the Cold are you on about, dwarf?" Allystaire said, while Idgen Marte lowered a knee to the ground and watched Torvul carefully.

The dwarf shrugged and lifted his jug again. "Nothin'. Back to the matter at hand. These Braech-types, they're just after getting' what they can because it's there and someone else might get it if they don't, yes?"

"And what of dwarfish gods," Allystaire needled gently. "What wisdom would they have?"

"There aren't any dwarfish gods. Not so's you'd understand," Torvul replied, his tone shifting from genial drunk to belligerent drunk, and back, at the speed of his words.

"Fair enough. Commune some more with the gods of the bottle then," Allystaire said. He turned to Idgen Marte, who finally sat down, though she worried her bottom lip with her teeth. "I think I made an enemy in the Choiron Symod, back in Bend. He did not seem a man like to let a slight rest."

"So is this just about you, then?"

"Not at all. I think it is about the Mother. I think maybe Braech, or His Church, fears Her. Fears what we will do for Her."

"There're only two of us," she pointed out, shaking her head, her braid brushing against her back. "What threat can we pose?"

Torvul chuckled and toyed with the cork of his bottle, then thumbed it loose and tossed it away into the darkness. "You two're plenty enough threat. Murder kings, you had even the bare bones of a plan. Topple empires. Maybe found one." He laughed sharply, a little drunkenly, and tapped the bottle he held with loose fingers. "Cold help us all you two get that idea in your heads, start a dynasty, raise terrifying children together. You lack somethin' though," he frowned, holding up a finger to bid them wait while he first raised the bottle to his lips for another big nip.

As he lowered the bottle, the upraised finger tapped against the side of his head. "Brains. S'what you're lacking. If the only plan you can ever come up with is walk straight at 'em and count on pounding 'em into jelly, well, there'd be a lot of dwarfish generals who'd approve of the way you think. And every single freezin' one of 'em is dead. Dead as a played out ore vein."

"Your poi—" Allystaire started, but the dwarf cut him off with a sharp gesture of one flat hand.

"My point is that a half-decent schemer will best you, and with little enough effort."

"I am not a subtle man. I have no time for schemes, and have never known one that was good for stopping a hammer blow."

Idgen Marte had been chuckling helplessly during the dwarf's prating, but cut in now. "Stop it, the pair of you. We need to decide what to do next, after we return this lot to Grenthorpe."

"We keep following the map," Allystaire replied.

"Been doing that for almost two months now, and we've not found—"

"We follow the map." Allystaire's tone brooked no argument.

"What map?" Torvul sat up a bit straighter and set aside his mostly empty jug of spirits.

"None that you need to see. The map has Londray on it, aye? Then we make for it, stopping as needs be on the way."

Idgen Marte flopped to a seat on the grass and rested her forehead in one hand. "And what if they're waiting for us there? Or on the way?"

"I told Symod to get out of my way once. I will tell him again," Allystaire said solemnly. Then he leaned forward and put a hand on Idgen Marte's shoulder. "Faith. He will not stop us. He cannot."

Idgen Marte raised her head and her eyes shone for a moment in the dim, guarded firelight. She started to say again, "Near two months and we've not found—"

Allystaire cut her off a second time. "Faith," he repeated. "We do not labor in vain. Nor will we find a fight we cannot win. If the Sea Dragon Himself should find us on the road, I will shatter his jaws and you will rend his belly." He waited a moment and said, "Aye?" with a slight tilt of his head.

She smiled, an expression he could barely see, nodded and patted his hand, and murmured, "Aye."

He stood up. "To bed with us, then. Well, to bed with the two of you. I will take the first watch."

"I'll join you in it," Torvul said. "Got a potion I aim to drink. Keep me from bein' hungover. Just means I stay up a few more turns."

"Why in the Cold would it mean that?"

"Horrible nightmares. Just horrible. Side effect. Know what a *yumunavith* is? Eh?"

"No."

"Then you've never been chased by one down a dark mineshaft that ain't been properly shored up. Like I said. Horrible."

In a few moments, Idgen Marte had scurried up a tree with her hammock and the dwarf returned from his wagon clutching a small bottle that smelled foul from three yards. He raised it to his lips and took a large gulp, with no apparent trouble swallowing it. He sealed the bottle, tucked it into one of his many pockets, and drifted over toward Allystaire's shadow. "You out to declare war on the Church of Braech?"

Whether the potion worked or not, Allystaire wouldn't have wagered, but the dwarf's voice was less thick with drink than it had been moments before. "Not if I can help it, no," he replied tiredly.

"They may not be giving you a choice." The dwarf sniffed, spat, and stamped his feet as if putting feeling back into them. "They can bring a lot of force to bear. Lot of warriors eager to gain Braech's favor. Lot of priests they say have his powers of will, or weather, or sight. And there's the Berzerkers. Heard of 'em. Never seen 'em."

Allystaire's memory flitted to the assize back in bend, to the terrible weight that pressed down upon his mind and even his body; he was briefly chilled by the thought. "The Berzerkers I have not seen. But I have met such a priest, I think. He told me Braech favored me and wanted my service."

"I can see why he would," the dwarf remarked thoughtfully, strolling up to Allystaire's side and once again uncorking his foul potion. From mere feet away the stench was almost overpowering, but the dwarf sipped it resolutely before sealing it again. "Braech favors bold action, strength, and resolve. Whatever you lack, Sir Allystaire, you've got those. Still, I suppose he was surprised to learn your services were already, ah…engaged, as it were."

"At that moment I had not yet met the Mother." Allystaire reflected a moment. "I was already serving Her, mind. I just did not know it."

"Well that doesn't make any damned sense."

"Makes perfect sense from where I stand."

"Now that's going to require—"

Allystaire turned to the dwarf and shook his head, waved one hand dismissively. "No it is not. Ask Idgen Marte if you must. She is the storyteller, not I. There will be plenty of time on the road tomorrow. Now, we walk and we watch. Aye?"

"You walk, I'll watch. My legs are too old and besides, I can perch up on the wagon with my bow and have a good view."

"How are you going to shoot anything in the dark, if it comes to it?"

"You don't know much about dwarfish bows, do you? Dark is no obstacle. Heh." Torvul walked off toward his wagon, chuckling. "Dark. As if that mattered," he muttered to himself. Allystaire thought he caught the word *savages* as the dwarf's dim outline merged with the darkness of the surrounding trees.

Then, with the shuttered fire the dimmest of glows behind him, the paladin began walking a slow circle around the camp and the sleeping folk within. He could feel Idgen Marte's presence above him in the trees, though she was sleeping, and he fancied perhaps he could hear Torvul occasionally sighing atop his wagon, or adjusting some piece of his gear. Mostly, though, he watched the darkness around them with careful eyes, shield and hammer at the ready, while six young men and women slept peacefully for the first time in days.

Allystaire had stood many a watch during his days on campaign, but none that he could recall felt so much like what he ought to be doing, rather than simply what he was doing; there was the fire and those who slept near it, there was the darkness surrounding them, and between them, the paladin.

CHAPTER 31

Interlude

The Marynth Evolyn hurried through the central chamber of the Temple of the Sea Dragon. Her steps were not as measured nor as calm as when last she had walked underneath the statue that loomed in its center, and her sea-green robes were muddied near to the waist. She shivered as the bursting waves brought a chill promise of the winter to come. Nearly two weeks had passed since she and Ismaurgh had fled the paladin at the camp outside Grenthorpe, on foot and with little to provision them. She did not pause to reflect upon the statue of the Dragon Rampant, the Lord of Waves, Father of Storms, Master of Trade and Accords. She barely eyed it as she hurried down the corridor, fighting off a sudden urge to kick one or both of the figures that followed her into the crashing waves beneath them.

Her guardsman, similarly dirtied to the tops of his calf-high boots, proceeded rather more slowly behind her, dragging an even dirtier shape behind him on a length of rope; once or twice he paused and aimed a kick that sent the bundle of muddied robe perilously close to the edge of the tiled walkways and the roaring waves beneath.

Evolyn led them down the warren of hallways, turning with an unerring sense of place and direction. She paused at the end of a corridor of thick stone, still lit with the thick stubs of white wax candles.

"Wait here. If I call for you, come, and bring the beggar. If I am to be given to the waves, Ismaurgh, kick him into the surf and flee." She stepped closer to him and her cheeks colored faintly. "You have been a good servant." She turned, her hand lingering on his arm for a moment, and entered the heavy, iron-banded oak door they had stopped a few paces from.

And you've been a fine lay, Ismaurgh thought, *but I ain't about to say that. Touching how she can make her cheeks color like that, though.* He leaned against the wall, idly toed the tied-up shape that had fallen to the ground in front of him, and launched a swift kick into its ribs.

Once inside the door, Evolyn continued down a shorter, slightly darker corridor and knocked at a similar door. It opened without a word—filling the doorway before her was the Choiron Symod, dressed as usual in his robes, his amulet of office sparkling in the light of a three-sconced candelabra clutched in his left hand.

"Marynth Evolyn. I understand that you come before me a failure." Symod's voice, as always, rolled through her body with a profound force, and she found her eyes lowering toward the stones beneath her feet. He stepped out of the doorway and she stepped quietly into his private chamber.

"Not entirely a failure, my lord choiron," she said, albeit meekly. "I have brought you valuable information."

"You were meant to bring me Coldbourne in chains. Or confirmation of his death," the choiron said, drawing out the sounds of his last few words till they hung, resonant, in the stone walled room.

"I know that, Choiron. I have failed you and failed the Father of Waves. Yet the information—"

"I have all the information I need! The man is dangerous. His Goddess is dangerous. She must *not* be allowed to bring her paladins into this world. I have found the text I sought. You do not understand the ruin this could mean."

The Marynth lifted her gaze to his and swallowed once, widening her eyes a bit to appear, if only slightly, vulnerable; few men she knew could resist such a look, even a man like Symod. Notwithstanding, she was afraid. Afraid of what she had seen. Afraid of the eyes that had stared at her through the man he condemned as he wrapped those hideous bonds around his wrists.

"Choiron, this Goddess already has brought Her paladin into this world. I saw him. I saw his powers. I saw him crush a giantkin's arm as a child might squeeze mud between his fingers. I saw him crush out the life of the men I hired. I saw him heal wounds. There is no doubt, Choiron. A paladin walks this world again. And yet." Evolyn tried not to smile, kept her head down, tried to seem contrite and thankful for the opportunity to speak. "I think I know how he may be overcome. I think his Goddess has left him vulnerable."

The choiron's face stiffened into a mask of anger, his lips compressed, his cheeks taut. But his eyes were cautious, wary. Even a bit afraid. "What else have you brought me out of the disaster you have made?"

"I brought the one we sought to be our instrument."

"He lives?"

"Indeed." Evolyn closed her eyes and thought deeply for a moment, about the man outside. He was repulsive in many ways, and yet he was lean and strong and skilled with his hands. In many ways. After their hasty coupling two nights hence, she could still touch his mind. *Come in. Bring the priest.*

There was a knock on the door, and then it opened inward with Ismaurgh's leather-gauntleted fist on the end of it. He shoved the rumpled shape to the floor and pulled back its hood, revealing the mud-spattered, glassy-eyed face of Rede.

"The paladin was merciful, I see. He is a fool," Symod said, as he bent forward and held the candelabra lower to examine Rede. The former priest, like most, shied away from the choiron's gaze, but Symod reached out a thin, strong hand and drew his chin up as he continued, "Rede. Eye of the Mother. We have much still to discuss. If you would save your life, you will make yourself useful to us. Your brother in faith may come to regret his mercy."

* * *

Baron Lionel Delondeur rode at the very tip of his vanguard, green banners with the sand-colored Tower streaming above the mass of men. A small knot of knights and officers formed his retinue, but as was the baron's habit, a troop of common soldiers rode along with them. Some ferried orders and dispatches back and forth from his retinue to other lords and commanders scattered among the two thousand that strung along behind him, but others were simply given the honor of accompanying the baron home at the end of the campaign season.

One such soldier, wearing a green tabard over well-scoured mail and doubled-green-and-white bands tied around his left arm, rode just behind the baron's party, competent if not entirely comfortable in the saddle. A few wisps of blond hair escaped his tightly cropped coif, which made his fine-boned face seem younger and more delicate than it was. Unlike the other soldiers and the knights, he was silent and sober as sloshing skins were passed around him. Lightly armored riders pounded up along the column to call out that Luden Thryft had turned for his home along with his levees, or that the Sixes and Sevens or the Copper Halves were turning aside and wished to pay the Baron their compliments on his wages and wish him luck in the winter. When each warband was named, the men around him cheered or rattled gauntlets and vambraces against the edges of their shields. He dutifully raised his voice with the others, though with little enthusiasm, letting it blend into the din.

Lionel turned in his saddle and waved the mailed, blonde soldier to his side, and the ranks of knights parted to let him pass. As the soldier reached the baron, Delondeur urged his white charger ahead a bit, forcing the soldier's lesser bay to work a little harder to keep pace.

"Bannerman-Sergeant…?"

"Chaddin, my lord Baron Delondeur," the young man replied. "And it is only Sergeant."

"It's Bannerman-Sergeant if I freezing well say it is, eh?" The baron turned in the saddle—for all his age he was still the model of a horseman, able to ride with both hands occupied, using just his knees—and flashed a brilliant smile full of straight teeth at the younger man. Chaddin respectfully inclined his head to avoid meeting the baron eye to eye.

"What post would you like over the winter, Bannerman-Sergeant Chaddin? You've earned the right to ask."

"I'd prefer to stay in the city, my lord," Chaddin answered. "Guard the walls, command a patrol of Greenhats, perhaps."

"That's not glorious work, lad," Lionel said gruffly. "Even so, it needs doing, and a willing hand is a welcome one. I cannot promise you a posting in the Dunes itself," he went on, raising a hand and waving it indistinctly in the air.

"Londray itself would be all I would ask, my lord," Chaddin replied, his words careful and slow, his eyes still respectfully low.

They were interrupted by the approach of a rider wearing the light De-londeur green and the soft leather cap and short sword of a messenger. "M'lord baron," he called out. "The Long Knives send their compliments and their respect and desire their release be made official 'pon your Lordship's word."

Delondeur shared a brief, toothy grin with Chaddin before turning to the messenger, shaking his head with its great mane of greying blonde hair. "No, no lad, I think not. You tell Captain Tierne and his men that quartering the winter in Londray would see them well supplied with the weight to hold up the bars and keep the girls bow-legged. I may have work for them before the winter's out, eh?"

Chaddin grimaced but swallowed the expression as quickly as he could, recovering the professional calm of his features as the messenger knuckled his forehead, sawed at the reins to turn his small and nimble mount, and dashed off.

"Might not be an easy fortnight of it if you do command some Green-hats, Bannerman-Sergeant," Lionel remarked drily. "Not with the bulk of the men all waiting it out with drink and dice and women. Fistfights mostly, but a few yards of steel get wet every year. Ah, but what am I saying? You're a soldier, you know the way of it."

Chaddin remained silent, and Lionel heaved a deep breath. The road had long since turned their direction northwest, and now topping a small rise, they got their first glimpse of Londray Bay; the city that was named for it squatted over it like a gargoyle. Commanding the best passage from the coast to the rolling hills and brief mountains of its interior, the city was curtained by towered walls rising over the pebbly cliffs along the coastline.

"You can smell the sea even from here, eh Bannerman-Sergeant? I sailed it once, in my younger days. To Keersvast. Meant to go the lands be-yond, south of the Archipelago. Other countries of strange folk and strange tongues, the Concordat. The fiercest of women and finest of minstrels, or so they say, in Keersvast. Never made it, though—the tundra called, with its giants and the elves. Still, I wonder: ought I have taken Delondeur to sea? Conquered other lands?"

"Mayhap my lord," Chaddin answered. "There seems plenty left to conquer here," he added somewhat unconvincingly.

They rode on in silence for a few more moments, then the baron reined in. "Is there, Chaddin? Eh? How long were we at it this time? Soon as the spring thaw, all through the summer. Five months? We could perhaps eke out a sixth if we wished, but that canny old bastard Innadan won't give us a straight battle. And I've no desire to burn out vineyards all winter for fuel."

"Why not, my lord? Certainly that would starve Innadan's coffers—"

"Then what would we drink in the years to come, eh? Say what you will about those weak bastards, they make the best wine in this—"

He paused on the verge of saying, Chaddin was sure, *kingdom.*

"In this part o'the world. What have we conquered? Did we push the border a few miles? Could we push it a few more next year? At that rate my grandson might, when he is my age, ride in victory into that pile of rocks Hamadrian Innadan calls the Vineyards. Or Innadan's grandson might do the same to the Dunes. "

Chaddin frowned and swallowed once, buying time to think. This, he thought, was new territory. "Perhaps we could sue for peace over the winter, milord. If we sent an emissary under a branch of peace…"

The Baron Delondeur thought on this a moment in silence. He kicked his horse back into motion, and slowly his retinue all followed suit, their bigger and stronger horses leaving Chaddin and his troop of soldiers behind; kicking into speed was an effective dismissal of the bannerman-sergeant.

Lionel reflected, as he rode, about the bargains he'd made. About the man with the glowing fingertips working somewhere in the bowels of his castle. *Working, Lionel? Is that what you call it?* He wasn't sure if the voice asking him that was his own, or his father's. It made little difference.

He thought again of the letter he had burned. Coldbourne's arrogance choked him with anger. And bitterness—three times they had met on the field, army to army, with that broken-nosed, jumped-up peat digger leading the Old Baron's host, and once with him at the head next to the Young Baron. Each time Delondeur had come away more bloodied than Oyrwyn. And here Coldbourne was yet again, making demands.

The chafing arrogance of Coldbourne's letter was so like him. And yet, what stories had come to the baron this fall, stories of his own lands, his own people…that was not like Coldbourne at all.

"No other man ever got the better of me twice. And none four times. And none in my own bloody land!" Lionel's words had begun as a whisper but ended a roar, and he spurred his horse to a gallop, leaving his knights and captains struggling to catch up to his anger-fueled haste while Chaddin and his soldiers fell further behind.

* * *

Waiting inside The Dunes, once more secreted in its deepest, darkest tunnels, Bhimanzir was again at work. The similarly robed, bald-headed youth stood beside him, handing him tools and attending upon the sorcerer's commands.

The youth no longer fumbled for the tools the sorcerer bade him fetch. Holding a knife carefully with his fingertips, he placed the smooth bone hilt carefully into Bhimanzir's casually outstretched hand.

The woman tried to scream. In fact, her mouth and her eyes were both opened wide and full of pain, but no sound emerged. A dark and shimmering red light hovered around her mouth, swallowing up all the sounds she made; similar lines of blood-dark light bound her to the table.

Bhimanzir harrumphed quietly as he continued to cut, eventually peeling open the woman's abdomen. He leaned over the spilled viscera, inspecting it closely.

"The divinations agree," he muttered. "The Mother. This is new, though," he mused, as he probed at a rope of the woman's entrails with the tip of his knife.

Next to him, the boy flinched only slightly. His eyes, wide and slightly almond, were fixed on a point on the damp stone wall. Something in him forced him to turn and look at the woman's face.

She was not a particularly old woman, but her face bore a tale of hard work down the years. He watched her pant and scream silently as her innards steamed on the table. He forced himself to watch the pupils in her eyes contract and the light in them dim until it was gone.

Bhimanzir continued to mutter aloud. The boy caught something about an "ancient enemy"—then the sorcerer was laughing.

"As if any enemies are left to frighten the Knowing."

The sorcerer poked and prodded a few moments more. "Still. It deserves attention. I must speak with Gethmasanar. The idiot knight's tendencies can be exploited, surely. And of course he must be taken and studied."

"Of course, master," the lad echoed, even as he stared at the woman's slack eyes and still features.

CHAPTER 32

Daft

The three of them made a small and dismal column—the two humans mounted and the dwarf on his wagon. They followed a thin and none-too-well maintained dirt track that was threatening to become mud as a warm rain fell around them.

"Never get used to the way summer fights its ending up here," Idgen Marte grumbled, riding alongside Allystaire on her courser. She had pulled a light, hooded cloak from her saddlebags and worked at arranging its peak above her head with one hand.

"What do you mean?" Allystaire looked at the smattering of first fallen leaves on the dirt track they followed, frowning. He fiercely ignored the rain, letting it pelt off his face and shoulders.

"It's autumn. Even the trees know it. And yet still the heat would like us to braise in our saddles."

Allystaire turned toward her. "Surely a southerner is not telling me it is too hot for her."

Idgen Marte sniffed. "In my part of the world, the seasons go gracefully." Then she added, "And spring lasts longer than the two bloody weeks between the snowmelt and the pounding summer sun."

"Seasons at all are an abomination, you ask me," Torvul called out from behind them. The dwarf had reins gathered in one hand. He guided his harnessed team with practiced ease and a light hand. The whip sat almost unused on the bench next to him, along with his cudgel and an earthenware jug. He paid as much attention to the rain as did a rock. "Weather should be hot and dank and dark at all times."

Idgen Marte laughed at the dwarf's jibe, but Allystaire's face was dour, grim beneath his broken nose and angry blue eyes, his jaw taut with tension. He suddenly pounded a balled up fist into his thigh and muttered, "I never should have let him go. He should have been brought back to Grenthorpe to face those people."

Idgen Marte reined in, and the dwarf tugged his team to a stop. Sensing his rider's anger, Ardent stamped at the ground.

"We agreed, Allystaire. If he'd been meant to die, the Mother would have told me. He was judged, and he was punished."

"Might've wanted to make sure of that one," the dwarf offered, his tone reasonable, mild, the companionable suggestion of the man who is rather certain he is the smartest one in the room and sees no need to point it out. "Not good policy to leave enemies behind you."

"He should have answered to the folk he wronged." Allystaire was insistent, and rather than meet the gaze of the woman or answer the dwarf, he stared off into the trees flanking them.

"He answered to the Mother, and he will not find Her justice pleasant."

"I'm not sayin' I agree with Idgen Marte here, or quite buy all this Mother business the pair of you are selling, but didn't you, just the other day, speak eloquently to me of the difference between the law and justice? Seems to me that tossing the man to a mob, no matter how good it may have felt, would've been neither." The dwarf rested his rein-wrapped hands on his knees as he spoke, eyes moving speculatively from the woman, to the man, and back.

"Eloquently?" Idgen Marte practically chortled the word, her mount tossing its head as if echoing her laughter. "Him?"

"Well," Torvul, said, shrugging his shoulders expansively, "maybe the compliment will inspire him to aim higher in future."

"I am right here," Allystaire replied, his lips curling in anger around his teeth. "I am not an animal to be spoken of as though I cannot comprehend."

"Then stop sulking like a kicked dog," Idgen Marte said sharply. "The matter is done with. When Rede finds a bed this night, like as not his sleep will be tortured with memories of his sightlessness. It has been so for better than a week now. That the people of Grenthorpe did not flock to the Mother is not to be fixed by killing him."

Allystaire sighed and balled his fist again, raising it as if to pound it into his thigh, then dropping it, flattened, to his side. "He poisoned the well before we ever got there," he admitted.

"We did the good that we could. That's all we can do."

"It was not enough."

"Speaking of beds," Torvul said, raising his voice pointedly above the brewing argument, "we ought to be after finding ours, eh? Not so very many turns of daylight left. There's a decent village with a perfectly agreeable inn but a couple of turns ride ahead. Called Hillendale, or something. Such imaginations you people have. Still, their inn has the only tolerable beer in this barony outside of Londray."

"I could do with a night in bed," Idgen Marte nearly sighed. "Allystaire?"

"I never sleep in a bed anyway," he said laconically.

Idgen Marte rolled her eyes and tugged the head of her horse, turning it away and back up the road, throwing back over her shoulder, "Then sit on the floor and stiffen your back, you bloody martyr." She was quickly out of sight around a bend, the hoofs of her courser pounding into the dirt.

"Just because you're a masochist fool doesn't mean the rest of us are," Torvul chided. "Besides…I think maybe the lass might not, ah…" The dwarf cleared his throat delicately.

"Spit it out, dwarf."

"I think perhaps she's tired of having the bed to herself, as it were."

"She is free to fill it however she pleases," Allystaire said, his voice skin-chillingly cold.

"Are you daft? A eunuch?" Torvul shook his head, spat to the dirt, and *tched-tched* his team into motion with a light click of his tongue accompanied by a lighter flick of his wrist. "Never mind. I already know you're the first and if you're the second it's too pitiful to know. I hope you're just a prude."

"I am neither a eunuch nor a prude."

"Least you're not arguing on daft," Torvul said. "Maybe you can learn."

"Why are you still here, dwarf? Why do you still follow me, if you find me so contemptible?" Allystaire nudged Ardent with a heel and thundered off, his countenance as dark as it had been before.

The dwarf chewed hard on the inside of his cheek for a moment, and when the paladin was out of earshot, murmured, "Haven't got anywhere else to be."

* * *

The village was precisely where Torvul remembered it to be, and the three travelers rode into its outskirts as the last bit of sunlight was sinking below the nestling hills. When a single finger of vanishing light danced across his face, Allystaire paused and took a deep breath and closed his eyes, gathering himself.

He slid off his horse and remained that way, eyes closed, breathing softly but deeply, unspeaking and unmoving. He did not hear the Mother's voice, as some part of him hoped, but did, perhaps, feel the ringing chime of one single note of the music that seemed to fill his mind in Her presence, however distant. *I am sorry, Mother*, he thought. *I should not question Your justice.* The apology, however, rang a bit hollow; with a grimace he added, *Yet I am as I was made and as You found me. It is hard to see one who has wronged Your people in Your own name go free.*

Allystaire was jolted out of his reverie by Idgen Marte's hand upon his shoulder. "We can't kill everyone who wrongs our people, Ally," she murmured—too softly, he hoped, for Torvul's ear—"any more than we can save everyone who needs us. Don't let it consume you. We have too much work to do."

"Because of him, Grenthorpe will not know the Mother," Allystaire replied, though his voice was calm and his jaw had finally unclenched.

"They don't have to worship Her to be Her people," Idgen Marte chided him. "Nor to be ours."

He nodded, finally, with another deep exhalation, letting out the tension and the anger he had been carrying all the day. "True. Thank you for reminding me."

"My job," she smiled, letting go his shoulder with a pat and picking up the reins of her horse.

Something jolted him suddenly, and Allystaire fixed her with a questioning look. "Ally?"

She grinned lopsidedly at him, stretching the taut, whitened skin of the scar descending from a corner of her mouth. "It's what Garth called you, aye? Thought mayhap it's what friends…" She shrugged and turned away, still grinning.

Allystaire went and picked up his own reins as Torvul's wagon rattled past him, the dwarf clucking at his team, and then at him. "Daft."

The wagon rolled along into the village square with Allystaire and Idgen Marte walking to either side of it, and Torvul holding forth. "Folks here probably haven't seen a dwarfish wagon in some time. Like to be a mob scene all demanding pots mended and tools fixed. Wanting emetics and potions to stir the ol' kindly feeling, poison for the rats and something to clear the dog's eyes—"

"And all you've got that ain't poison is those dwarfish spirits, which might as well be, so what are you going to sell 'em?" Idgen Marte looked up at him, grinning a bit wickedly.

The dwarf's expression darkened, and he rolled off a string of grim noises that sounded like stones being cracked apart by fast-freezing ice.

"If you are going to curse, do it in a language we can understand." For the first time in many turns, Allystaire's voice carried a hint of laughter in the feigned reproach.

The dwarf spat to the side of his wagon and said, "There's no proper curses in your northern human tongues, anyway."

"Eh?" Idgen Marte and Allystaire chimed in unison as they turned to face Torvul.

"There's no word in your tongues for, ah…" The dwarf paused, wrinkling his heavy brows. "A vein of ore that can't be extracted without crashing the tunnel. Well there is, I just said it, but it's a bit unwieldy. Lacks impact and verve. And I have to add another word to say whether it's silver or tin or…" He shuddered and hoarsely whispered, "gold." Then he shook his head as if to clear it of a horrid vision, and both humans laughed, though Torvul looked on their mirth with dismay.

By now they had reached the outside of the largest building in the square; it boasted three stories, dozens of rooms, thick glass windows along the front, and a cluster of outbuildings spreading behind. The scents of woodsmoke, horse, wet hay, and cookery on a large scale seemed melded together in an inescapable scent that all three recognized simply as *inn*.

As they pulled up short of it, Torvul said, "Odd that no one's spotted us yet. Not exactly dark. And you can joke as you like, but usually the moment I roll into a village this far out in the hinterlands I'm mobbed. By the children, at least."

The lights of fires, lamps, and candles shone through windows in the buildings that surrounded the green on three sides, and in some of the closer outlying houses, but although the trio hadn't been quiet in their approach, no faces had peeked out through curtains or lifted the flaps of hide or oilskin to look at the new arrivals.

"Probably all after their dinners. Time we were after ours," Allystaire said. He started to walk closer to the inn's door, lightly tugging on the reins he clutched in one hand. The huge grey destrier refused to move. He tugged again and the horse gave a slight negative whicker, stamped a hoof, and tried to tug out of his grip. "Ardent," Allystaire admonished gently. "Nothing to fear here. Calm."

His words, or at least his tone of voice, had some mitigating effect on the animal's mood and, though still shying, the horse followed his master's steps. Allystaire grounded the reins and stepped lightly on them, then approached the door, knocked politely but loudly, and stepped back.

The door opened slowly, and the man standing on the threshold was unmistakably the innkeep: portly, balding, red-cheeked, and apron-clad. He simply stood, however, staring at them. There was light at his back and darkness fast approaching out of doors, so Allystaire couldn't make out his features entirely, but the stiffness with which the man held himself appeared odd.

"Evening, goodman," Allystaire said warily, standing up a little straighter, his scalp tingling slightly. "Have you rooms and space for our animals? Three travelers and five animals all told."

"Three…three?" The innkeep dragged out his second iteration of the querying word, and his voice was rather hoarse. "Three travelers? Is one of you a dwarf?"

"Aye, goodman, a dwarf indeed and to your luck an alchemist, a handy fellow with every tool known to man and several dozen yet unknown in this benighted but charming country…" The dwarf trailed off as the innkeep's head turned sharply toward him, and a flash of pale, sickly yellow, so brief it seemed a trick of the light, blazed in his eyes.

The innkeep's mouth opened wide, stretching so far that they heard the bones of his jaw creak in protest, and an unearthly wail, an ear-splitting sound, emanated from his mouth. Their animals screamed in a unified protest, and the paladin himself quailed and stepped back away from the door, clutching at his ears.

"What in the Cold…" As Allystaire turned toward Torvul, who'd been stunned into silence, he heard Idgen Marte's long and very slightly curved sword whisk against its sheath as it was drawn free. The innkeep, his eyes now pulsing with the sickly yellow light, was drawing a deep breath, his jaw still nearly obscenely open, preparing to unleash another wail. *Bugger that*, said a dry, practical voice in Allystaire's thoughts, and he stepped up and drove a fist hard into the man's stomach, stepping forward and turning his body into the blow by pivoting on one foot. The intended wail became a choking gasp, the punch sending the aproned man stumbling backwards.

When Allystaire turned back toward Idgen Marte and Torvul, he saw every door and every window on the square open, each one framing the same pulsing flashes of yellow—dozens of them, always in pairs, at heights ranging from his waist to his head.

Torvul cursed again in dwarfish, and the words required no translation. Then, his voice thick, he cried out, "*Sorcery!*"

CHAPTER 33

Something of Ambushes

In contrast to the brightly lit houses of the village square, the more outlying houses were completely dark, save for one. A thick, sickly yellow glow—just like the pairs of eyes that were even now advancing on Allystaire, Idgen Marte, and Torvul—filled the interior of the house and spilled through its oilskin windows. It was not the glow of lamp, hearth, candle, or rushlight.

Instead, the glow emanated from a single figure that hunched over a large family dining table, the surface of which was slick beneath his hands. Thick, dark liquid pooled in dents and marks on the table's surface. The glow rose from beneath his fingernails, from his eyes, and faintly from behind his clenched lips.

The simple farmhouse was a scene of unimaginable gore. Several bodies lay motionless—a few large, some much smaller, none with all their limbs intact.

The robed and hooded man who stood amidst this nightmare was wet to the elbows from the blood that he swirled and pushed upon the table with his glowing yellow fingertips. His eyes were narrowed in concentration and his thin lips moved in a constant, incantatory susurration.

* * *

"Sorcery and no freezing mistake about it," Torvul yelled. "And powerful stuff."

The innkeep Allystaire had punched had recovered his footing, and now he lurched forward clumsily, almost drunkenly, reaching for the much larger man. His strong hands found no purchase on the scored and pitted metal of the paladin's armor. By the time his fingers, groping almost blindly, started to find a grip near the underarms, Allystaire had picked him up by his collar and belt, lifted him a foot off the ground, and flung him, as carefully as he could manage in such a moment, back into the inn, from which were emerging more ensorcelled townfolk. Women, children, men young and old began closing in with the same half-drunken walk as the innkeep.

With the first man tossed away from him, Allystaire's hand curled under the heavy head of the maul he wore on his belt, pulling it free and slapping the metal-banded, polished wood of the haft across both of his hands. "These folk—are they dead, or do they live?"

Torvul stood and braced one foot on the front of his wagon. He'd wrapped the reins around one fist, while the other grasped his bronze-capped head-knocker. "They live, but their minds aren't their own. Cuttin' a way out would be easiest for such as the pair o'ya."

"Idgen Marte," Allystaire called out, seeing, in his peripheral vision, the swordswoman brandishing her sword. "We are leaving. Now. We are not cutting anyone down."

"I was afraid ya'd say that," Torvul said, limbering up his arm with a few tentative swings of his cudgel.

"Alchemist, can you do anything for them?"

"Even if I were in good form these days, no. Sorcery needs be met with sorcery, leastways it does now. Or you kill the sorcerer, I s'pose."

"Then we will find him. *Ardent*," Allystaire bellowed at his mount, which had flattened its ears and was stamping at the ground and whinnying nervously. "To me." The horse dutifully trotted over and Allystaire swiftly hauled himself into the saddle, switching the hammer into his right hand. He saw Idgen Marte slide into her own saddle. "How easily can you turn that wagon, dwarf?"

"Quicker'n you'd imagine," Torvul answered. He sat back and flicked the reins, setting his ponies into motion.

The villagers were closing in from all sides; forms had squeezed out through the windows of the inn.

Allystaire's mule stepped away nervously and finally bolted. Idgen Marte cursed and kicked her heels into her courser's flank, starting off after it. The smaller, heavily laden animal had set a course straight into a knot of village folk, and though Idgen Marte caught up to it quickly and seized its dangling lead, by the time she had started to turn both horses, the glowing-yellow-eyed mob was upon them.

"Dwarf, your cudgel!" Allystaire slid his hammer back into the ring on his belt and extended his hand.

Torvul's throw was true—the stout length of wood *thunked* into Allystaire's hand even as his eyes turned to look for it. He spurred Ardent, and the huge destrier gathered itself in a great muscled leap, then charged, neck extended. Allystaire leaned low in the saddle, shifting his weight to the right, cudgel held at head-height of a man.

Idgen Marte was trying to bring the flat of her sword into play, but the thin curved blade didn't have enough surface area to work well as a bludgeon, and while he could see her blows stinging, and in one case opening a thin line of blood across an outstretched arm, the pain didn't seem to frighten the villagers away.

He had one moment of brief thought. *Please, Ardent, do not crush any of them*, before man and horse crashed into the crowd.

Perhaps the horse heard his thoughts, guessed his intent, or felt some subtle shift of weight or mood. Regardless, the horse did not simply crash straight through the crowd. At the last moment it turned sharply and smacked its flank and hindquarter into the mass of bodies. Allystaire swept the cudgel out in a wide blow—forceful, but not enough to crack heads or spines. *These are innocent people*, he reminded himself. *These are* my *people*.

The combined weight of horse and man, and Allystaire's work with the cudgel, sent many of the stumbling crowd flying and others tripping over them. Idgen Marte wasn't yet free, though, as two of them had hands on her legs and were trying to drag her from the saddle. Fortunately they were to either side and so pulled against each other. Her sword raised, she had just turned her wrist to slash down at one of their hands, leading with the edge, when Allystaire cracked the villager on the back of the head with his borrowed club.

The yellow points of light in his eyes winked out, and the man sank to the earth like a stone. Two other villagers tripped over him reaching for Idgen Marte, who kicked her way free of the villager on the other side and smacked her horse's flank with her other heel. The knight and the warrior, their mounts and packhorse, pulled away from the crowd, but better than three dozen folk still barred their way. Torvul had not been idle, though. Driving his wagon straight onto the green, he'd given himself space to move and forced the mobs to shift course. He was rummaging in his many pouches and tossing tiny, easily broken vials at the crowds that were converging.

Two that landed near each other immediately puffed smoke, soon followed by man-high walls of bright blue flames. Others landed among the crowds themselves, in one case smashing over the head of one of the taller folk. Smoke and vapors began to spread, filling the edge of the green with a thick, clinging, and choking cloud of fog that lay heavily over the heads of the yellow-eyed horde.

"Around them, quickly! While it lasts!" The dwarf pointed to a gap that the crowds had left open when they followed him onto the green, and he whipped his team frantically. His small, sturdy ponies could get up good speed, and, driven by fear and flame and the insistence of their riders, Idgen Marte's courser and the mule, and Allystaire's huge stallion flanked it to either side, and they sped off into the night, leaving blue flames, lurching yellow-eyed villagers, choking fog, and chaos behind.

* * *

The sorcerer lurking in the gore-strewn house did not rage. He did not pound the table or kick the remnants of the peasants he'd slaughtered. He laughed and glided out of the house, trailing sickly yellow vapor from his fingers, eyes, nose, and mouth. He held out his hands and murmured, and the blood on them vanished as if polished away by scrubbing sponges. His robe wrung itself out and dried, and he walked into the night, still chuckling softly.

He made a point of leaving the farmhouse a scene of bloody horror.

"Oh the fools, the fools," he said aloud as he opened his eyes wide, raised a hand, and folded the darkness of the night in on itself, stepping through the space he had bent. Tiny jewel-like points of glowing light—red, green, and dark blue—waited in the darkness beyond. "Fools! They rode away without defending themselves," he said, laughing again.

In the distant village, glowing yellow eyes went dark, blinked, and the possessed villagers passed out *en masse*, falling in heaps on the grass and the mud. This scene played out for the robed and hooded figures occupying the space into which the sorcerer had transported himself. Pairs of red and blue lights that seemed to hover in the air followed the action on the village green, as if a window to the field simply hung before them.

No lights illuminated the place, natural or man-made, except that which emanated from the men within, if men they were. The plain stone walls were tightly and expertly worked and lacked doors or windows; it was a place that only a man or woman who had drunk of the power of sorcery could find.

"What precisely have you achieved, Gethmasanar?" The voice that spoke was a hollow, creaking rasp. "You knocked a village of peasants senseless. Well done. Bhimanzir's apprentice could manage the same with a cudgel." The unblinking, brilliantly blue points of light focused intently on Gethmasanar's yellow eyes, with fingers that leaked the same light interlacing beneath the point of a chin. These seemed to waver and smoke, as though light was not merely projecting from within the body that contained it, but leaking.

A choked, angry sound emanated from Bhimanzir, whose red fingertips drummed on the arm of a chair.

Some of the sneer drained from Gethmasanar. "Watch and learn. He may demonstrate his powers. We wait and watch."

"Should have destroyed him if there is any chance—"

Bhimanzir was instantly cut off by two others—the rasping, nearly empty voice as before, and another, deeper and more resonant, a voice that vibrated between two pitches in a manner impossible for a normal human throat.

All three of the other sorcerers straightaway fell silent when the inhuman voice spoke, and all of them turned their eyes to the hazy, green-rippled outline from whence it issued.

"Silence, Bhimanzir," it thrummed. "You are not given leave to speak. The results of your haruspicy are known to us…" Here the voice paused, but there was no inhalation, no sense of indrawn wind, only a gathering of thoughts. "We do not yet know if he is the threat we have come to destroy. Silence, the rest of you. Silence, and watchfulness."

The room fell utterly silent, save the sound of breathing, a sound that could only accurately be said to emanate from two of the figures within.

* * *

The horses were all lathered by the time they drew to a halt well outside the village. A few distant lights and the suggestion of buildings were visible. All of them were breathing heavy. The horses were tired and still frightened, eyes rolling and ears back.

Idgen Marte was the first to speak. "What the freezing, bleeding Cold was *that?*"

"Sorcery," Torvul answered. It had grown too dark for their expressions to communicate much to each other, but they could imagine the grim, sour cast of his face in the single uttered word. "Sorcery," he repeated with conviction. "I've seen it a time or two."

"What can be done about it?" Allystaire tossed the cudgel back to Torvul and began stroking Ardent's neck with one hand.

"Depends. That many folk under the sway, it's one powerful bastard. Or it's a number of them working together. Neither is good news."

"That did not answer my question, dwarf."

Torvul sighed heavily, and wood clacked against wood as he set his cudgel down in his seat. "No, it didn't. I think you'll mislike the answers."

"Out with it."

"Fine. There isn't much, really. If it's one sorcerer, you can find him and kill him. If it's a gaggle of 'em? Try and lay low till they're gone."

Allystaire snorted. "I have seen sorcery before. It did not look like that."

"What'd it look like then?"

"Fire. Gouts of it. At a battle."

"I can make fire and I can make it look like it's coming from the air," Torvul replied. "Sorcerers don't call fire. Not like you mean. What'd the man doing it look like?"

Allystaire shrugged and slid off his horse, patting its flanks. Idgen Marte clutched her reins and joined him in front of Torvul's wagon. "What you would expect. Older chap. Robes stitched with glyphs and a long rowan wand…"

"Not a sorcerer," Idgen Marte commented, quiet, but insistent. "I saw them, in Keersvast, in the war with the Concordat. The Archipelago was crawling with them then. They don't look like old men, and they don't carry rowan wands."

"She has the right of it," Torvul said, slowly climbing down off the wagon to join them. "What you saw, if he was anything, was a thaumaturgist. Not the same thing."

"Explain the difference, and quickly. We cannot stand around here all night."

Torvul sighed and crossed his thick arms over his barrel chest. "You expect me to condense distinct schools of magical theory into something you can understand?"

Idgen Marte snorted and gave Torvul's forearm a quick slap, her arm an indistinct blur in the darkness. "On with it."

"Fine, fine. What you should do is borrow some of the texts in my library," he said, hooking a thumb over his shoulder at the wagon behind him. "But I'm guessing you can't read dwarfish marks. All right then. Magic, which is an altogether poor term for what we're dealing with here, well, imagine it's a deep underground lake. So deep and so dark that only a few are brave enough, gifted enough, or foolish enough to go seeking it. A thaumaturgist, he travels down to the lake every so often, bottles some of it up, brings it home, and puts it in new vessels. This was your man's wand, d'ya see? A vessel full of the stuff that he could call upon."

"Fine. Thaumaturgists bottle the stuff up in their devices and amulets. What of sorcerers?"

"Sorcerers bathe in the bleeding lake. They live in it, leastways in part. One half of a sorcerer is there, and one half is here, walking around with you and me. And not the better half."

"That kind of power drives a man to madness or to horror or both," Idgen Marte remarked. "In the war down in Keersvast, it chilled my blood to see them at work. Didn't matter what side they were on; I stayed well away from 'em."

"Whether it's the power that makes them what they are, or what they are makes them chase that kind of power, well, that's hard to say. What's certain is they aren't here for any good purpose."

"Why are they here?"

Torvul leaned forward and poked a broad, lightly scarred forefinger against Allystaire's armored chest. "You, it looks like. Probably hired."

"Seems farfetched."

"How many people did we piss off this summer, Allystaire?" Idgen Marte asked him, her voice still carrying a tiny, whispery note of fear.

"Many. But who among them would have the kind of weight to hire anyone with that kind of power?"

"Probably not the Baron of Bend," Idgen Marte said. "The Church of the Sea Dragon, then. Or—"

"I cannot conceive of Lionel Delondeur hiring someone who could or would do that," Allystaire cut in. "He is not a good man, exactly, not nearly the best he could be. Yet there was always something decent in him. Something I felt kinship with, even when we led armies against each other. He wanted the best out of his men, but also the best *for* them."

"A man can want to be loved by his folk and still pay wages to a dungeon full of torturers and a stable full of killers if it means they stay *his* folk," Torvul noted flatly.

"We can sort this out later," Allystaire said, with a note of finality. "We have to go back."

Torvul groaned. "I was afraid you'd say that. Why? We don't know where the sorcerer or sorcerers are, or entirely what they're capable of."

"One sorcerer or many, those people back there are my people. He cannot be far away. Time for both halves of him to drown in that lake you spoke of."

"That was a metaphor," Torvul protested.

"I am not—"

"…a subtle man. Metaphors are probably not beyond him, dwarf, but he mostly ignores 'em." Idgen Marte cut through Allystaire's reply with a smirk.

"Well you're gonna be a dead man if you go charging back there," Torvul spat. "A sorcerer won't stand still while you level your lance and spur your horse, and he won't challenge you to a wrestling match like that gravekling. We already know what he can do to the minds of an entire village; like as not if that sorcerer gets close enough, he'll just set up camp in that thick head of yours and walk you straight off a cliff. Yes, and they can do it, too, if that's how they choose to direct their magic," he finished, raising a hand to forestall Allystaire's protest.

"Then how do we fight them?" Allystaire's hands curled into fists at his sides and he rocked forward on his feet, his body rippling with tension.

"You *don't*," Torvul said, pointedly. "Or you hire another sorcerer to fight him for you."

"Are they all for hire then?"

"Everyone's for hire when you've enough weight behind the offer."

"Well what are they, then? A guild?"

"Nobody really knows, Allystaire," Idgen Marte said quietly. She stood in front of Allystaire and fixed his eyes with hers. "Many words and many pages have been wasted in guessing, but they keep their policy close. Why they've come north to the baronies, I couldn't guess. But Torvul has a point." She laid a hand lightly on his arm. "That village was a trap. We escaped it. Run back into it, with a sorcerer waiting, and you'll die."

"If he was so powerful, how did we escape in the first place? There has to be a reason the trap was constructed in the manner it was," Allystaire said. Suddenly, he shook his head. "It was not meant to kill us."

"And you're the expert on sorcerers now?" Torvul smugly recrossed his arms over his chest.

"Not at all. Ambushes, though? I know something of ambushes If a sorcerer wanted us dead, then…" Allystaire waived a gauntleted hand, searching for a word, "cloud the mind of the innkeep, not the entire village. Let us in, give us a room. Murder us in our beds. Bring down the inn around our ears and burn it. More effective, with less effort. He did not want us dead. Caught, perhaps," he conceded, "but not dead."

Idgen Marte turned toward Torvul. "Now he's the one with the point." She frowned. "Not used to sayin' that."

"Well, go on. You look mighty pleased with yourself, so finish up," Torvul growled.

"It's too dark to see his face from that far," Idgen Marte retorted.

"I can imagine it well enough!"

"If they really wanted us caught, there would be pursuit. Surely he could drive them a half mile or so, based on what you tell me. If they did not want us dead and they did not care much about getting us caught, then they wanted to learn something."

"Such as?"

Allystaire shrugged, the pauldrons of the half-suit of armor he wore clanking softly. "They knew how many we were; the innkeep said as much. What we are capable of, or what we were willing to do, or something none of us can guess. His ambush was too clumsy to be anything but a probe."

"So what could he have learned?" Idgen Marte worried at her bottom lip.

"Whatever he learned, it is not as important as what he is about to learn."

"Stones above," Torvul moaned.

"And that is what?" Idgen Marte tilted her head to one side.

"He will learn that I do not abandon my people. And if he lingers, he will also learn what an angry Goddess has to offer him."

"You're just gonna walk back in there?" Torvul threw up his hands. "Just slit my throat now, be done with it."

"No. Idgen Marte is going to walk back in there. You are going to think of what good you might be with your potions and poisons."

"What makes you sure either of us will do any good?"

"Faith."

* * *

They walked back to the village, leaving the horses lightly picketed in a well-protected strand of trees. Before they had walked away, Allystaire had taken Ardent's head between his hands and spoken directly to his destrier. "Guard. Watch. Wait," he had said. *And felt less silly than I ought to have done*, he thought, as the trio of them crept up on the village.

They did not follow the road into it this time; they crossed over it and marched well out of sight of it while keeping it on their right. Rather than approach the green from its western side, they would approach from the south. Idgen Marte led the way, sword in hand, followed by Torvul, and then Allystaire; the latter received more than one dirty look from the dwarf, who managed to move along a good deal more quietly than Allystaire, with hammer, shield, and half of his plate armor, could manage.

The fact that the paladin could even see the dwarf's face was a minor miracle, in its way; the alchemist had produced a bottle of a potion from his cart, rubbed it in his own eyes first, and then offered it to them without a word of praise for its merits.

Much to his own shock and Torvul's apparent indifference, Allystaire had immediately begun to see as though there were brightest, clearest moonlight; it wasn't as bright as day, but it was a great and welcome improvement.

Waiting for my eyes to start melting, he thought grimly, remembering his previous experience with the dwarf's promises of bottled miracles. Nevertheless, they tromped on until Idgen Marte's hand suddenly raised and stopped them; then she skittered away, sword held low at her side.

Potion or no potion, she disappeared from his vision almost as soon as she stepped away. *Shadow of the Goddess,* he thought approvingly, smiling just a little. The thought that she might walk into a scene of carnage quickly settled his mouth back into its familiar thin line.

Just as quickly as she was gone, even before Torvul had a chance to wax chatty, she returned, sword sheathed. "Come and see. No need for quiet, I think."

Torvul let his crossbow dangle against his chest from the strap worn over his shoulder. Allystaire kept his hammer in his hand, however, until he walked the few yards onto the southern edge of the green and moved quickly past the buildings bordering it.

Prone and limp, the forms of the villagers that had attacked them a turn ago lay scattered haphazardly. Allystaire immediately slung his hammer and trotted to the nearest one, pulling off his leather gauntlets as he went and stuffing them into his belt. He slid to his knees at the side of the nearest form, a peasant woman, still young, with long, loose dark hair, robed and dressed for bed, it appeared. He pressed his left hand to the side of her neck and let his eyes drift lightly closed. As he moved, he silently mouthed a quick litany: *Please, Mother, please Goddess, please do not let them be dead.*

As soon as he reached the woman, he felt the faint fluttering of her pulse, not so much with his fingertips as with some sense that lived and moved within him, in his mind and body. A sense of the woman he touched, of her frailties relative to him or to Idgen Marte, of the thousands of ways she might be hurt.

And with that sense came a kind of compassion that, if it was not without pity, was also not without admiration for being willing to live the life she faced. Somehow, with that sense, he guided just a touch of energy into her, just a fraction of life, and she sat bolt upright in his arms, gasping, mouth wide in horror.

"Still here, still here," she moaned, "still watching! Still the blood and the awful yellow fire!" Her body shook and she tried to scramble away from Allystaire in fear, beginning a keening wail, her hands bunching into fists and striking uselessly, weakly at his armored chest.

Idgen Marte had flown to his side and, knowing well enough what he could and couldn't do for the woman, he let go and scrambled aside. The tall warrior gently placed a hand upon the village woman's head and spoke in hushed, soothing tones that Allystaire could not quite catch. The woman's eyes, wide and rolling in fear, suddenly slid nearly closed and she slumped against Idgen Marte, though she did not fall back into a faint.

"Still watching," she murmured again quietly, a muted sob. "Awful yellow eyes. Watching. There." The woman pointed, and all three of them turned their faces to the direction she pointed.

Had it not been for Torvul's potion, none of them would have seen it; a patch, less than a pace on any side, of darker darkness floated in the air, hidden by night's own shadows. But they did see it, and all three of them stood at once, Idgen Marte gently setting the woman down, and all three reached for weapons.

Idgen Marte's sword cleared its sheath first; Torvul's crossbow was suddenly leveled and bolted, and Allystaire's hands filled with hammer and shield. He opened his mouth and shouted, "You craven. If hiding behind these folk have done them any lasting harm, then enjoy the last days of life your cowardice has bought. We do not fear you. The Mother does not fear you."

"And we will find you," Idgen Marte added, her voice little more than a steely hiss.

* * *

When the half-armored man, the dwarf, and the Concordat woman suddenly stood and stared straight into their scrying portal, the sorcerers, gathered in their dark spirit-room continents away, showed no signs of concern.

But when the paladin spoke, suddenly he was not a man half-armored in steel and leather and holding a heavy but plain maul; the hammer in his hand glowed with a light like the noonday sun and its terrible brightness was thrown back at them by the mirror-bright armor that he wore. The woman, too, had changed, and in fact they could not see her except as an outline, a hazy shadow thrown by the brightness of the man's armor. The vision lasted but an instant, but the overwhelming brightness of it sent each of them reeling, and their scrying view seemed focused on the surface of the sun itself.

The portal shut off with a wave of bilious, pulsing green fingertips.

"That was unexpected," the lead sorcerer said in his dual-pitched voice.

"They are dangerous. I see Bhimanzir's point, now." This from the sorcerer who leaked blue energy, his own voice half-empty, hollow. "This human ought to be destroyed."

"Better he were brought to heel. Isolated. Captured, studied. If there is power there, its source must be understood." This from the voice to which they all hearkened.

"He claims it is a goddess, Eldest." This, from Gethmasanar. "A new deity. Or an old one."

"Nonsense" warred with "Ridiculous", but as soon as the voice that was almost two voices spoke, the other three hushed and listened.

"Gods, as these people would have them, do not exist. And what deities there *are* do not grant such power as that. Perhaps in his native ignorance, he thinks he has spoken with some deity. We will know better when Bhimanzir has done his work." The green eyes flitted to focus on the shadow that had been silent since his earlier chastisement. "Return to your baron. Counsel him. Compel him if you must; be certain to turn him against this man. Under no circumstances shall he be allowed to gain a refuge or accrue a following to his novel superstition. Be vigilant; watch and wait to see what his motives and means are."

"If I may," Bhimanzir said, and waited for the other sorcerer to incline his head in permission, "I think it likely that his motives are precisely what he says they are."

"Then it should be no great difficulty to outmaneuver him."

Bhimanzir lowered his head. "As you say, Eldest," he said through gritted teeth.

"Surely others will move against him. Perhaps we can use them as well. And Bhimanzir? If your apprentice shows no command of his will, then soon it will be time to make such use of him as you can."

Gethmasanar broke in angrily. "No. I tell you, I have felt the brush of his will. If he can be made to see, to understand. There is a pathway to power in that boy that could burn us to a cinder. Grind us to dust. Reduce our minds to puppets. Even yours. He must be counted among The Knowing."

Slowly, the deep and poisonous green smoke that filled the very wide eye-sockets of the Eldest moved slowly through the darkness till they focused upon Gethmasanar, who met the gaze steadily. "Very well," the sorcerer thrummed. "Another season, perhaps. Now, Bhimanzir, go."

The sorcerer stood, feeling the shame and the envy of being the least of the gathered powers. His red-glowing fingers curled into fists as he stepped into darkness and disappeared.

* * *

The night air was cool, but as it went on, Allystaire began to sweat. He'd set down his shield and unbuckled his sheathed sword from his back, but the hammer still rode on his hip and his shoulders ached with the weight of his armor. There had been no indication that the affected villagers were likely to wake up on their own, but neither was there any sign of them getting worse, so in the end there was nothing for it but for him and Idgen Marte to move among them one by one.

A half dozen or so slightly dazed peasants already sat at one corner of the green under Torvul's nervous watch. Allystaire knelt at the side of a child whose form had been buried beneath two larger forms; judging by the red hair the child and the woman shared, he thought it reasonable to assume them mother and son.

His fingers felt for the pulse. It was there, but faint, and once again, with something that was slowly becoming practiced ease, he extended his inner sense into the child's body and touched it, very lightly, with a flicker of the Mother's radiance. The boy breathed in sharply, his eyes fluttered, and, his mouth opened in a wordless cry. Idgen Marte was ready and reached for the boy, quieting his mind and returning him to calm with her own Gifts. She helped the boy to his feet and began to walk him over to Torvul, whose face was set in a grimace of displeasure. The two exchanged words Allystaire couldn't hear.

He stood and stretched his back, covering a yawn with the back of a fist, and was still yawning when Idgen Marte approached him. "Dwarf says he doesn't like how exposed we are out here in the middle of a field."

"Nor do I. Shame these villagers lacked the decency and foresight to be ensorcelled and then dumped in the middle of a defensible position, eh?" He shook his head to clear the weariness and said, "Let us push on while he grumbles; he excels at it, after all."

"His potion is still working and my eyes haven't grown a cataract yet. Give him credit for that."

"I will—when I do not think it will start him reaching for our purse." Allystaire bent and began carefully to feel along the neck of the next prone villager, a large man, thick-necked and broad-shouldered, who needed turning over. He was a dead weight, and of a size with the paladin himself.

Idgen Marte snorted and squatted next to him. "He could reach for our purse all he likes; there's hardly anything keeping its sides apart."

"I have some gemmary put away."

"What is it with you and jewels?"

Allystaire ignored her question and pushed a bit of the Mother's power into the man's body, through his pulse, and the man came awake with wild, angry swings of his tree-trunk arms that sent the both of them sprawling onto their backs and scrambling away. The man roared to his feet and then stared, blinking at them.

"Neither of you've got yellow eyes," he shouted, curling his fists and dropping into, Allystaire noted, a competent boxer's stance. "Are ya the man's servants? Stand to and answer me!"

"Had to be the blacksmith'd wake up angry," Idgen Marte muttered as she rolled to her feet, holding her hands out, palms up.

Allystaire was slower to get up, but when he reached his feet, he did the same. "We are here to help, goodman smith," he said, his voice heavy with fatigue. "If the man with the yellow eyes is your enemy, then he is ours as well."

The man who, as far as Allystaire could tell, was staring into the darkness at two shadowy, threatening figures, wavered, but did not drop his hands. *Don't make me have to punch it out with you in the dark and the mud*, Allystaire thought wearily.

"That bastard said he was our friend too and the next thing he's…he's in my head…Fortune, what was he?" The man spat and shook, furious and terrified.

"He was in your head, aye, and now he's gone," Idgen Marte said matter-of-factly. "And if we wanted to hurt you, or rob you, why bother to wake you?"

"Look to the southwest corner of the green, goodman," Allystaire said. "A dwarf waits there, watching over such of your villagers as we have awoken. See that dim lantern light?" Allystaire turned and gave the dwarf a wave, and Torvul, his vision similarly brightened with drops of his own potion, lifted a dim green lamp and waved it; the blacksmith saw it, and his hands dropped to his sides, but he didn't yet move.

"The dwarf could use your help," Idgen Marte said, "getting folk settled. They're calm, but not all awake. Give us your patience and all will be explained, I promise." She waited a moment, then added, "And he's got dwarfish spirits; looks as though a tot'll do you good, eh?"

The promise of spirits got the blacksmith in motion and heading toward the distant twinkle of Torvul's tiny green-tinted lamp. "Dwarfish whiskey's good then?" he asked as he passed. Allystaire and Idgen Marte both mumbled their assurances, and the man sauntered off to join the dwarf.

* * *

The village, it turned out, was called Hilgensdale, and the beer was indeed fairly drinkable, as Idgen Marte and Allystaire sat in its inn, exhausted, with the full light of early morning filtering through its exposed windows, the glass having been shattered, or oilskin torn, when ensorcelled townfolk had crawled through them. It had taken most of the night and a good deal of energy to get the village back on its feet, and with the help of Torvul and the blacksmith, who turned out to be called Haight, those who'd fallen lifeless upon the green had all gotten back on their feet and off to beds.

Torvul had insisted upon sleeping in his own bed in the back of his wagon, while Allystaire and Idgen Marte had both gotten such sleep as they could, in spare rooms on the inn's second floor. Both found themselves awake and aware, if barely, after only a few turns.

"Are we doomed to be up with every dawn," Idgen Marte wondered aloud, as she filled their second mugs from a jar of beer left upon the table. "Because I can't think of too many worse punishments."

Allystaire thought a moment before answering, arms crossed over his chest. "It is hardly dawn. And surely we will get none of Her work done by having a lie-in."

Idgen Marte punched his forearm lightly. "Might get it done better if we were rested."

Allystaire snorted and was about to reply when the door swung open and Torvul stomped in, carrying a mug that trailed steam and the strong scent of robust tea. "So," the dwarf grumbled, "how long are we going to be staying in this dungheap before pushing on to Londray?"

"Mind your manners, alchemist," Allystaire snapped. "The villagers are likely to be up and about any moment."

Torvul took a healthy swig from his mug, heedless of its heat. "I could talk any of the townfolk into seeing it a compliment," he noted at length. "And some of 'em are already up. I saw some dust trails, off in the distance. Today's apparently a market day, so every turnip and mangel grubber'll be coming in. Good day to get out quietly in the hubbub."

"Better day for you to sell some spirits, mend some pots, sharpen knives and the like," Idgen Marte pointed out. "All those beets'll be silver in some farmer's palm soon."

"Surely even a mangel-farmer has use for some of my tinctures, my elixirs and potions…"

"I do not even know what a mangel is," Allystaire said, standing up slowly, stiffly, then holding out a warning hand, first finger extended, to both Idgen Marte and Torvul. "Nor do I wish to know. Nor do I wish to see you selling any of your poisons here today."

Torvul's free hand pressed to his chest in an aggrieved, dramatic pose. "Poisons? Why, Sir Allystaire, my life's work, reduced so callously. I don't recall poisoning your eyes last night."

"So that makes one, of two attempts, that worked. Bad odds for folk who cannot afford the loss. Start hawking your medicines, dwarf, and I will tell them all what happened in Grenthorpe."

Torvul was about to respond when a hue and cry rose in the green outside; a man, tall and lean and dressed in plain wool, came running onto the churned grass and stopped, yelling breathlessly. "Murder! Murder at Edvar's farm! Please, anyone. Murder!"

Torvul quickly gulped the rest of his tea and calmly hung the mug from one of the many wire loops on his jerkin, while Allystaire and Idgen Marte blew past him for the door, the woman outpacing the knight by several steps.

He shook his head and slowly turned to follow them, muttering to himself, "Never going to make color or weight following this pair, you know. Time to get back on the road, right?" His tone was almost imploring, but he didn't answer himself, only sighed and trotted after them on his shorter, stouter legs.

CHAPTER 34

Assassin

The interior of the cottage was a scene of slaughter, with bodies and pieces of bodies strewn about the flag-stoned floor, the table, and the hearth; pools and stains of blood darkened every surface, its heavy copper stink unavoidable.

"I'm their hired man, m'lord," the tall and skinny peasant man was explaining to Allystaire, who stood in the midst of the carnage, jaw taut and nostrils flared. "Came at dawn to help them load and drive for the market today. Cuisin's m'name. Edvar were a good man, m'lord, with no enemies." Cuisin stood pale and wide-eyed outside the door, explaining everything in a shocked rush.

"Torvul," Allystaire asked, his voice so calm and so even that he frightened even himself. "Sorcery?"

"Aye," the dwarf replied, and Idgen Marte nodded her head in assent.

"Why?"

The dwarf cleared his throat, then spoke, breathing carefully through his mouth. "Power his spells, my guess. Lot of folk for him to control…"

"So they were just wood on the fire, so to speak?"

"The analogy's not perfect, but you've the gist."

Allystaire nodded faintly. "How do we find him?"

"Now, you've got to understand—" Torvul began in a conciliating tone.

"Understand this," Allystaire interrupted calmly, even as his hands curled into fists and his blood pounded in his head. "This sorcerer was here for me. For us. Our Gifts. Our power." he said, indicating Idgen Marte with a wave of a hand. "I mean him to have it. Every freezing bit. And before I am done he will know the fear these folk have endured, I promise. I swear it on the Mother's Gifts to me."

Allystaire's vow sent a charge rippling across his own skin, and he knew instantly that Idgen Marte felt it as well. It was if a chime played faintly and distantly, yet he was able to hear it and knew that it signaled something.

Torvul started slightly, throwing a look back over his shoulder at Cuisin's pale face, then spat to the ground and spoke without looking at Allystaire or Idgen Marte. "You're a fool to swear an oath like that. Whatever power you've got, it'll not stand to such as him."

"Cease your nattering, dwarf." Allystaire strode out of the house, careful not to disturb any of the ghoulish remains. "In this matter, be with me, be in my way, be out of it—but whatever you choose, *be silent*."

Allystaire deliberately uncurled his fists, but he loomed over the dwarf as if daring him to speak again. Then he turned his eyes toward Cuisin and said, "If you can tell me where in the house they kept bedding, blankets, and such, well, we can use them. And we will need shovels, mattocks, and the like later today."

"Beggin' yer pardon, m'lord, but who are ya?"

"I know it is all a bit of a blur, goodman, but we are here to help," Allystaire replied, as he walked back into the morning sunlight with the lanky farmhand. "My name is Allystaire," he began, but his words were cut off by a rush of air and a hard thunk.

Suddenly Cuisin collapsed in a heap, clutching at the fletchings that sprouted from the meat of his thigh.

Allystaire dropped to one knee beside the man, settling his left hand over the wound. He began searching for the special connection the Goddess's Gift had taught him to seek. He felt the man's spirit, terrified at the mutilation he'd discovered, doubly so at the wound he'd taken. Allystaire reached into the well of power the Goddess had granted him and started to draw Her healing from it like water, to pour it over the wound.

The healing essence seemed to sizzle like water thrown on a grease fire. Something foul rose up and pushed it back at him. He knew he could heal the wound itself, draw the bolt, but there was something wrong in the wound, something that had been carried by the bolt. Something Her Gift would not touch.

"Poison," Allystaire suddenly yelled. He turned to where Idgen Marte and Torvul had come spilling out of the doorway. "Alchemist! What can you do for a man that's been poisoned?"

The dwarf had unlimbered his crossbow and dropped to a knee, scanning the distant rise of hill and trees beyond. Idgen Marte's sword was in her hand before the whisper of her draw reached Allystaire's ears.

Allystaire lifted his hand, motioning toward the treeline. "It must have come," he started to yell, when once again the air was sliced by a bolt.

His eyes widened in shock as he saw it pierce his left arm between the elbow and wrist. Its barbed, bloodstained end protruded an inch past his skin.

His mouth dropped open and his face blanched, and he held his hand up to his eyes, staring in disbelief as the blood began to pour from the wound. The shock didn't last, though, for soon he was dropping to the ground and curling around the wound. *Got to get that out,* he was thinking. *Clean through the muscle, I think. Good. That's good. Not in the bone.*

Idgen Marte and Torvul exploded into action around him. Idgen Marte leapt to his left, putting herself between him and the direction of the bolt, her sword held in a crosswise guard. The dwarf, meanwhile, rushed to Allystaire's back and seized the shield that was hung there by a strap. Torvul slid a knife from one of his sleeves and he sawed quickly through the leather.

Idgen Marte's feet shifted and her wrists tensed, then flicked, moving faster than the eye could follow, and there was a clang. A third bolt dropped to the ground a few feet away, deflected by her lightning-quick sword.

"Heal yourself, Allystaire," she half-yelled. "Do it!"

Not even sure if I can, Allystaire was thinking, but then he tried to flex his wrist so that he might touch his fingertips to his palm, gritting his teeth against the expectation of pain, and found himself surprised that there was no pain.

But he could not move his hand.

He looked down at his arm; a purple-black cloud moved beneath his skin, and then his entire arm went limp. He heard Torvul shouting at Idgen Marte, felt the strap that kept his shield across his back give way, and the dwarf leapt in front of him, crouching beneath the shield and holding it across both of them.

"Go! Go! Find the archer! I'll deal with this," the dwarf shouted, and Allystaire looked up and saw Idgen Marte disappear in a bound. A dim shape flitted in his sight under the eaves of an outbuilding built into the side of a small hill on the farm, then again at a stand of trees.

"Cuisin," Allystaire managed to say, though he felt his tongue growing thick and his head swimming. "Torvul…" He swallowed hard, swayed on his knees, felt the dwarf's free hand seize the collar of his shirt and hold him in place. "Got to help him. Help Cuisin first."

"You fall over boy, I can't pick you up. Stay awake." Torvul's hand darted away from his collar and slapped him lightly across one cheek.

"P—poisoned…Torvul." Allystaire used his right hand to lift up the dead-weight that was his left, showing the dwarf the wound, the impossibly-fast moving blot beneath his skin. The blood flow was nearly stopped around the bolt. "Cannot heal him."

The dwarf's eyes widened and he swallowed hard. "Whore's Kiss," he breathed. "Priceless stuff, that," but even as he said it, his hand had let go of Allystaire's collar and was fumbling among his pouches. "I don't…my potions haven't…"

"Have to," Allystaire mumbled, falling forward against Torvul's shoulder, the dwarf grunting under his weight but managing to hold him up with one side of his body while continuing to rummage. "Have to, Torvul," Allystaire muttered again, his eyes drooping and the flesh of his hand turning a vile purple.

"'It's a tough poison, lad. I've got…" The dwarf plucked from his pouches three small bottles and one wax-besmeared jar full of tiny, dried red filaments. "I—this might be beyond my art now.. And I haven't enough for…" he added almost pitiably, his eyes flitting toward Cuisin, who lay crumpled on the ground a few paces away.

* * *

Idgen Marte ran as fast as the Goddess's Gifts would carry her, faster than anyone who didn't know how to look could possibly have seen. She moved from shadow to shadow at the speed of her own thoughts, and a wood, even a small wood, casts myriad shadows.

She moved in a circle around the clumps of trees, darting from the shade of one to another in a blur. The outline of the swordswoman would appear and then vanish, her passage marked by the puff of yellowing leaves pulled from their branches by the force of her advance. She remained in each spot just long enough to orient herself, then darted to another shadow.

Eventually her outline must've made a tempting enough target, for suddenly the solid sound of a crossbow discharging rang out, followed straightaway by a shattering of bark as the bolt skidded across a trunk. Idgen Marte paused, her right hand still holding her sword, but her left had darted to the back of her belt and produced a compact knife, the tip of the blade held between her first finger and her thumb. Her arm, straight as a board, cocked back and then came down; the blade left her hands, and she grimaced in an angry satisfaction when she heard a muffled grunt as the blade struck home.

Then she was under the tree she had thrown toward. The bowman, stretched out across a limb above, scarcely had time to register her presence when, with both feet and one hand, she bounded up the limbs until she reached him and launched a sharp kick to his face. He tumbled out of the tree to the ground, his bow clattering away, and she dropped lithely from the trunk, rolling on one shoulder to break the fall.

She came up on her feet, and the sword whipped to the edge of the man's neck as he was just starting to roll over and reach for the thick-bladed shortsword on his belt. Her knife protruded from one of his shoulders, and she placed the tip of one boot upon the hilt and pressed lightly.

"Come with me peacefully, answer every question put you, and you'll get a clean death, at least. Touch one finger to that hilt and I'll see how long it takes me to make my knife and my sword meet in the middle." To add weight to her claim she leaned forward ever so slightly on the knife's hilt, and the man groaned in pain and threw his arms to the sides.

"I yield," he moaned. "Not that it'll do y'any good. Whore's Kiss'll have done its work by now."

Idgen Marte's eyes widened, and she rammed her foot down on knife-hilt until the sole of her boot pressed against his chest. He screamed and tried to roll away as the knife plunged into his shoulder. "You have a purgative, or, or an answer for it?"

The man's face blanched beneath its layer of dark stubble and sweat and he shook his head side to side. "No. I was ordered not to carry one."

Idgen Marte leaned down over him, bending her arm at the elbow so that her sword still lay lightly across his neck. "By who? Remember what I said about answering questions."

CHAPTER 35

Power, of a Kind

Torvul set down the bottles he'd pulled from his pouches, turned and seized the rim of the shield in both hands and pressed it into the dirt, silently thanking the rain that had softened it. With the shield standing on its own and giving the slumped over Allystaire some cover, Torvul rose from his knees into a deep squat.

His old knees protested, and he grimaced in pain as, hunched over, he walked to Cuisin's side, grabbed his collar, and dragged him over to lie next to Allystaire beneath whatever cover the paladin's shield offered.

When Torvul felt the shield bump against his back he slumped back to his knees and reached for his bottles, palming them all in one huge, long-fingered hand. He got one uncorked, his hands moving steady and true, and poured it over Allystaire's wound. The flesh sizzled where the yellowish liquid met his blood, and the paladin let out a low moan.

"Him first," he repeated, his words mumbled into the dwarf's leather-clad shoulder. "Potion worked last night," he mouthed. "Faith, Torvul," he groaned out. "Faith."

With a deep sigh, the dwarf slipped his sleeve-knife back into one hand and quickly cut away the homespun trews Cuisin wore, exposing his wound. While the farmhand bled freely, and the wound in his leg was angry and raw, there was no matching cloud of purple moving beneath the skin. The scent that rose from it, reminiscent of berry-wine gone to vinegar and then something worse, told Torvul what he needed to know.

"Moon Shadow's Dust," the dwarf muttered aloud. Then, suddenly frowning, "Ah, freeze—"

Cuisin began to spasm, his arms and legs punching and kicking forcefully at the air. Torvul curled instinctively around the bottles he held and let Allystaire slide to the ground. He fumbled in his palm, came out with a blue cut-glass bottle, then threw himself onto the farmhand's thrashing chest and managed to wedge his elbow under the man's chin, pinning his head to the ground.

With Cuisin still spasming below him, Torvul pulled out the bottle's stopper with his teeth and upended it into the man's open mouth. Then he jumped back, knocking the shield askew in the process.

Cuisin's spasms slowed and slowed until they were simply twitches rippling down his limbs, and Torvul turned his attention back to the more gravely poisoned Allystaire.

His eyes had closed and his cheeks grown even paler; flecks of spit gathered in the corners of his mouth as he mumbled incomprehensibly into the ground. Torvul had a job of hauling the heavy, armored man back up to lean him against his chest.

He began a steady stream of dwarfish cursing, all thick guttural sounds crashing into and rolling over one another, and eyed the hissing steam that had risen from Allystaire's wound where he had poured the first potion over it. The purple stain, lurking under the paladin's muscled, bristly-haired forearm like a brooding sea monster, now extended almost from elbow to wrist.

Torvul took a deep breath and said, "Sorry lad. This'll hurt. If it works. Even if it doesn't." He seized Allystaire's wrist in one hand and lifted his arm, using the other to push the bolt forward into the wound. Allystaire moaned and his body shook violently, almost knocking the dwarf to his haunches. When enough of the shaft was clear, Torvul wrapped one hand around the base of it, then the other atop the first, careful to keep his hand clear of the bloody steel tip, then clenched his teeth and began to pull his hands in opposite directions.

Dense muscles rippled along the dwarf's thick arms and the bolt head snapped; Torvul left the top lying at his feet, then reached for the fletchings and pulled it free. Blood glugged from the wound, but not much. The Whore's Kiss was squeezing shut the veins and deadening the muscles, and Torvul knew that even on his greatest day as an alchemist, with his finest equipment in a workshop of clean marble and silver instruments, he might not have been able to do this.

Yet he pushed aside the thought and tried to replace it; *Faith*, he thought. *The lad's got it in me or he wouldn't have let me hang about. Time t'stop lying to myself about what he is. Faith—at least in him, if naught else.*

He added aloud, "Lady or Mother or Goddess, if you're real, which I have my doubts on, and you've taken a shine to this man, mayhap you could do him a favor now, eh?"

Torvul selected the third jar. The oldest one he carried, the one he wasn't sure why he still kept. Behind its clouded glass and beneath its ancient, crumbling cork, it was hard to say what it contained. It appeared to be a small pile of reddish-brown dirt.

He tried to unstopper the jar, but couldn't, so he bent down, seized a rock, and chipped at the top until it cracked and broke free. He upended the bottle into his other palm and stared hard at it.

Dirt, dark red and smelling of mold, settled coldly in his palm. He narrowed his dark, deepset eyes, hunting for something amidst its granules and clumps. Using the tip of one finger, he stirred it around until the loosely packed earth revealed a half-dozen tiny filaments, curled and withered and brown.

Torvul closed his eyes and began to sing.

The song was not in a language Allystaire or Cuisin or Idgen Marte or anyone in the village would've known. It was the same low-pitched and guttural tongue the alchemist had cursed in just moments ago, but no one would've mistaken this song for something vulgar. The first few words were halting, his voice stilted and unused to it. Then he took in a deep breath and tried with renewed vigor. The song flowed like water over stone, the words forming an unbroken line of sound, the dwarf's voice a low and rumbling and not unpleasing bass.

His singing voice could've filled the hall of the largest castle Allystaire had ever known. Even deep in the torture of the poison coursing through him, the paladin's eyes flickered and his head lifted feebly, so powerful was the call of the dwarf's song.

Torvul's eyes remained shut, but the song grew steadier, stronger, as something began to stir within the dirt on his palm.

Slowly, the tiny filaments uncurled and lengthened. As they grew, their color began to shift from a dark and dry brown to a vivid red. They lightened to orange, then finally to a delicate, glinting gold.

Torvul carefully plucked one filament with two fingers, grimacing as he did, his song drawing to a close. *Ought to be plucked from crystal bottles with pure silver tweezers*, the alchemist thought, as he carefully lifted the tiny golden thread to Allystaire's wound.

As if drawn to the wound and the poison within, the shining fiber suddenly straightened, pulling Torvul's hand to the wound. He let it go, and it flew straight into the wound, dissolving as soon as it touched the paladin's skin.

He slowed his song, coughing a bit for breath, careful to angle his face away from the hand on which he still held a few precious golden threads.

"Could be the last dwarfish medicine in all the world, lad," the alchemist croaked, his voice gone a bit hollow. "It had better work."

With his free hand, Torvul pulled a silver flask free from a pouch on his belt, unscrewing it with the finger and thumb of the same hand he held it in. He lifted it to his own lips and took a quick swig, then poured a measure of it over both wounds.

After a faint hissing, another voice, hoarse and weak, suddenly intruded on the dwarf's thoughts.

"Last in the world, eh? Must have been worth…worth a fortune." Torvul's eyes lifted sharply from the wound and met Allystaire's hard blue eyes, bloodshot and wearied, but alive and aware.

Torvul's hand immediately shot out and grasped Allystaire's left wrist. The paladin winced sharply, groaning as the dwarf, fingers pressing none too gently, lifted his arm up to eye level. The cloud of purple beneath his skin was visibly retreating. Torvul bent even closer and sniffed carefully.

He released Allystaire's hand more gently and sat back on his haunches, practically collapsing, and lifted his dark, deepset eyes, mystification quickly overcome by joy.

"Well I'll be dipped in shit," Torvul said, dazed. "It worked."

"What worked?" Allystaire fell, slumping forward over his legs, holding his left arm out awkwardly. Suddenly, he forced himself back up on his knees. "Cuisin? Where is—"

"Already dealing with him," Torvul said. Leaning over the lanky farmhand's outstretched leg, carefully slid another tiny gleaming thread into the poisoned wound. "His wasn't quite as critical as yours. The poison, anyway. I haven't done for his bolt yet but I'd like some help with that."

"I can handle it once I have my arm back," Allystaire croaked.

"And as to your first question," the dwarf grunted, pushing himself cautiously back to his feet, "this." He held out his carefully cupped hand. "This is what worked. The *hluriankathaum*. Ah, in your tongue: the sovereign antidote, proof against all poisons, infections, and rot." He stared in wonderment at his palm for a moment, then said, "Ask me later, I'll explain more."

The dwarf carefully pulled free one of the last few bottles that remained pouched on his jerkin, flicked it open, poured out its contents, and delicately slid the remaining few filaments into the emptied bottle, along with the few grainy clumps of dirt that had clung to his palm during the healing. "Never thought t'see its like again," he muttered. He carefully secreted the bottle.

Meanwhile, Cuisin had sat up, hands reaching for the wound on his leg. Torvul moved to his side, placed his huge hands on the man's chest, and guided him back toward the ground. The farmhand made no fight of it. "I dosed him pretty well for the pain and constricted the bleeding. He won't know for a turn or two that he's got a bolt in his leg."

"What was done to us?"

"You were poisoned." Torvul regained his feet, bent down and gingerly retrieved the top half of the bolt he'd snapped off, holding its broken shaft by thumb and forefinger. He raised it—beneath the blood, the barbed steel head bore a veneer of thin but sticky blue liquid. "Whore's Kiss, we call it in the trade. A right nasty mixture of things, expensive, known to few, and not, to your luck, an instant killer. A paralytic. He," the dwarf pointed, to the dazed Cuisin, "was shot with Moon Shadow's Dust. Causes strong and violent convulsions. An odd combination. Our man has exotic tastes and deep pockets."

Allystaire sat absorbing the information while forcing himself to look at his blood-smeared wound. *Not the first time you've been shot, old man*, he thought, but there was something disconcerting about the lingering weakness in his hand. He could move his fingers again, lightly, but trying to curl his arm resulted in a stab of pain.

"Bolt missed the bones, I think, or nicked them lightly. Fortune knows how." Torvul carefully toed away a divot of sod, bent down, and began rubbing the head of the bolt into the dirt. "Can't burn this; smoke'll kill you faster than any other way." Then he turned and looked toward the slight rise into the woods where Idgen Marte had disappeared. "She must've found the bowman."

"She did. She is on her way back." Allystaire's voice, deprived of its usual potency, still came out in a kind of croak. *How do I know that exactly? Question for another day.*

As if cued, Idgen Marte appeared, leading the would-be assassin with her sword point resting at the precise juncture of his skull and his neck. In her other hand she gingerly carried, by the stock, the crossbow that had fallen from his hands when she'd kicked him clear of the tree.

He was a compact man, neither small nor large but with an easy grace and an apparent vitality. His long hair was tied in a neat queue and his face covered by a few days' worth of stubble. His deceptively simple-looking clothing was colored grey and dark green and would pass, from a distance, as the raiment of a forester. Up close, it was too well-tailored, with hints of silk beneath the cuffs. The knee-high boots were made of supple leather that few lacking a title could afford.

The corner of his quilted jacket was torn and bloody, where Idgen Marte's throwing knife had wounded him, and where it was still buried.

Allystaire forced himself unsteadily to his feet. *You've lost more blood than this in a tourney joust,* he thought, and rebuked himself into putting some strength in his knees. He caught Idgen Marte's face before she composed it into her usual smirk; was that a flash of fear he had seen? *Not likely.* He cleared his throat as he sought what to say, but his thoughts were driven away by Torvul's sudden yelling.

"Where did you get *that*?" He pointed at the crossbow Idgen Marte carried in her left hand. He rushed to her side and seized the weapon, holding it up to inspect. It was long and slim; the stock was a dark varnished wood, with a thin, twisting spiral for the hand and wrist to slip through and against which the arm would brace. It looked like a branch that a vine had grown into, then been cut out of by a patient woodcarver. The top of it bore a number of small, hinged pieces, not unlike Torvul's own bow.

"I bought it," the bowman said. "From one of your kinsmen, no doubt. All of you link-grubbing dwarfs are kin, right?"

Torvul swung his dangerously glittering eyes from bow to bowman. "These aren't sold. Not ever. Not to…" Here he paused and looked from Allystaire to Idgen Marte and then back to the man. "Not to such as you."

"We can deal with that later." Idgen Marte drove her boot straight into the back of the assassin's knee, and he fell roughly to the ground, crying out as he threw out his wounded arm to cushion his fall. "We need to know who hired him."

"No more of that," Allystaire said, in as sharp a tone of command as he could muster. *Voice is still plenty sharp,* he assured himself, and indeed, Idgen Marte flushed slightly but didn't respond. He could feel her roiling anger, see the tension in her limbs, the unusually tight grip on her sword hilt.

He walked up close to the prisoner, taking him in, sizing up his green eyes and the defiant set of his jaw. He seized the man's chin, but the assassin tore free of his grip with a sharp tug of his thickly muscled neck. Allystaire reached out again, and the man suddenly cursed, his composure shattering in a rush of anger.

"I've been told what you do, sorcerer. I won't give in to it. My mind is my own! I'll not have it torn open for you to paw through!"

Allystaire's eyes rolled lightly, and he suddenly wrapped his right hand firmly around the man's neck. "I do not care what you have been told, what you want, or what you think about the sovereignty of your mind. If what they told you is that I will drag the truth from you and that I may hang you for being what you are, well, they were not wrong. Now then, what is your name?"

Allystaire tightened the grip of his fingers, though he was careful not to choke the man. He narrowed his eyes and directed his senses from his mind, through his hand, and into an awareness of the other man—it was like and yet unlike the times he had healed wounds. He gained a fuller awareness of the man, felt the pain that pulsed in his shoulder, the knife that still lodged there, the other smaller injuries he'd sustained in falling out of the tree, and the well-concealed fear that made his heart beat just a bit faster than it should.

"Dunlir." The man swallowed dryly, his throat moving against Allystaire's palm.

"All right, Dunlir, why poison me?"

"Specific orders: Whore's Kiss, and it had to be in your left arm."

"That answers how, not why. Who gave those orders to you? Who hired you and why?" Allystaire felt a resistance beginning to build against his questions, and Dunlir's eyes shut tightly, his teeth ground together, and his lips began to turn white. Allystaire concentrated more intently, his owns eyes screwing shut, pressing his mind harder against the assassin's.

"Is...Ismaurgh. Man I've known a long time. Said your left arm needed the poison. That was key. Without it, no chance."

Allystaire's eyes flew open when Dunlir answered him, and he looked to Idgen Marte, who was as shocked as he was, and as frightened. *Someone knows too much about the Mother's Gifts*, he thought. *And has thought of how to counter them.*

"Who is this Ismaurgh? Who employs him?"

Suddenly the resistance became a wall that shot up so quickly in front of Allystaire that he had no time to react. Dunlir began thrashing violently, foam flecking the corners of his mouth, and Allystaire stumbled away. He quickly recovered and wrapped his hand back around the thrashing man's throat, but Dunlir had lost all sense of himself and fallen to the ground. Allystaire fell roughly onto one knee beside him. Before even asking a question, there was the sense of some huge, powerful will not only resisting him, but actively pushing back against his queries.

Idgen Marte rushed to the thrashing man's other side and laid her hands upon him, trying to calm him, but to no effect; he thrashed and flopped like a fish pulled onto a dock. Allystaire lifted his still weak left arm and laid it upon Dunlir, reaching out for whatever injury was at fault, but found nothing.

"It is in his mind!" Idgen Marte shouted, as a stream of foam-flecked gibberish began to issue from Dunlir's mouth, his face darkening to a deep purple, and once again she reached for him; Allystaire resorted to simply pressing against the man, laying his hands on Dunlir's arms and pinning them to the ground.

Idgen Marte's eyes closed, and Allystaire could feel her reaching out and suddenly being swatted away like an insect. Her eyes rolled beneath their lids and she crumpled to the ground. The thrashing assassin forgotten, Allystaire lunged to her side, catching her neck in his left hand. He felt a steady pulse, but her breathing had slowed significantly; she was deeply unconscious. Meanwhile, Dunlir had begun to heave and groan, and emitted a terrible gurgling sound as foamy liquid began to gush from his mouth. Allystaire was aware of a smell like the sea, followed by the sharp twang of a bowstring, and feathers sprouted from the very center of Dunlir's head. All thrashing ceased.

Allystaire sat up on one knee, carefully lifting Idgen Marte into a sitting position, cradling her with his weakened arm and his chest. Torvul stood but a few feet away, the assassin's crossbow quivering in his hands from the bolt it had just fired.

"A mercy killing," the dwarf said thickly. "He was drowning, drowning from inside his own body. How, I don't know, but it hasn't got the stink of sorcery."

"It was Braech," Allystaire said darkly. "The Church of the Sea Dragon was behind this."

"The Father of Waves and I are destined to be at odds, it seems." A voice rang across the morning like a clear bell, with tones as pure and bright as polished silver. Allystaire's head snapped up, Idgen Marte stirred in his arms, and Torvul's jaw dropped as an intensely bright ray of the sun suddenly resolved itself into the glowing, vibrant form of the Goddess.

Allystaire was already on one knee, and Torvul quickly joined him, setting aside the crossbow. The dwarf did not, however, avert his eyes, even as the Mother's approach brought with it a nearly painful radiance.

"Strength, freedom, a man striving to do what he can because he can... these sound so noble until one realizes that strength is so often an accident of birth," She mused. Her eyes fell with pity upon Dunlir's corpse, and She shook her head sadly. "He was not a good man and I do not think you could have saved him. I think, my Knight and my Shadow, I would have seen you bring him to his end. But a more just end, a cleaner end than this." She was suddenly standing before Allystaire and Idgen Marte, and Her hands rested atop their heads.

Allystaire's body thrummed with the power of her touch, and the weakness of the poison, the ache in his knees and his back, melted before its heat. Idgen Marte, too, stirred and sat up of her own power. In his mind, he heard the Goddess's voice.

Your death was too near today, My Arm. I am proud of you, and I love you, yet there is so much more *I must ask of you that I fear that you may not love Me. You may regret, when these trials come before you, what I have made of you.*

"Never," Allystaire answered aloud, tears gathering in the corners of his eyes at the ferocity of his denial. Her presence was so enormous, so powerful, that it drove away everything but the desire for Her voice, Her touch, the suggestion of Her love or approval.

He knew, dimly, that Idgen Marte was hearing Her voice as well, but not the same words he heard. Then the Goddess turned from them and was standing in front of Torvul, who watched Her warily.

"Do you still discredit Me, Son of the Earth?"

"I'd say things are leaning in your favor, Lady," Torvul replied a bit hoarsely.

The Goddess threw back Her head and filled the field with a pealing laughter like sunlight being fractured by the brilliance of polished crystal.

"It is that very Wit that has brought you before me, Mourmitnourthruk-acshtorvul. Today, you valued the life of two men beyond any price of gold. I know the words you sang when you healed them, and I know how long it has been since you sang them. I know how much it has hurt you." She reached down and took Torvul's hands in Her own, and stood the dwarf up on unsteady legs, though Allystaire knew from experience that the Goddess could have lifted any of them as they might lift a child.

Allystaire looked to Idgen Marte and she nodded; they walked off; when the Mother ordained one of those She had Called, She did so for the chosen one's eyes and ears alone.

* * *

Whether it was a few minutes, or a turn of the glass, Allystaire could not have said; he and Idgen Marte did not speak. Such was the daze that the touch of the Goddess brought upon them both that they simply wandered out of sight. Yet soon enough they knew they were called back, and they found the door of the farmhouse open and radiance streaming out of its windows. Wide-eyed, they hastened through the door.

They found the Goddess standing just inside, turning Her head as She surveyed the carnage within. And then Her shoulders shook, and Her face lowered into Her upturned hands, and She wept.

In Allystaire's ears, the sound was the very death of joy; it was silver harp strings curling and popping in a fire. Deep inside him the anger that he had known when using Her Gifts in battle began to hum in his veins, and because he had no means to vent his rage, perhaps it made him bold, but for the first time in his service to Her, he spoke unbidden.

"Goddess," he said, his mouth dry, his voice raspy, "I will tear apart the world of men to find the man who has done this thing in Your sight, to find the man who has made You weep."

She turned toward him then and took Her hands from Her face. "And that, my Knight, my Arm, my First Paladin, is why I chose you." She held up her right palm, and a few shimmering teardrops lay upon it; She tilted Her hand, extended a finger, and a single drop rolled down and toward the floor. When it landed, the room flashed in a light so bright that Allystaire felt certain he should be blinded; Idgen Marte clutched at his arm in the wake of it, but when he blinked his eyes open, he found, first, that he saw.

Second, the room had changed. What had once been a charnel house of body parts, of blood and gore, was now immaculately clean. Five corpses, one a man of Allystaire's age, one a woman of similar years, and three children, lay in repose on the floor. Their skin was waxy and pale, but their wounds mercifully hidden behind white burial shrouds. "A small mercy, but it is all I can give to them now," She said softly. "It is not given, even to me, to pluck back a spirit from the next world." Her voice, Her face, were shot through with sadness, but resignation.

"Mourmitnourthrukacshtorvul," She said, turning toward the dwarf and extending Her hand, palm up, with a tiny radiant pool of glistening tears still in it.

The dwarf knew precisely what to do; he retrieved an empty bottle from a pouch on his jerkin, uncorked it, and held it toward Her. She bent Her hand, and the tears slid from Her palm and neatly into the bottle. "These are not miracles," She said then, gently. "Yet all just and earned tears have power, of a kind. Perhaps, my Wit, in your new work you may find a use for them."

Then She addressed all of them. "The world notices your coming, my Chosen, my Servants—and the powerful begin to fear you. The folk of this village come now, and you must minister to them as you are able, but you must not tarry here. There is much work for you to do, and it lies distant. You must make for My people places of Light in this world. You must show them that there may still be brightness in the face of a gathering darkness."

Allystaire, Idgen Marte, and Torvul turned and followed as She moved through the door of the farmhouse, and a gathering of townfolk with mattocks and shovels gasped as Her radiance greeted them, and many fell prostrate before Her, tools clattering to the ground.

"Do not hide your eyes from Me, good people," She said, though Her voice was already growing distant, her brightness dimming. "I am the Mother, and I do not demand your fear and prostration. I bring you love, and hope it is returned; my Chosen Servants are come to bring you hope." She turned to indicate Allystaire, Idgen Marte, and Torvul, and then vanished in a brief flash.

"Tough one to take the stage after," Torvul muttered, He wiped the back of one hand against a dab of wetness at the corner of his eye and added, "Dusty in here."

* * *

Turns later, the cleaned, wrapped bodies had been lowered into a family grave. Allystaire had helped with the digging as much as his weakened arm would allow, and Torvul had proven himself a more able hand with a spade than any other present. Idgen Marte had spoken with Cuisin, calming him, for the man had started to go to pieces once the shock had worn off and the reality set in. Then she had spoken with other victims of the previous night, among whom she still mingled.

Allystaire silently sat with Torvul near the hearth, upon which the innkeep had laid and stoked a blazing fire, as if preparing for a cold night. In fact it had made the room so warm that Allystaire suddenly stood and walked across the stone floor, his boots clomping loudly against the general silence, and began carefully pushing aside the thin hides that covered the windows. A chiller air immediately began to fill the room, and he returned heavily and wearily to his seat. Suddenly he winced and set his left elbow gingerly upon the table.

"Y'know boy, all I really did was stop the poison. You still took a bolt to the arm. You're damned lucky that it doesn't seem to have shattered the bones, but still, we'll need to do something more about it." Torvul's hand was curled reflexively around the handle of a large clay mug, and a similar one, foam still sloshing at its rim, sat in front of Allystaire.

"I have taken wounds before. And I heal fast."

"Not fast enough," Torvul insisted, rapping a scarred knuckle on the table. "Tomorrow you won't be able to strap your shield around your arm. You lost blood; believe me, a lot of it soaked into my boots. I'm at the limit of what I could do. Your turn at playing chirurgeon now."

Allystaire turned his grimacing face to the dwarf. "I am reluctant to use the Mother's Gifts on myself, and frankly, I do not know if I can."

"Pssst. Nonsense." Torvul took a long draw off his beer and gave the mug a shake to determine its fullness. He set it down and reached out to hook Allystaire's with two fingers. "You lose blood, you can't be drinking beer. Now, are you going to sit there and mope and brood, or are you going to heal yourself?"

"I am not brooding," Allystaire protested, curling his left hand into a weak and white-knuckled fist.

"If you aren't yelling or preaching or killing something, chances are you're brooding," Idgen Marte put in, suddenly arriving at the table and plopping into a seat. In her right hand she clutched two clay mugs of a piece with Allystaire and Torvul's; in her left, a smaller mug with no foam topping it, which she set before Allystaire. She slid it in front of him; he sniffed the air, and his eyes widened.

"Innadan brandy?" He lifted the mug to his nose and inhaled deeply. "The real kind, not the pomace. Where in Cold did you find this?"

"Back in Ashmill Bridge. Grateful innkeep."

"The one with the thieves living in his cellar?"

"The same," Idgen Marte replied with a nod. She leaned across the table and placed her free hand lightly on Allystaire's left arm, near his wound. "I know it isn't a day of celebration, but it seemed a good time. Besides," she added, leaning back, "I've got to sew that up, and nobody ought to take my stitching sober."

"Your stitching did not hurt last time."

"You were unconscious," Idgen Marte noted. She lifted her mug and sipped.

"Are you two still talkin' about wounds?" Torvul snorted, and tucked into his own mug.

"Leave it, dwarf," Allystaire barked, before finally taking a careful, savoring sip of the brandy Idgen Marte had brought him, his eyes dimming briefly in pleasure.

"Well why should she need to stitch it if you'll just heal it yourself, anyway?" Torvul wiped foam off his mouth with the back of his hand.

"I have never tried to heal myself," Allystaire replied, "and even if I could do as you say, I cannot reach the wound itself."

Torvul gave Allystaire a flat, disbelieving stare, his lips pressed into a thin line, and finally said, "Son, how in the Cold did you live this long in the paladin trade without me?" Then he held up a hand to forestall the answer that Allystaire was about to spit back at him. "Why've you never tried to heal yourself?"

"Does not seem the Goddess would give me a Gift like that for my own use."

"Hard to do Her work if your arm's off, though, isn't it? Why in the Cold would the Lady not want you able to tend to yourself if you've a need? That's foolish talk."

"Fine," Allystaire said, and flexed his arm, as if trying to place his hand against the wound itself. "Even assuming I can, how do I reach the wound?"

Torvul sighed, pushed back his chair and hopped off of it. He walked around to Allystaire's side of the table, took his left wrist in one strong, rough hand, and guided it over to the skin of his right arm. "Did She ever tell you you had to touch a wound in order to heal it? The body's all of a piece, boy. Different bits, yes, but all working together. Do it."

Allystaire sighed and settled his fingers against the skin of his right arm; his left arm was still weaker, a little cold to the touch. He slowed his breathing, closed his eyes, and tried to sense himself, his own hurts, expecting failure.

It was remarkably easy. He could feel the hole in his muscles in his left arm, the damage the poison had done before Torvul had been able to stop it. His senses extended so far that he could feel the accumulation of the years in his knees and his back, what years of wearing armor had done to his shoulders, the twisted places where blades and maces and arrows and lances had left their marks. *Could I sweep all of that away?* The Goddess's song thrummed in his head and his hand, amplified by the fact that he was healing himself. *Have the strength of my youth back, unwounded?*

Allystaire felt as though the healing was quick. He poured the song, the compassion he knew the Mother felt for the wound he had taken in her service, into the injured arm. Muscle knit; where bone had chipped, it smoothed itself and strengthened. He felt the wound closing, felt the skin mending itself, and he stopped just as the puckered whiteness of a new scar appeared on his flesh.

"Why'd that take so long?" Allystaire was suddenly jolted back into awareness by Idgen Marte's query, which sounded dim and distant to his ears.

He blinked his eyes open. Torvul and Idgen Marte crowded him, staring with concern in their features.

"What? It took as long as it typically does."

"You were gone for a span, lad. Didn't answer us, either. Stones above, I would've had time to go get another beer. And drink it. And then get another after that, and I wouldn't have missed anything."

Idgen Marte seized his left arm and held it up, running her fingers over the skin where the wound had been. "Why'd you leave a scar instead of just mending it?"

Allystaire thought on this for a moment, and, after shaking his arm free from Idgen Marte's grasp, he paused for a quick sip of brandy. "I was lost for a moment. Feeling the wound, feeling all the small hurts I have gathered up in my life."

Torvul's thick brows knitted closely. "Fix all that up while you were in there? Stones above, what I wouldn't give to have the sprightliness of youth about me again. Just shave seven or eight decades off like a beard—"

"Seven or eight decades? How old *are* you?" Idgen Marte, ever curious, was quickly distracted.

"Old enough. My folk live a long time. Enough about me, though," Torvul said, pointing with his near empty mug at Allystaire. "So, you do it?"

Allystaire shook his head. "No. Healing the wound I took, well, Torvul… you were right about that. The others, though? I thought, what if I could take them away, have the strength of my youth again? Take what I know now with what I could do then…" He stopped, downed the rest of the brandy. "I realized what a terrible idea it was."

"Cold, Ally, if I'd half as many scars as I know you do, I'd be in a dress somewhere, embroidering—" Idgen Marte stopped cold, searching for a word. "Whatever it is that rich cows in smothering dresses embroider. How could it be a terrible idea?"

"When I was given my first command by Gerard Oyrwyn, I was younger than many of the knights who were told to hop to my word. The Old Baron told them all, to forestall the grumbling, that the reason he had put me in charge was because I knew the most important lesson a fighting man could ever learn: that fighting hurts."

"Not if you do it right," Idgen Marte retorted.

"Still, he was making a point; all these scars, these old wounds, they all taught me something. They are *why* I know what I know now. What would I be if I took them away?" Allystaire shook his head and stood, slowly and heavily, wearied by healing himself and by a day of exertions. "I would be no paladin if I let myself forget what it means to be hurt. Goodnight."

He turned to Torvul and extended his right hand. The dwarf raised a brow, but stood, and clasped Allystaire's arm, hand to forearm. Allystaire smiled faintly and said, "We have had our arguments these days, Torvul. We must be brothers now, with all that entails. Some of my words were meant to cut, and were not worthy of me. Or of you." He gave the dwarf's arm a pump, then let it drop.

"There is much to talk of in the morning, but now, I am for bed." He stumped heavily out of the room and slowly up the stairs, which creaked under his weight.

The other two watched him go, and Torvul drained the last bit in his mug, then tilted it toward him and eyed its empty bottom disapprovingly. "How in the Cold do we live up to him?"

"Live up to what the Goddess asks of *you*," Idgen Marte replied. "Whatever Gifts She bestowed, whatever charges She laid on you, they're different to what She gave him, different to what She asks of you."

Torvul set down his mug and let out a slow, somewhat shaky breath. "There's a reason She called him first, though."

"She didn't," Idgen Marte pointed out. "But you've not met the Voice yet." She shrugged and gathered up double handfuls of mugs to carry back to the weary innkeep, who leaned sleepily against his bar. "No doubt there're reasons She called us when She did. I won't lose sleep over it."

Torvul shook his head. "Not what I meant. You just *want* t' follow him after a bit, don't ya? You're around him for a time, you see that he means precisely what he says, he'll do what he dares, that he doesn't give a good Cold-damn who's standing in his way, and he was probably like that before the Lady's favor. Now with Her behind him, what chance does anyone stand?"

"What does that mean?"

"It means he could be the best thing to ever happen to the baronies. Or the worst. A stone pulled from the right place can start an avalanche that'll bury a nest of trolls. Old dwarfish saying, that. There's a another side to it, though."

"Oh?"

"Once you start it, you can't guarantee it'll bury only the trolls."

CHAPTER 36

Of Songs and Singing

Dawn was slow to come the next morning. Allystaire stood outside the inn, facing east, watching slow streaks of yellow and orange reach tentatively into the persistently dark blue of the sky above him. *Thornhurst is to the east,* he thought, *and the Mother's temple, and Mol.* Then suddenly, he said aloud, "Cold! How did that place come to seem like home? And why do I long for the wisdom of an eleven-year-old lass?" He shook his head as if to clear it and looked back to the darkened windows of the inn.

The morning was chill, and he was glad of it, for he wore as much of his armor as he could stand: dark and scarred breastplate over-hanging his shoulders, lower guard of his vambraces on his forearms, leather-and-iron gloves, plates sewn onto a knee-length leather kirtle around his waist. His helm was tucked under his right arm and his shield hung from his left.

"Dressed for business, are we?"

Allystaire smiled and replied without turning around. "I am a vigilant man. And yet you always manage to sneak up like a footpad on a drunk merchant."

"Drunk merchants are more careful with their links than you are with your life." Idgen Marte rapped a hand against his armor. "Not taking any chances today? But then, no greaves, no chausses…"

"Long way to ride today, and besides, greaves and chausses are freezing near useless unless you know you are staying horsed. Too hard to move on foot."

"Best you start wearing all of it, or nearly all, I think," Idgen Marte replied. "You know you could've sensed me coming if you'd been thinking on it. I know I'm not the only one who feels that sometimes."

Allystaire shook his head. "You are not. When it seems like it matters, on watch, or in battle, if I concentrate even for a moment, I know precisely where you are. I suspect if we work at it, we can learn to know more than that. Probably Torvul and Mol, as well. Just have to try it and see."

"And there have been times I have heard words you thought, but did not speak. What do you make of that?"

"Nothing, until it happens when we mean it to, and not just when we are close to the Goddess," Allystaire replied. "I think it likely that She has given us these other Gifts, and simply not spoken of them. Mayhap they are just a result of being connected through Her. I am not made for such metaphysical theorizing."

"Well I'll theorize alone or with Torvul if I have to, but if these other Gifts, or these accidents, whatever they are, if they can help stop days like yesterday, then we need them."

"Yesterday worked out fine."

Idgen Marte strode around to face Allystaire directly. "*Barely*. Had the assassin time for another shot, you'd be dead. Had they been smart enough to send two or three, you'd be dead. And make no mistake," she added, raising a fingertip to the level of his chin, her cheeks darkening a bit, "*they will now*. They were watching or listening somehow, and they know what happened, and they'll not make the same mistake again. I won't have this end because you're being careless or lazy or just thick."

Allystaire took this in quietly, and then carefully reached out and lowered Idgen Marte's hand from his face. "You know I am not any of those things. Not even thick. And you know also that if I did die, that this, whatever it is, does not end."

"There's meant to be five of us," she insisted, pulling away her hand and rapping on his breastplate with a knuckle. "And you, we can't spare."

"We do not even know who the fifth of us will be yet."

"Doesn't matter," she insisted with a shake of her head. "I know what I know. Without you, what would we have? I've stood at the head of men in battle, but I'm no leader. Nor is Torvul. Mol is brilliant and stubborn and wonderful, but she's still a lass of less than twelve summers. Besides," she went on, a bit of her signature grin twisting the corner of her mouth, "I'm not done finding out where your story is going."

"It is not a story."

"It will be when the bards get ahold of it. Just wait."

Allystaire sighed and rolled his eyes, and Idgen Marte turned from him to face the oncoming sunlight.

"Where are we riding, then?"

"Londray," Allystaire responded with finality.

Idgen Marte merely nodded and started back to the inn, its windows now fully bathed in the glow of sunrise. "I'll go wake the dwarf."

"The dwarf is already awake, thank you." Torvul's voice boomed from the front step of the inn, and he was already dressed in his traveling jerkin and using his cudgel as a walking stick. "Though don't get used to it. I mean to address this rising with the dawn business with Her Ladyship at the first opportunity. After we go over this plan to ride straight into Londray."

"Torvul," Allystaire said, turning his face from the sun, which had grown much brighter since he first stepped out, "I have thought on it, and it is where we are meant to go. Listen," he went on, forestalling the dwarf's argument with a raised hand. "Listen, and you might learn something. We have two sets of enemies—that we know of. Could be more, but two we can identify: the Church of Braech, and the sorcerer. Both powerful, both dangerous. The latter mayhap more of both. Yet we can precisely locate the Church and not the sorcerer. That means we go there and clear the board, then marshal ourselves to face the enemy that remains. If I were caught between two armies in hostile territory, it is exactly what I would do."

"What if the sorcerer strikes back at these folk again, hrmm?"

The paladin shook his head quickly, lips pressing into a thin line. "He had all day yesterday if he wished. And they are not his target. More than likely by staying here we would be putting these folk in danger."

Torvul stopped, as Allystaire's hand fell. "Well," the dwarf murmured, "you aren't as dumb as you are ugly, I suppose. Let's wait till the village is up, though."

"Why?"

"You've words to say to them, and I've something to give them. And if you'll excuse me, I'm going to go make it."

"Please tell me it is not dwarfish spirits."

"Of course not. Potions."

"Do try not to sicken them all."

"Potions'll work fine."

"What makes you certain of that," Idgen Marte called after him, as the dwarf started for his parked wagon and, no doubt, the tools and workshop within.

The dwarf turned back and smiled wryly, but brightly. "Faith."

* * *

Torvul was gone for long enough to leave Allystaire and Idgen Marte to bargain and pay for provisions for the road out of their dwindling supply of silver links. When the mule was loaded and the horses ready, Torvul finally emerged from his wagon, cradling a small crystal bottle in his right hand.

"Well, have you said what needed saying?" He eyed Allystaire with furrowed brows.

Allystaire blinked in surprise. "The only words I have said this morning have been about what biscuit, beer, and meat they could afford to sell us."

Torvul's lips compressed in frustration. "So these people have seen some of their own murdered, and their minds turned into a sorcerer's toys, and you mean to ride away like it was just a quick stay? Leave your links on the table and tie the tent closed on your way out, eh?" The dwarf stopped, hefted his potion, and turned away, grumbling.

"What can I say to them that the Goddess did not already say?" Allystaire's question was as much to Idgen Marte as to Torvul, for the dwarf was already stumping up the stairs and throwing open the door to the inn.

"Probably not much," Idgen Marte said, but then she gave him a shove in the back anyway. "But best to give it a try. The Goddess can be a bit overwhelming; compared to Her, even you aren't likely to give them a fright."

With a deep breath, Allystaire followed the dwarf inside. The proprietor, whose name they'd learned was Henrik, was up and about, as were his wife and children, going about the morning tasks—laying fires, preparing bread, sweeping. *The endless sweeping. Cold, I'd go mad*, Allystaire thought. Torvul had cornered Henrik by the bar.

"Of course you're the headman hereabouts. Man who makes the beer is always in charge," the dwarf was saying, as Allystaire and Idgen Marte stopped a few feet away.

"I don't actually make it, I just buy—"

Torvul interrupted with a brusque wave of his hand. "Doesn't matter. Your place has excellent beer and you're the one who puts it here. Point is, folks are gonna come." He lifted the crystal bottle in his hand and pointed to it. "See this? Something for your village, for the farms about." He slid it into one of the pouches on his jerkin, unhooked the pouch, and set it down carefully on the bar. "There ain't much of it, so you'll need to be careful with it."

"Right," Henrik said, laying his hands one atop the other on the end of his broomstick. "What…what is it?"

"*This*," Torvul said, gently fingering the bag, "is a *revolution* in agriculture, my good man. An absolute guarantee of bumper crops, no matter the ground, little matter the rain. This potion, small in volume though it may be, is a piece of craft and power so ingenious it…" His voice began to pick up speed and volume, and his hand lifted in an expansive gesture.

From a pace behind, Allystaire cleared his throat and shifted his weight so that his riding boot tapped on a flagstone.

Torvul paused in mid-gesticulation, and stopped. "Listen, Henrik. I know it's too late in the year to do aught about this year's harvest. This is for next year's. When you gather your seed corn, you take this bottle, and, by the *drop*, mind you, the merest drop you can coax out of it, and it'll be tiny, I designed this bottle myself, you see, and the neck impedes the movement of liquid—"

Allystaire began gathering his breath for another interruption, but Torvul stopped himself short. "Sorry. By the drop, you mix this in with each farm's seed corn, or turnip tops or mushroom spawn or potato eyes, whatever it is they're growing. Stretch it as far as it'll go. Next year's harvest will be more than you'll know what to do with."

"Beggin' your pardon, dwarf, but what d'ya know of farming?" Henrik's wife, Nora, a short, thin, hard-worked woman with ash-blonde hair going grey, ducked out of the kitchen behind the bar with her arms floury up to the elbow, wiping them on her apron as she came. "And what do you think happens if we have a good year? D'ya think we get to keep any of it? With no end of war in sight, how many new taxes d'ya think you'll bring down on us?"

Allystaire stepped forward and seized the moment. "Goodwife, who is your lord in these parts?"

"S'Lord Carrinth of Ennithstide," the woman said, her mouth twisting as though she'd like to spit.

"Does he use your people ill? Mistreat them?"

"No more'n any other, I 'spect," she replied, her eyes shifting nervously. "I mean no disrespect, m'lord."

"I am not a lord," Allystaire said, attempting a reassuring smile. "And you shall not offend me by speaking ill of any man who deserves it, be he ever so great in the eyes of law. Listen to me now; there is a village a good ride east and north of here, the other side of the mountains, called Thornhurst. The Mother's Temple rises there even now. If this Lord Carrinth, or his soldiers, or his agents, come to you asking a tax you should not or cannot pay, if they use you ill or ply strength and fear to keep you hungry, you send word to that village, and it will come to me. And no matter if I am in some far-flung corner of the world, I will come back here, I will go to Lord Carrinth, and I will take back every link, every crumb, every ounce you are owed. And if I must leave Ennithstide a smoking ruin when I do, then so be it. You are people of the Mother now, if you wish to be; this potion is one of Her gifts to you. My protection is another."

The woman's eyes hadn't lost their nervous cast as Allystaire spoke. "D'ya mean that, m'lord? You'd come fight for us for…for what?"

"I would fight for you, good lady Nora, because it would be the right thing to do. Because no one else has. Because the Mother calls me to. Pick the answer that suits you. All are true."

When Allystaire called Nora 'lady', at first she gasped in fear. And then, for just a moment, her blue eyes showed the tiniest hint of a tear in each corner. Allystaire gently laid one gauntleted hand on her arm and squeezed lightly, then stepped back.

"Now we must go," Allystaire said. "Know this; I will forever regret that I was not here a day sooner. I will remember what happened here, and I will find the man who did it, and he will face the Mother's justice. And you, remember Thornhurst. Send someone there, if you can spare him, and tell him to speak with Mol, the Mother's priestess there. If there is any help you need, and it is in Mol's power to grant, you will have it."

Allystaire turned to leave, and Torvul pointed a thick finger at Henrik. "Remember—careful hand with the drops. It'll work on any crop you mean to grow."

"What do I owe you, m'lords?"

Allystaire and Idgen Marte glanced at Torvul as the question was asked. The dwarf simply shrugged his broad shoulders. "It's free. Just mind it well." With that, he stumped on out the door, his thick boots ringing hard on the stones. Idgen Marte and Allystaire headed for the door, but Torvul's head and shoulders suddenly burst back through it.

"And another thing," the dwarf called out, squeezing between the paladins and walking back to the bar, "I'm not accusing you of anything, but you need to know. Since that is freely given to you," he raised a hand and pointed one finger at the bag and the bottle inside, "it must be freely given by you. The moment anyone tries to sell it, tries to take links in exchange for its power, the magic in it will be not destroyed, but changed. You would not like to see what happens to fields sewn with seed cursed by that potion if gold or silver changes hands for it. Understand?"

The dwarf barely waited for Henrik to nod enthusiastically before he turned and made haste through the door again. He was but a few steps beyond it when Allystaire and Idgen Marte heard him bellow.

"You two are a festering carbuncle on the ass of progress. Get out here already."

Idgen Marte gave Allystaire a light shove, laughing, and he went, shaking his head, into the bright morning sunshine, where the dwarf was already turning his team for the road.

They mounted, Idgen Marte on her courser, Allystaire on the broad-shouldered destrier. Ardent whickered happily and tried to tear off down the road; Allystaire felt the huge muscles beneath him gathering, but he gave the horse only enough head to catch up with Torvul's wagon.

"I know what you're going to ask, and I'll save you the trouble," Torvul said. "Potion'll work. I promise."

"That is not what I was going to ask," Allystaire returned mildly. "Your potions worked when the villagers were ensorcelled, and they worked when I was poisoned."

Torvul coughed delicately, his eyes narrowing as they focused on the road ahead. "Well, in point of fact, in the interest of precision and truth, they didn't work when the villagers were ensorcelled. They were supposed to be smoke and noise. Not flames."

Allystaire stifled a laugh by coughing into a gauntleted fist. "Well. No, Torvul, the question I was going to ask is about the, ah, the price."

"Prices are between me and Her Ladyship," Torvul replied. His lips clamped shut.

Allystaire raised a conciliatory hand from the reins. "Then I take back the question. If it concerns your Ordination, then it remains yours in private, unless you choose otherwise."

Torvul was quiet, and Allystaire rode beside him in silence. For a few minutes, the only sounds were the occasional chattering of birds, the roll of Torvul's wagon's wheels along the road, the clomping of horseshoes, the jingle of harness. Finally the dwarf broke the silence.

"There is somethin' I need to do when we get to Londray. It's about the bow that assassin carried."

"What of it?"

"It's Dwarfish make. Old Dwarfish make. I need t'know who sold it, and when, and if there are more."

"There are plenty of crossbows in the world."

Torvul turned his gaze from the road, and Allystaire saw a glimpse of stone and iron in his expression. *"Not like that there aren't.* My bow is a little bit alike to it in the same way that a noble maiden's first palfrey is alike to that monster you're riding. I need to know who, and where, and how many. I'm gonna need your help with it. Aye?"

"Aye," Allystaire nodded.

Allystaire let Ardent run for just a few moments then, and the restless horse soon pulled away from the wagon, but with a few yards distance he reined in and slowed the destrier's pace to a walk. They passed the time, and several miles of road, in watchful silence.

* * *

They made camp that night before twilight, which meant few turns on the road, as the days were growing short. The land was hilly, caught between the mountains that divided Barony Delondeur in its middle and those that guarded its coast, and the terrain offered them a sheltered and elevated spot to park the wagon, though little cover was afforded by the increasingly leafless trees. The horses and the mule were picketed and calm, and Torvul was busy starting a fire in the light-shielding brazier he had brought out of his wagon.

"Just what else have you got in there?" Idgen Marte asked, as she leaned casually against a pile of her saddle and some baggage, legs stretched out in front of her and crossed at the ankle.

"Wouldn't you like to know?" Torvul struck something against the side of the brazier and soon light flared within it, and in moments a full fire was burning away on whatever fuel he'd added. "Stones but it feels good t'have the touch back," the dwarf murmured. He stepped up and entered his wagon again.

Allystaire had been rooting through a pack, and came to the fire with hard squares of salty biscuit and leathery strips of meat and handed sizable portions of each to Idgen Marte. "Torvul certainly has a lighter step since…"

"Didn't you?" She nibbled cautiously on the end of a biscuit, turning her head to the side in order to bite with her grinding teeth.

"Not as such. Felt rested, I suppose. He seems a full ten years younger."

At that, Torvul emerged from the door of his wagon and hopped down lightly, two crossbows held in his bent arms—his own, and the one they had taken from the would-be assassin.

"More'n ten years. Thirty, if it's one," the dwarf said. He approached the fire, set down the bows, and reached for the food Allystaire offered him. He took one tearing bite at the meat and quickly spat it out, his face twisted in pain, and tossed the remnant to the ground.

"New rule," he said, spitting again. "You're no longer responsible for food."

"Ask me to cook and I'll feed you your tongue," Idgen Marte warned him. "You're taking it on yourself."

"I'm the only one who can be trusted with it, apparently," the dwarf replied, eyeing his forsaken jerky and biscuit balefully.

"Many a time on campaign I have eaten worse, and been glad of it," Allystaire replied. "I suggest you make yourself used to it, for we have little silver left, and no gold."

The dwarf waved a hand dismissively. "We've plenty. Just wait till we get to Londray and I'll fit out my kitchen proper. You'll see. Now, to important business."

He held up his own crossbow, its plain wooden stock resting on the palms of his hands. "Helped a weapon-crafter of my own caravan make this. I have this," he flipped a large, clear crystal set in a brass ring and hinged on the top of the stock, "for measuring distance." He gently eased the ring down, seating it snugly into a recess cut into the stock. "And this." Another, much smaller crystal set in a silver ring; the crystal itself was a dark red, and cracked. "This is for the dark. It doesn't work too well, but a decent bowman can make use of it. Otherwise, well, it's your basic crossbow. I've toyed with trick bolts, y'know, filled with alchemical whatnot. No more accurate than just trusting my good right arm, I've found." He set his bow down and reached for the longer, slightly thinner one.

It was, Allystaire noticed for the first time, not simply a darkly burnished wood, for no wood could have been that rippling dark blue color. The spiraling stock of the weapon seemed made for a short, fairly thick arm to slide into it.

"This weapon is from the Homes, from before we took to wagons. If any dwarf still living knows how to make one, and much less can find the *mchazchen*—that's the stone it's made from—"

"You can't make a bow out of stone," Idgen Marte protested. "That's absurd."

"And yet here it is." Torvul cleared his throat, briefly glared at the warrior, and resumed, "If any dwarf still living knows how to make one, then he is older or cleverer than he has any right t'be." He reached up and flipped up no less than four separate crystal lenses. Unlike those on his bow, these were smooth and clear as glass. "Measuring distance, wind, darkness, fog, cover, terrain, armor. There's very little that can stop such a bow. This weapon was fashioned with a potent and forgotten magic, and best it stays that way."

"I have a question, Torvul. And I mean no offense by it," Allystaire said quietly. "If the weapon is so very powerful, and your people had the making of them, what did defeat you?"

"I never said we were defeated," Torvul answered evenly. "Only that we left the Homes behind. And when we came up, and took to wagons, one thing every crafter agreed upon, every soldier who carried such as this," he hefted the bow before setting it down at his feet, "was that we'd not sell them at any price. Not at any measure of desperation."

"Agreements like that are made to be broken," Idgen Marte said. "You can't expect everyone to simply give their word and mean it."

"You don't know much about dwarfs," Torvul said sternly. "It was entered into The History by the Loresingers. Every dwarf in every caravan carries that in his soul and is reminded of it at every Singing. Had that changed—had *any* dwarf consented to sell these—then *every* dwarf would learn of it, and fast. So if it's happened, it's been since…" Here the dwarf paused and drew in a heavy breath. "Since I left."

"History? Loresingers?" Idgen Marte sat up, her half-eaten biscuit forgotten, and leaned forward with an eager curiosity.

"One thing at a time," Allystaire said, forestalling her questions with an upraised hand. "It could have been taken as a prize on a battlefield."

Torvul smiled faintly. "Don't you think we took that into account? If that happened, the magic of the bow simply wouldn't work, and he'd only be able to point it and shoot. There are steps that have to be taken, lessons; this was given or sold by a dwarf."

"How do we know he was not just pointing and shooting?"

Torvul turned to Idgen Marte. "How far would you say an ordinary crossbow can shoot, and hit what it's aimed at?"

"Three hundred span or so, if the bowman knows his business. Bit more if he knows and is damned lucky."

Torvul nodded. "And how far away was the assassin using this?"

Idgen Marte paused to consider, then said carefully, "A lot freezing further than that."

"Right." Torvul reached down and flipped up one of the ring-set crystal lenses. "The only reason he could even see you, Allystaire, was because the bow was working for him. He was too far away, the elevations were all cocked, and he was hanging in a damned tree. No normal crossbow makes that shot, not even if you're strung up like a target at a fair game and he got forty bolts at a copper half. You have to see that." Torvul closed down one lens, the large clear one, and flipped up another of bright peridot hue. "And you—" he pointed at Idgen Marte, "since the Lady's Gift, how many have seen you coming when you meant them harm? I'm guessing the answer is one, and it's him. And didn't you stop to wonder why he could even see you?" The dwarf tapped the ring with a fingertip and then pushed it closed on well-oiled, noiseless hinges.

"I'm sold," Idgen Marte said, leaning back again. "We'll do what we can. Where do we start?" Allystaire nodded his agreement and went back to chewing a hard, musty biscuit.

"In Londray. Bound to be some of my folk around."

"Good. Now that's settled, Loresingers. History." Idgen Marte made herself comfortable, uncrossed and re-crossed her feet at the ankles, and looked at the dwarf expectantly.

The dwarf sighed and rather nimbly tucked his legs so that he was sitting with his hands resting on his knees. "These are big questions, woman. But you've a right to know some things, I s'pose, and I'm not opposed to telling you a little."

"Torvul, trust me—if you start answering any of her questions, they will never, ever stop," Allystaire warned.

The dwarf shrugged. "I like t'talk almost as much as you like t'chew." He tossed his discarded biscuit toward Allystaire, who caught it in the air and, with the equanimity of a seasoned soldier presented with unexpected food, serenely began nibbling on it.

"Now. Songs. For such as you, they're what, a turn's entertainment? An old and twisted and broken story? For dwarfs, though, they're who we are as a people, who we have been; everything that we do, everything that we decide, our laws and our memories and our plans—all of these are sung by our Loresingers." He raised a hand to forestall further questions, for Idgen Marte was already leaning forward again, her mouth half open. "Every so often when caravans meet—it used to be a lot more often in the Homes—there is a Singing. Things are added to the History. Marriages, deaths, births, great events, new contracts, new creations." He paused here and looked to Allystaire. "I do like talkin' but it's thirsty work."

Allystaire snorted softly, but amiably, and pushed himself to his feet and walked over to Torvul's wagon, where wineskins and waterskins hung in sacks from pegs along the side. He returned with two, tossing one to Torvul and keeping one for himself. The dwarf nodded obligingly. He pulled off the cork, tilted his head, opened his mouth, and squeezed the back of the sack.

He suddenly sputtered and shouted, "Water! I said I was *thirsty*, not dirty." Allystaire, meanwhile, enjoyed a chuckle as he poured a good measure of sour red wine down his own throat before handing the bag over to the dwarf.

His thirst finally quenched, Torvul continued. "Now, then. That all might sound a bit boring to non-dwarfish folk such as yourselves, but I reckon the telling gets more interesting when I add this: when two Loresingers have sung together to add to our History, every Loresinger in the world knows what they have sung."

Idgen Marte sat bolt upright, sputtering in disbelief. "But that's impossible."

"Says the woman who is the handpicked servant of a newly woken Goddess," Allystaire pointed out quietly.

"Talkin' sense for once," Torvul said, nodding in Allystaire's direction. "I don't understand how it works, but it does; without it, we'd long since have dispersed, I s'pose. We've not got the Homes, but we have the History, and it keeps us one." A pause. "Most of us."

"What was the song you sang when you healed me," Allystaire asked suddenly. "I heard your voice, and though I had no idea of the words, I felt… anchored. Drawn together with you, somehow."

"Ah, that, well. That's just a song all dwarfs know."

"The Goddess made mention of it when She came for you," Allystaire recalled. "She said it had been a long time since you sang it."

"She also called you something long and like to crack my jaw if I attempt to pronounce it," Idgen Marte put in.

"Mourmitnourthrukacshtorvul," the dwarf said, nodding. "That is my name, my real name, as given by my family."

"I can see why you go by Torvul," Idgen Marte chortled.

"Yes, I take pity on your poor, all too human powers of elocution. Now, as for that song Her Ladyship mentioned, well." Torvul reached for the wineskin and half drained it before going on. "Songs aren't just for the Loresingers. Every caravan has a song; every city in our Homes had one, every family. We sing them to remind each other who we are, what we are. It is how we know we're dwarfs. It is how we feel at home when we have none. And I've long suspected it's how we power our magics—obviously the Loresingers, the weapons—but even the alchemy." He jabbed a finger at the air. "I could never quite prove it, but now…"

"The song," Idgen Marte nudged him on.

"Ah, right." Torvul rubbed his bald pate with one big hand. "Well, the song I sang was a family song. A song of bonding, usually sung every night. I hadn't sung it in two years."

"You have been apart from your caravan for two years?"

"I've been apart from my caravan for five," Torvul answered. He gave the wineskin a shake, found it too empty to suit him, and tossed it to Allystaire. "I'm done with questions for the night. Time for bed. I'll take the third watch." With that the dwarf got up and moved off, leaving behind his brazier.

"I will take the first," Allystaire said, as Idgen Marte watched Torvul trundle off. Soon the fire was banked, the remains of food and drink cleared, Idgen Marte ensconced in her hammock in a tree, and Allystaire was standing alone.

When he strained to listen, he thought he heard, very faintly, the sound of Torvul's rumbling voice singing in his strange and mournful-sounding language.

CHAPTER 37

A Realization at Londray

After two solid days and half of a third of travel without cease, they reached Londray. The city lay on the curve of a roiling bay where the Western Sea and the Ash River met. The effluvia from the city itself turned the brackish bay into a malodorous stew, the stench of which had Torvul complaining before any of it was even in sight.

Great cliffs running north and south of the city ensured that it sat in the only natural harbor for miles, and the mountain range that divided the barony in half could be seen to the east, grey-capped and not a far ride. The city itself sprawled over and around its curtain wall, cobbled together out of the grey-white stones of the surrounding cliffs. A seawall rose against the bay, and a forest of masts crowded its quays, flying the flags of a dozen lords, the barony itself, and distant nations.

"It has grown since last I saw it," Allystaire said, as they sat on a rise in the road looking far ahead. "Never a good idea to have your folk spilling over the walls like that. Lionel is getting complacent," he continued to muse aloud, folding his hands atop the pommel of his saddle, "though he has good reason to be somewhat less than vigilant."

"What d'ya mean?" Idgen Marte, who had been ranging around behind him and Torvul's wagon, pulled her mount next to his.

"Look." Allystaire pointed to the huge, gleaming walls of a castle that squatted in the northwest corner of the city. "The Dunes. His seat, and the nut you have to crack to take this city. It is nigh impossible to besiege the place as is, but even if you do, in order to bring anything in range you have to get through the city itself and thousands—"

Suddenly Allystaire's thoughts broke off and his hands squeezed together into fists, his shoulders trembling with the force of an onrushing anger. "Through thousands of the city's folk. And for years, for *years* this is how we have fought."

"You didn't invent the rules, boy," Torvul said.

"You didn't build a castle that way, either," Idgen Marte pointed out. "This Lionel's great-great-grandfather or somethin' like it did."

"I spent years, *years* trying to plan how to take this place. Years of my life, and I thought of everything—where and when to cross the mountains, how to maintain supply, what to do about the harbor, whether or not to try and force the mouth of the Ash. We in Oyrwyn were never much for boats, so we were exploring alliances, hiring warbands. I thought of everything."

He turned his face to the sun that shone on them and on the city, though without much heat. "Yet I never thought of the folk. It was a task, a game even. I counted the lives of my men, and yes, sometimes the enemy's, but not—" He stopped, his jaw clenched, and shook his head.

"It'd be the baron's decision to put the lives of his folk between an army and his walls, or not," Torvul said. "You didn't make the rules," he repeated.

"That changes nothing. It is, and always was, despicable." Allystaire practically bit the words as they passed his lips.

"Time to make some new rules, then," Idgen Marte said.

They sat in silence for a moment, till Torvul spoke up. "I think we ought to discuss how we mean to get into the city, and out. You give me some time to work on it, I could make the both of you unrecognizable. I'm a peddler, you're my guards. Sit still and let me do the talking."

"No." Allystaire cut him off with a single syllable as implacable as the mountain range to the east.

"Listen to sense, lad, you can't just walk in to the city and announce yourself."

Allystaire turned to face him. "Torvul, you do not understand. I cannot do this."

"Now is not the time for your honor to rear up—"

"Torvul. This is a condition the Mother has laid upon me. No lie may pass my lips. If a guard so much as asked my name, I would have to tell it to him."

The dwarf blinked in astonishment, taken aback by Allystaire's answer. "You mean, no matter what question is put you, you must tell the truth?" He shook his head in slow, open-mouthed horror. "That is…I can't imagine…" He put a hand to his forehead, paled. "I'm dizzy."

I can't even tell if he's joking, Allystaire thought, but said, "I have another way in. One that will not require a lie."

He reached inside one of his bracers and pulled out a crumpled parchment. "This is the letter the Choiron of Braech wrote to Rede, promising him recognition and aid in establishing a Temple of the Mother in Londray. I happen to think Londray could use a Temple of the Mother, and so much the better if it begins under our administration than his. What say you?"

Idgen Marte laughed, and Torvul nodded admiringly. "Well, you've got sand. I'll give you that. Say that gets us through the gate. What happens if word gets to the baron?"

Allystaire thought on the question for a moment, pursing his lips. Finally, he tapped one gauntleted hand on the pommel of the saddle and said, "His own sense of himself would demand a face-to-face talk. And if he wanted me dead he would try to do it himself, the right way. Well, the formal way. A challenge, seconds, the list, a herald to judge—all of it. Knowing him he would make a festival of it."

"And could he?"

"Kill me?" Allystaire leaned back in his saddle. "It is a Delondeur tradition to undertake great errantries in youth. Go hunt gravekmir with the elves, for instance. Sail to Keersvast and lead a mercenary ship for a season or two. Lionel was no exception. He was deadly with a lance and as good a horseman who ever lived. They say he spitted a gravekmir through the throat at one pass. Yet that was a long time ago, and his swordsmanship always depended upon the edge, all grace and style and flourish."

"So? What's all that mean?"

"My swordsmanship depends upon the head of my hammer, and Delondeur is more than a score of years my elder. If it came to it, I would kill him." Allystaire paused. "He might make me pay for it, but he would die."

"Are your sort allowed to bring hammers to duels?" Idgen Marte spoke up, shifting restlessly on her saddle.

"If he issues the challenge, I may bring to it any weapon I wish."

"Not too sure o'yourself, are ya? Him being a Giantslayer and all." Torvul leaned forward in the seat of his wagon, peering at Allystaire.

"He killed a gravekmir with eight feet of good ash topped with a foot of steel, from horseback, in full charge. I killed a gravekling from my back with my empty hand, the rim of my shield, and my boot. I would say that makes us even."

"The Goddess was with you then," Idgen Marte pointed out.

"And She would not abandon me now if I fought him for the right reasons." Allystaire gave his head a quick shake and frowned faintly. "Do not misunderstand me; I do not want to fight him. Lionel was…" He sighed, shook his head. "I thought, and still think, that he wanted to be a better man than most. That he tried; he cared for his men and his lands in much the same way the Old Baron did in Oyrwyn. I am less certain of that now. Yet I will not seek out a confrontation unless he forces it on me, or it becomes a necessary part of the Mother's will."

"What if he knew—not suspected, not ignored, but knew—what was going on in Bend?"

Allystaire's frown darkened into a scowl. "Then I will kill him, if I have to take the Dunes apart stone by stone." Then he gave his head a quick shake. "This is all irrelevant. We have to get in first. Come along already."

Torvul twitched his reins and started the wagon rolling again; Allystaire and Idgen Marte moved their mounts to either side of the wagon, on the very edges of the road. What had begun outside Grenthorpe as a dirt track had become something approaching a proper road, with a raised middle and a bed of stones that should've been more tightly packed, but were a considerable improvement over the mud, dust, and wheel-ruts of the dirt tracks.

Though the city seemed to loom near, it still took the better part of a turn to join with the queue lining up outside its gates. While they had encountered little to no traffic, foot or mounted, excepting the occasional galloping message-rider, a number of folk in carts, horses, and on foot were gathered on the eastern mountain road. Merchants, farmers with goods to sell, and more than one young man or woman come to the great city of Londray from their own towns or villages or farms.

They fell into line not far behind one such group. There was little mingling; as Idgen Marte stepped lightly off her mount, and Allystaire slid carefully off of Ardent's saddle and landed with a heavy rattle of armor and a grunt, one of the youths in front of them cast a backward glance. The lad's eyes widened as he took in their weapons, their armor, the size of the destrier. He turned back to his companions and there was quiet muttering, then the boy approached them.

"Come for the armin', m'lord?" He gestured to Allystaire's lance and the pennant affixed. "I dunno yer sigil, but are y'lookin' t'hire men-at-arms?"

"Arming?" Allystaire's eyes widened, and he felt Idgen Marte stiffen at his side.

"Aye, m'lord! Baron Delondeur has put out the call fer volunteers, though he don't say why. We think maybe he means t'launch a winter campaign to catch the bastards in Oyrwyn sleepin', or they mean t'do the same t'us and he wants t'be on guard."

Allystaire turned to Idgen Marte with a frown, then back to the lad. "Well, as you can see, I am already armed." He rapped a gauntleted knuckle against the head of his hammer. "And I am here on other business. If there is war here this fall or winter, I want no part of it."

"Wouldn't y'want to earn glory, m'lord?" The lad's cheeks were spotted with downy fuzz that matched the sandy color of his hair. "Set Oyrwyn cowards right?"

Anger flashed in his mind but was quickly washed away with the thought he'd voiced to Garth not so long ago. *If I have any friends left in Oyrwyn, I do not want them.* He studied the lad a moment, as he turned back around, noting the thin knife on his belt, the old and soft boots, the way his wrists stuck out of the plain homespun tunic.

"What is your name, lad?" Allystaire could hear Torvul's repressed groan as soon as he spoke.

The lad turned to face him. "Marcel, m'lord. Of Ennithstide."

Allystaire nodded faintly and approached him; he had almost a score of years on him, four inches of height and five stone in weight. "How do you expect to win glory, Marcel of Ennithstide?"

"With the sword, m'lord, or the spear! I'll kill enough Oyrwyn sons-of-whores to earn a place in the world—"

Allystaire cut him off with a raised hand. "Have you ever held a sword? A spear? A bow?"

"I've used my da's bow for hunting…"

"Oh? And where is it now?"

"Back home."

"I see." Allystaire sighed briefly. "Marcel, I have been at war, and seen war, longer than you or your friends have been alive. I know how it works; you will not be given swords or bows. Spears, mayhap, or halberds, but more likely daggers, a handful of javelins, and a leather jerkin that will no sooner stop a tree branch from scratching you than it will ease the blow of a sword. And in the field you will be run out ahead of the actual fighting men and told you are a skirmisher, or a scout. Mayhap a kern if the man in charge of you prefers. And the knight or bannerman who commands you will know that he has found the enemy when—from atop his mount—he *sees you die.*"

Allystaire emphasized *atop his mount* with a finger jabbed into Marcel's bony chest, and the lad quailed under the sudden anger in the paladin's face, but Allystaire continued.

"You will take an arrow—in the eye and straight into the brain if you are the luckiest of the lucky. In the neck is a good, quick way to go; I expect it burns and the choking panic is awful, but at least a man bleeds out fast that way. Mayhap you will live through your first fight, kill a man, even. And perhaps get a scratch from a dagger or take a javelin in the meat of the shoulder, no great wound, you think. And unless a veteran takes a moment to pour boiling wine into the wound for you that very instant, in the morning it will start to itch. And then next day it will be hot. And in three days time, perhaps five, perhaps a week, you will die in the screaming agony of wound-fever, shitting blood and losing your mind."

Marcel's face blanched with fear, but still Allystaire went on.

"If you are truly unlucky, you will survive almost an entire campaign. You will eat rotten food, march until your boots fall apart and your very clothes unravel, until your muscles scream to simply be allowed to lie down and die. You will watch your friends die and in your dreams you will see the faces of the men you kill. And then in some battle, a knight of Oyrwyn will ride straight over you. Or perhaps one of Delondeur's knights, in his haste to join the combat, will decide that the loss of a peasant kern is easier to bear than missing his chance at glory, and his horse's hooves will crush your back, and if you do not die with the taste of your own innards in your mouth, then you will be sent home, a cripple, a legless wreck, to sit in the village tavern and be pitied just enough to be allowed to drink yourself into an early grave. Women will not line up to mount your cock and men will not sit at your elbow to hear your stories. They will not sing any songs or compose any tales in your honor. They will turn their faces away in shock, and shame, and fear."

Allystaire paused, and realized now that Torvul, Idgen Marte, and all the boys of Marcel's group were staring at him in varying degrees of shock, fear, and wonder.

"That is your glory, Marcel of Ennithstide. Were I you, I would go home and back to my father's boat or my uncle's farm or the village mill, or wherever it is you came from. And if men come waving the flag and promising the baron's link and glory, remember what I said. If they press you into service, well, Marcel, there is not much you can do about that. But do not do the baron's bloody work for him, eh?"

With that, Allystaire turned away from Marcel and spat, walked back to Ardent, and patted the horse's neck. Within a few moments he heard the clamor of many footsteps and felt the rush of half a dozen lads fleeing the gates of Londray as if fleeing the mouth of Cold itself.

He turned and watched them disappear in a field, and then heard Torvul clear his throat. "Can ya use that trick to clear us all the way to the front? Handy if you could."

Allystaire didn't answer; he continued to watch the disappearing backs of the boys who had stood, mere moments ago, in line in front of them, and thought perhaps he heard, or felt, a tiny hint of the Goddess's music.

* * *

The small contingent of guards watching the gate were bored, sloppily dressed, and poorly armed. They wore the colors of Barony Delondeur, as well as the arms—a tower of a light sandy color on a bright green field. One unarmored man, in matching livery with a stripe on his arm and a cudgel holding down a stack of papers, sat at a folding camp table, with four flanking the thrown-open gates and several more patrolling the sloping stone walls above.

Allystaire and Idgen Marte led their horses next to Torvul's wagon, while the dwarf remained perched upon his seat. When they pulled up, the man at the desk droned questions at them without bothering to look up, meanwhile dipping the worn tip of a quill into a bottle of ink.

"Names."

"Mourmitnourthrukacshtorvul," Torvul said brightly, fluently chewing upon each twisting syllable.

The man's quill stopped upon the parchment, and his eyes fluttered in frustration.

"Ya can just write Torvul, sergeant. No one'll know the difference but us," the dwarf offered in a conspiratorial whisper.

The sergeant nodded and quickly scratched some lines. "And you two?"

"Idgen Marte."

"Allystaire."

The sergeant looked up when Allystaire answered, his eyes instantly focusing.

"Allystaire of?"

"Thornhurst," he answered, with deliberate care.

"I didn't know Thornhurst grew knights. Thought it was mostly cabbages and gap-toothed farm girls, when it's anything at all."

"Times change," Allystaire replied drily. "Though I am not a knight in the way you mean."

"Got a knight's weapons. Knight's mount. And that pennant." He peered at it as the wind teased it. "Dunno those arms. You're a liegeman to the Baron Delondeur?"

"No."

"Then to who?"

Allystaire smiled faintly, the half-formed and sometimes chilling expression that rarely touched his dark blue eyes. "No man."

The sergeant stood from behind his desk and looked up at Torvul. "All three of you together?"

The dwarf nodded. "Aye, sergeant. We share the road together, have for a good bit of it now. I'm here to take in supplies, do some trading. I've useful potions, unguents, solutions, tinctures, brews, philtres—"

The sergeant spat. The bored gate guards were more interested now; hands were tightening on spearshafts and mail was clinking as their weight shifted.

"I didn't ask, dwarf." The sergeant studied the three a while, waved them in, and watched them disappear through the darkness of the gatehouse. All other traffic was held up; finally, he sat down, wrote hastily on a piece of paper and folded it carefully in half, twice. He stood again, while merchants and farmers grumbled at the delay, and yelled, "Runner."

In a few moments a lad no older than twelve emerged from the gatehouse wearing the green and the tower. The sergeant handed the paper to him. "The Dunes. For the Baron. Go." The lad nodded and went back through the gatehouse; soon he was seen dashing atop the city wall along the parapet.

* * *

"Grand old city, this," Torvul was saying, as he drove his wagon slowly and carefully down the grand central street of Londray. "The buildings are hardly falling into each other, the lanes are near wide enough to squat in and the gutters aren't choked with garbage. Just sort of, decorated, I s'pose. Arranged, as it were. But…" The dwarf sat up straight in his wagon and sniffed the air, his eyes drifting half-closed. "D'ya smell that?"

"The harbor?" Idgen Marte and Allystaire answered in unison, and Torvul shook his head sadly.

"No! The rivers of weight. Silver links enough to forge a hauberk of them. Enough gold t'choke a troll with…ah, I s'pose that one loses something out of Dwarfish. Ya see, trolls will try to eat metals on occasion, so a big enough lump…" Torvul waved a hand vaguely in the air. "The place is ripe with links, and I—"

"Cannot touch any of it, best I can see," Allystaire finished the sentence cheerily. "At least, not in exchange for your craft. Am I correct?"

Torvul's face suddenly fell and he slumped in his seat, sullenly flicked the reins. "You're a cruel man, to remind a friend of his burdens so readily."

"There's more than one way to make some weight," Idgen Marte replied. "No reason you can't exchange honest work for—"

Torvul halted his wagon and stood so that he could look down upon the warrior with a scowl that could've shattered shields. "Mind your tongue, woman. We'll have none of that vile talk."

Idgen Marte laughed full-throatedly. "I don't like it any better than you. And yet we need to find some weight somehow."

"We will not be swindlers, but neither are we common laborers. The Goddess will provide," Allystaire put in. "And besides, I remember Torvul admitting to having a bit put by here and there in his wagon."

Allystaire paused and looked off to the harbor; afternoon sunlight gleamed off of the roof of the temple of Braech, probably the second largest building, after the Dunes, in the city. The roof was a bright metallic blue and sculpted as a wave curling and rising threateningly above all who entered. Above everyone in the city, truthfully, for it could be seen from the gatehouse itself, though only just.

"Rumor has long held that sapphires, tourmalines, agates, and lapis lazulis are crushed into the paint of that roof," he said, raising a hand to point. "Probably untrue, yet it is very bright."

"How d'ya think Her Ladyship would feel about sackin' the temples o'sworn enemies?" Torvul was rubbing at his chin with his fingertips.

"Probably poorly," Allystaire said. "She did not seem happy to be at odds with Braech. More like, ah…" He shrugged slightly. "Resigned, I suppose."

"Ah well. Perhaps another day. Now I have to see whom among my folk I can contact. And I've ingredients t'buy. And," Torvul pointed one thick finger at Allystaire. "If y'don't mind, toss me your gauntlet. The left one."

"Why?"

"Trust me, boy. I've a mind to do some tinkering and I think I can get what I need here when I go t'make contact with my own people. Where are you bound?"

Allystaire simply lifted his now bare hand and pointed toward the distant blue gleam that was the Temple of Braech. Then he took Ardent's reins and tossed them toward the dwarf, who caught them reflexively. "Horses will not be of much use. Find an inn with a good stable, or a hostelry that will not try to steal him."

Torvul nodded and gave the reins a gentle pull; Ardent whickered and tugged back, the reins almost slipping from the dwarf's strong hand. Allystaire placed his bare hand on the horse's neck and murmured. The giant grey calmed and went placidly along with Torvul's wagon. Idgen Marte tied her reins along the back of the wagon, next to the pack mule's lead.

With that the dwarf rumbled off down the Main Street, and the other two took off for the southwestern corner of the city, to where the Temple District lay.

CHAPTER 38

Paladin and Priestess

"Just gonna walk straight in?" Idgen Marte and Allystaire were watching the Temple of Braech from the shadow of a nearby temple minor. He hadn't paid any mind to whatever the sign at the front of it proclaimed in flaking paint and crude idolatry. That it was in a cluster of buildings squatting this close to Braech's Temple meant that it was sponsored by the Sea Dragon's Church, and would likely disappear within it in a few months. The temples dominated this particular part of the city, defining points of a triangle, with Braech's hard up against the water, a plain square of black basalt devoted to Urdaran to the southeast, and the light and airy silver-and-white of Fortune's Temple directly north of it.

"Idgen Marte, in the months you have known me, have I done anything else?"

"No, but you haven't planned on walking into the primary Temple of Braech in this Barony. There are bound to be temple guards, possible Braech-sworn knights, maybe even islandman crews.

"Have you seen a great deal of traffic in and out of the place?"

"No."

"I doubt there is an islandman crew in the barony right now, much less in that temple. Sometimes you are overly cautious." He pushed off the edge of

446 – DANIEL M. FORD

the building and some of its brickwork flaked away at his touch, which drew a backwards look and a frown. "Shoddy work."

"What do you expect a rented temple to be made of?" Idgen Marte stepped forward and grabbed Allystaire by the arm. "And stop tryin' to distract me. Sometimes *you* are not cautious *enough*. You haven't any idea what you're walking into, or whether you can walk out."

"Which is why you are here, yes? If it goes wrong, you will find me, and we will find our way out." He reached up and took her hand, gave it a companionable squeeze, and let it go. "Faith, Shadow of the Mother."

She sighed and nodded. "Faith," she agreed. Then she watched as he walked brazenly into the temple of their enemy.

* * *

The first hint the Marynth Evolyn had that things in the Temple were amiss was the sound of clattering metal and shouts and the heavy thud of a fist against flesh. Ismaurgh burst into her study so quickly that she did not sense his coming. He slammed her door and threw down the bar to bolt it and leaned against it, heaving for breath.

"He's here," he was saying, wild-eyed. "I sent two guards to detain him. They didn't even slow him down."

She took a deep breath, maintaining the equipoise and composure expected from a priestess of Braech, and set down her quill and quickly gathered up the papers upon which she had been making notes, stuffing them into a drawer of her desk. She had just drawn forth a long, curved knife from another drawer when the door pressed hard against the bar with a booming rattle, and a voice called from the other side.

"You can unbar the door and we can speak like civilized folk, or you can keep it up and I will treat everyone in this building as an enemy. Your choice. But I *will* see the choiron. You have a count of five." There was a brief pause, then in the same commanding, powerful tone. "*One.*"

There was barely a pause before "*Two,*" which was quickly followed by a loud, rattling blow against the door, which sent splinters flying and cracked two of the stout planks.

"*Three.*" Another heavy blow, and the blunt head of a maul poked through a crack in the door.

"Your bow," the Marynth Evolyn hissed, and Ismaurgh, color quickly draining from his face, patted his hip. The priestess rose from her chair, stalked to his side, and slapped him across the face with her open hand.

Even as she did the boards of the door rattled with the force of another clout. The head of the hammer wedged through the door and ripped another plank away as it was pulled clear. An armored arm slipped underneath and worked the bar loose from its brackets, and the broken door swung open.

"Four and five," the paladin said.

For the first time, the Marynth saw him close, with her own eyes. From a safe distance, through the eyes of a sword-at-hire whose mind she'd dominated with salt-water, he seemed dangerous, yes, but not so commandingly present.

He was, she realized, arrestingly unattractive. With an oft-broken nose, scars about his eyes, blocky cheeks, and the dark hint of perpetual stubble around his chin, he would turn few heads. His eyes, though, were a dark and piercing blue, and standing there in his grey and scarred armor, hammer in hand, with a cold and deadly anger radiating from him so vividly, he was terrifying.

In that moment, when his eyes met hers, the Marynth Evolyn knew she had been judged. *Braech help me, this man will kill me, and he'll be right to do it*, she thought, but then Ismaurgh leapt to the attack with a long knife drawn from his belt. She knew instantly his strike was doomed, for he'd pounced like a street-brawler, slashing across the chest, and the point of the knife simply skirled against the thick steel of the paladin's armor.

Her guardsman and lover was lucky, perhaps, in that he'd immediately gotten within the arc of the paladin's hammer, so he was safe from the weapon's head. Not, however, from its iron-clad haft, which the armored man raised and brought straight down onto the crown of Ismaurgh's head. Her guard staggered and fell to one knee. The paladin changed his grip, freeing his left hand, grabbed the back of Ismaurgh's hair and simply smashed his face, with no small amount of force, against his own breastplate.

Ismaurgh cried out, crumpled, with the sound of broken bones, a ruined face, and a smear of blood on the paladin's armor.

"Where is Symod?" With Ismaurgh out of the fight, those cold, hard, blue eyes focused on her, and she shivered and half-fell back into her seat. "Put your hands where I can see them," he quickly spat out, advancing until he stood over her desk, resting the head of his hammer threateningly on its edge. "And answer my question. Where is he?"

"You. You can't simply kill me," she sputtered, forcing herself to meet his gaze, sitting up straight and placing her hands deliberately upon the wooden surface of her desk, as if she had a say in the matter.

"No. Yet it may be that I can do much worse. Answer me."

"He is not in residence; he has left to attend to an oath-breaker."

The paladin's head tilted to one side, his lips pressed into a thin line. Her eyes flicked to movement behind him, and she suppressed a smile as she saw Ismaurgh climbing, albeit unsteadily, to his feet, his second knife drawn and clutched in his right hand.

Her eyes had given him away, for the paladin instantly turned, weapon at the ready. Seeing Ismaurgh with knife in hand, he wasted no time, quickly driving the butt of his hammer into the guard's stomach. The paladin caught him as he began to fall and dragged him in front of the desk. He placed Ismaurgh's hand, still clutching the knife, on her desk, wrapping his left hand around the wrist, and raising his hammer with the other.

"I will heal him before I leave, but I will not be backstabbed while I speak to you." The hammer rose in the air and then descended heavily against Ismaurgh's hand, crushing it to a pulp against the thick wood of the desk. Ismaurgh cried out, but swiftly and mercifully fell into a swoon upon her floor.

"Monster," she breathed, regaining some of her innate imperiousness. "He was trying to defend me."

"He is a murderer, and a man too afraid of me to try and kill me himself, except at desperate need. And after locking himself in a room with a priestess to protect him. Such courage, such boldness. Braech must be *so proud* of His Church. Cravens and employers of assassins."

Evolyn's fingers curled against the wooden surface of her desk and her knuckles whitened. She forced herself to sit upright, to not peer over the edge at Ismaurgh laying upon the floor, but suddenly her vision was filled with the impossibly eye-drawing presence of the paladin, as he leaned forward and set the head of his hammer on the desk between them. His scarred and beaten face loomed over hers. His brows were as much scar as they were grey-flecked dark hair, and his nose splayed hard to the left. His hair was carelessly shorn above a creased forehead that bore the same hard marks as the rest of his face. His jaw quivered with a tension that shot up into his cheeks as he stared down at her. She felt almost physically assaulted by his simple, unblinking glare.

Still, she had borne worse. *Are you not a student of a better and a harder man than this?* She met his stare with her own, set her chin, and said in a voice that did not quaver, "I am Lady Evolyn Lamaliere, daughter of Lord Lamaliere of Tideswater Watch, a Marynth of the Church of Braech, Second Seat in this Choironal to the legendary Symod, and if you think you can stare me into fear, you will be staring till we are both dust. Speak your piece on behalf of your up-jumped spirit or demon and then be gone before I turn the power of the Sea Dragon upon you."

As she spoke, confidence filled her, and her voice rose, and finally so did she, extending one hand toward the paladin, whose left arm suddenly shot forth and seized her wrist, transfixing her with an immoveable grip.

"The man Rede. Why did you promise him a temple to the Mother?"

She tried to gather her will, to bring the power of Braech to bear upon him, to force him away. To her shock and dismay, she found herself answering his question without dissembling. "This is the nature of temple politics. We thought it would be useful. If a new goddess is indeed risen, her church could be beholden to us…"

His hand tightened around her wrist and Evolyn gritted her teeth against the pain of his grip, afraid that she would cry out, but his hand relaxed before her bones could snap.

"You would try to enslave even Her. I should kill you, and everyone in this temple wearing your robes," he growled, before clearing his throat and shifting his grip, but Evolyn did not, for a moment, imagine that she could move her hand.

His voice was low, rumbling with his anger. *Not without melody*, she thought, *a voice that could shout commands or orders and be heard at great distance. A voice meant for a more handsome face.*

"Why were assassins sent against me, and what did they know?"

"Because I watched you destroy the mercenaries, and kill the gravekling with your bare hands, and it seemed that you healed with your left."

"And the poison? Where did it come from?"

"Ismaurgh knows a useful apothecary."

"Where is Symod?"

"He took a crew of Dragon's Scales and set sail. Some matter of a broken Oath to be punished and—"

"*Where*," he bellowed, before she finished, and tightened his hand around her wrist again, leaning forward till she could smell the mingling of iron and leather and horse upon him. Evolyn could no more resist his question than the beach could repel the waves, yet she smiled as she answered.

"Upon a ship; at sea; on a river. In the embrace of the Father of Waves if the journey has been poor. *I do not know.*"

He released her hand and she caught herself before she fell back into her seat. There was a clattering of boots in the corridors outside, and she smiled more widely. His face shot to the broken door, then back to her, and he hefted his hammer once again, menacingly.

The Marynth Evolyn began praying silently, expecting that she would die very soon. *Father of Waves, Master of Trade and Accords, Dragon of the Sea, your faithful servant begs to be embraced…*

She saw that he hesitated before he chose his next words. "If ever we cross paths as enemies again, Marynth, I will kill you. Why I do not do so now, I do not know; perhaps it is that there is a strength and a dignity in you that is hard not to see. Perhaps you remind me of my sister." He shook his head, looking almost disappointed. "You could do great things in this world, Lady Lamaliere, if you would but choose. You still might." He looked to the hallway and hefted his hammer in both hands.

"Choose this, now; order the guards in the hallway to allow me to leave, and I will heal this man Ismaurgh, as I said I would. Know that if you refuse, you are ordering them to their deaths. They are ornamental, and I would break them as easily as I would a lady's bauble."

"There are at least a half dozen of them."

"Then there will be at least a half dozen corpses in your hallway. I did not come here to kill un-blooded tradesman's sons playing at being guardsmen, but I will."

Evolyn thought for only a moment before calling out. "Guardsmen. Stand down. This has been a mere misunderstanding. You will allow Sir…"

"Allystaire," the paladin volunteered.

"Sir Allystaire to leave." The Paladin nodded, shifted his hammer to his right hand and then to his belt, and bent down to Ismaurgh's side. She crumpled into her chair, even as she heard Ismaurgh moaning and the paladin asking some insistent question, to which her guard responded with a mumbled street name. Then Allystaire swung Ismaurgh up onto his feet, clutching the front of his tunic with both hands, and tossed him roughly against her desk. Papers, pens, inkbottles, paperweights, and arcane instruments scattered and broke upon the ground as Ismaurgh fell backwards over her desk.

To his credit, her guard tried to scramble back to his feet, but the paladin was on him again, grabbing his collar with his left hand, and raising his his gauntleted right hand, balled into an iron-banded fist, threateningly.

"And you. You coward. You ought to die here today, but I said I would heal you, and I did. Understand something, you craven pig. Weapons are forbidden you from now on. To have one to hand in my sight is to die, as swiftly as I can manage. And I will be watching."

Ismaurgh said nothing as Allystaire straightened; slowly and carefully the guardsman pushed himself off the desk and tried to stand up straight.

"Go for your knife," the paladin nearly whispered. "Do it. Bend and put that blade in your hand and die like something resembling a man. I will make it quick. Or go on living, knowing yourself such a coward that even though you hired men to assassinate him, the Arm of the Mother thought killing you a waste of his time." His gloved hand descended to the haft of his hammer and began to loosen from its ring.

Ismaurgh dropped his eyes to the ground and turned halfway, his one good eye tightly shut.

Then Allystaire stood, turned his eyes back upon the Marynth Evolyn for a moment, and left. She listened to his boots ringing on the tiles as he moved off down the hallway, heard the clatter of guards as they raced for her study.

Suddenly Ismaurgh snarled and bent to pick up his knife, half-lunging toward her shattered door.

"Don't," she ordered. "You are no match for him." Ismaurgh glared at her, then collapsed into a spare chair against one wall, as Evolyn considered the paladin's words to her. *You could do great things in this world, Lady Lamaliere, if you would but choose*, rolled across her thoughts in his deep and flowing voice.

CHAPTER 39

An Invitation

Idgen Marte was waiting for him in an alley when Allystaire strolled out of the temple, and the two of them put some distance between themselves and Braech's glittering hall before they spoke.

"Symod?"

"Gone, with a crew of islandmen, to punish an oath-breaker, she said."

"She?"

"The Marynth Evolyn, Lady Lamaliere of Tideswater Watch, daughter of one of Delondeur's more powerful lords," Allystaire replied, pausing to think a moment. "I did not know the Sea Dragon had priestesses."

Idgen Marte sighed heavily and wheeled around to face Allystaire, stopping him short and staring at him eye to eye. "Don't tell me you were, ah, impressed by this Marynth Evolyn? What in Cold is a Marynth, anyway?"

Allystaire shrugged, armor clanking. "Damned if I know what their titles mean. And yes, I was impressed, though not how you think."

"'Course not. You'd be blind to an incarnation of Fortune if she strolled up to you naked," she said, rolling her eyes.

"Violence was afoot. There was no time to notice any of that."

"Just how much violence did you do?" Idgen Marte stepped away from him and started walking again.

"Very little. Nothing permanent. I even healed a man on the way out."

"Who?"

"The one who hired the assassin and supplied him with the poison."

"And you let him live?"

Allystaire reached out and grabbed Idgen Marte by the shoulder, turning her around to face him again. "I will not murder a man I have already defeated. Execute for a heinous crime I know he has committed, yes, but simply crushing his head while he writhed on her floor in pain, no. I wanted him to know he was beaten and that he could be again. Nothing was gained by killing him."

"What about her?"

He sighed and dropped his gaze as Idgen Marte's brown eyes searched his face, and she scowled. "You couldn't, could you? Because she's a woman."

"No. Because there was something in her. A kind of strength," he said thoughtfully. "Not unlike you," he added, lifting his eyes to meet hers again. "Not unlike my sister. Planted in different soil, she might have been one of us. Mayhap Symod's way is not entirely hers. Not yet."

"You're a fool. And when I have to kill her, I'll remind you of that." Idgen Marte slid quickly past Allystaire and strode angrily down the alley until it spilled out into a wider thoroughfare. Allystaire was close behind.

"This city's too...too tidy," Idgen Marte was saying, as Allystaire reached her. "Look at these main streets. Not narrow enough. No squatters, no beggars, signs everywhere you can see." She pointed to a tall post at the nearest corner; it bore signs pointing in every direction, with painted symbols for those who couldn't read; a threaded needle, a wine jar, a bushel of wheat, and a hammer pointed west, east, south, and north, respectively.

"There are no beggars on these streets because they are swarming around the army camps along the walls," Allystaire pointed out. "Trust me. They are here."

"How d'ya know?"

"Because I probably made half of them," he replied. "When a soldier is too hurt to soldier anymore, he is likely too hurt to work. What do you think becomes of them then?"

Idgen Marte was silent a moment. "Still, the place feels unnatural. A proper city needs to grow up on its own, like a person does. Develop scars and boils and ugly places and cowpaths that become streets. This smacks of too much lordship."

"The Delondeurs have ruled here for hundreds of years, an unbroken line. Bound to happen."

Idgen Marte spat and pointed north. "We ought to be after Torvul, now. Figure he'll be there."

"I would try the wine jug."

"Well we've already established that you're a fool," she replied somewhat bitterly, and strode off without another word, leaving him to follow fast at her heels once more.

It was perhaps half a turn of the glass before their ears began to catch the sounds of ringing hammers and pumping bellows, and the scents of smoke and hot metal filled the air.

Allystaire suddenly realized that Idgen Marte was no longer looking at the signs or pausing; she was simply walking with determination and speed. He said, "You do not need to guess where he is. You can sense it, aye?"

"Try it yourself and tell me," she replied, her voice still short and angry.

Allystaire focused, inwardly, and realized he quickly felt, as much as saw, Idgen Marte's presence a pace away. He knew how fast she was moving, where she was going, and most of all, that she was angry. He could have closed his eyes and kept pace with her, followed her. He tried to push that feeling outward from her and found that he could, indeed, sense another presence, like a bright and sparkling point of light in the map of his mind.

"Goddess," he murmured, smiling despite himself. "Is there no end to Her Gifts?"

He was distracted by the new intricacies of this sensation when he suddenly felt Idgen Marte come to an abrupt halt. He shook his head to focus. The road ahead was barred by a squad of brightly-mailed, green-tabarded soldiers—a dozen in all—carrying spears, shields, and an assortment of swords, maces, and axes.

One, with the a black bar across the top of his shield and twined bands of rank around his upper arm, stepped forward and spoke loudly and nasally. "Sir Allystaire Coldbourne, lately Lord of Coldbourne Hall, former Castellan of Wind's Jaw Keep, and war-leader of Barony Oyrwyn: our Lord Baron Lionel Delondeur wishes your presence for a private audience in his keep." A beat. "Immediately."

By the time Allystaire's hand had dropped to the haft of his hammer, Idgen Marte's sword had cleared its sheath. He hadn't even registered the whisper of metal against leather.

Three feet of curved steel, gleaming and deadly, hung in the air inches from the bannerman-sergeant's eye. Idgen Marte had simply slid across the intervening distance, gliding into a fighting stance, feet spread, weight shifting, with a light but firm grip upon the hilt of her weapon.

"And what if he doesn't come," she asked, calmly, evenly.

"Then we're to make him," the bannerman-sergeant replied.

If the sight of bared steel frightened him, his face didn't betray it. He had, Allystaire thought, a kind of professional resignation. *He'd rather be doing something else. Yet he'll do this because he believes he must.*

"D'ya think ya can, sergeant? Willin' t'die to find out?" Idgen Marte taunted.

"Stay your hand," Allystaire called out sharply. "And think this through. Could we cut down this dozen, we would still not make it past the ward gates between here and the outer wall, and we could never force a crossing there."

"I asked *him* a question," Idgen Marte insisted, her blade still and gleaming.

"I think your lord spoke sense just now, woman," he replied, with the casual aplomb of a man who's had blades pointed at him before. "And I think if I died in finding out whether you could cut us down, I'd only be doing what I was sworn to do: carry out the orders of my Lord Baron." The bannerman-sergeant swallowed once, his eyes moving to the blade, then back to Idgen Marte. They were dark green, unruffled, and set in a face that was hard to age, given the way it was framed by a mailed coif.

Looks on the young side to have rank. Eyes aren't young, though, Allystaire thought, then nodded very lightly as he came to a decision. He strode carefully to Idgen Marte's side and reached up to her sword with his armored right hand and pushed it gently downward. She looked to him, eyes wide in anger, but he forestalled her.

"They have done us no harm, made no threats, drawn no weapons. I will go with them." She opened her mouth to protest, and he shook his head quickly. "They said Lionel wanted an audience with me, and they came with courtesy, not chains. I will go." *Goddess grant that I am right, and this one boon.* He focused, for a moment, narrowed his eyes and leaned closer to Idgen Marte, and thought. *If you hear this, sheath your sword and find Torvul. Wait till morning. If you have not heard, do as you think best.*

You're a fool, he heard, almost immediately. *And if I don't see you by the morning I'll kill everyone in this city wearing Delondeur green.* But she slid her sword back into its scabbard and backed away, nodding.

The bannerman-sergeant took a breath, but otherwise showed no signs of relief. "Your servant may accompany you, m'lord."

"She is not my servant," Allystaire replied. "She is a friend, and has other business." At this, Idgen Marte nodded and turned on a heel and disappeared into the crowd.

Allystaire fell into step beside the bannerman-sergeant. "What is your name, Bannerman-Sergeant?"

"Chaddin, sir," the man replied, briskly.

"Chaddin of…?"

"Of Londray, I suppose, m'lord."

"You have no surname or place?"

"None that I care for," he replied. His clipped and forceful tone indicated that the conversation was over. The bannerman-sergeant picked up his pace, and soon he and Allystaire were surrounded by the green-cloaked and tabarded soldiers.

Allystaire looked back into the crowd—futilely, he knew, for Idgen Marte had melted into it as soon as she stepped away, as completely gone from his vision in an instant as if she had slipped underwater.

And so I am alone, he thought, *for the first time in months.*

Never alone, rang the smallest echo of the beautiful voice he longed, every waking moment, to hear.

CHAPTER 40

Every Link of the Cost

The columns along the polished marble floor of the Great Hall of the Dunes were decorated with the banners and weapons of defeated enemies. The smooth, sand-colored walls bore tapestries depicting hundreds of years' worth of Delondeur victory.

Though none against Oyrwyn, Allystaire thought, immediately chiding himself for the flush of pride he felt.

Looming menacingly over the Seat of Station at the far end was the polished skull of a Gravekmir. The creature alive and intact would've stood twelve feet tall or more, with protruding teeth, a sloping forehead, and arms that could tear a man like a piece of bread. Beneath the massive skull lounged Lionel Delondeur, the man who, in the errantries of youth, had killed the giant, along with, Allystaire knew, countless other men and beasts.

Lionel looks older, Allystaire thought. Statesmanlike silver had chased all traces of blond from his hair, and his face was as lined as parchment that had been crumpled and then unrolled. Lionel still looked every inch the warrior, though, with his sword leaning against his chair, his shoulders unbent by the mail he wore, his green silk cloak casually tossed over one shoulder. The many windows in the hall were thrown open to admit great streams of light, the cries of gulls, and the briny odor of the bay. A table sat next to the Baron

Delondeur's chair, along with a cut-crystal decanter of wine and a pair of pewter goblets.

No other guards were in the room besides the detachment of three, headed by Chaddin, which had brought Allystaire to the audience.

As they approached the seat, Allystaire took a moment to study Chaddin's face again. Something about the man's features was niggling at his perceptions, but the professional distance he'd maintained was impenetrable, so he simply shook his head and turned to face the baron.

Lionel stayed seated, shifted in his seat so that he leaned back a bit, studying Allystaire's face. "Coldbourne," he finally said, his tone all companionable-old-soldier on the surface. Beneath it, though, lurked a kind of ice. *Fear, or anger, or both,* Allystaire thought.

"Baron," Allystaire said, inclining his head only the barest inch. He kept his eyes level, though, locked on his old enemy.

"What in the Cold are you doing in my barony, you old Oyrwyn dog?"

"Things that need doing," Allystaire replied simply.

"I'm going to need more answer than that, Coldbourne."

"That is neither my home nor my name anymore. Allystaire will do."

Lionel sat up straighter, the goatee at the end of his chin bristling a bit. "Oh, the writs announcing your exile reached the Dunes while I was in the field this summer, don't doubt it. Yet the name suits you. Northern, simple, honest, and ugly." He squinted faintly. "The years haven't improved you on that score, I see. When *is* the last time we were face to face?"

"Innadan's Tourney. Seven years ago now."

"Ah, back when that runt Hamadrian had the idea of bringing us all together in the name of peace. Fool." The baron turned and filled his goblet with wine, but held it without drinking. "That long though, eh?"

"In the years since, you had your chances to see me up close. I do not recall your being too eager, though," Allystaire replied, and he couldn't help the tiny trace of a smile that ghosted along the left side of his mouth.

The baron covered a sudden flush in his cheeks with a deep gulp of wine, then set down the cup and stood. "Too busy dealing with Innadan. I'd have given you a good thrashing eventually." Before Allystaire could reply, he went on. "I still need a better answer. What are you doing in my barony?"

Allystaire remained silent a moment, thinking on his answer. "I would say the work of a Goddess, but you would not understand what I meant. Let me say, then, that I have been doing the work I ought to have been doing these twenty years and more, now. The work you ought to do."

"Shattering the bones of my knights so badly they die when we peel off their armor? Rousing my rabble into froth? Building some temple out in a shit-step town in the Ash River valley? You presume to tell me what I *ought* to do?" Anger started to get the better of him now, and the baron pushed himself to his feet, slowly, though he stood blade-straight once he was up.

"Your knight was pressing your own people," Allystaire countered. "And I gave him fair warning. The raising of a temple is only partly my doing, a very small part. And I do have to wonder, Lionel, how the men beside me think of hearing you call their kin your rabble."

"You might do well to remember that I have a title," Lionel shouted, taking a step toward Allystaire.

"I have not forgotten it," Allystaire replied, voice calm, face unruffled. "I do not see a reason to use it until you remember what titles mean." He felt and heard the guards at his sides and behind him shifting their weight, heard their gear clanking softly.

Delondeur was dead silent as he approached to within a step of Allystaire. The baron surpassed Allystaire in height; closing in forced the paladin to tilt his head.

"Having a title means that the people are not *your* rabble. It means that you are *their* baron. That difference is something all of us forgot long ago. Might be that we never understood it to begin with."

"You've gone soft. The man I remember wasn't afraid to torch a village or question a captive if need be."

"I burned villages, aye," Allystaire replied. "Though I always gave orders that houses, and not people, were to burn, I cannot be sure they were always followed. I put men to the question, though I always told myself it was for a greater end." At this, he paused, shook his head and snorted slightly, lips curling in disgust. "These are pathetic excuses; I will pay every link of the cost of my sins. You will bear the cost of yours as well, *Baron Delondeur*," he went on, twisting the title into something near a curse. "What will matter to you in the end is whether you will pay it willingly, or whether the Goddess wills that I take it from you."

Lionel's flushed cheeks turned to a bright, angry red, and he strode forward, his arm lifting to deliver a blow, but Allystaire's left hand darted forward and caught the man's arm by his thickly muscled wrist.

The guards exploded briefly into motion but were stilled with a quick wave from the baron's free hand, though Bannerman-Sergeant Chaddin drew his sword and held it still and at guard, carefully watching Allystaire.

The baron was not a weak man, but Allystaire was near twenty years his junior, and heavier, if shorter. Slowly, tightening his left hand around Lionel's right wrist, he was able to forcefully push the baron's hand backwards. *Hope it doesn't show*, Allystaire thought, as he bent the baron's hand toward his forearm, working hard to keep the strain from his voice.

"I am not powerless rabble you can slap with impunity, Lionel," Allystaire said, and he leaned forward, pressing harder on the baron's wrist, so that the other man had no choice but to fall, hard, to one knee, or have his wrist snapped. "Now that I have your attention, I have a question for you."

"To the Cold with you, Allystaire" Lionel grunted, teeth clenched in pain. "Guards, do nothing," he spat. "I will deal with this landless exile myself."

"Bend, Lionel. The man who had set himself up as a baron there. The slave trade, operating in your own barony." Allystaire's voice was rising with every word, till it resonated through the columns of the hall. "Your own people, chained, and sold. How much did you know of it?" As he asked, he pushed his senses into Lionel's mind, forcing the truth out of him. It needed surprisingly little force, Allystaire noted.

"I knew all. Collected gold from that Windspar fool. Ships need oar-hands and we've too many mouths to feed as it is. I mean to shut it down when the war is done."

Allystaire leaned forward with anger flooding his veins, and he thought, of a certainty, that he was going to kill Lionel Delondeur, today, right now, this moment, in the seat of his own power.

The thought fueled his anger as he shouted. "When the war is *done*? When will it *ever* be done?" He meant to snap the baron's arm, for a start, and see where his mood led him from there, but suddenly his grip was pulled free and his arms were slammed against his sides by an unearthly force, immeasurably stronger even than the gravekling he had wrestled against.

"When the assistance I provide leads to its end," said a new voice Allystaire didn't recognize. "And I needed many of the captives. Useless, hungry mouths who would not help win this war, petty though it be." From behind one of the columns strode a figure, robed and hooded, his extended hand glowing dark red at the tips of his fingers.

Allystaire looked down and saw bands of pulsating red energy encircling his hands; he tried pressing against them and found moving his hands as likely as shoving over a castle wall.

The sorcerer stepped closer to Allystaire until the paladin could see into the depths of his hood: a pale-skinned, unlined face, with thin red lines of energy pulsing through the whites of his eyes like fiery veins. "Just as I told him to bring you here so that I could see you face to face. We have a lot of work to do."

A tiny bolt of energy flew from the sorcerer's hand into Allystaire's chest, as if his armor weren't there. He was suddenly wracked with a pain that was everywhere in his body—his bones, his skin, his muscles, his vitals. Just as soon as it had come upon him, it was gone. His feet were pulled an inch from the ground, and his ankles constricted as his wrists were bound together.

Under his hood, the sorcerer frowned; his lips were thin and almost yellowish, and even in a frown they parted to reveal small, pale teeth. "That is unusual. There is much I have to know."

The Baron Delondeur rose to his feet and massaged his right wrist with his left. He offered Allystaire an angry, but triumphant smile. "You see the Black Horse of Tarynth over there, Coldbourne?" He raised his left hand, pointing to one of the trophies hung on the columns lining the hall. Rent and stained dark brown on one corner, it had once been a deep purple and featured a rearing black horse. "It is the last one in the world. I paid a bounty to find and burn the rest of them, to drive them from the world, as I did to the family that once flew them. All that remains of them are scattered across my southern plains."

Lionel dropped his hand and simply enjoyed the scene of Allystaire held motionless and impotent in the air before him. "Before I pass this seat onto whichever son proves his worth, Innadan and Harlach, Varshyne and Telmawr will join it. Oyrwyn, last, if the Young Baron doesn't simply bend his knee. There will be a king again, and it'll be a Delondeur. This country will be mine."

Delondeur turned, waving dismissively. "Take him. Do what you must to learn what you need. But he does not die unless I am there to see it."

Allystaire felt himself lifted further into the air as more red clouds flowed from the fingers of the sorcerer, and he heard the guards fall in beside him as he was carried backwards out of the hall. "You made your choice, Lionel," Allystaire bellowed, taking brief solace in the fact that he could still speak. "Remember it when the Goddess's justice finds you, Li—"

His mouth suddenly slammed shut, and the breath was driven out of his lungs. Mute and powerless, Allystaire turned his thoughts inward as he was carried through the halls. *This*, he thought, with sinking certainty, *is going to hurt*.

The End of Book 1 of the *Paladin Trilogy*

Acknowledgments

Thanks to Andrew for taking a chance on me and my fantasy superhero origin story. Thanks to Rion for pointing me to SFWP. Thanks to all my beta readers; Jacob, Stephanie, Josh, Andy, Jason, Yeager, Caren, and Sarah. This is a much better book than it would otherwise have been because of you. Thanks to my mom for having wondered, loudly and often, why I wanted to study fairy tales and write poems at graduate school, but never trying to stop me. Thanks to Westley and Hector for being editor cats. Thanks to Karen and Kyle for their dedicated work on the book. And last but never, ever least, Lara; for putting up with day after day of me talking about the book, complaining about the book, whining about the book, disappearing every night to work on the book, for believing in the book when I wouldn't. This book wouldn't exist without you. I wouldn't have had a reason to write it.

About the author

Daniel M. Ford was born and raised near Baltimore, Maryland. He holds an M.A. in Irish Literature from Boston College and an M.F.A. in Creative Writing, concentrating in Poetry, from George Mason University. As a poet, his work has appeared most recently in *Soundings Review*, as well as *Phoebe, Floorboard Review, The Cossack,* and *Vending Machine Press*. He teaches English at a college prep high school in the northeastern corner of Maryland. *Ordination* is his first novel.

THE ADVENTURE CONTINUES...

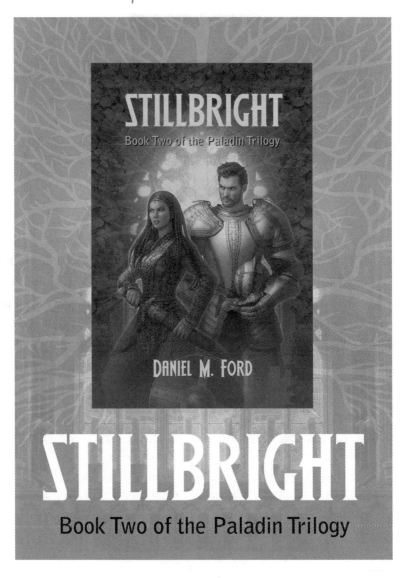

STILLBRIGHT

Book Two of the Paladin Trilogy

AVAILABLE IN 2017

Santa Fe Writers Project

sfwp.com